C0-ATS-628

Studies in Fifteenth-Century Stagecraft

Studies in Fifteenth-Century Stagecraft

J. W. Robinson

Early Art, Drama, and Music
Monograph Series, 14

MEDIEVAL INSTITUTE PUBLICATIONS

WESTERN MICHIGAN UNIVERSITY

Kalamazoo, Michigan 49008-3851
1991

BRESCIA UNIVERSITY
COLLEGE LIBRARY
72313

© Copyright 1991 by the Board of the Medieval Institute

ISBN 0-918720-38-9 (casebound)
ISBN 0-918720-39-7 (paperbound)

Cover design by Linda K. Judy
Printed in the United States of America

Contents

Illustrations

Foreword

When John W. Robinson died suddenly of a heart attack on 25 February 1986 at the age of 51, a fine scholar of the theater was lost prematurely. His critical mind was ever alert and his energy always unfailing in the service of scholarship. On the day before he died, he had written a letter to me enthusiastically accepting the task of reviewing an edition of an early sixteenth-century playwright for *Comparative Drama*; because his understanding of the theater of the sixteenth century—and also of earlier centuries—in England was uncommonly acute, he was immediately missed. He was never one to see play texts merely as literary exercises, but rather he insisted upon regarding them (correctly) as destined for actual production by living actors. His students at the University of Nebraska-Lincoln commented about how he was able in his classes to make drama "come alive."

Very fortunately, at his death Professor Robinson left a manuscript on the theater of northern England, a work which he had been long in forging and which was to be his major scholarly accomplishment in this field. In earlier and more ambitious plans for the book, he had written that he saw his task as effecting a marriage between "the theatrical and the dramatic." There is, he felt, too great a division between practitioners of the theater and literary scholars, who tend not to communicate with each other. "I find it useful," he wrote, "to analyse early plays thinking of them as scripts for performance, looking into each play for the 'sub-text,' and for signs that the audience is taken into account, and considering the auspices and occasion for the play, the staging—the *decor simultane* or Place and Scaffolds (even if only general rather than detailed certainty can be achieved about this matter)—music, costuming, and established iconographical and theatrical traditions." But also "as an integral part of the same endeavor, the plays must . . . be analysed as dramas, and the sources and analogues, plot, irony, characters, language, imagery, and theme of each play probed." He had intimately studied the West Yorkshire region (formerly the West Riding)—the home of the dramas in the Towneley Manuscript (now Huntington Library MS. HM 1)—as well as the theatrical and intellectual context of the plays themselves. He was especially interested in the works written by the dramatist we know as the "Wakefield Master." His insights into these religious plays, often drawing on the literature and art with which the playwright was familiar, were penetrating and wide-ranging in their scope. He was, I am convinced, the very best reader to date of the Towneley plays as well as of the work of the dramatist known as the York Realist.

The liveliness of the York Realist and the humor of the Wakefield Master—the plays by the latter form the focal point of this book—demonstrate that religious drama need not be dull or somber. The York Realist is characterized by an attention to specifics that produces exactitude of iconographic detail, while the Wakefield Master achieves, as I have argued elsewhere, a form that engages what has been called the "double vision" of comedy—seeing the grotesque and serious simultaneously. The absurd happenings of shepherds thus become the background for dramatic action that stands as a reflection of events at the very center of history. On a page at the beginning of his manuscript, Professor Robinson had appropriately copied out the following verses from John Bunyan's *Pilgrim's Progress*:

> Thus by the Shepherds secrets are revealed.
> Which from all other men are kept concealed.
> Come to the Shepherds then, if you would see
> Things deep, things hid, and that mysterious be.

Thomas Bestul, kindly acting as Professor Robinson's literary executor, has been responsible for the formidable job of preparing the manuscript of this book for submission to the Early Drama, Art, and Music Monograph Series and also for having the text

Foreword

transferred to computer disks. Since Professor Bestul's expertise is not medieval drama, it was necessary for me to see that missing footnotes were supplied, citations checked, and emendations made where scholarship had advanced in the period since Professor Robinson's death. In this task I was kindly aided by Kay Chase, an assistant librarian who gave cheerfully of countless hours of her time and ultimately proved invaluable since much of the work needed to be done at a time when the Western Michigan University Library, while its building was in process of being rebuilt, was necessarily a closed-stack facility. Professor Robinson was a careful and exacting writer, and we have attempted to work together to produce a book that would reflect his scholarly standards.

It should be noted that in one respect especially recent research has necessitated some changes in Professor Robinson's manuscript. At the time of his death, the Towneley plays were widely believed to be the Wakefield cycle presented in that town at Corpus Christi each year. That he had some doubts about this connection is clear; in one of his footnotes, he had written: "It is perhaps unnecessarily scrupulous to point out that the only good evidence that the Wakefield Master's plays were in fact ever presented is their eminent playability . . . ; the same is true of *Everyman*." But the link with Wakefield has now been much weakened. While there was a Corpus Christi play at this location in the sixteenth century, it was certainly not the cycle of plays included in the Towneley manuscript since the records in the Wakefield Burgess Court rolls that seem to support the connection have been found to be forgeries by the local historian, John Walker (see the summary of the evidence in Barbara D. Palmer, "'Towneley Plays' or 'Wakefield Cycle' Revisited," *Comparative Drama*, 21 [1987-88], 318-49). Hence it has seemed wise not to label the plays in the Towneley collection as "Wakefield cycle" or "Wakefield plays," as was the case in Professor Robinson's manuscript—an emendation that, meticulous scholar that he was, he would have made had he lived to see the book through the press. The "Wakefield Master," however, is the name by which the great dramatist who produced the Second Shepherds' play correctly continues to be known.

Another alteration that has been made in the process of seeing Professor Robinson's book through the press has been the adopt-

Foreword

ing of A. C. Cawley's edition of the plays of the Wakefield Master for quotations instead of the facsimile prepared by A. C. Cawley and Martin Stevens. Citations of other plays from the Towneley manuscript are to the Early English Text Society edition of George England and A. W. Pollard. The quotations in Professor Robinson's manuscript were as yet unchecked against the readings in Huntington Library MS. HM 1, and on the whole agreed with Professor Cawley's readings in essence except for an occasional minor disagreement with regard to spelling or punctuation. We have also decided that for typographical reasons the Middle English thorn and yogh would be transcribed by their modern equivalents.

In addition to those noted above or listed in Professor Robinson's Acknowledgments, the following helped in various ways to transform this book from manuscript to an actual publication: Sarah Brown, of the Commission on Historical Monuments of England; William Wanbaugh, graduate student in Medieval Studies; and Candace Woodruff, of Medieval Institute Publications. Barbara Palmer also provided invaluable advice during the process of editing.

CLIFFORD DAVIDSON

Acknowledgments

I wish to recognize in connection with this book some early personal obligations to Canon Sidney John Burling, A.K.C., and Mrs. Burling (and the St. Francis Players); my late sister, Freda, and the Wanstead Players; the late Bertie Campbell, Esq., B.A., C.B.E.; and my late mother and father, the former disapproving of the stage, the latter a Yorkshire monologist and prestidigitator of local fame. I also owe much to my teachers, Professor Peter Bayley and the late Professor James Arnott. More recently, I have benefitted from the hospitality of Mr. Hedley Sharples, M.A., and Mrs. Martha Arnott (who gave me some of her late husband's books); Professors David Lampe, Jan McDonald, and Derek Pearsall, who allowed me to try out some of my ideas in the form of lectures at the State University College of New York, Buffalo, the University of York, and the University of Glasgow; and Professor Clifford Davidson, who allowed me to present papers at the annual International Congress on Medieval Studies, sponsored by the Medieval Institute, Western Michigan University. For answering questions and sharing their knowledge I thank Mr. Bernard Barr, Sub-Librarian of York Minster; Mr. Peter C. D. Brears, F.S.A., Director of Museums, Leeds, who by his sudden, indeed shaking, laughter solved at one stroke the question of the meaning of "like fulling-mill clogs," who is probably the first person since the Reformation promptly to have understood this amazing simile, and who prepared the drawing on which figure c is based; Mr. Peter Gibson, M.A. (Hon.), F.S.A., the Chairman of the York Glaziers Trust, who led me through the "tradesmen's entrance" to York Minster; Dr. Richard Marks, Curator of the remarkable Burrell Collection, Glasgow, who allowed me access to the files relating to the ala-

Acknowledgments

baster carvings; Jane Oakshott (Mrs. Rastell), a director following adventurously in the footsteps of Poel, Monck, and Browne, who gave me some of her souvenir programs; Professor Barbara Palmer, who shared with me her wide knowledge of religious art in the West Riding; Mr. William M. Roberts, the archivist of the University of California, Berkeley; Professor John Scattergood; Mrs. Meg Twycross, a notable scholar-director; Rev. Michael Wittock, Rector of St. Oswald's, Methley; and Mr. C. Wilkins-Jones, Norfolk County Local Studies Librarian. My chief debt is to Professor A. C. Cawley and Dr. Richard Beadle, whose editions of the plays of the Wakefield Master and of the York plays have made this book much easier to write than would have been the case without them. My debts to others who have written about these plays, and produced them, especially in recent years, are many, and I gratefully acknowledge them. I have been inspired by Professor A. C. Sprague and by the example of fellow members of the Society for Theatre Research, and have benefitted, in various ways, from the comments of my students and my colleagues, among them Professors Thomas Bestul, Robert Haller, Robert Knoll, and Paul Olson.

Except for Chapter II, a short version of which was published in the *Journal of English and Germanic Philology*, only very small sections of this book, since rewritten, have previously appeared in print. I am grateful to the editors of *ACTA 12: The Fifteenth Century, Folklore, JEGP, Medieval Drama: A Collection of Festival Papers* (1968), *Modern Philology* (and the University of Chicago Press, publisher), the *Proceedings of the Eighth International Patristic, Medieval, and Renaissance Conference, Theatre Notebook*, and *Theatre Survey* for permission to reuse this material.

This book is dedicated to my wife, Ella, whose relentless love and heart-felt logic have made it possible.

J. W. R.

Introduction

I suspect that from any height where life can be supported there may be danger of too quick descent. —Dr. Johnson, *Rasselas*

My purpose is to expound *as plays* the New Testament plays of the Wakefield Master and some of the related York plays, including two by the York Realist. These are the two medieval English playwrights who produced distinctive and distinguished bodies of work; further, their exclusive or main concerns, the Nativity (and Incarnation) and Passion (and Redemption), are the chief subjects of late medieval art and drama, and the key events and dogmas of the Christian faith.

Medieval biblical plays were written to be performed, but even after almost a century of revivals it is not uncommon to find them considered as literature only, and questions concerning their performance regarded as trivial. Only such a limited approach could lead to the conclusion, recently expressed, by a literary scholar, that "there are no fifteenth-century dramatic masterpieces."[1]

Revivals are often illuminating, but medieval plays have undergone since 1901 the same vicissitudes Shakespeare's plays have endured since the Restoration. They have been performed in theatrical conditions they were not written for, made to take second place to the theatrical arts, rewritten and rearranged with scant regard for their integrity, imitated, subjected to ideological modernization, and (their texts restored) performed as practical experiments to test hypotheses about their original staging—but encumbered (a point not infrequently made by observers) with modern audiences. Nevertheless, in the course of this steady flow of assorted revivals, the plays have proved themselves to be pow-

1

Introduction

erful and as resilient and as actable as Shakespeare's. Something of their authentic effectiveness has now and then, from the early years of this century to the present day, been revealed.[2]

The Wakefield Master's plays have sometimes been treated sentimentally but have generally fared well in revival, the York series of Nativity plays less so, and the York Realist's plays in the York Passion series not well at all. The first revival of a medieval English biblical play was inauspicious. As an afterpiece to his celebrated production of *Everyman*, "under the shade of the venerable walls of the Charterhouse," opening on 13 July 1901, William Poel presented the episode of Abraham and Isaac which forms somewhat more than half the fourth play in the Chester collection. The style was Pre-Raphaelite; Eastern costumes were borrowed from Holman Hunt's studio, and Isaac was played by a "prepossessing young lady."[3] For some years nothing was heard in the south of the York plays or of the even more vigorous plays of the Wakefield Master, although as early as 1899 it had been suggested that his plays of Herod the Great or the Buffeting of Jesus might supplant the Roman comedy customarily performed at Westminster School, and in 1902 an article in the *Era*, the stage newspaper, praised the Second Shepherds' play.[4] It was left to Leeds University to take matters in hand, and it did so with panache. In a lecture delivered to the annual meeting of the Yorkshire Dialect Society in 1905, Professor F. W. Moorman claimed for the Wakefield Master a powerful and influential position in English drama (a point impossible to prove, but for which there exists more evidence than Moorman adduced) and concluded: "It is probably from three to four hundred years since the Second Shepherds' play was last acted in Yorkshire"—or anywhere in England, for that matter, he might have added. "Why should it not be acted again?" Let it be performed, "reviving as far as possible the conditions under which the old Miracle plays were acted."[5]

Accordingly, a group of students presented the play as part of the annual open-house of Leeds University Union on 8 February 1907, providing, it was generally agreed, the most interesting part of the evening. The original "conditions under which the . . . plays were acted" were scarcely fully apparent, since the play was performed in front of painted canvas scenery, the *Gloria* was sung by a choir of women students accompanied by particularly brilliant "magnesium lighting," the shepherds had a "magnificent collie" dog (not called for in the script) to keep them company, and at the end of the performance a curtain fell. Even so, a sense of shepherd life on a Yorkshire moor was conveyed, and the performance was nothing if not lively: Mak and Jill (played by a male) "threw themselves into the farce with unflagging spirit. The former was especially good in his bare-faced and plausible denials of the theft, his injured innocence, and his frantic efforts, unfortunately fruitless, to prevent the unveiling of the cradle and its bulky occupant. The latter was excellent in his unwonted character of the new-made mother; and once only, by a somewhat masculine flounce onto the bed as the unwelcome visitors approached, did he betray the full extent of his imposture." The play was sympathetically conceived as "rolicking farce merging at the end into rapt devotion."[6]

The Headmaster of Wakefield Grammar School, Matthew Peacock, who by 1901 had argued that the Towneley plays were in fact the Wakefield plays,[7] persuaded some of the senior boys to present the Second Shepherds' play in the school hall for two consecutive evenings, opening on 1 April 1910. Before a large audience the Headmaster spoke eloquently of the "genius" of the playwright, his "dramatic power, forcible language, and decided originality." The parts of both Jill and Mary, following an English tradition of female impersonation originating in the Middle Ages or earlier and unbroken since, were taken by males, the shepherds were "witty, sarcastic and sententious" and also offered their gifts to the Christ Child in addresses "beautiful in idea and expression"; however, the angel did not appear, singing instead from "behind the scenes," and between "each of the first six scenes" baroque music was played on the organ.[8]

As the Leeds University students gallantly recognized, London and Chester "had the start on us by a few weeks in performances of the same kind"; they refer to the less spirited work of Nugent Monck (1877-1958), the most significant director of early plays between Poel (1852-1934) and E. Martin Browne (1900-80).[9] Monck and his English Drama Society (founded after Poel's Elizabethan Stage Society disbanded in 1905) presented a condensed and bowdlerized version of the series of four Nativity plays in the Chester collection on a curtained stage at the Old Music Hall, Chester, 29 November 1906, with the approval of the Mayor and Archdeacon, and at Bloomsbury Hall, London, 4 December 1906. The London critics, who found this revival to be a "perfectly well-intentioned sham," objected to the lime-light, darkened auditorium, incense, organ music, and "a shepherd boy of an incorrigible Pre-Raphaelitism, with a strong tinge about him, too, of an Aubrey Beardsley"; the episodes of Joseph's doubt and the birth of Christ were omitted.[10] Monck similarly managed to weaken the Second Shepherds' play itself, which he took south, first anticipating the Wakefield boys with three matinee performances at the large Gaiety Theatre, Manchester, opening on 28 February 1910. The stage was curtainless, but in the interests of solemn artistry and sentimentality the "buffoonery" was subdued, the first shepherd slept in a fine "pose" illuminated by lime-light, Mak wept as he carried the lamb back to the fold, making a "conclusion perfectly beautiful and symmetrical," and the audience was puzzled and respectful.[11] Monck subsequently took the play to Norwich (Blackfriars Hall, 26 December 1910), where he again slighted the text but possibly to better effect: at "What the dewill is this? He has a long snoute!" (l. 585, "devil"), which was delivered as a shout, "pandemonium broke loose, in one of the most murderous free-fights ever shewn on the stage. By a stroke of inspiration the action was not allowed to cool, but went straight to the *Gloria in Excelsis*, which rang out over the tumult and stilled it; and the Angel appeared."[12] At the small Abbey Theatre, Dublin, Monck then opened with the play on 23 November 1911. Yeats was dissatisfied, although he had himself once contemplated writing a "medieval" biblical play, and his friend Katharine Tynan had written the first plausible imitations, which were followed by the cult of numerous original "mystery" or "miracle" plays (often performed by church groups) against which T. S. Eliot rebelled, seeking modern religious plays. Anticipating Eliot, and rightly sensing that the appeal of the Second Shepherds' play is local as well as universal, Yeats asked Padraic Colum, the author of *The Miracle of the Corn*, an Irish "miracle play" (Abbey Theatre, 22 May 1908), to "go over all these [mystery] plays and turn them into Irish plays."[13]

Monck and others continued to produce and direct single plays, especially the Second Shepherds' play; it was not until 1958 that a version of the Towneley collection approaching completeness was performed. At the suggestion of the Bishop of Wakefield, who was perhaps prompted by the example of nearby York (as was, probably, the Wakefield Master himself), the students and staff of Bretton Hall College of Education performed twenty of the plays in the College grounds, on 4-6 July 1958. The text was prepared by the director, Martial Rose; at least three of the Wakefield Master's plays were performed: the play of Noah, the Second Shepherds' play, and the play of Herod the Great—his play of the Buffeting of Jesus, however, was alternated with the play of the Scourging because presented together "the impact was so horrific." The whole performance throbbed, in the words of the director, with the "reality of human experience."[14] Much the same version, directed by Colin Ellis and Sally Miles, was performed by professional actors, at the Mermaid Theatre, London, opening on 5 April 1961, but with less success, the cast managing, according to the critic Irving Wardle, little more than "stained glass posturing and numb-skull knockabout"; the Second Shepherds' play was taken to be the occasion for raucous humor only, and Christ, to my surprise, died on the Cross with his back, perversely, to the audience.[15] The following year, the Lambeth Dramatic Club performed a three-hour version of the plays in front of the choir screen in Westminster Abbey, 16-21 July 1962; this production was "often deeply moving" and "cut deepest" in such episodes as that of the shepherds at the Nativity, where a "naive earthiness is accepted into worship," although the "lively horseplay of Noah and his wife" was less easily accepted.[16]

When all five of the Wakefield Master's plays were first performed—on Corpus Christi day, 1967, again at Bretton Hall, the entire Wakefield collection being presented, directed by John Hodgson, using the text modernized by Martial Rose—the play of Herod the Great proved to be the most forcibly effective of all.[17]

Rose formed the hypothesis that the Towneley plays were originally all presented in one place rather than on pageant wagons moving from station to station. Jane Oakshott of Leeds

Introduction

University countered with a presentation of the complete plays (except for the First Shepherds' play) for the Wakefield Festival on 28-29 June 1980, by twenty-nine separate companies, each representing a putative trade guild and each performing its play at three separate stations, the first adjacent to the cathedral. These hypotheses, related to arguments about the original processional method of presenting the York plays, hardly affect the exposition in the following chapters since I am concerned with single plays, not whole collections; but it is relevant to note that the processions of each cast from the station where they had just finished playing to the next provided, according to one observer of the Wakefield production, a "valuable insight into the way it must have felt to be in a medieval town on the day of a performance, with so many actors engaged and so many dramatic episodes in the corner of one's eyes: the sense of endeavor and participation was remarkable";[18] and also that similar comments about the "communal spirit" or sense of "common experience" are invariably made in connection with other large-scale productions which involve a variety of acting companies united in one enterprise—indeed, the first Bretton Hall production was undertaken to provide a unifying common purpose for the newly-founded college.

More relevant for my purpose are the observations that the text used in the 1980 production (barely modernized, by Peter Meredith) revealed the remarkable strength of the language of the Wakefield Master, and that those performers best succeeded who allowed the text to work for them and who refrained from diluting their monologues with unnecessary business.

> [T]he amateur players of the Second Shepherds' Play—which is all too often turgidly performed—showed an equally intelligent and sure-footed understanding of what they were saying and doing. The shepherds played a persuasively rustic comic routine, allowing the text to dictate expression and business, rather than adding them as distracting extras. The convincing solidity of the rough and dirty costumes also made a moving theatrical contrast with the silk and satin of the Virgin and Child, emphasising the contrast in tone between the two parts of the play.[19]

Introduction

What seemed to me the best efforts of the next production of the entire collection (minus the Second Shepherds' play), performed in the quadrangle of Victoria College, Toronto, on 25-26 May 1985, using a moderately modernized text by David Parry (Alexandra Johnston, dramaturge; Garrett Epp, artistic director), again came straight from the text: Cain's self-satisfied smile as he carried off Abel's body; Noah's enormous sigh as he thought of what his wife would say; Herod's clear manic-depression; the startled look on the knights' faces as they learned they were required to prepare for battle; Christ dragged through the audience. The least satisfactory effects resulted from the imagination of the director rather than the mind of the playwright: the herald pretended he had to improvise his long speech since Herod's arrival had been delayed (recalling all the tricks directors have played with the long speech by the archbishop in *Henry V*); and Annas illogically asked, "Why standys thou so styll?" (l. 246) even while Jesus was being pushed and pulled about by the knights. One of the hypotheses (associated with Richard Southern's thesis propounded in *The Medieval Theatre in the Round*, 1957 [revised ed., 1975]) tested in this production concerned the placing of the audience; they moved freely between five stages on the perimeters of the quadrangle to stand near the play being performed and, since one play might occupy more than one stage, and since characters often approached their stages from the front, were frequently jostled by the actors—an effect only sparingly called for in the text.

The York Historical Pageant, acted in York on 26-31 July 1909, included a performance on a wagon of a shortened version of the York Shepherds' play, preceded by an abbreviation of the annual proclamation announcing the plays and the placing of a city banner beside the wagon. The city was proud of such authentic historical details in its Pageant, and memories of the Shepherds' play may have lingered at All Saints, since in the Historical Pageant it was imagined that a fifteenth-century Rector of All Saints, North Street, was in attendance at the performance of the play.[20] At any rate, some years before 1925, a performance of Paul H. Wright's version of the York sequence of Nativity plays (based clearly on the original text, but with some rearrangement and shortening) had become an annual event in the life of All

Saints Church, North Street, York. In 1925 this production was overshadowed by the arrival in York of Dame Ellen Terry. She had come to see a production of an amalgamation, in eight episodes, of the York and Coventry plays of the Nativity by E. K. Chambers; when this was first produced, at the Everyman Theatre, Hampstead, on Christmas Eve, 1920, she herself (aged 74) had played the part of the Prologue, costumed as a nun. At York the play was performed at the Guildhall (opening on 5 January) by the amateurs of the York Everyman Theatre, and directed by Edith Craig, Ellen Terry's daughter. Edith Craig (1869-1947) also specialized in directing out-of-the-way serious plays. She had learned from her brother Gordon's direction of Housman's *Bethlehem* (Imperial Institute, London, opening on 17 December 1902), for which she helped make the colorful costumes,[21] and at York showed her skill at "fine grouping and contrast of costume and color," and was careful to make sure that the dialogue was not "unduly stressed." Students and members of the congregation of All Saints presented their less ambitious production with the "utmost dignity and reverence" on a stage (with a curtain) erected before the altar, affording the "congregation" a clear view. Special lighting was used to good effect and certainly authentically when, at the Nativity proper, "an unearthly light fills the place and makes Joseph's lantern superfluous"; but in contrast to the medieval productions Joseph "showed commendable restraint in the hour of his distressing discovery"—necessarily so, since the long complaint with which he begins the play of Joseph's Trouble about Mary was omitted, and his questioning of her much abbreviated—and the birth of Christ took place behind closed curtains. The extreme liveliness apparent in the early Yorkshire revivals of the Second Shepherds' play is not called for by the York plays, although the published text of the All Saints version contains many stage-directions indicating the emotions behind the words of the actors; rather, the script of the York play of the Nativity is especially noticeable for its restraint and beautiful patterning. Even the latter was supplanted by posing and remains absent from the curtailed version of this play performed since 1951 at the York Festival.[22] Like the Second Shepherds' play and other plays by the Wakefield Master, the York series of Nativity

Introduction

plays has remained in the amateur repertoire. For some years, for example, they were performed annually at Christmas time in St. Mary's Church, Aldermaston, by members of the Atomic Weapons Research Establishment and others, directed in 1959 by Patricia Eastop;[23] in the fifteenth century as well the plays were felt to be an antidote to a crumbling world order.

No public performance of a medieval Passion play took place in England until after the Second World War, and the plays of the York Realist have not fared well. E. Martin Browne, who early in his career advocated planning scenes according to "contemporary pictures" in order to arrive at beautiful compositions—and, in reaction to some of the Craigs' work, speaking the lines "to bring out the meaning" as well as, in reaction to some of Poel's and Monck's work, avoiding "monotony or chanting"[24]—and who directed the York plays for the York Festival in 1951, 1954, 1957, and 1966, believed that they "are not sophisticated and do not demand subtle acting . . . but always . . . ask for a fine sense of rhythm in the speaking, strength in movement, and above all a direct and simple sincerity born of faith."[25] He therefore established for the York Festival a style generally regarded since as "slow-paced, reverent, dignified, and stylishly archaic,"[26] with occasional novelties. The York Realist demands more than this. It is impossible to gain much, if any, appreciation of his work from the York Festival performances. One of his characteristic effects, for example, is iteration, and this is necessarily missing from Canon J. S. Purvis' text, which is condensed so that it can be played in three or three-and-a-half hours; in addition, the heads and tails of the plays, important for their meaning, are often lopped off.

Thirty-six of the York plays, including five by the York Realist, were performed, very successfully and with a gripping effect, directed by Jane Oakshott (using the complete texts modernized by Canon Purvis), in the pedestrian precinct of Leeds University on 17-18 May 1975, as part of the centenary celebrations of the University. The entire York collection of plays was performed (planned by Alexandra Johnston, artistic direction by David Parry) at the University of Toronto on 1-2 October 1977. At both Leeds and Toronto the plays were performed on wagons (12′ by 6′), each by a different company of actors, and each at three different stations.[27] At Leeds, where, it may be said, the York plays were first revived in conditions approximating those of York in the Middle Ages, the thirty-six different companies came from, among others, twenty different university departments and twelve city groups. An attempt was made, as in the case of fifteenth-century York, to match the special interests or abilities of the company with the subject of their play. Thus, members of the Department of Physics performed the play of the Creation (originally produced by the Plasterers); members of the dramatic society of a Leeds department store (in a spirit, perhaps, of jovial self-criticism) performed the play of the Temptation of Adam and Eve (originally produced by the Coopers); members of the Department of Psychology, knowledgeable about hidden guilt and naked depression, performed the play of the Expulsion of Adam and Eve from Eden (originally produced by the Armorers, a guild able to supply the angel, who plays the major and sternest part, with his armor and his sword); members of the Department of Metallurgy made gilt crowns for their play of the Magi (originally produced by the Goldsmiths); members of the Department of Civil Engineering performed the play of the Crucifixion, which calls for a "gynne" (l. 197, "device" or "engine") for raising the cross (originally produced by the Pinners, who made sharp-pointed metal objects such as are needed for boring holes and nailing); and members of the drama society of St. Mary's Church performed the play of the Death of the Virgin (originally produced by the Drapers, who could see to it that Mary was attired and covered in a comely manner on her death-bed). According to the director, "the very appropriateness of the play for certain groups helped to give those groups a sense of purposeful corporate identity which supplied a strong motivation for performing that particular play, and performing it well."[28] This particular (and important) effect was missing from the production at Toronto.

Apparent at both Leeds and Toronto were the excitement and grandeur of the rumbling wagons, especially in the more confined space at Leeds; their surprisingly large capacity; the ease and speed with which it proved possible to prepare them at each station (a preparation covered, at least at Toronto, by the mono-

Introduction

logues with which many of the plays, including all but one of the York Realist's, begin); the usefulness for the performance of the small area immediately in front of each wagon; and the prevailing festive or holiday mood. Unfortunately, the plays of the York Realist, except his last, were among those forced indoors by torrential rains at Toronto and performed in makeshift conditions. The play of Christ before Herod was, in any case, calamitously under-rehearsed. Despite these disadvantages, the performance of the series of plays by the York Realist impressed itself on the audience, according to one observer, as portraying "Christ as victim of the human desire for law and order, complacency, and the status quo"—an effect true, I believe, to part of the playwright's meaning. The Realist's last play, the Death of Christ, proved powerful—the audience was by now filled with a sense of complicity in his death, and some of them wept—even though the actor playing Jesus failed to address his words to the audience, an effect almost certainly called for in the script.[29]

Earlier in 1977, *The Passion*, "a selection from the York Mystery Plays" by Tony Harrison (the Yorkshire poet) and "the company," directed by Bill Bryden and Sebastian Graham-Jones, was performed at the National Theatre (in the small Cottesloe Theatre), opening on 21 April, so successfully that it became for a time a part of the permanent repertoire of the National Theatre (joined thereafter by versions of the Nativity and Last Judgment which include episodes from collections other than York). This 1977 production perhaps owed something to the first "trendy" revival (of the Chester plays, in a circus tent, with rock music, at Chester in 1973, directed by James Roose-Evans)[30] and possibly also to Joseph Papp's notorious or celebrated version of *Hamlet* (The Public Theatre, New York, 26 December 1967).[31] *The Passion*, with a candid and refreshing absence of piety, but on the other hand possibly disingenuously, is meant to show the faith of a people in action, not the faith of the audience, although the "complicity" of the audience, by their silence and proximity, in the killing of Christ noticed at Toronto also occurs at the National, especially since the Cottesloe is adapted to "promenade theatre." The play is presented in an "aggressively demotic" modern setting; members of the company, dressed in the "various uniforms and overalls of carpenter, painter, butcher, fireman . . . gas fitter, construction worker, etc.," chat (or are instructed to) with members of the audience, who stand (no seats are provided) while the play, interspersed with songs accompanied by traditional tunes rearranged as popular music, proceeds around and among them, Yorkshire accents being much in evidence. One is somewhat confused, turning round to find Albert Finney monotonously, and with mild anger, addressing nobody in particular. *The Passion* is essentially a radically shortened version of the York Realist's work; it keeps an abbreviated version of the important exchange between Pilate and his wife (as does Canon Purvis in his short version)—and legitimately adds a fine mayoral complacency for the former, as well as a belch for Caiaphas as he drinks from a large goblet—but, as at Toronto, the audience is most seized by the play of the Crucifixion, almost completely preserved by Harrison (and only slightly less so by Purvis) and characterized by a "complex mixture of unawareness and cruelty"[32] on the part of the torturers, a play which cannot with confidence be claimed to be the work of the York Realist but which was assumed to be so in the publicity for *The Passion*, and quickly declared by Benedict Nightingale, the dramatic critic, to be "the first unqualified masterpiece of the British theatre."[33]

Numerous revivals have briefly shone, to vanish into oblivion, but the record shows that the most sucessful performances—or moments in performances—seem to have occurred when the texts of the plays have been trusted, or at least when an attempt has been made to catch their true spirit, to approach them with humility (in Jane Oakshott's words). The plays of the Wakefield Master and the York Realist are not only among the most complicated medieval biblical plays, but are particularly to be relied on, since these two playwrights knew—as I hope to demonstrate—in detail exactly what they were about. Their scripts, particularly the former's, are as replete with implicit directions for action as Shakespeare's. In no need of gratuitous theatricality, they both seize to full advantage the theatrical resources at their disposal, and both write with a distinct purpose and for a particular audience.

Putting the play and the players together has been said to be a hopeless task, producing only "phantoms,"[34] and it is certainly true that a detailed reconstruction of a medieval (or Elizabethan) performance is impossible. The business of the playwright—his highest art—is to write for performance, however, and I hope to show that the meaning and effect of the Wakefield Master's and York Realist's plays will not appear unless they are approached with the understanding that they were performed, with some idea of how they were performed, and with some appreciation of what they meant to a medieval audience. Their meaning is embodied or made palpable in performance; their effect results from a confluence of the playwright's art, the art of the players, and the minds and feelings of the audience. A surprising number of points become clear if the plays are analyzed from this point of view.

Using mostly medieval sources (and generally avoiding non-medieval English terms with unhelpful connotations, such as "act," "actor," "theatrical," "scene," "scenery," "drama," "dramatic," and "character," but not ignoring the twentieth-century revivals), trying to keep to the path between scepticism and credulity, and hoping that my opinions, unlike those manufactured by Rasselas' man who was eminent for his knowledge of the mechanic powers but who in an instant dropped into the lake, will sustain my flight, I therefore consider, in the case of the eight plays studied in some detail in the following chapters, the elements essential to their performance: a playwright; sponsors; a place (with some spectacle and music); a plot made out of a story or out of interpretations of a story; a script with sources; players (in costumes) capable of expressing the meaning of lines, and doing any necessary "stage business," and so representing the persons in the plot; and an audience to respond to the meaning (or, rather, multiple meanings) of the performance, and to share in the purpose of the playwright, sponsors, and players. I have in this way been able to find some keys with which to unlock the practices of the Wakefield Master and the York Realist, and have been able to reach many conclusions which seem to me to be indisputable. Too little, however, is known in detail about religious, social, economic, and agricultural life—not to mention the art of plays—for certainty to be asked in all particulars. I have distinguished between what I regard as certain and what is probable, and have tried to keep to a

Introduction

minimum any observations based on the merely possible.

In the first chapter I outline the particular interests and skills of the Wakefield Master and the York Realist, and describe the circumstances surrounding the original presentation of their work; offering, in the case of the Wakefield Master, examples from his play of Noah, which I do not subsequently discuss.

Introduction

Fig. a. Map of the West Riding

Chapter I

The Wakefield Master and the York Realist:
Playwrights, Playing, Players, and Audience

*And David and all Israel played before God with all
their might.—1 Paralipomenon* 13.8

Two Playwrights. The Wakefield Master, who consistently
writes in a particular stanzaic form[1] and has a pronounced aptitude for proverbial language and an interest in contemporary rural
life, with which he manifests a detached sympathy, unarguably
wrote five of the biblical plays in the Towneley manuscript: the
play of Noah, the First and Second Shepherds' plays, and the
plays of Herod the Great and the Buffeting of Jesus. His work is
thus much more in evidence in the Nativity than in the Passion,
but he also added passages, identifiable by their stanzaic form, to
all four other plays of the Passion in the Towneley collection; except in the case of the play of the Scourging, to which he contributed twenty-eight stanzas and which follows his play of the
Buffeting, these passages are very short. He also contributed one
stanza each to the plays of the Pilgrims, the Ascension, and the
Killing of Abel (a play sometimes wholly attributed to him because of its general style) and forty-two stanzas to the play of the
Last Judgment, more than doubling its length.

The Towneley manuscript was written by one hand, perhaps
at a date well into the sixteenth century,[2] and it appears to reproduce the Wakefield Master's plays from very good copies and
with only minor inaccuracies. Their language and some allusions
to style of clothing indicate that he wrote his plays during the

17

fifteenth century.[3] Precise dates are mere guesses; an hypothesis, which I follow but which is not essential to my analysis of his work, is that his plays were in part inspired by analogous plays in the York collection, and I consequently favor a date later in the century. If he wrote many decades before his plays were copied into the manuscript, someone took care to preserve fair copies of them.

His title, the "Wakefield Master," first given to him by Charles Gayley in 1903, with a lower-case "m," and in 1907, with an upper-case "M,"[4] is cautiously avoided by, among others, the expert editor of his plays. I adopt it with no hesitation since he has demonstrably and brilliantly mastered the art of writing plays for performance. If, as is possible, he influenced the work of other playwrights he can be termed a "Master" also in the sense of that word as it is used by art historians; and if he learned something about playwriting—particularly plotting—from the York Realist, he is revealed to be a pivotal figure among medieval playwrights.

The York Realist's work can also be identified on stylistic grounds only. He writes true or functional alliterative verse in rhyming stanzas, but unlike the Wakefield Master uses different stanzaic forms for each of his plays, except for the plays of the Conspiracy and Christ before Herod; and he has a strong interest in argument and debate as well as in contemporary upper-class life, which he satirizes. For these two reasons he is generally agreed to be the author of eight of the ten York plays about the Passion (and to have added a beginning to a ninth, the play of the Road to Calvary, which is not otherwise in functional alliterative verse). The subjects of the five other York plays written in functional alliterative verse do not allow scope for his brand of "realism," but it is possible that he wrote them also; and the one play of the Passion which contains no such verse, the play of the Crucifixion (which because of its blasé cruelty has proved so moving to twentieth-century audiences), shows many signs of it, although no sign of his characteristic "star system." It may most reliably be concluded that his work consists of at least the series of eight Passion plays. Their single authorship seems to me to be indubitable. He composed them before 1463-77, the date of the single manuscript, British Library MS. Add. 35,290, written by one main hand, in which they are reproduced, especially five of them, from very imperfect copies. Speeches are misassigned, the stanzaic pattern often breaks down, lines are missing, and meter and sense can be unclear. It is certain that the scribe in no case had in front of him fair copies of the original texts; the passage of time, permitting ad hoc revisions and repeated and careless copying or memorizing of the texts, can account for these defects, and the York Realist was therefore perhaps at work some decades before 1463—but probably not before 1422, when a play was written of the Judgment of Christ before Pilate, which his play on the same subject appears to have subsequently replaced.[5] He therefore appears to have been at work early in the middle third of the fifteenth century. Neither his language nor any internal allusions permit a more precise dating.

Perhaps the Wakefield Master was his younger contemporary. His title, the "York Realist," was first provided, again, by Charles Gayley in 1903, with a lower-case "r"; I elevated this to a capital "R" in 1963, for reasons which have inevitably led to disputes about the meaning of his "realism" and to legitimate assertions that his religion subsumes it[6] (as well as to rather indignant, and unnecessary, claims that the Wakefield Master is the better playwright), but there are still good reasons, related to his treatment of the Old Testament, to keep this title. (The term 'York Master' has been pre-empted for a tenth-century York limestone carver.)

The work of these two geniuses, whose identities are unknown but who must have been clerics, might well have spread over a number of years or decades. More important, they are the first English writers to be gifted with an amazing aptitude for writing for performance.

The Purpose of Playing Biblical Plays. Biblical plays in the vernacular had been performed in England since the twelfth century "en l'onur Deu," as the Anglo-Norman play of the *Resurrection* says.[7] The phrase recurs in 1399 in connection with the York biblical plays, financed by the commons and craftsmen of the same city "en honour & reuerence nostre seignour Iesu Crist."[8] In about 1335 Robert Holcot, the English Dominican, adapting a phrase used with reference to *2 Kings* 6.21-23 by St. Thomas

Aquinas to express his approval of religious plays (*Alii ludi sunt qui ex gaudio devotionis procedunt*), sanctions plays performed by Christians, *ludus deuocionis et gaudii spiritalis*.[9] This phrase is Englished in 1405-10 in *Dives and Pauper*, Pauper approving of plays "don principaly for deuocioun & honest merthe,"[10] or spiritual joy (*MED* mirth n 2a) (there is no reflection of the Horatian *dulce et utile* here), and the York biblical plays are said in 1422 to have been instituted *ob magnam deuocionis causam*.[11] The performances are thus intended to be essentially forms of worship and expressions of spiritual joy and devotion. The representation of Christ suffering in silence amidst the worldly and cruel bustle of the plays of the Passion at York, and the prayers (to mention only one example) with which Noah begins and ends the Wakefield Master's plays of Noah clearly indicate that he and the York Realist share this religious purpose. When the plays were eventually banned it was because they were no longer understood to serve this purpose but to pervert it; in 1576 the ecclesiastical authorities decided that the Corpus Christi play at Wakefield contained "many thinges . . . which tende to the Derogation of the Maiestie and glorie of god."[12]

The performances at York were also good for the economy. The same document of 1399, which speaks of the honor and worship of our Lord, goes on to mention the "honour & profitt de mesme la Citee" (the two thoughts and phrases are also found together in similar contexts in the records of other cities, including Beverley[13]) and the visitors who travel to the city to see the plays. In 1426 Friar William Melton complained that the performances were the occasions of too much eating, drinking, general clamor, and holiday-making;[14] Chaucer (generally critical of the biblical plays) has the Wife of Bath attend "pleyes of myracles" to lead on her young lover—she would not have disappointed this meddling friar.[15] The Wycliffite treatise written in opposition to biblical plays in general (1380-1410), though it does not mention any particular plays or places, complains, among many other things, of the high prices charged for refreshments on the days of the performances and of the effort made to increase business beforehand so that money is available for the expenses of the play.[16] The general economy of York, the second city in the kingdom,

suffered a serious decline in the fifteenth century, when the performances seem to have been at their height (the same situation
prevailed at Coventry in the early sixteenth century),[17] and the
corporation and guilds had therefore a worldly motive for ensur-
ing that the performances continued and increased in splendor. It
may well have been partly as an anodyne to decreasing prosperity
that the York Realist was encouraged or welcomed (or hired) to
write his relatively grandiose plays, most of which, like the other
York plays, are keyed to the craft guilds financing them just as, at
the same time, as has been pointed out, the Minster and the parish
churches of the city were, at considerable expense, made more
glorious by the addition of new painted glass windows. Historians
consider the fifteenth century to be an age of piety,[18] and civic
prudence and pride were not incompatible with the religious purposes of the performances. The two motives probably melded into
one in the minds of the citizens, especially members of the corporation which controlled the plays and the master craftsmen who
produced them. God had saved and destroyed cities before.

By contrast, Wakefield, which has given its name to the
Wakefield Master, was little more than a very small township at
the beginning of the fifteenth century, though it had grown to
larger proportions by the end of the century, prospering with the
increasing woolen industry in the West Riding, although the area
remained overwhelmingly agricultural. During the third quarter of
the century the parish church was extensively rebuilt and em-
bellished, and Wakefield became a center for the woolen industry
but, although it had a Burgess Court by the fourteenth century,
remained unincorporated as a town, had no trade or craft guilds,
and was governed under the authority of the steward of the Lord
of the Manor of Wakefield, of which the town of Wakefield was
only a very small part. By the early sixteenth century it flourished
entirely by cloth manufacture ("Al the hole profite of the toun
stondith by course drapery," wrote John Leland) and most of the
inhabitants were connected with the industry, which was run by
small clothiers.[19] Before 1576 the town had "a plaie commonlie
called Corpus Christi plaie."[20]

It is not clear for what reason the manuscript of the Towneley
collection was written, but scholars in the past frequently held

Chapter I

that this collection represents in some form the Wakefield "Corpus Christi plaie" and more firmly that it includes plays previously presented, singly or in groups, as "clerks' plays"—short, self-contained religious plays (a common genre in England from the thirteenth or fourteenth century[21])—in the West Riding, among them the plays of the Wakefield Master: hence the anomaly of two Shepherds' plays. It was possibly when the collection was first mooted that he made his additions to the seven other plays. The Towneley series of Passion plays are held together by a unique understanding of Pilate,[22] which the Wakefield Master noticed and developed. His plays show no connection with guilds or with metropolitan life; on the contrary they reflect the concerns of an irregularly governed agricultural community with troubles and difficulties of its own, to which his plays offer solutions.

Biblical plays are entertaining. During the performance of the Anglo-Norman *Adam* not only does a choir sing seven responsories, but devils scatter across the playing area banging metal pots together, and a moving serpent (*serpens artificiose compositus*) suddenly appears. At Beverley (not thirty miles east of York) in 1220 a presentation of a play of the Resurrection, possibly a version of the Anglo-Norman play, drew a crowd motivated, according to a contemporary, by delight, or curiosity, or devotion, *delectationis . . . seu admirationis causa, vel sancto proposito excitandae devotionis.*[23] Robert Holcot also approved of plays presented for human consolation and relaxation. Most medieval biblical plays provide liveliness, invoke joy or laughter, and arouse curiosity. Music and song, for example, are called for in the scripts of about one in three of them.[24] Angels playing musical instruments are a favorite subject of late medieval English artists, including those who worked in York and in the West Riding, and angels are often required to sing in the plays. The York Realist has no occasion for music or song, plays of the Passion being normally unaccompanied by them, unless to lend worldly glory to Christ's enemies; the Wakefield Master, on the other hand, was knowledgeable about music and is, for example, very particular about how the *Gloria* is to be sung in his two Shepherds' plays, well in accordance with his century, of which the first half was one of the greatest ages of English music. Costumes were also a source of attraction. The many evil persons in the biblical plays and immoral ones in the morality plays provided an opportunity for the legitimate display of the exaggerated and fashionable clothing worn in both town and country and frequently denounced in the fourteenth and fifteenth centuries. The Wycliffite treatise seems to complain that the players' costumes encourage proud "aray" among members of the audience; the Wife of Bath obliges, wearing one of her bright scarlet gowns on her outings.[25] To make one of his points, the York Realist's plays require especially splendiferous costumes for the wicked, particularly Herod; and the knights of the Passion in both his and the Wakefield Master's plays probably wear gleaming bosses and girdles on their armor. The Wakefield Master, who has an eye for appropriate ornaments, depicts Caiaphas, for example, in every way as "a prelate, a lord in degré" (l. 154), and he is equally interested in the tattered and unusually muddy tunics of his shepherds as well as their mysterious satchels.

On the one hand the Wycliffite treatise claims that the players and their patrons make their plays ends in themselves, using biblical subjects merely as a means to indulge their pleasure in playing,[26] like Absolon in the Miller's Tale, who took the part of Herod merely "to shewe his lightnesse and maistrye" (I.3383, "agility and skill") and to impress Alison; on the other, York records of the extant play of the Crucifixion (the play notable for the combined ignorance and callousness of its speakers) refer in 1422 to the "holy words of the players," *ludencium oracula*.[27] The purposes of playing were no doubt mixed, but they certainly included the desire to entertain, the wish to find or show solutions, in personal reformation, to the problems both urban and rural of this world, and the absorption of these two motives in the impulse to worship God and express joy and devotion, an instinct fully shared by the York Realist and the Wakefield Master, although in the latter the desire to entertain was especially strong. No other English biblical plays are as hilarious as his, as some modern audiences have been fortunate enough to discover.

"Scaffold," "Place," and "Pageant." Biblical plays were usually presented outdoors according to a system of simultaneous

staging best referred to as the Place-and-Scaffold method, borrowing the terminology used in the *Castle of Perseverance* (probably written before 1425) and elsewhere. A Scaffold apparently was normally a raised wooden construction, the permanent home of one of the chief characters and not interchangeable with the Scaffold of an opposing character. The Place was a flat area, representing nowhere in particular, except the earth, or anything characters called it, or the area just outside whatever the Scaffold was meant to represent. Thus the Wakefield Master's play of Noah requires three Scaffolds representing respectively Heaven (high up), Noah's house, and the Ark; the Place represents the earth, the area outside Noah's house, the distance between his house and the Ark, and the ground and green fields of Armenia. All medieval English religious plays, from the earliest to the latest, can be presented according to this system, and a large number, including the Wakefield Master's and York Realist's, contain clear indications in their scripts and occasional stage-directions that they were.

External evidence reveals that the York (and Chester and Coventry) plays were presented on moveable wagons, or "Pageants," which were at least sometimes framed by four posts and a covering, but the essential features of the Place-and-Scaffold system still pertained. The Pageant might contain one or several Scaffolds, the area between and in front of them constituting the Place, which might (as has seemed natural in some revivals) overflow into the street. Thus the York Realist's play of Christ before Herod, presented on its Pageant, requires one Scaffold, representing Herod's court; the Place represents the street adjacent to the court.

What can be known about the Scaffolds must be largely deduced from the scripts, although full descriptions (dated 1433 and 1526)[28] of the York Pageant, which was especially lavish, for the play of the Last Judgment indicate that, with representations of Heaven, a rainbow, and Hell, it attempts to reproduce the arrangement of the Last Judgment as it was commonly painted, especially on chancel arches (as, for example, in St. Gregory's, Bedale). It is therefore not unreasonable to regard paintings and carvings, or parts of them, as providing analogues for Scaffolds. That paintings, carvings, and plays often had common literary sources points to the same conclusion. The one Scaffold, representing the stable, required for the York play of the Nativity is thus in all probability a three-dimensional version of the numerous depictions of it in fifteenth-century English and Northern European art (fig. 1). The Scaffold inhabited during the trial sequence by the York Realist's Herod which represents his court, both his private chamber and the presence chamber, contains his throne, judgment-bar, bed, and something (presumably a table) to hold his wine jar, goblet, scepter, and enormous sword; and somewhere at hand (in a chest?) are a white garment and tunic. It has an entrance from the Place and can hold nine people. Such phrases as "gois abakke" (l. 141), "drawes you adrygh" (l. 159, "stand aside"), and "Comes nerre" (l. 236, "come nearer") probably imply crowding rather than spaciousness, and Herod's carelessness with his sword might legitimately cause some consternation. Artists frequently crammed this and similar episodes into the small spaces afforded by the pages of a book, tablets of alabaster, roof-bosses, and misericords. The frame of the Pageant, it has been observed of a modern production, gives the sense that what is shown constitutes the "inner reality of things,"[29] especially, it might be added, since in the case of this play the audience is said to occupy a "broydenesse" (l. 1, "spacious area"). The Wakefield Master's Scaffolds are generally less crowded, but they can be equally as solid and elaborate. It is impossible to tell whether his plays were presented or meant to be presented on Pageants, but the Place is more fully used in his plays than in the York Realist's and appears to be larger. The Wakefield Master's plays require from none (if my inferences from the script of the play of Herod the Great are correct) to three Scaffolds, the York Realist's from one to two (or possibly three).

Both playwrights were skilled at making the most of their Scaffolds (particularly, perhaps, their doors, bed, and thrones) and also of the relationship between the Place and the Scaffold. The obsequiousness and hypocrisy of Caiaphas and Annas are well expressed—for example, in the exchange in the York play of the First Trial before Pilate (ll. 275-79)—between them (in the Place, or barely in the Scaffold) and Pilate, complacently ensconced on his Scaffold, which contains his judicial bench:

Chapter I

Pilatus.	Come byn, you bothe, and to the benke brayde you.	*in bench hasten*
Caiaphas.	Nay gud sir, laugher is leffull for vs.	*lower lawful*
Pilatus.	A, sir Cayphas, be curtayse yhe bus.	*must*
Anna.	Nay goode lorde, it may not be thus.	
Pilatus.	Sais no more, but come sitte you beside me in sorowe as I saide youe.	*say*

(ll. 275-79)

Similarly, but with a very different meaning, God, in the Wakefield Master's play of Noah, descends from the Scaffold to stand in the Place by Noah (*Gen.* 6.9, "Noe . . . walked with God," *cum Deo ambulavit*), who responds: "I thank the, Lord so dere, that wold vowchsayf/ Thus low to appere to a symple knafe" (ll. 172-73), thus providing, since "low" is both literally and figuratively true, one of the many Christological references in this play; none of the five other English plays of Noah explicitly demonstrates God's humility in this way.

The audience stood or sat as close to the Place as possible. In some cases (for the presentation of the *Castle of Perseverance*, for example) they appear to have surrounded it altogether, but the effects of the Wakefield Master's and York Realist's plays depend so frequently on facial expressions, small movements, and the positioning of the players that anything more than a semicircle or horseshoe for the audience seems undesirable, to say the least, despite some modern experiments to the contrary. (It may be, however, that the devotional—or festive—spirit, was so active in some instances that some felt it sufficient merely to be in the vicinity of a performance.) The back of the York Pageant for the play of the Last Judgment was covered with a red cloth, and the sides were also hung with cloth, thus making it impossible to see the presentation from behind or from the side.

Evil characters—the Devil in the opening lines of the York play of the Temptation, for example—sometimes enter the Place by shoving their way, or pretending to, through the audience. The York Realist's scripts never call for this effect; the Wakefield Master makes use of it on one (very appropriate) occasion, in his addition to the play of the Scourging when the knights drag Jesus through the audience to Pilate's Scaffold, and where the crowning with thorns is later performed in the Place, referred to by the knights as their "ryng" (l. 227), or the area in front of the Scaffold.

The members of the audience did not have a passive role. When not being verbally abused by tyrants, they were listening to God the Father proclaiming his Trinity and his might, hearing a sermon delivered directly to them, listening to a proclamation being read out to them from the Place, being appealed to as "man" by Jesus speaking mournfully from the cross or after he had risen, being confided in, in a neighborly manner, by persons more like themselves—Joseph or the shepherds, for example—or, at the end of the performance, being blessed by one of the holy characters or cursed by one of the devilish. In general the Place and Scaffolds must have lent themselves to such forms of direct address, which are very common in medieval plays. Again, the Wakefield Master and York Realist take full advantage of this tradition. They are acutely aware, for example, of the ludicrous and terrifying nature of the tyrannical speeches, to which they give greater intensity than is usual and whose meaning they deepen; and simple direct address is hardly ample precedent for the competing comic monologues, embarrassing moments of public exposure, of Noah and his wife, each overheard to the other's disgust. Proclamations in the two early morality plays are, as stage directions indicate, read out "down stage" in the Place by an official, probably turning now this way and now that;[30] probably the herald (heralds were commonly used for embassies in fifteenth-century England) in the Towneley play of the Magi does the same (ll. 73-84), to be followed by the Wakefield Master's more elaborate and pointed version of the same episode in his play of Herod the Great. Thrice, in the plays of the First Trial before Pilate (ll. 370-79), Trial before Herod (ll. 375-78), and Second Trial before Pilate (ll. 264-67*sd*), the York Realist shows, amidst some impatience and confusion, the busy, repetitive, and legalistic forms of this world by having Jesus and any witnesses called to the "bar" with an official "Oyez" (as was the custom, both in real life and in romances) pronounced to this crowd, the audience.

Other features common to medieval religious plays resulted from the system of simultaneous staging. Performances, for example, began with all or most of the characters who belong in the Scaffold already in them, or with a procession of all such characters, who entered the Place and then repaired to their respective Scaffolds.[31] Jill, for example, must be in her cottage Scaffold when both the play of Noah and the Second Shepherds' play begin, and Christ, of course, is already on the cross, surrounded by the other characters, when the York Realist's play of the Death of Christ begins. The system generally made it possible for the audience to see different or opposing characters simultaneously, as in the narrative paintings, retables, diptychs, and series of carvings skirting the altar of a well-furnished church, which provide good analogies to the idea of simultaneous staging. The opportunity to present obvious contrasts—between Jill and Mary, or between a snoozing Pilate and an exhausted Jesus brutally kept awake—or to reveal a universal view—God sees the stubbornness of Noah's wife—is not lost on the York Realist or Wakefield Master.[32]

Again, as in the longer liturgical plays, the system of Place and Scaffolds also called for a large number of greetings, farewells, and journeys. Much of the dialogue consisted of one great character formally greeting another at his Scaffold or bidding him a stately farewell, or of characters talking about journeys to be undertaken (or talking or singing as they undertook them by walking across the Place). There are thus ample precedents for the constant comings and goings in the York Realist's plays, and for the way in which he has endowed this activity with elaborate (and often blasphemous) politeness, but none for the sense of inconvenience, the logistical obstacles (which, as I shall show, have spiritual significance) he has introduced. He tends to show departures and arrivals, the Wakefield Master longer journeys, over which he takes some care. In the explicitly devotional parts of his plays, they tend to be symbolic; in the ostensibly farcical parts, real. Both the York and Towneley shepherds reach Bethlehem ("about a mile" distant from the fields, according to general understanding[33]) in a minute or two while they sing, and their journey carries some of the moral force of journeys in the older morality plays: salvation is quickly available. Time and space are more real (as is necessary for farce) in the Wakefield Master's play of the Buffeting and the first parts of his Shepherds' plays and his play of Noah: Chaucer's Miller's old John the carpenter, who has seen a play of Noah (perhaps his guild produced it), readily believes that the world will be drowned "in lasse than an hour" (I.3519, "less"), and in the Wakefield Master's play time is seen as pressing. Noah and his wife—the latter awkwardly carrying a distaff with flax on it, a spindle in use, and a reel half-wound (ll. 298, 338, 364), and periodically frantically dropping them, or getting tangled up in them, no doubt (l. 324), and their sons and daughters carrying their possessions (l. 316)—move quickly across the Place from their House Scaffold to the Ark Scaffold (ll. 334-35), wordlessly, in a grim hurry.

Both the Wakefield Master and the York Realist write explicitly for the Place-and-Scaffold method of presentation and show themselves thoroughly at home with its possibilities. In their own ways, they both make fuller and more adventurous use than other medieval playwrights of the system of presentation they inherited. The ease with which the Wakefield Master in particular uses or manipulates the Place and Scaffolds, and fits his plots and themes into them in clever and unusual ways, amounts to genius. Both his and the York Realist's plays provide examples to support Allardyce Nicoll's general thesis that playwrights do their best work for given theatrical conditions, not when they can pick and choose among a variety of radically different possibilities.[34]

Story, Plot, and Meaning. The plots of the plays of the Nativity and Passion, which are expansions and sometimes re-orderings and alterations and selections of the stories told in the Gospels, including some of the apocryphal gospels, are partly shaped by the exigencies imposed and opportunities opened up by the system of presentation. The English tradition, first apparent in the thirteenth century, of beginning plays with tyrannical speeches, for example, provided occasions for speeches by Christ's enemies, which could be filled with phrases (such as "by Mahound's blood") suggesting ironic contrasts to the real power of God or the mildness of Christ, and thus the meaning of the play could be introduced.[35] The York Realist begins eight plays in this way and the Wakefield Master three (the play of Herod the Great, the Conspiracy, and the "Talents"). Again, a literary tradition of complaint and satire proved useful for some of the plays of the

Nativity, since the shepherds and Joseph were poor men. Their plays could thus begin with gloomy monologues which form a contrast to the joy which eventually prevails; the York play of the Nativity and the Wakefield Master's two Shepherds' plays begin in this way.

The plots are also heavily controlled by medieval interpretations and re-tellings of the Gospel stories. The Franciscan *Meditations on the Life of Christ*, a long work written in the late thirteenth or early fourteenth century and once attributed entirely to St. Bonaventura (1221-74), pervasively influenced both artists and playwrights. An abridged translation into English by Nicholas Love, Prior of the Carthusian House of Mount Grace in Yorkshire from 1409, circulated widely during the fifteenth century, especially in Yorkshire. It contains many passages analogous to the biblical plays and describes episodes in the life of Christ in expansive and vivid detail; these devout "imagined representations," as the author calls them, are exactly what most of the plays provide. Of the offering of the three Magi, for example, the author of the *Meditations* comments: "Regard them well as they reverently speak and listen; and see the Lady as, with great modesty in speech, her eyes always turned to the ground, she finds no pleasure in speaking much or in being seen."[36] Such passages provide clues to the organization (not to mention the playing) of the plays; the *Meditations on the Life of Christ* and some of its many vernacular descendants, such as the long and popular *Northern Passion*, certainly influenced the work of the York Realist.

Much of the *Meditations on the Life of Christ* is incorporated in the even longer fourteenth-century *Vita Christi* by Ludolphus of Saxony, who died in 1377. This work is more densely written and more learned than the *Meditations on the Life of Christ* (which is itself, however, by no means unlearned, making frequent reference to the Old Testament, for example) and provides not only devout "imagined representations" but also frequent intellectual interpretations, based on numerous patristic and scholastic commentaries. Copies of this work were widespread on the continent (it was printed as early as 1472), and it was certainly known, although probably less well known than the *Meditations on the Life of Christ*, in fifteenth-century England.[37] The great learning of Ludolphus probably provided the Wakefield Master with food for thought; he appears to be dependent on the *Vita Christi* for the plots and themes of his plays of Herod the Great and the Buffeting, and to quote from it.

The plots and themes of the plays of the York Realist and the Wakefield Master depend on their ability to see the Nativity and the Passion and their significance from a less direct angle than earlier or simpler playwrights. The York Realist's plays form a sequence whose full significance is not revealed until the last play, the play of the Death of Christ, an effect clear even if not all his plays are performed in any given year; the Wakefield Master's are self-contained, providing their own keys and conclusions. The indirections, more complex than the contrasts provided at the beginnings of simpler plays, are not inventions but expansions of brief clues found in medieval interpretations of the Gospels (and in the Gospels themselves), especially in their references to the Old Testament. The two playwrights never fail to express in detail their obvious interest not only in contemporary social conditions but also in the use of less immediately obvious messianic passages in the Old Testament, especially from the books of *Isaias, Jeremias, Job*, and *Psalms*, which they tend to take literally rather than figuratively or allegorically—a practice more common in late medieval works of art[38] than in biblical plays. They both "unmetaphor" the language of the Old Testament mercilessly, and this literalizing is what makes possible, for example, the York Realist's inclusion of four humorous going-to-bed episodes (*Job* 33.19) in his plays.

The unmetaphoring is the justification for the term 'York Realist,' especially if, as is possible, he taught the trick to the Wakefield Master, who goes further than the York Realist into the realm of literalizing biblical and ecclesiastical language ("the hand of God," "the head of the Church") and who also takes some delight—probably because the Bible itself was generally considered to be full of riddles, and perfect love (*1 John* 4.18), itself a riddle (as Langland says, B XIII.167)—in melding, with his literal use of the Old Testament, not only the activities of daily life but also proverbs, catch-phrases, literary works, games, popular tales, meaningful names and puns, which he generally not only mentions but has his players enact. Like Solomon, the Wakefield Master multiplies riddles in parables, and is to be wondered at for his "canticles, and proverbs, and parables, and interpretations"; *Ecclesiasticus* (47.18) thus provided him with warrant, if he needed it, for his complicated and ravelled activity. He was also surrounded by an analogous *modus operandi* in carvings (especially misericords) and glass-paintings in churches and yeomen's houses in Yorkshire, including the West Riding. He must have seen and known of some of these teasing visualizations, which were very common in the fifteenth century, and most examples of which were made from the fourteenth to the early sixteenth centuries.

The turbulence of domestic life and labor interested him as much as it did the designer for the carvers from Ripon who, working at Beverley in 1520, on two adjacent misericords showed a woman pulling a man's hair, a dog stealing food from a pot, a woman grinding with a hand-mill, a boy splitting logs, the man wheeling his wife in a barrow (one way to get Jill into the ark) while she pulls his ear, a man lifting a beam, and a woman holding a dog by the neck.[39] Proverbs, such as "shoeing the goose" (Whiting G389; fig. 2),[40] "putting the cart before the horse" (Whiting C60), and "to know a goose from a swan" (Whiting G387), are also carved on misericords in Beverley; the latter might particularly have interested the Wakefield Master (who shows a ram confused with a lamb): a jester (echoed by the one in the next seat who sees one thing and says another, unable to make up his mind) is flanked by a goose in the left supporter and a swan in the right.[41] Foxes and geese are very frequently carved on misericords, the former often representing friars and the latter gullible persons (Whiting G377, 384, 385, 393; fig. 3), a proverbial configuration (Whiting F605) spoken backwards by Cain in the play of the Killing of Abel (l. 84). Many of these *jeux* need have no religious significance except insofar as they show how little the world of man is, but sometimes the religious point is made directly, as in a lost glass-painting, in the West Riding, which dramatizes the proverbial expression "God speed the plough" (Whiting G239) by showing a plough drawn by four oxen led by an angel with another driving behind.[42] (Cain's plough horse, Donning, moves promptly only when the name of God is invoked, ll. 33-34). A catch-phrase is suggested by the supporter on a misericord showing a man with his head in a sack (fig. 4), especially since his fellow in the other supporter is spearing a snail; they are responding inadequately to the center-piece, which shows a man entangled by two dragons.[43] Popular and literary tales also find a place here, as they do in the plays; a version of the Man of Law's tale appears in the roof bosses of the Bauchon chantry in Norwich cathedral, and the tale of the Clever Daughter (smarter than Moll) in a misericord (c.1445) in St. Mary's, Beverley.[44] Rebuses were common, not only in church art (a glass painting in York Minster visualizes the name "[Tun]er,"[45] for example, fig. 5) but also on the badges worn by the retainers of the lords of "Bastard Feudalism"[46] (who interested the Wakefield Master); he can similarly show his people who have special names, such as Daw and Froward, acting according to their meaning. Puns are not unusual and sometimes have religious significance. Did the Wakefield Master chuckle at the small fifteenth-century glass painting in the window of the housebody (the main room, in which the food was cooked, the family dined, and guests entertained) of the yeoman's house (now Shibden Hall) some fifteen miles from Wakefield of the chicken-toed devil carrying off a large fish (a sole or soul?)[47] (fig. b). At some moment, at least, pondering one of the ubiquitous depictions of the Agnus Dei in a church (for an example in York Minster, see fig. 6),[48] and musing on a West Riding sheep on a moor or hillside or on the tale of the stolen sheep, he was inspired to see a connection between the two, a walking pun. As Pauper explains to Dives, St. John is painted bearing "a lomb wyt a cros in his lefght hond & his fyngyr of the ryght hond thertoward in tokene that he shewydde Godys lomb,

Fig. b. Chicken-toed devil, Shibden Hall, Halifax

Godys sone, that deyid for us on the cros."[49]

Like many medieval writers and thinkers, including the cleric who wrote the founding sermon, which is organized around the number seven,[50] for the York Guild of Corpus Christi in 1408 and the authors of a number of poems of the alliterative revival (and like James Joyce, who divided the history of early English drama into six days, the Elizabethan forming the glorious sixth[51]), the Wakefield Master was interested in numerology and plots his plays accordingly. Few other biblical plays appear to be composed numerically, at least beyond an elementary level of threes and nines. None of the eight York Realist's plays is so organized, although if the same playwright also wrote the other alliterative plays in the York collection it was he who gave God, in the play of the Fall of the Angels, nine whole stanzas, five before the fall of Lucifer and four after, symbolizing his trinity (9 being a fuller expression of 3, its root) or the nine orders of angels worshipping him in this play, or both; and he who took care to divide the play of the Assumption of the Virgin (whose prosody is very similar to that of his play of the Death of Christ) into three equal parts of eight stanzas each, on the analogy of the work of God, who "ordered all things in measure, and number, and weight" (*Wisdom* 11.21), as St. Augustine, Christianizing the Pythagorean sense of the universal significance of numbers proclaimed,[52] or as the priest of the temple in the York play of the Purification explains, "In nomber, weight, and mesure fyne/ God creat here al thyng, I say" (ll. 5-6). Literary numerical composition tends, as in the York plays and Dante's *Divina Commedia*, to be concerned with symmetry or equality rather than inequality, but the Wakefield Master uses numbers to determine and control the long length of that indirect part of the play which consists of the preliminary and horrifyingly wrong version of the "imagined representation," or the jokes palely pointing to divine joy. For example, in his play of Noah he adopts (as the characteristically accurate title of his play—*Processus Noe cum Filiis*—indicates) the established idea (found also in the York play on the same subject) of letting Noah's family relationships reflect, at first distortedly, his relationship with God. The play contains 558 lines, divided into sixty-two stanzas. The second eruption of fighting between man and wife occurs near the very end of the first three-quarters of the play; Noah's three sons, speaking in harmonious rotation (ll. 415-17), as is their habit—they do so three times in the play (the York Realist has some interest in such regular rotation of speeches, but generally avoids it)—then begin the forty-seventh stanza, to conclude the three-quarters. It is only then that Noah and his wife discover matrimonial peace and affection; and they begin to work as a team in the line which exactly begins the final quarter of the play: Noah says, "We will do as ye bid vs; we will no more be wroth,/ Dere barnes" (ll. 418-19), and the mood of the play changes for the better. It is also in the line (l. 466) which exactly begins the final sixth of the play that Noah declares, speaking both geographically and spiritually, that the ark and his family have arrived on the "hyllys of Armonye." The pun ("harmony" and "Armenia") seems clear, being also made in the speech of welcome (l. 24) addressed to Queen Margaret, who is said to be bringing peace between France and England, in 1445 from the Noah's ark set up on London bridge;[53] the Bible itself contains many such significant names, as the playwright must have known. This method of controlling the plots of his plays and adding to their meaning (for the denominator—4 and 6 in the case of the play of Noah—always has symbolic value) is characteristic of the Wakefield Master; the numbers used in his other plays are different, and in one, the play of Herod the Great, deliberately absent (unless I have failed to detect it), although that play contains his most explicit reference to biblical numerology.

The apparent disproportion, practical ingenuity, and complicated allusiveness characteristic of Gothic art are fully manifest in the plots of the York Realist's and Wakefield Master's plays, and no less in the language of their scripts. Both give them an unusual richness.

The Scripts. Medieval plays are written in verse, usually stanzaic, and in the best plays, especially those of the Wakefield Master and York Realist, the prosody and diction, however elaborately wrought, are good guides to the players. Both playwrights adapt features common in medieval poetry, particularly the poetry of the alliterative revival, for the special needs of playwriting. For

Chapter I

example, stanza-linking by repetition (or concatenation) is used, as it is, sometimes mechanically, in earlier or simpler plays,[54] to lend forcefulness to monologues and spirit to passages of dialogue. The Wakefield Master's repetition is not usually direct or immediate, as the following examples from the play of Noah show:

Vxor.	In fayth, yit will I spyn;
	All in vayn ye carp.
3 Mulier.	If ye like ye may spyn, moder, in the ship.

(ll. 359-61)

Noe.	I see toppys of hyllys he, many at a syght;	*hills high*
	Nothyng to let me, the wedir is so bright.	*hinder*
Vxor.	Thise ar of mercy tokyns full right.	

(ll. 469-71)

Noe.	Doufe, byrd full blist, fayre myght the befall!	*thee*
	Thou art trew for to trist as ston in the wall;	*trust*
	Full well I it wist thou wold com to thi hall.	
Vxor.	A trew tokyn ist we shall be sauyd all,	
	Forwhi	*because*
	The water, syn she com,	*since*
	Of depnes plom	
	Is fallen a fathom	
	And more, hardely.	*certainly*

(ll. 514-22)

Noe.	All ar thai slayn,	
	And put vnto payn.	
Vxor.	From thens agayn	
	May thai neuer wyn?	*escape*
Noe.	Wyn? No, iwis, bot he that myght hase	*has might*
	Wold myn of thare mys, and admytte thaym to grace.	*been in mind loss*

(ll. 546-52)

The tone of voice required in the response—here conciliatory ("spin in the ship, if you like"), interpretative ("these"), reinforcing ("true"), and instructive—is easy to infer, and the thought and feeling flow easily in the words. The last example, the one piece of mechanical repetition in this play, comes in the final stanza, proclaims the message of the play, and also (in a way characteristic of the Wakefield Master's work) helps to tie it together, answering Noah's preliminary and despairing comment that they shall "neuer wyn away" (l. 24). (Perhaps the Wakefield Master heard this word rhyming through the York play of the Building of the Ark, l. 32, and the Flood, ll. 167, 267.)

The dialogue in the York Realist's plays similarly follows along with the repetition, in the play of the Conspiracy ("learn," "teach"), for example:

III Doctor. But Judas, we trewly the trast,
　　　　　For truly thou moste lerne vs that losell to lache,
　　　　　Or of lande thurgh a lirte that lurdayne may lepe.
Judas.　I schall you teche a token hym tyte for to take. . . .
　　　　　　　　　　(ll. 252-55)

What seems like mechanical repetition in the play of the Remorse of Judas in fact shows Pilate stung into action:

Kayphas. He claymes hym clerely till a kyngdome of Jewes
　　　　　And callis hymselffe oure comeliest kyng.
Pilatus.　Kyng, in the deuillis name? . . .
　　　　　　　　　　(ll. 102-04)

This effect is found in some earlier plays, the *Pride of Life* (ll. 166-67, 218-19), for example. In the York Realist's play, where he is seeking a different effect, the concatenation is more ornate and chiming, as in the York play of the Nativity, where an effect of solemn joy is sought. In the case of monologues, there is also no mechanical repetition between the end of one stanza and the beginning of the next.

Like the earlier *Castle of Perseverance*, the plays of both the York Realist and Wakefield Master are written in complex stanzas closely related in form to the rhyming stanzas of poems written within the traditions of the northern alliterative revival. The first part of the stanza (the frons) is in long lines, and is followed by shorter lines (the "bob and wheel"). The Wakefield Master's stanza, $aaaa_4$ b_1 ccc_3 b_2, with loose stresses and some ornamental alliteration (a complete example is quoted above, from the play of Noah, ll. 514-22), never varies; the first four lines have internal rhymes, and so this stanza may also be regarded as having thirteen lines, rather than nine (and thus no symbolic significance associated with the number 9 can be safely attributed to it).[55] The York Realist's stanzas are similar, but only because they also generally descend from longer lines to shorter; his stanza which is perhaps closest to the Wakefield Master's occurs (consistently) in his play of the Death of Jesus. These two playwrights, unlike the authors of some of the poems of the alliterative revival, and unlike the author of the *Castle of Perseverance* (whose bobs, for example, are often otiose), seldom if ever seem to produce a line merely to keep the form of the stanza. On the contrary, as in the case of the concatenation, these elaborate stanzaic forms are, unlikely as it may seem, caused to lend themselves to the give-and-take of the dialogue and the chain of thought of the monologue.

The Wakefield Master takes more positive advantage of his stanza than the York Realist although the latter can use, for example, the frons in the opening monologue to express a complete thought, or the short line for a disputant to slip in a quick objection (by Caiaphas in the play of the Conspiracy, l. 94, for example), or the last line to carry an obsequious assent or determination (by the second knight and Herod in the play of Christ before Herod, ll. 120, 148, for example), to be followed up by the next speaker at the beginning of the following stanza. The Wakefield Master's bob is never a mere filler, and frequently continues the sense of the frons into the wheel, the whole stanza thus forming a complete thought, with no repetition:

Noe.   Angels thou maide ful euen, all orders that is,
To haue the blis in heuen: this did thou more and les,
Full mervelus to neuen. Yit was ther vnkyndnes
More bi foldys seuen then I can well expres,
Forwhi   *because*
Of all angels in brightnes
God gaf Lucifer most lightnes,
Yit prowdly he flyt his des,   *departed his seat*
And set hym euen hym by.
            (ll. 10-18)

The bob, in fact, is often of crucial importance to the meaning, and requires stressing: "For euer" (1. 23), "Allway" (1. 59), "And make end" (1. 104), "Bot, wife" (1. 239).

The wheel is for swelling feelings: anger, despair, regret, indignation, and pomp—feelings which then can reach a climax in the last line, or subside there:

Noe.   And now I wax old,
           Seke, sory, and cold;
           As muk apon mold
           I widder away.

                       (ll. 60-63)

Deus.   All shall I fordo
           With floodys that shall floo;
           Wirk shall I thaym wo
           That will not repent.

                       (ll. 114-17)

Deus.   I am God most myghty,
           Oone God in Trynyty,
           Made the and ich man to be;
           To luf me well thou awe.

                       (ll. 168-71)

Noe.   For she is full tethee,   *bad-tempered*
           For litill ofte angré;
           If any thyng wrang be,
           Soyne is she worth.

                       (ll. 186-89)

Here, and perhaps even more so in the Master's other plays, the prosody will work for the player.

More frequently than earlier or simpler playwrights, and out of their sense of the forcefulness of individual human beings, the York Realist and the Wakefield Master constantly give their stanzas and lines to more than one speaker, normally at moments of excitement, intense emotion, disagreement, or busy action. Since their plays are full of such moments, monologues and prayers are their most common unshared stanzas. The York Realist has a

Chapter I

number of extra-metrical lines (in Judas' argument with the Janitor in the play of the Conspiracy, l. 184a, for example), but the Wakefield Master never alters or abandons his stanza. If numbers control his plots, his one stanzaic form controls the voices of his people and helps them to express themselves; it probably also assisted the players to memorize their lines.

The Gospels and meditations are rather sparing of dialogue, and the playwrights are here necessarily inventive. The Wakefield Master (some 3,524 lines) has a rich vocabulary of perhaps 3,000 or more different words, and the York Realist (some 3,270 extant lines) is probably not too far behind, although he repeats words more often than the former; the comparison with Chaucer (some 8,072 words) whose work is of course much more copious (more than 43,000 lines) is favorable.[56]

The diction of both the Wakefield Master and the York Realist is either dignified or low. In the case of the Wakefield Master, the dignified can verge onto the aureate and abstract, but is more usually plain, nearing the simple-minded, according to the speaker. Gib's adoration of the Christ Child in the First Shepherds' play shows the range of dignity the playwright achieves:

Hayll, kyng I the call! Hayll, most of myght!	*thee*
Hayll, the worthyst of all! Hayll, duke! Hayll, knyght!	
Of greatt and small thou art Lord by right.	
Hayll, perpetuall! Hayll, faryst wyght!	*creature*
Here I offer:	
I pray the to take,	*thee*
If thou wold, for my sake—	*would*
With this may thou lake—	*play*
This lytyll spruse cofer.	

(ll. 458-66)

This lyric, adapted to the context of the play, necessarily expresses what the old man thinks and feels, and thus takes note of both King and Baby. The result is a brilliant and moving example of the *sermo humilis*, the mixture of the humble and sublime, the style born in the New Testament;[57] the same effect is found also in the York play of the Nativity.

The Wakefield Master's low diction is his richest. He uses

The Wakefield Master and the York Realist

some forty proverbs, and about seventy-five proverbial comparisons and expressions, far more than the York Realist, who uses about five and thirty-five respectively.[58] These fit the mood of the speakers, always either fallible or wicked, who also express agitation and rage with abusive epithets, expletives, and interjections, as in the following exchange (a whole stanza):

Noe.	We! hold thi tong, ram-skyt, or I shall the still.	*Ooh! ram-shit thee*
Vxor.	By my thryft, if thou smyte, I shal turne the untill.	
Noe.	We shall assay as tyte. Haue at the, Gill!	
	Apon the bone shall it byte.	
Vxor.	A, so! Mary, thou smytys ill!	
	Bot I suppose	
	I shal not in thi det	
	Flyt of this flett:	*place*
	Take the ther a langett	*thong*
	To tye vp thi hose!	

(ll. 217-25)

The York Realist's speakers are hardly less full of interjections and expletives: "Heres thou not, harlott? Ille happe on thy hede," says Caiaphas to Jesus in the play of Trial before Annas and Caiaphas (l. 305). A stock of abusive epithets particularly but not uniquely associated with the plays grew up in the fourteenth and fifteenth centuries. They are especially applied to Jesus by his enemies. Their origin is the Bible, where Jesus is said to be "mocked" and "reviled" and is specifically called a "robber," "deceiver," "criminal," and "wicked" man, and where Paul (in *Acts*) is called a "babbler" "pest," "ringleader," "promoter of sedition," and a "mad" man for Jesus. The *Meditations on the Life of Christ* adds "fool" (no doubt conscious of the injunction "Do not say, 'thou fool'"; see *Matt.* 5.22) and the Old Testament prefigurations of Christ many more, especially the Hebraicism, a "byword, song, and reproach." Such terms as "losel," "harlot," and "lurden" are common in the plays. The Wakefield Master's Herod and Caiaphas have their full share of such terms for Jesus, but it is the York Realist who specializes in them; he uses some fifty different terms of abuse for Jesus, about half of them frequently. Since his verse is alliterative, they are usually found in alliterative phrases such as "on-hanged harlott" and "mummeland myghtyng." Such diction is clearly a conventional sign of the function or nature of the speaker,[59] but these terms still require *hauteur* or venom in their delivery, according to the context; the torrents of indiscriminate abuse ("madman," "traitor," "wretch," "criminal," "scoundrel") are punctuated by the apt nonce term: "sawntrelle" ("saintling"?) which is not recorded elsewhere. Perhaps it is legitimate to see Caiaphas momentarily fishing in his mind for the right mot for Jesus hanging on the cross, "Thou saggard" (l. 82). We hardly need Chaucer's Parson to remind us that, despite the high worldly station of Christ's enemies, "chidynge may nat come but out of a vileyns herte" (X.630-31); he offers crooked and drunken "harlot" as examples.

A characteristic feature of the usage of both the York Realist and the Wakefield Master is the sudden change of tone, expressed by the quick turning from dignified to low; another is the misappropriation of well-established dignified expressions, often alliterative, for low purposes, a good sign of hypocrisy or a good source of humor. Thus, the exchange between Noah and his wife, quoted above (ll. 217-25), follows closely on Noah's dignified exchange with God (ll. 163-81), and Pilate's wife responds to his noble-minded beadle with words which reveal her villain's heart:

Bedellus. My Liberall lorde, o leder of lawis
　　　　　O schynyng schewe thet all schames escheues,
　　　　　I beseke you my souerayne, assente to my sawes,
　　　　　As ye are gentil unger and justice of Jewes.
Domina. Do herke howe thou, javell, jangill of Jewes.
　　　　　Why, go belte Lorosonne boy, when I bidde the.
　　　　　　　　　　　(ll. 55-60)

Of his wife, Gib, in the Second Shepherds' play, says,

　　　She is browyd lyke a brystyll, with a sowre-loten chere;
　　　Had she oones wett hyr whystyll, she couth syng full clere
　　　Hyr Paternoster.
　　　　　　　　　(ll. 102-04)

Here the heroic and sometimes mock-heroic expression "browyd lyke a brystyll" is not only incongruously applied to a woman, but yoked to the low "wett hyr whystyll," which happens also to alliterate, and is followed by what in another context could be a plain but dignified religious expression, to "syng full clere/ Hyr Paternoster," itself, in the present circumstances, an activity of doubtful sanctity.[60]

Many phrases or short passages are incorporated into these plays (as they are also in earlier plays) directly from the Gospels. Thus the York Realist's Jesus prays, substituting "pain" for "cup": "if it possible be this payne myght I ouerpasse" (Agony and Betrayal, 1. 58; from *Matt.* 26.39, *si possibile est, transeat a me calix iste*, and *Mark* and *Luke*). And the Wakefield Master's Herod learns that the three kings have gone "Anothere way" (1. 147, from *Matt.* 2.12, *per aliam viam*). The language of the liturgy and the Old Testament has also flooded into these plays. The dignified language is always allusive, as is normal in religious poetry; in Gib's address to the Christ Child, quoted above, "kyng," "Lord," "most of myght," and "perpetuall" are biblical (*Isa.* 9.6-7), and "knyght" and "duke" liturgical.[61] The misappropriated dignified language is no less resonant of the Bible. Not only is the "Peace!" so commonly issued with disdain from the mouths of the tyrants an obviously devilish version of Jesus' words "Peace be to you" (*John* 20.19) and of the liturgical kiss of peace (while at the same time a reflection of contemporary language and social life [*OED* peace sb 14 and v.1]), but much less common expressions also have the same effect: in the Trial before Herod, the York Realist's Herod terrifies dragons (1. 11) not only or mainly as a ridiculous hero of romance but because the sins of the Jews have turned Jerusalem into a den of dragons (*Jer.* 9.11), which the true King (not Herod and certainly not the man with his head in the sack) shall crush (*Ps.* 73.13-14). This process has been taken further by the Wakefield Master, as might be expected, since, as I have suggested, types of the Old Testament have insistently infiltrated the fifteenth-century world of his plays. As a result, each is almost a short "cycle" of plays. Many of the phrases used by his chief persons—the shepherds, Herod, and Caiaphas—come from messianic passages in the Old Testament, mixed up with fifteenth-century alliterative collocations (and his proverbial, half-proverbial, and low expressions), with the result that, despite the freedom and feeling with which his speeches appear to flow, they are almost mosaics. Chaucer and Langland provide precedents, especially the latter.

His plays may or may not (in the nature of language it is frequently impossible to be sure) be full of colloquial expressions—"not in your debt," "now it is twice," and "as ever eat I bread" might be examples.[62] If they are, rhythm and rhyme have been imposed upon them, or they have been chosen because they already have these features. It is probable that the diction of his plays (like that of the York Realist's) is more ornate and formulaic than at first sight appears; together with his rigid adherence to his chronically rhyming stanzaic form, the result is an allusive language brimful of artifice and pattern. The carving is rich and subtle. Nevertheless, it is a language indubitably meant for speaking and playing, since countless expressions call for a particular tone of voice or for some accompanying action. It is difficult not to think of the players as taking full advantage of these scripts; the condition of the manuscript of the York plays, particularly the series of plays of the Passion, suggests, in contrast, that the players had more difficulty with the York Realist's language, which, with the alliterative revival, was gradually becoming archaic during the fifteenth century.[63] It seems possible that as the decades went by, some of the York players understood only the gist of what they were saying. Some annotations in the manuscript (in the play of the Building of the Ark, especially) are modernizations. John Clerke, assistant or deputy clerk to the corporation, who in the mid-sixteenth century apparently kept an ear open for unauthorized deviations from the official copy of the plays (the extant manuscript), must, however, have understood all the words and phrases.[64]

The Players. Little can be made of the greater success northerners and amateurs appear to have had with the plays in the twentieth century than southerners and professionals! All actors pretend to be someone they are not, and medieval players approached their scripts in this spirit. The few stage-directions in the Wakefield Master's and York Realist's plays are sufficient to

indicate that business called for in the dialogue was performed—the norm in England for a long time, as the Anglo-
Norman plays (which have full stage-directions) and other early
plays show. The extant accounts of money spent on *properties* (a
word which had its theatrical sense by the early fifteenth century,
OED sb property 3) for performances of plays whose scripts are
probably those extant[65] further reveal that business was done in
deed rather than mimed. Thus when Herod, in the York Realist's
play of Christ before Herod, calls for wine, it would be safe to
infer that he receives and drinks it (or colored water, like the cold
tea used for whiskey on the modern stage) even if John Clerke
had not so noted (l. 42*sd*) in the manuscript. When Gib begins the
First Shepherds' play, he may, therefore, be reasonably supposed
to be holding a box of dice (l. 38) around which he wrings his
hands in grief, "My handys may I wryng and mowrning make"
(l. 28)—although there is always the possibility that the latter, and
other such very common phrases, are only metaphorical. That
words and actions went together (not always the case in simpler
plays) is indicated by many passages in the York Realist's plays
(in the lines spoken by the knights indicating that they have a
firm hold on Jesus, for example) and in the Wakefield Master's
(in the exchange between Noah and his wife, quoted above, for
example, during which, if their dialogue is to make sense, they
must hit each other).

The playing, apart from doing any concomitant business,
must have chiefly consisted of expressing—in the right tone of
voice, and with a corresponding look on the face, and gestures
(probably generally demonstrative) if needed—the meaning of the
words. The look, of course, is changeable, but for the wicked it is
usually fierce or gloating and sometimes was accentuated by
masks or face-painting, following an English tradition of caricature; for the holy it is serene and modest, as in the pictorial and
written analogues—imagine God as "seated on a raised chair, with
benign face, compassionate and paternal. . . . [A]nd Gabriel, with
glad and joyful face," says the *Meditations on the Life of
Christ*—and certainly sometimes accentuated by gold masks or
face-painting (see fig. 7):[66] an immobile mask can be very ex-
pressive—a turn of the head, for example, becomes unusually

significant, stirring yet distant, recognizable yet mysterious (fig. 8). For the fallible the look is usually at first gloomy, although, in line with a growing interest in the fifteenth century in individual personalities and portraiture,[67] they are more variable, and, particularly in the Wakefield Master's plays, may have more than one side to them; they are not associated in the records with masks or face-painting.

Stressing the words which especially carry the meaning is suggested by the prosody in the case of both playwrights. Better a live actor than a carving, Reginald Pecock suggested in c.1449,[68] but it is impossible to tell how much extra emotion was indulged in by the players, either when speaking or when silent. Movement and loquacity without purpose were not thought to be decorous in the Middle Ages, and certainly the frequent short heaves of pain indulged in by Christ on the Cross in some modern revivals seem out of place, although the Passion plays all make, like Gothic art generally, a strong point of stressing Christ's humanity. On the whole, it is probable that the players avoided looks or gestures unless directly called for, although there is some evidence of ad-libbing. In the York Realist's play of Christ before Annas and Caiaphas and in his plays in general, there is a constant flow of short comments, sometimes with almost a staccato effect, from minor characters, who must have been on their toes to keep up the pace. Pacing is also noticeably important for the dialogue (and all the monologues) in the Wakefield Master's plays, as Noah's wife is cajoled into the Ark, for example, or as the shepherds one by one recognize their stolen sheep. That a formal and pictorial quality predominated may well have been true of plays which focus rather directly on the "imagined representation" (including the York play of the Nativity and the Chester play of the Purification, most convincingly directed in this style by Meg Twycross[69]), but does not seem right, except for the climactic and devout passages, for the plays of the York Realist and Wakefield Master, unusually replete as they are with the unholy and agitated ways of wicked and fallible men and women.

The York civic authorities were concerned that the plays be presented well; the annual proclamation called for "good players well arayed & openly ["clearly," *OED* 3] spekyng," and later in

The Wakefield Master and the York Realist

the fifteenth century provision was made for auditions before four "of the moste Connyng ["expert," "dexterous," *OED* cunning 2] discrete and able playeres within this Citie."[70] Female parts were generally played by men or boys; presenting the plays was essentially a male enterprise, and men's voices carry much more clearly in the open air than women's;[71] there is no reason to suppose that the players in the York Realist's and Wakefield Master's plays were not all men or boys. It is not clear from the accounts at York that, by modern standards, many rehearsals were held; this suggests that the emphasis was on getting the properties in place, basic "blocking," learning the lines, speaking them loudly, and perhaps the prompt picking up of cues.

The first known record of the presence of a professional troupe of players at York occurs in 1446 (in 1426 in England, at London[72]), but such troupes would not have performed the York Realist's plays, in some cases because (in contrast to the Wakefield Master's plays) their casts are large, ranging up to seventeen speaking parts. Further, each of his plays (except the play of the Death of Christ, for which his intentions were different) has one main part, which dominates the play, and one or two secondary parts (including that evil pair, Caiaphas and Annas), followed, usually at a long distance, by numerous minor parts. For example, in his play of the Conspiracy, his first and shortest play, out of 294 lines, Pilate speaks 106, Judas 72, and the rest of the cast of ten speakers anywhere from thirty-one (the Janitor) to four (the third doctor); in his following six plays, the main characters are Jesus (131 out of 305 lines, not counting 40 lost lines), Caiaphas (129 out of 395), Pilate (209 out of 545), Herod (220 out of 423), Pilate (141 out of 389), and Pilate (165 out of 485, not counting 54 lost lines). The secondary characters may have set speeches or whole stanzas to deliver, but the minor characters are often confined to single lines scattered throughout the play; in the play of the Agony in the Garden and the Betrayal, the fourth knight speaks only one line and the fourth Jew only two—he concludes the performance with them: perhaps he was an important member of the guild whose ambitions to play had to be accommodated (although the manuscript may be corrupt here, and so deceptive). It is thus a reasonable guess that some expert player was engaged to direct the play and to undertake the main part (possibly, in the early years, the author himself), the other parts being assigned to persons associated with the guild producing the play; in 1449, one Robert Clerk, presumably a cleric expert at plays, was paid eight shillings for taking charge of the play of the Coronation of the Virgin,[73] and a few similar payments at York are recorded later in the fifteenth century, none, however, for the York Realist's plays. It is nevertheless difficult to imagine the York Realist writing his long parts, including his tyrannical speeches (which are, however, not half so long as the Wakefield Master's), unless he knew competent players were available, but nothing is known about who played his plays—except that they played on behalf of the guild producing them, which, with the auditions, may have led (as at Leeds in 1975 and Toronto in 1977) to a certain amount of constructive rivalry among the players.

Internal evidence, on the other hand, shows that the Wakefield Master knew the players for whom he was writing, and suggests (but does not prove) that they formed a small troupe of skilled men. If my inferences are correct, his plays are the first in the history of English playwriting written for a particular group of actors—a strong and recurrent element in the history of English plays, easily documentable from the sixteenth century onwards. The parts of John Horne, the second shepherd in the First Shepherds' play, and of Christ in the play of the Buffeting call for an unusually tall actor, who is referred to in the Second Shepherds' play as having long legs (l. 565).[74] The conclusion, that the playwright knew who would be playing these two parts—or knew whom he had in mind to play them—is inescapable, since nothing in the plot of the First Shepherds' play requires a tall person.

In contrast to the York Realist's there are few single star roles in his plays. They have up to five main parts each, and some minor parts; two require six players, and the others seven, nine, and ten (the Killing of Abel requires only four). Some of the minor parts (the Virgin Mary and the angel, for example) are among those requiring the greatest skill, especially if, as is again probable, they were played by men and boys. All the players need a strong "stage presence" and a strong sense of "address." The recurrence of certain kinds of parts in his plays and the repeated

The Wakefield Master and the York Realist

need for certain playing skills also suggests that he worked with a stable band of players, or at least that he heavily rehearsed ad hoc groups he gathered about him. A "cheeky boy" (Jack, Daw, and Froward) is required in three of the plays (four, if Pikeharnes in the play of the Killing of Abel is counted): they and their cousins (e.g., Mirth in the *Pride of Life*, the doctor's boy in the Croxton play of the Sacrament, and, I think, the servant in the York Realist's play of the Death of Christ) are related to the servants of Roman comedy, which was studied in medieval England, including Yorkshire,[75] and to the fool of the English folk plays (of which there are no medieval versions extant). A comic female impersonator, referred to as "Jill," is required in two plays. A singer, capable of great rhythmic virtuosity, is needed to play the part of the angel in two. At least three of the other players had to have good singing voices, able to perform Three Men's Songs; the same three had to be good comic monologists, and two of them polylogists, able to "do voices." One had to be capable of deliberately bad "acting" and some, probably, of performing conjuring tricks. Comic routines such as vain escapes, foolish miming, drunken addresses to the bottle, transparent lies, loud tuneless songs, face-pulling, howling, tumbling, and beating, all requiring much practice and some skill, occur in all his plays. At least one "stage-hand" is required.

Troupes of play-loving clerics are recorded in the West Riding in the fourteenth century and later; a troupe of four from Snaith, twenty miles east of Wakefield, for example, traveled to Cowick in 1323 to play "entreludies."[76] If these plays were indeed originally "clerks' plays," they were written for clerks available to play them and ready to do so with the necessary enthusiasm.

Paid entertainers, frequently referred to in the Middle Ages as minstrels and jesters, were not uncommon throughout medieval England, some in the service of noble households, others less established, the latter sometimes dispossessed or negligent farmers or vagabonds, at least some of them from Yorkshire. Their chief business was to recite narratives, but miming also appears to have been central to their work; their skills ranged from the dignified to the scurrilous and are sometimes of the kind required for the successful presentation of the York Realist's and Wakefield Master's plays. They probably entertained those who attended the half-yearly fairs at Wakefield in the fifteenth century.[77] They played the harp; danced; indulged in slapstick clowning, contortions, and tumbling; performed amorous skits (at York in 1447-48 they are recorded as playing "Ioly Wat & Malkyn"[78]); acted out comic monologues and polylogues; worked puppets; did hat-tricks and other conjuring tricks (at Whitby Abbey in 1394-96 several were rewarded, comprising dancers and one "ludenti in sacco"[79]), including turning sticks into serpents; juggled; walked on stilts; rope danced; trained animals (horses, bears, monkeys, and dogs); threw out plays on words; imitated the various classes of society and drunkards and idiots; indulged in absurd boastings; engaged in insults, mockery and satirical sallies; told indecent stories; made animal noises and disguised themselves as animals; motioned obscenely with their bodies; and emitted low and repulsive but probably musical sounds from them. Langland touches the extremes in his list:

> Y can nat tabre ne trompy ne telle fayre gestes,
> Farten ne fythelen at festes, ne harpe,
> Iape ne iogele ne genteliche pipe,
> Ne nother sayle ne sautrien ne syngen with the geterne.
> (C XV.205-08)[80]

Some were women. Some wore masks. Some adopted professional, odd, or national names—Clod, Jack the Juggler, Lobe, Pearl-in-the-Egg, Reginald the Liar, Robin the Ribadour, Scot the Fool (not to mention Mak), and Swagger.[81] Their costume was distinctive. It is probably alluded to in the Towneley play of the Creation, where the fallen angels become devils "tatyrd as a foyll" (l. 137, fantastically dressed like a Fool, perhaps a proverbial comparison—*MED* fol n 3). Depictions of them abound on misericords (fig. 9) in representations datable from 1305 to 1520, and also elsewhere; a fourteenth-century corbel in St. Catherine's Chapel, St. Mary's, Beverley, contains an example. The Fool wears a characteristic costume and holds a bladder. Their baubles are often mentioned.[82]

Closely related to jesters and their activities, at least in the minds of those who disapproved of them, was the habit of pulling extremely silly or grotesque faces, with protruding tongues and bulging eyes (perhaps Gib and John Horne confront each other in this way); again, these faces are common on misericords (fig. 10) and corbels.[83] Sinful deeds listed in a long and popular penitential manual (c.1440) link all these activities together—"pleyis & iapys of vanytees," "feynyng foly countenaunce," and rewarding "iogoulours & mynstrallys for iapys & veyn-talys."[84] The carvings and glass paintings (like the puns, scenes from domestic life, proverbs, and other *jeux* described earlier) are generally not easily seen with the naked eye, corbels, tracery lights, and especially roof bosses being normally too distant to be seen clearly. Misericords are the exceptions, easily detectable. It is as if the second estate, comfortably lounging or purely and liturgically exalted in the chancel, sat on and prayed for mercy for the follies and struggles of the third estate and for the activities of their own lower members, both nestled beneath them. (Devotional subjects—scenes from the New Testament and angels—are found on misericords, but are far less common than scenes from daily life, and are more usually and more symbolically to be found far aloft in tracery lights and roof bosses.)

The Wycliffite treatise complains that playing biblical plays is the same as "japinge";[85] the Wakefield Master seems to have gone one better and borrowed from the repertoire of minstrelish accomplishments to help him demonstrate the foolishness or wickedness of some of his characters, who indulge in many of the same spirited feats as the minstrels. He may, despite frequent ecclesiastical injunctions to avoid them, even have had in mind borrowing a minstrel or two for his troupe, not necessarily the "j ludenti de Wakefeld" who visited York and was well rewarded with sixpence for his efforts in 1446.[86] The Wakefield Master's all-embracing versatility is again apparent.

Most of these skills are not called for in other fifteenth-century biblical plays (although Moses does a trick—condensed to the wand-trick within the powers of conjuring from *Exod.* 7.10-12—in the plays); and neither are most fifteenth-century playwrights (including the York Realist) so obviously and consistently concerned with keeping the audience happy as is the Wakefield Master. His "applause traps" are unusual in biblical plays (although *Mankind*, c.1465-70, often assumed to have been performed by a commercial traveling troupe of players, provides a playful instance, to introduce Tutivillus, ll. 451-74): Noah, perhaps with the enormous sigh of the 1985 production, uniquely warns the audience of his wife's recalcitrant spirit (ll. 183-89), thus building up her part much as Maria gives advance warning of Malvolio's yellow stockings to increase the humor in his arrival. This is human comedy, not the laughter of surprise. Two passages of what amounts to self-referential pirandelloism (in the Second Shepherds' play, ll. 563-65, and the play of Herod the Great, ll. 347-70) are unique[87] and also argue for an advanced sense of entertainment and a sophisticated sense of playing as well as for a strong confidence in the abilities of the players; whether clerics or minstrels or neither, it seems clear that originally they formed a stable and skillful little band.

The Audience. The York Realist acknowledges the presence of the audience by his direct addresses to them when, as usual, they become both onlookers and characters, and also by his brief but pointed allusions to the craft of the guild members attending the Pageant, as they had been instructed to do.[88] The population of York was about 11,000 at the end of the fourteenth century; it declined steadily during the fifteenth century,[89] but the audiences were surely numerous, as Friar Melton's comment suggests, particularly at the first and other advantageous stations,[90] and particularly when royalty was in attendance, as in 1487. There are over three hundred speaking parts and many "extras" in the York plays, and others are needed to move and tend the Pageants. Some members of the audience of a particular play might therefore be related to those connected with the production of it, or themselves associated with the production of other plays, or related to those who were (as is sometimes the case in the recent large-scale revivals); their presence, together with that of any experienced visitors, must have added a spirit of festivity, community, and friendly criticism to the sense of devotion manifested by some in the audience. In East Anglia in the early sixteenth century, audiences sometimes wore favors, or badges, for the occasion[91] (like the buttons worn by supporters at modern festival productions), but there is no evidence that they did so at York. And despite the crowds the York Realist's plays appear more remote—overwhelmed, perhaps, by the majesty of the Minster—than the Wakefield Master's. Their language is less familiar. As years went by, the performances perhaps began to appear archaic; in one sense, E. Martin Browne's York Festival style can be said to be not so inappropriate after all.

The York Realist makes no local allusions; the Wakefield Master, however, possibly copying morality plays or minstrels' skits, both of which contain topographical allusions,[92] has not merely anglicized his story (as do most of the biblical playwrights) but localized it. He is the first English biblical playwright to do so. Cain cynically asks to be buried at Goodybower, a close in Wakefield, at the "quarell hede" (1. 367), or at the top of the quarry pits there, with some point since in the play he is a very poor tither and the rector's great tithe-barn was nearby (or possibly, with equal point, at an ale-house named the Quarry Head there—for the existence of which, however, there is no evidence). The shepherds in the First Shepherds' play wash down their feast with ale from Hely (1. 244), presumably a village named Healey in the West Riding; the corn mill where Slowpace in the same play (1. 126) has had his corn ground could be in Horbury or Wakefield.[93] Coll, in the Second Shepherds' play, has been looking for his lost sheep on the rough moorland around Horbury (1. 455), three miles southwest of Wakefield, where there was a chapelry of All Saints, Wakefield, and also a notable "crokyd thorne" (1. 403, "crooked thorn-tree") where he and his two colleagues agree to meet. Herod's fame extends from Egypt to "Kemptowne" (1. 47), perhaps a local West Riding village.[94] In the Wakefield Master's addition to the play of the Last Judgment, the second demon says that the way to the Judgment is "vp watlyn strete" (1. 126, "Watling Street"), the Roman road which ran near Wakefield and which was used in the Middle Ages.[95]

There are no sayings or activities related to the woolen industry in the York plays or in the Towneley plays written by playwrights other than the Master, but perhaps taking his cue from the references in the York plays to the occupations of the guilds producing them, the Wakefield Master does not hesitate to embrace the local industry. Women did the hard and not very profitable work of spinning, as they do in two of his plays. Noah's wife is not a spinner in the other English plays, in which she has other excuses for not wanting to board the Ark; Mak's wife works at her spinning late at night, "a penny to wyn," she says (Second Shepherds' play, l. 299, "earn"). Similarly, proverbial sayings related to wool occur in these plays: "Ill-spon weft, iwys, ay commys foull owte" (Second Shepherds' play, l. 586, and the play of the Killing of Abel, 436; Whiting W 571); "I haue tow on my rok more then euer I had" (Second Shepherds' play, l. 389; Whiting T 432); and the related "Ther is garn on the reyll other" (Noah, l. 298; Whiting Y5). The hilly areas of the West Riding owed their prosperity to the invention and necessary use of the fulling mill, of which there were many in the Wakefield district, one (owned, as usual, by the Lord of the Manor and repaired in 1429) on the river Calder at Wakefield and another by the ford at Horbury;[96] in a local and suitably technological variation of a common satirical observation Tutivillus (in the Wakefield Master's part of the play of the Last Judgment) describes a fashionable sinner (also called Jill—"Jelian Iowke"—l. 317, Jilly the lazy one—*MED* jouk) as dressing and walking so preposterously that his buttocks "lowke/ like walk-mylne cloggys" (l. 314, that is, that he casually minces along, his buttocks each rising and falling in turn at some speed like the two blocks, beneath the twin hammer heads, beating the cloth in the tub, on the two shafts of a fulling-mill, fig. c), "his tayll when he Wryngys" (l. 313, "writhes"). A medieval etymology for "Tutivillus" itself was "decaying threads of cloth";[97] they, like ram shit, must have littered the townships and villages where these plays were probably performed. Agricultural problems related to the rise of the woolen industry (such as the real or potential shortage of land for tillage) also form a part of his plays. The Wakefield Master can, therefore, be said to know his audience well and to be interested in them and their way of life, both in the sense of wanting to entertain them and also, given the themes of his plays, in the pastoral sense. He has been in their houses, watched them at work and play, and is far from remote from them, peasants, yeomen, tradesmen, clerics, manorial officials;

The Wakefield Master and the York Realist

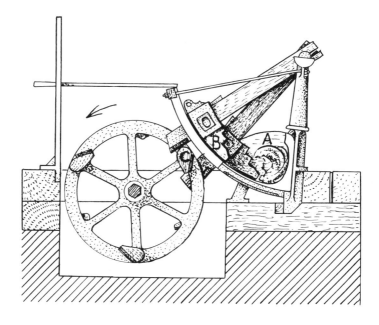

Fig. c. Fulling-mill clogs. Box (A) in which cloth is beaten and turned by the two clogs (B) raised in turn by tappits (C) mounted on a wheel powered by an adjacent waterwheel. Drawn from a mid-nineteenth-century example, which worked on exactly the same principles as those used in the fifteenth century (no surviving fifteenth-century examples are known). In the nineteenth century the desirable speed was forty strokes per minute (hence "casually minces"). Drawn by Peter C. D. Brears, F.S.A.

men, women, children, and babies; the sly, daft, humorous, athletic, lazy, and those hardened by the bitter weather.

The plays of the York Realist and Wakefield Master are not primarily educational or didactic; rather, they simultaneously challenge thought and call for an emotional response. Their plots are so contrived that, from the point of view of the audience, keys are needed to unlock them; this problem is solved by both playwrights in essentially the same way, by repetition: they repeat their hints (Noah and his wife have two rounds of fisticuffs rather than the usual one), and it seems safe to conclude, on the analogy of the Bible (the Fathers and late medieval teachers encouraged alternative interpretations of biblical passages), that

their plays (as good plays do) provoked and were meant to provoke their audiences to thought. At least some members of the
Wakefield Master's audiences could have followed his key
points, but none unaided could have understood all the implications of his plays. It is not hard, however, to see that they are
full of elusive implications, and that these are discussable. At the
conclusion of the play of Noah, for example, the well-instructed
might have noticed that it is Jill (unbiblically, *Gen.* 8.6) who
advocates sending forth a raven, and nodded if they knew of St.
Augustine's etymological explanation that since the raven cries
"'Cras! 'Cras!'" it is the great procrastinator; perhaps Jill is still
up to her tricks. Others would have known that the Ark is a type
of the Church, which must be entered now, and the Flood both a
sign of baptism—and sign of God's wrath, evident also in the play
of the Expulsion of Adam and Eve from Eden (now missing from
the Towneley manuscript) and the play of the Last Judgment. In
connection with the play of the Expulsion, some may have gone
beyond recognizing Jill's spinning as a piece of social caricature
and recalled that Eve, who also caused her husband so much
trouble, was forced to take up spinning when she was expelled.
The dimensions of the Ark, carefully given in the text, provide
further points for discussion. If the water was fifteen cubits
higher than "all hillys" (l. 442, "hills"), had that to do with the
height of the Cross on Calvary? Thus the early Fathers' commentaries, which had a long life in the Middle Ages and were filtered
through the various versions of the *Glossa Ordinaria*, not infrequently finding their way into vernacular sermons and lives of
Christ (and the *Vita Christi*), provide some of the dimensions for
the debate which follows the play. The need for obedience to
God, eventually so bravely manifested by Noah, who may well
have worn fifteenth-century clothing, would have been clearer
and understood by more members of the audience, even while
they laughed as Jill sat on him (l. 409). What old John the carpenter, who seems to have seen a Shepherds' play as well as a
play of Noah ("Nowelis flood," *Canterbury Tales* I.3834),
thought of it is not recorded—perhaps he learned only not to star-
gaze (I.3457-61). One chief effect of the semi-obscure morality
and obscure typology of the Wakefield Master's and York Realist's

plays is to produce first puzzlement and then enlightenment, progress analogous to spiritual progress.

They also call for an emotional response to the human life of Christ such as had been especially expected of Christians since at least the time of St. Anselm (1033-1109) and St. Bernard of Clairvaux (1090-1153). At the sight of a play of the Passion some men and women, according to the Wycliffite treatise, were frequently "movyd to compassion and devocion, wepinge bitere teris"[98]—as some members of modern audiences are, unprompted—the same tears encouraged by the writers in the meditative tradition, called for in religious lyrics, socially acceptable in the late Middle Ages, and spiritually efficacious. The image—including the living image—of the dying Christ was capable, when one was near it and in prayer, of producing many years of pardon, as evidence from Yorkshire and elsewhere shows;[99] but one old northerner, who was even less well-instructed than old John, remembered only that at the play at Kendal there "was a man on a tree, and blood ran down."[100]

There is no record of how audiences responded to the threats (whose purpose, contrary to what has sometimes been assumed, was certainly not always and never exclusively to quell the hubbub of a noisy audience) directed at them by Herod and Pilate. Derisive laughter at such creatures was considered by some to be divinely sanctioned, and audiences may have whistled or hissed, medieval English ways of expressing disapprobation (*MED* hissen v b)—as some modern audiences do, prompted by claques. They may equally well have prayed that they would not become subject to these monsters and, like them, become children of Cain, however strong the element of absurdity, mockery, and even teasing may be in some of these speeches.

The meditative writings were originally addressed to those in the religious life, but the translations and vernacular offshoots were intended for a lay public, possibly a privileged elite. Meditation, or thinking about the life of Christ and imagining it to oneself, was considered to be the highest form of the Active Life, and is recommended by the author of *Meditations on the Life of Christ* for several reasons: to avoid "trivial and transient things"; to bear "trials and tribulations"; to follow the "perfection of

Chapter I

virtue": "Where can you find examples and teachings of charity, of great poverty, of faultless humility, of profound wisdom, of prayer, meekness, obedience, and patience, and all the virtues to equal those in the holy life of the Lord, full of all virtues?"[101] The performance provides for their audiences desirable opportunities for active devotion and adoration. At the Nativity they can, like the shepherds, spend time especially contemplating his divine face; at the Passion they can watch Christ "attentively" and not be repelled at the cruelty of his audiences.[102] They can see in Mary and Jesus decorous behavior suitable for a Christian, and feel in the fallible (like themselves) members of the cast, such as Joseph and the shepherds (these latter especially interested the Wakefield Master), the changes leading to the road to Bethlehem. Above all, the devout must "be present."[103] It is not a question of "accepting into worship," as in some ecclesiastically sponsored revivals, the "naive earthiness" of the shepherds, but of feeling relief that they manage to change.

Although the feelings of the members of the audience are clearly meant to be engaged by these plays, they are not meant to be indulged at the expense of all else. The two playwrights remain firmly in control of their material, and, while encouraging thoughtfulness—and the worship and devotion which impel all biblical plays—they discourage the kind of extreme and even hysterical emotionalism frequently invoked by pious art, including a number of plays (the sixteenth-century Yorkshire plays of Christ's Burial and Resurrection, perhaps from the Carthusian house at Kingston upon Hull, among them), as the Middle Ages drew to a close.

The songs of worship and blessings, with which many of the performances, like sermons, conclude, may well have quelled any impulse on the part of the audience to applaud; and the curses with which others, including five by the York Realist and the Wakefield Master, end may have had a dampening effect. There may be abundant cause for laughter driving the course of the performances of the Wakefield Master's plays, and some in the case of the York Realist's, but there is none at their conclusion, where it is overtaken by joy (as in the play of Noah, where the pun is a blessing), or holy satisfaction, or derision, or temporary terror. These were representations of serious and ultimate truths and desirable norms, not escapes into darkened auditoria. Applauding at the end of a performance is not recorded in England until the mid-sixteenth century, when it is associated (and then not invariably) with the new indoor drama of humanism. At modern revivals, especially during the earlier part of the twentieth century, audiences often refrained (sometimes by request) from applauding, but they normally do so at the more recent festival productions.

Joy prevails in the York play of the Nativity, a work simpler than the plays of the York Realist and the Wakefield Master; it contains plenty of matter for thought, but is easier to understand and lovelier, although hardly less cleverly plotted, than the work of those two pre-eminent playwrights.

Chapter II

The York Play of the Nativity

Virgo . . . dixit illi: Bene veneris deus meus, dominus meus et filius meus.—St. Bridget of Sweden

According to the *Meditations on the Life of Christ*, the devout are permitted to construct their own "imagined representations"; this text indeed sometimes shows the way by offering its own alternatives:

> I shall tell them to you as they occurred or as they might have occurred according to the devout belief of the imagination and the varying interpretation of the mind. It is possible to contemplate, explain, and understand the Holy Scriptures in as many ways as we consider necessary, in such a manner as not to contradict the truth of life and justice and not to oppose faith and morality. Thus when you find it said here, "This was said and done by the Lord Jesus," and by others of whom we read, if it cannot be demonstrated by the Scriptures, you must consider it only as a requirement of devout contemplation. Take it as if I had said, "Suppose that this is what the Lord Jesus said and did," and also for similar things.[1]

With this license, artists and playwrights generally pick and choose from among previously established ways of envisioning their holy scenes. It is possible to enter the workshop of the playwright of the York play of the Nativity and see him selecting and controlling his material and shaping it into a brilliant and lovely play. He is especially interested in the version of the birth re-

The York Play of the Nativity

vealed in the recent past to St. Bridget of Sweden, which appears to have been important in York, but he is not overwhelmed by it. Her simplicity but not her aristocratic taste appealed to him. He was also conscious of other versions of the birth, aware of the guild of Tile Thatchers, for whom he was writing, concerned that his play, although simple, be rich enough to provoke thought, and careful not to slight the Passion implicit in the Nativity. Above all, he aimed, with grace and dignity, to inspire "honest mirth," joy. His play is one of the shortest at York (154 lines), has only two speakers, Mary and Joseph, and can have taken only about ten minutes to present, yet his management of the story is remarkable, and his play is far superior to the two other (and much longer) English plays solely concerned with showing the birth of Christ. It is not possible to identify him as the playwright of other York plays, although his consistent seven-line stanzaic form appears in three other York plays (including the middle section of the Shepherds' play), his quotation from St. Bridget occurs also in the play of the Flight into Egypt, and the irony associated with his Joseph resembles the irony in the play of the Incredulity of Thomas (ll. 96-126). If it is permissible to assume that the original players had direction from someone knowledgeable about this script (perhaps the playwright), it may be possible to come close to seeing this play as it was presented in fifteenth-century York.

The York records are almost silent about this play—there is no mention of its Pageant or properties—and what can be said about its stagecraft must be deduced from its sources and the text itself, which is a good one. It is a record of what was performed under the auspices of the guild of Tile Thatchers when it was copied into the Register (1463-77) and for some unknown number of years earlier; at an undiscoverable time after 1477 the play was wholly or partially revised, and a second version, no longer extant, was from then on presented.[2] The Tile Thatchers were associated with both versions throughout the life of the York plays, or at least from 1415, sometimes in conjunction with the Plasterers (who had their own play, the play of the Creation). By the early sixteenth century, some similar craft guilds—the Slaters, Tilers, Roofers, and Daubers—were helping the Wrights (Carpenters) sponsor the play of the Nativity at Chester.

The story on which the York play is ultimately based is told in *Luke* 2.6-7: "And it came to pass while they were there, that the days for her to be delivered were fulfilled. And she brought forth her firstborn son, and wrapped him in swaddling clothes, and laid him in a manger, because there was no room for them in the inn." How is this brief narrative to be turned into a plot and dialogue? The play opens, like many English biblical plays (ten in the York collection), with a prayer—from Joseph, but it is a prayer mixed with a complaint. The Gospels record little more than that Joseph was a just man (*Matt.* 1.19), but *Pseudo-Matthew* (known in medieval England through the agency of the *Life of Saint Anne* and some sermons and liturgical plays, if by no other means) depicts him as old (old enough to be Mary's grandfather), humble, suspicious, fearful, given to weeping and trembling, but busy as a carpenter and willing to keep Mary.[3] He thus vacillates throughout the York series of Nativity plays, now churlish and grumbling, now contrite and solicitous, as in the play of the Flight to Egypt. The *Meditations on the Life of Christ* imagines him before the birth as "seated, downcast perhaps because he could not prepare what was necessary."[4] His opening speech in the play is well balanced; although he manages to rescue himself from whining, his faith is not now quite firm enough, not steadfast (ll. 1-28), somewhat as in Noah's long opening prayer-monologue in the Wakefield Master's play. In York and other English art Joseph sometimes appears as small or in the background, still "last," and rather ignored; he frequently wears a thick long cloak, sometimes red or brown, against the cold, and carries a staff or crutch; he is invariably old, as he is in the play (fig. 11).[5]

"No room for them in the inn" has become "So mekill pepull is comen to towne/ That we can nowhare herbered be" (ll. 10-11); and Joseph can see no solution but to take shelter with "there bestes" (l. 14, "these animals") "because of the crowds," says the *Meditations on the Life of Christ*.[6] When the play begins, he and Mary are therefore standing by the stable, about which he now comments as they enter; with a professional eye, he looks about them, putting down the pack he is probably carrying (if there has been any carry-over from the reference to the pack at the end of

The York Play of the Nativity

the preceding play at York) but still leaning on his crutch or staff (l. 74):

And yf we here all nyght abide
We schall be stormed in this steede,   *place*
The walles are doune on ilke a side,
The ruffe is rayued abouen oure hede,   *torn open*
Als haue I roo.   *as I hope to have peace!*

(ll. 15-20)

The connection between the craft of the Tile Thatchers and the subject of their play is thus soon clear. The only Scaffold required for the presentation on their Pageant is this tumble-down stable, its walls collapsed—so that it is open to public view—and its roof split. Such a stable is normally the site of the Nativity in English and York art and also in work by the fifteenth-century Flemish painters (fig. 1). Real fifteenth-century Yorkshire stables probably normally had thatched or tiled roofs and wood and clay or wattled sides and could be rather flimsy;[7] a large, almost life-sized model of one would not have been difficult to put together. The Place is the area on the Pageant outside the stable, which perhaps stands in the middle, occupying most of the space.

The apocryphal cave, found in the *Meditations on the Life of Christ* and in St. Bridget's *Revelations*, has been decisively rejected in favor of something more English; but of the four English plays which depict the Nativity it is only in the York play that the poor condition of the stable roof is mentioned. The Tile Thatchers can do no better, so to speak, than present a play whose one Scaffold is covered with a dilapidated roof. On the other hand, the condition of the stable not only indicates the poverty of the place in which the King of Kings is born—and poverty, as the *Meditations on the Life of Christ* says, quoting St. Francis, is "the peculiar road of salvation"[8]—but the hole in the roof is also needed for the star to shine through; what is required (it was perhaps felt) is a roof in which a hole has been deliberately made—some roof-work fit for the miraculous Nativity. A fifteenth-century Norwich glass-painter certainly thought along these lines. In his Nativity angel roof-workers pull a hole in the thatch to let the light from the star shine through onto the baby (fig. 12). A neat, square hole is another miraculous coincidence sometimes found in fifteenth-century English and other art.[9] The Tile Thatchers at York (and Chester) had the special ability to build such a roof complete, with a section professionally and miraculously missing. Perhaps the Plasterers (and Carpenters) felt the same way about the gaping holes in the walls. The subject of the play is thus a cause of both pride and shame for the guilds of craftsmen—both pointedly useless and pointedly useful—associated with it.

St. Bridget's vision of the Nativity, which draws on the *Meditations on the Life of Christ*—which in turn draws on St. Bernard's sermons on the Nativity—was granted to her in Bethlehem in about 1370, and her account of it caused a widespread shift in the iconography of the Nativity during the first quarter of the fifteenth century.[10] Her *Revelations* were well known in fifteenth-century England. Henry V established Syon Monastery of the Brigittine Order in 1415, and in the north her *Revelations* were equally influential. A selection in English was copied by a northern scribe before 1475, some of the brethren at Syon were Yorkshiremen, and English translations were bequeathed in Yorkshire in 1468 and 1495.[11] Two of the York plays give Mary the same words she is given by St. Bridget with which to address her Son; and John Bolton (d. 1445), Mayor of York in 1431, owned a manuscript Hours of the Blessed Virgin Mary written in York or Yorkshire in about 1420,[12] one of whose many illuminations is a rare full-page portrait of St. Bridget (fol. 108ᵛ). She is robed as a nun, seated in a chapel, quill in hand; the foreground is green, with flowers.

Having got his play underway with a complaint and prayer from Joseph (about whom St. Bridget says only that he was "an old man of great honesty"), the playwright proceeds (uniquely among English playwrights) to plot his play mainly but not exclusively or slavishly according to St. Bridget's vision. In the play Mary says that "the tyme is nere" (l. 34, "the days . . . were fulfilled"), and Joseph goes into the Place from the Scaffold to fetch some "light" (l. 43); while he is gone, the baby is born (l. 56), radiating light (l. 111); Mary worships him (ll. 57-63), then takes him in her arms (l. 66), and then dresses him (l. 67);

The York Play of the Nativity

Joseph returns to find the stable filled with light (ll. 92-93); Mary lays the baby into the crib (l. 118); finally, Mary and Joseph worship him (ll. 143-52).

This is a very distinctive sequence of events, differing from previous versions, and it is St. Bridget's. It is therefore not unreasonable to go a step further and conclude that she may well have been followed in some matters about which the script of the play provides no information. Mary (played by a male) might wear St. Bridget's white cloak over a robe or tunic (for which St. Bridget names no color, but which is blue, beneath the white cloak, in a painted window, about 1430, of the Virgin and Child in All Saints, North Street,[13] and blue in the Nativity in the Bolton Hours, fol. 36). She is visibly pregnant; St. Bridget "saw the child in her womb move." Just before the birth, Mary removes her white cloak to reveal "beautiful golden hair falling loosely down her shoulders"; her long hair is a prominent feature in York, English, and Northern art (figs. 1, 11)—the actor wore a wig, such as is recorded in some of the accounts of expenses for plays.[14] The *Meditations on the Life of Christ* records that she is now fifteen years old. When she speaks as a mother and wife, she is gentle and "mild"—the favorite epithet for her in fifteenth-century English writers. In the play she is cheerful, full of faith, and courteous: "Ye ar welcum sirre," she says (l. 84), to bring Joseph in from out of the darkness, rounding off his two worried stanzas (ll. 71-83).

The painting by the Master of Flemalle (fig. 1) shows not only Mary (with her long hair) and old Joseph kneeling as best he can, but also two women (midwives) and four angels. The effect, even without the shepherds who have arrived too promptly, is crowded. The York playwright sought to reduce the number of events that had accrued around the story and yet to demonstrate with great force its meaning. The theme of the play—the contrast between the feebleness of human endeavor and the miraculous and powerful intervention of God—is implicit in the sources of the plot, an uncluttered and economical amalgamation of the story as expounded by St. Bernard, told in the *Meditations on the Life of Christ*, and revealed to St. Bridget.

These meditative versions of the Nativity had been, when the

Chapter II

York play was written, rivaling for up to 250 years or more the legendary versions which medieval playwrights normally followed. The York playwright, perhaps in order to stay close to a version felt locally to be more up-to-date, authoritative (and certainly more graceful), has broken away from many well-established traditions. In particular, he has abandoned the traditional midwives or midwife (who was, however, restored to the lost York play of the Nativity).[15] These legendary women play a significant part in the other plays of the Nativity. They frequently appear in the liturgical *Officium Pastorum* and *Officium Stellae* (and so perhaps appeared in these Offices at York, recorded in the fifteenth century, whose texts are lost),[16] and it is presumably partly because of this liturgical tradition that (even though there are no liturgical plays of the Nativity proper) the vernacular plays commonly include the miracle of the midwife whose hands were paralyzed which is recounted in the apocryphal gospels. In all the other English and in the early French and Provençal plays of the Nativity the midwives appear or are at least mentioned. They were useful to the playwrights in various ways. In the plays which actually dramatize the paralyzing of Salome's hand, they provide ocular proof of the Virgin birth. A further point made in most of the plays is that the presence of the midwives is, at such a miraculously swift, painless, and non-mucilaginous birth—an idea important to St. Bernard and the *Meditations on the Life of Christ*—unnecessary. In the N-town play of the Nativity Mary smiles because she is so independent of them (l. 176*sd*). In the York play she, all alone, has "grete joie" (l. 50), a word probably deliberately chosen since what is happening to her is one of her "five joys" so frequently enumerated in the fifteenth century—by Jesus in the York play of the Coronation of the Virgin (ll. 113-28) and in many carols, for example.

The midwives were found especially useful in connection with the problem of what to do with Joseph during the actual birth: he can be conveniently got out of the way by being sent off to fetch them. According to *Pseudo-Matthew* 13,

> And there she brought forth a male child. . . . For the
> nativity of the Lord had already come, and Joseph was

The York Play of the Nativity

gone to seek midwives. When he had found them, he
returned to the cave, and found Mary with the infant she
had borne.

The effect is the same in the *Protevangelium* (18-19). This arrangement, made into a plot, is first found in *La Nativité Nostre
Seigneur Jhesu Crist* (played in Paris in about 1343);[17] in this
play Mary sends Joseph out. She says:

> Joseph, alez me tost la hors
> Aucune ventriére amener: *quelque*
> Car je senz bien que delivrer
> D'enfant me fault.
>
> (ll. 77-80)

Similarly, in the Ste. Genevieve *Nativité*, Mary sends Joseph to
fetch Anastasia to act as midwife and also says that it is not fit-
ting for him to be present at the birth. The same arrangement is
found in the English plays (excepting York) and is so convenient
that there is some justification for supposing it to have been the
norm at least in England by the early fifteenth century. The midwives are also frequently mentioned in English sermons and narratives, and they are seen in paintings.

However, some English sermons and narratives, following St.
Jerome and other early fathers, reject the story of the midwives as
fanciful, and neither the *Meditations on the Life of Christ* nor St.
Bridget mentions them; and following these two authorities and despite the strong playwriting, homiletic, and pictorial tradition, neither does the York playwright. Without them, how is the miraculous
nature of the Nativity to be demonstrated? And with no midwives,
how is the redundancy of human effort to be shown? And with no
midwives to fetch, how is Joseph to be got out of the way at the
critical moment? On the economical solutions to these questions of
plot and meaning hinges much of the success of the York play.

On hearing that Mary's time is near and that she can travel no
more, Joseph (his doubts about her now safely out of the way—in
the preceding play—and loving her solicitously and beyond
words, as the *Meditations on the Life of Christ* reports, and overcoming his handicaps) says:

Chapter II

Than wolde I fayne we had sum light,
What so befall.
It waxis right myrke vnto my sight,   *dark*
And colde withall.
I will go gete vs light forthy,   *get for this reason*
And fewell fande with me to bryng.   *fuel*
(ll. 39-44)

Now, while he is out looking for earthly light, it ironically happens that the Light of the World is born. In the midst of his shivering and stumbling search in the Place for light (like his Tudor descendants, the actor must act as if he is in the dark) a great light shines, and Joseph returns to Mary to find out what it is (ll. 81-83). That the contrast between the two kinds of light is not coincidental is confirmed by St. Bridget's account of the Nativity, where the same point is made. She says that Joseph

> went outside and brought to the virgin a burning candle; having attached this to the wall he went outside so that he might not be present at the birth. . . . [S]uddenly in a moment she gave birth to her son, from whom radiated such an ineffable light and splendour, that the sun was not comparable to it, nor did the candle, that St. Joseph had put there, give any light at all, the divine light totally annihilating the material light of the candle. . . .[18]

These events have been managed more economically by the playwright, whose Joseph goes and returns once only—on his new errand, for light. It is possible, although there is no mention of it in the text, that the playwright meant Joseph, in the presentation of the play, to return to the Scaffold with a candle; countless paintings, following St. Bridget, show him with his candle (fig. 1). In any case, the contrast between divine and material light is kept, and turned into a piece of irony (a point not missed in the revivals in the 1920's at All Saints, North Street, York). Just as midwives are not needed, neither is earthly light.

In St. Bridget's account the source of the light is the baby Jesus. This notion is kept in the play: worshipping the baby, Joseph says, "Hayle my lorde, lemer of light" (l. 111). "Lemer" means "source or giver of light" (*MED*), and Joseph's words, in

The York Play of the Nativity

view of what St. Bridget says, must be taken literally: the baby, in the performance, is born lying in an aureole; he is so portrayed in many English paintings and carvings of the Nativity. If St. Bridget is being followed exactly by the players, Mary kneels with her back to the crib—which, if the crib is in the middle, suggests that she kneels "downstage" facing the audience—to pray, looking up, for Joseph and for grace (ll. 45-49); she then stands with her hands extended in ecstasy (ll. 50-51), and the baby appears at her feet in front of her, *statim*, suddenly: "Nowe borne is he" (l. 55). Coincidentally Mary, in many recent revivals, abandoning an earlier twentieth-century coyness, parts her cloak to reveal him on the floor. He is a carved figure of a naked baby surrounded by short rays (probably painted golden).[19]

The playwright has added a second fount of divine light—the star. The star, which according to the chronology of the story does not yet shine, and which is not mentioned in this connection by the *Meditations on the Life of Christ* or St. Bridget, is yet mentioned or shown as shining at the Nativity proper in *Pseudo-Matthew* (13), the *Golden Legend*, the Chester play (Nativity, l. 508*sd*), and other English works, and is shown to be shining above the stable immediately after the birth occurs in the performance of this play: in reply to Joseph's inquiry about the light, Mary recalls Balaam's prophecy "that a sterne shulde rise full hye" (l. 100, "A star shal rise," *Num.* 24.17). The miraculous effulgence which in *Pseudo-Matthew* (13) is said to fill the place of the Nativity is given two definite sources (the baby and the star) in the late Middle Ages; the two may be seen shining together in various paintings (English and others) of the Nativity. The dramatist is allowing for both sources and is stressing, by a modest but pointed piece of irony, one of his central symbols, which he presumably took from St. Bridget: material light—suggesting the limitations of unaided human endeavor—pales beside divine. Light is an Old Testament messianic image (*Bar.* 5.9, *Hab.* 3.4, for example) and sorely needed. St. Bernard compares the virgin birth to a star which sends forth its light without losing its radiance, and proclaims that we leave the world of shadows, the Place and the Scaffold before the birth (ll. 41, 63), guided by the great light, while the *Meditations on the Life of Christ* declares that

Chapter II

"Today the Sun of justice, which has been hidden behind clouds, shines brightly."[20] St. Bridget, and the playwright, have given distinct direction to this powerful image.

It is not, in the play, only light that Joseph sets out to find, but also fuel for a fire to keep the baby warm (ll. 42-44). St. Bernard, the *Meditations on the Life of Christ*, and St. Bridget all pity the baby suffering from the cold. The playwright is, therefore, again being economical with his movements between Place and Scaffold when he adds to Joseph's search for light the search for warmth. And again the efforts of this mere human being are forestalled and seen to be unnecessary, for it is actually the ox and the ass who keep the baby warm by deliberately breathing on him (ll. 130-33). This miracle, reported in the *Meditations on the Life of Christ* but ignored by St. Bridget, is shown in some of the other English plays but is not in those plays tied into the whole pattern—it is a separate event. Here, however, having decided to keep the particular legend (*Pseudo-Matthew* 14), the playwright anticipates it by giving Joseph an extra errand, and the miraculous warmth joins the miraculous light in one economical stroke of the plot to stand in contrast to man-made light and warmth. The supremacy of God over man in working the wonder of the Nativity is thus twice shown, and the unique motivation which the playwright gives to Joseph's one absence is twice, as it were, justified.

The pattern is further tied together by the two prophecies recalled in the play. In contrast to other plays and accounts of the Nativity which sometimes include what appears to be a miscellaneous selection of prophecies, the York playwright includes only the two that relate directly to his chosen pattern of contrasting light and warmth: Balaam's prophecy of the star, and Habacuc's (l. 137) of the baby lying between the beasts (3.2, reading, with the early Fathers, *in medio animalium*), which beasts, under the influence of *Isaias* 1.3 (as in *Pseudo-Matthew* 14), soon became an ox and an ass: "the ox knoweth his owner and the ass his master's crib" (fig. 13). This passage is the ultimate origin of Joseph and Mary's happy exchange:

Joseph. Forsothe it semes wele be ther chere   *mien*
Thare lord thei ken.

The York Play of the Nativity

Maria.	Ther lorde thai kenne, that wate I wele,	*know*
	They worshippe hym with myght and mayne.	
	(ll. 125-28)	

In the *Meditations on the Life of Christ* and St. Bridget's *Revelations*, Mary and Joseph have brought the ox and the ass with them, the ox to carry their modest baggage and the ass for Mary to ride; at the end of the York play of Joseph's Troubles about Mary (the preceding play), however, Joseph himself shoulders the pack (ll. 302-05), and there is no mention of the ass. It seems that the animals, in the York play, are already in the stable when Mary and Joseph enter it. Real animals were hardly used (they could not be relied upon to comfort or recognize "Ther lorde," l. 127); one common pattern in English carvings and paintings, including the full-page illumination in the Bolton Hours (fol. 36), is for the head only of the ox and the ass to appear (fig. 13),[21] and this arrangement, using models of the heads, would have been found convenient for the presentation of the play.

Thus, rather than pursue at random the legendary miracles of the Nativity, the playwright prefers to bring out in symbols the contrasts between God and man; he also exploits (like the poets and the preachers) the paradoxes of the Nativity—particularly the paradox of the Christ Child. Joseph is less like a husband than like an old man with a daughter; he calls Mary "doghtir" (l. 85), a denial of any carnal union and also merely an affectionate term— as well as a word particularly applicable to a devout woman (*MED* n 1, 2 and 3). He attempts to provide for her, but at the same time is dependent on her and turns to her for advice at every point. This mixture of human instincts is also what gives a touch of wonder to Mary's speeches to her baby. Here the play follows St. Bridget, who says: "When therefore the virgin felt, that she already had born[e] her child, she immediately worshipped him, her head bent down and her hands clasped, with great honour and reverence."[22] So, in the play, as soon as the baby is born Mary says a conventionally dignified "Hail" lyric to him:

> Hayle my lord God, hayle prince of pees,
> Hayle my fadir, and hayle my sone;
> Hayle souereyne sege all synnes to sesse,   *man sins stop*

Chapter II

> Hayle God and man in erth to wonne.   *dwell*
> Hayle, thurgh whos myht
> All this worlde was first begonne,
> Merknes and light.
>
> (ll. 57-63)

She is acknowledging the power of God, from the Creation (ll. 61-63) until now, recognizing his mighty presence, quoting (ll. 57, 59) *Isaias* (9.6), and not avoiding a full and ringing alliterative line (l. 59). The most high has himself built this humble place, as medieval writers commonly agreed. After this, St. Bridget says, Mary took the baby in her arms and dressed him in clothes "of exquisite purity and fineness." Her order of events is kept by the playwright, but the fine clothes have become the more usual "poure wede," following St. Bernard, who delighted in his sermons to ponder these rags (*pannus*) which he can ironically refer to as "silks," the *Meditations on the Life of Christ*, or any one of a number of sermons or carols. (At Chester, this is presumably where the Daubers—Renovators of old Clothes—came into their own.) The playwright has supplied Mary's modest and gentle supplication, whose mildness and simplicity contrast with her "Hail" lyric:

> Sone, as I am sympill sugett of thyne,   *subject*
> Vowchesaffe, swete sone I pray the,
> That I myght the take in the armys of myne   *thee these*
> And in this poure wede to arraie the.   *poor clothing*
>
> (ll. 64-67)

She picks up the small carved figure, complete with its short golden rays, and tenderly but tightly, as was the custom, wraps it in a cloth and binds it with ribbons or bands (so he lies in the crib in the illumination in the Bolton Hours, fig. 13, and in a fragmentary printed York Hours [STC 15929]) while she speaks; or perhaps, to stress the importance of this action, she binds the Christ Child in silence (between ll. 67 and 68, or 70 and 71). Joseph's "Hail" lyric, which is also very lofty and which emphasizes the traditional image of Jesus as "floure fairest of hewe" (ll. 106-12), is similarly followed, in his next speech, by plain and simple words (ll. 122-26). It is as if the playwright, by means of an abrupt change of diction between Mary's two contiguous and barely linked stanzas, has sought to represent St. Bernard's rapturous paradoxes, "wonderful mixtures": "God and man, mother and virgin, faith and the human heart, are joined as neighbours."[23] This effect appears to be special to the plays, although the numerous lyrics and carols of the Nativity which combine English and Latin form a parallel. There is a tension between the need to show that the birth was both *supra naturam* and *pro natura*, to use St. Bernard's words, or the idea that the birth was "Agaynst nature," as the carol says,[24] and the tendency of late medieval artists to humanize it; and so Mary can mix with her knowledge of the supernatural powers of the Son of God some pride in the human precociousness of her son: "This hase he ordand of his grace,/ My sone so ying" (ll. 95-96, "so young")—she might with advantage stress the last two words, giving the two lines a tone of complex wonder, the play equivalents, perhaps, of such an iconographic device as depicting a normal-looking baby who yet raises his right hand in a distinct blessing and waves his left hand at random in the air or both touches like an inquisitive baby and blesses the Magi's gift (fig. 11). At this moment in the play (while she is wrapping him up) Mary is necessarily holding the baby on her lap or knee, where Joseph first sees him, and where he can be seen in glass painting and carvings belonging to fourteenth- and fifteenth-century York, and which is a common position for him to be in when the shepherds and Magi visit him.[25]

By divine intervention the play, which begins with uncertainty, darkness, cold, and misery, ends with a sense of security, light, warmth, and joy—a foretaste of heaven brought within everyone's reach by the Incarnation. The prosody of the play expresses this meaning. Mary and Joseph seldom share stanzas, but when they are together again after the birth, a sense of excitement is conveyed by the rapid dialogue in stanza 13; then a sense of relief and harmony pervades the play—expressed by the way in which Mary and Joseph begin to echo each other. Mary's "Hail" lyric, for example, is echoed by Joseph's; Joseph's "Hail" lyric is deliberately added by the playwright to balance Mary's (in St. Bridget's account Joseph, returning at this point, merely weeps for joy). Mary's prophecy is also echoed by Joseph's, and toward the end of the play their speeches are linked by repetition and concatenation. The playwright has made a strong and harmonious pattern out of the responses of Mary and Joseph to the birth of the baby, a pattern which begins to be suggested by St. Bridget of Sweden, who concludes her revelation by saying that "together the two, that is, she herself and Joseph, put him into the manger, and on their knees they worshipped him with immense joy and happiness."[26]

And so at this point, the baby safely tucked up by Mary (ll. 118-20)—perhaps Joseph helps—and seen by his watchful but inexperienced parents to be safely asleep (l. 134), they probably kneel (as often in art, fig. 1) as they say their concluding prayers. The playwright has here put into Mary's mouth the words (also found in scrolls in paintings) that St. Bridget reports the Virgin as saying to her Son immediately after he was born: *Bene veneris deus meus, dominus meus et filius meus.*[27] In Mary's speeches changes are rung on these words (stanzas 9, 17), and the words themselves fittingly form part of the last, harmonious moment of the play:

Joseph.   Honnoure and worshippe both day and nyght,
            Ay-lastand lorde, be done to the
            Allway, as is worthy;
            And lord, to thy seruice I oblissh me
            With all myn herte, holy.
Maria.   Thou mercyfull maker, most myghty,
            My God, my lorde, my sone so free,
            Thy handemayden forsoth am I,
            And to thi seruice I oblissh me,
            With all myn herte entere.
                                    (ll. 143-52)

(St. Bridget's words also recur, in a similar context, in the York play of the Flight into Egypt, l. 26.) In contrast to Joseph's diffidence at the opening of the play, Mary now serenely asks her Son to grant his blessing on "vs all in feere"—that is, on all those present. The play, like many others that conclude with such blessings, thus finally opens out to recognize all those who have been

The York Play of the Nativity

following in their hearts this meditation on the Nativity shown outwardly to their eyes:

> Thy blissing, beseke I thee,
> Thou graunte vs all in feere.
>
> (ll. 153-54)

Well over half the York plays conclude with such blessings, which probably in most instances, and certainly in some, were given to the audiences.

It has been suggested that the appearance of a large number of carols and lyrics of the Nativity from the mid-fourteenth century onwards is due to the stimulation provided by the plays;[28] whether this is so or not, the poems can certainly serve in part as a commentary on this play, together with the *Meditations on the Life of Christ* and other theological and meditative works.

The Nativity is an occasion for sport and song, as the sixteenth-century carol written for a Lord of Misrule or King of Christmas makes clear:

> Make we mery, bothe more and lasse,
> For now ys the tyme of Crystymas.
>
> Lett no man cum into this hall,
> Grome, page, nor yet marshall,
> But that sum sport he bryng withall,
> For now ys the tyme of Crystmas.[29]

This is a point that the playwrights of the Shepherds' plays (including the Wakefield Master) understood. It is an occasion for "jubilation, gladness, and great exultation," says the *Meditations*.[30] A fifteenth-century carol expatiates on the hymn *Salvator mundi domine* found in the York Breviary for the first Sunday in Advent: "Make ye mery for hym that ys ycom,/ Alleluya Deo!"[31]

"Merry" (like "mirth") does not have exclusively worldly connotations. One can be, as was St. Thomas More, "merry in God" (*OED* merry 3 b), and the Nativity is also a special occasion for devotion, worship, and intimate meditation. Receive him devoutly, worship him, and pick him up and hold him, says St.

Chapter II

Bernard (*devote amplectimur cum Simeone sancto infantiam Salvatoris*), echoed by *Meditations on the Life of Christ.*[32] Since God has become a baby, it is now possible to see him, or see him "in the face," as the *Meditations on the Life of Christ* and some carols urge us to do, often: "Quene of heuyn and solace,/ Helpe vs to se God in the face."[33] Like Joseph in the play, we can "see the same in sight" (l. 141, "in sight" is not tautologous, but means "very clearly" or "in his presence," or "with my own eyes," or, indeed, "in the face"); and he is the best of children, "sweet Jesus," as the meditative poem "Swete Ihesu" (based on the hymn *Jesu dulcis memoria*) by the Yorkshireman Richard Rolle or one of his school reiterates,[34] accounting, probably, for Joseph's line (and Mary's word, l. 65) as he re-enters the stable: "O Marie, what swete thyng is that on thy kne?" (l. 87).

The paradoxes are a cause of wonder and are visibly central to the play. The Almighty Lord ("All-weldand God in trinité," say Joseph, l. 1, and Mary, l. 45) chose to be born in a humble stable to reprove the glory of the world; he had no bed, as both Mary and Joseph say in the play (ll. 24, 115), and "not a pylow to lay vnder his hed"[35]—notions to be seized on by the York Realist. The majestic Lord humbles himself, as a fifteenth-century carol, following St. Bernard, says: "The great Lord off Heaven/ Owr seruant is becom."[36] The possible lines of thought, many of them common, are numerous. There is no room at the inn, but there is always room in God's house, says Ludolphus.[37] He was born poor to make us rich, says a carol.[38] As Mary wraps him in rags while they watch, some members of the audience might remember that he is being wrapped in them so that they might receive "the stole of immortality" (unlike the Scribes "who desire to walk in long robes," *Luke* 20.46); and that his hands and feet are "tightly bound so that our hands might be led to good works and our feet directed to the way of peace," as the *Glossa Ordinaria*, quoting Bede, explains.[39]

The mirth is not only devout and thoughtful but also solemn. The sight of the Nativity inevitably leads to thoughts of the Passion, says St. Bernard, and scarcely a carol, lyric, or sermon on the Nativity fails to mention the Passion. The binding of the Christ Child is a particular reminder of the Passion, but this is

The York Play of the Nativity

hardly clear unless the play is seen. "He is made a little child," says St. Bernard, "His Virgin mother binds [*alligat*] his tender limbs with rags [*pannis*]. . . . In this you shall know that He comes not to lose you but to save you; to deliver, and not to bind."[40] The Christ Child is bound now, and will be bound on the Cross, and yet he himself is born to loose the bonds of our distress. Paintings and carvings of the Nativity, while like this play focusing on the main subject, sometimes unobtrusively contain small reminders of the Passion. A small cross, barely noticeable in the shadow, might be fixed to the stable wall; in a woodcut in a York Hours the baby's diadem has crosses on it.[41] Some members of the audience would have heard reminders of the Passion in both Mary's and Joseph's formal "Hail" speeches in the play: "Hayle souereyne sege all synnes to sesse" (l. 59) and "Hayle saueour" (l. 110). Jesus is also nourishment for us, as the *Meditations on the Life of Christ* says.[42] He is "blyesful fowde," says the fifteenth-century York carol[43] which uses as a burden a phrase from the Office of the Mass for Christmas Day; in Joseph's simple words "Wele is me I bade this day/ To se this foode" (ll. 90-91) there is, therefore, also a reminder of the Passion (and of the Eucharist) for some, since "foode," although primarily meaning "child" in this context, also, as in the carol and elsewhere in the York plays, means "sustenance" (it is the same word); the Wakefield Master probably found a pun here, as I hope to show.

Joseph's biblical (*Isa.* 11.1) metaphor for Jesus, "floure fairest of hewe" (ll. 106, 112), is used by St. Bernard and is common in religious poetry; it is often also applied to Mary to whom it may also in addition allude in the play, where it is the equivalent of the flowers found in many paintings and carvings of the Nativity—in the Bolton Hours, for example, where they dot the foreground and cover Mary's cloak (fol. 36).[44] Mary, being a virgin, bore Jesus "as a floure berith his odoure,"[45] and so for some members of the audience there may also be the fullest resonance in Joseph's "Hayle saueour" if they hear the word in its sense of sweetness, perfume, and delight as well as salvation (*OED* savour sb 2).

If, as seems likely, most members of the audience grasped the central ironies associated with Joseph's actions, he may be regarded as a figure for everyman and be said to represent, like a number of unsteadfast characters in the York plays, the Christian man *moyen sensuel*, the believer who does not quite have faith in miracles or in God's providence; in the Place, the bitter weather gets the better of his old bones, and he grumbles and stumbles as he goes about his futile task; but by the end of the play his spirit has been renewed and he has found God and his grace. He has been saved from "sorowes sere" (l. 32, "various") as if the leaking roof is, as Langland says, a metaphor for the many miseries that afflict us (XVII.335ff), the donkey-work of daily life and petty sorrows of everyday existence, sent by the Lord in his tender mercy to try us and perfect us; or even as if those (like Joseph) who are old and feeble and whom we should pity are metaphors for fallen man, for those who have not yet accepted Christ in their hearts (*Col.* 3.9-10)—another notion developed further by the Wakefield Master, particularly in the person of Coll, the old First Shepherd of the Second Shepherds' play. On the other hand, some may have recognized in Joseph a resemblance to old, just, and devout Simeon, with whom he was paired in a procession at Beverley in 1389,[46] and who "should not see death before he had seen the Christ" (*Luke* 2.26).

When Mary and Joseph both conclude the play by dedicating themselves to the service of God, the parental meaning (that they will rear him) can hardly be paramount; on behalf of the Tile Thatchers they are setting an example for everyone in attendance. St. Bernard says, so that Mary and Joseph and the infant lying in the manger may always be found in us, let us live soberly, justly, and piously all our days.[47] The baby instructs us in humility, mildness, and poverty. The Nativity occurs each day, explains Ludolphus, whenever anyone receives the "flower of the divine Word in his soul."[48]

In such ways and with varying degrees of piety, the audience, besides responding with joy to the subject of the play and with pleasure at its loveliness, can (as the *Meditations on the Life of Christ* says they should) ponder its significance and see a range of implications in it. The performance of even this relatively simple play, like the performance of the more complicated plays I explore in the following chapters, is meant to leave the audience devoutly thoughtful.

The audience at York was fortunate. It is as if the author of the N-town play of the Nativity would overwhelm his audience with the sheer weight of the evidence; he perhaps works from the narrative poem the *Life of Saint Anne*, expatiates on the compact legendary material in that poem (twelve lines of the poem become forty-four lines of the play, for example),[49] and even adds further to his play the miracle of the cherry tree. His Joseph and his midwives are garrulous. The author of the Chester play of the Nativity unimaginatively and at times abjectly follows the *Stanzaic Life of Christ* (ll. 209ff) which he had in front of him;[50] here there is not that artistic absorption of his material which may be fairly surmised in the case of the York playwright. The extremely lame ending of the Chester play, for example, may be contrasted to the fine rounding off of the York play, which seems to be due to an imaginative grasp of the episode as recounted by St. Bridget. The Coventry play[51] includes many subjects, from the opening prophecy by Isaias and the Annunciation to the Slaughter of the Innocents and the Flight to Egypt. It proceeds rather jerkily; the baby is no sooner, it seems, put into the crib to be warmed by the breathing of the beasts than he is taken out again (ll. 287-96). This play also lacks the even dignity of language that marks the York play. The Coventry play does have some shape to it, chiefly owing to the melodramatic contrast between King Herod and the King of Kings (quite possibly borrowed from the Wakefield Master, as I shall argue), but is crude—if vivacious—work when set beside the York play. In particular, the playwright rushes through the scene of the birth itself (ll. 180-203, 282-96), which he scarcely shows any interest in and which he does nothing with. The York play reveals a much stronger controlling intelligence than do the other English plays of the Nativity; there are no loose ends in the York play. One wonders how the revision could have been an improvement and what the two other recorded but lost Yorkshire plays of the Nativity (performed at Beverley in the fifteenth century, and at Wressle Castle, in the Earl of Northumberland's Chapel on Christmas morning early in the sixteenth century)[52] were like.

Chapter II

By carefully selecting and conflating his material the York playwright has succeeded in composing a dignified, compact, and rich version of the miracle of the Nativity. His play, deceptively slight, shows economical planning, workmanlike dovetailing, and careful balancing. He has adapted St. Bridget's revelation, increased the patterned repetition both in the actions and the prosody (an effect Edith Craig perhaps sought to mirror in production by symmetrical tableaux) in it, filled it out somewhat with some parts from earlier traditions, and stressed the paradox of the Christ Child. The legendary midwives and their functions have been replaced by symbols of light and warmth. He has incorporated his chief properties—the ox and the ass, the roof and the walls, the baby in an aureole (and perhaps a candle and an unlit fire)—into the central theme of the play: the ineffectiveness of human endeavor, the limitations of human nature, and, by implication, the consequent necessity for the Incarnation, which implies also the Redemption. The diction, always dignified (unless Joseph for a brief moment descends to low, l. 71), is both plain and lofty as well as resonant of present loveliness and future salvation. The very craft of the Tile Thatchers forms part of the unity of the play. Like the marriage and motherhood that are but are not, they are both effective and ineffective craftsmen, but Joseph's conversion and Mary's joy are plainly meant to be theirs and ours. Among the learned, there was possibly some satisfaction at the authenticity of the presentation.

Chapter III

The York Shepherds' Play and the First Shepherds' Play

Foolish men shall not obtain her. . . . For wisdom came forth from God.—Ecclesiasticus 15.7, 10

The extant text of the York Shepherds' play lacks about sixty lines (a leaf is missing from the manuscript), and one of the two key events of the play—the Annunciation by the angels to the shepherds—is thus absent.[1] The text otherwise represents the play presented from about 1415 to 1477 and sponsored by the Chandlers, or Candle Makers, under whose aegis it continued to be presented in a revised form, now lost, for the rest of the medieval life of the York plays. The connection between the craft and the subject of the play is to be found in the great star-light needed in the presentation; as in the case of the Tile Thatchers, the Chandlers are perhaps proud of their abilities but aware that their best efforts cannot meet the requirements of the story—in this instance, that the "brightness of God shone round about them" (*Luke* 2.9)—or express the metaphor of St. Bernard and the *Meditations on the Life of Christ*: "To the shepherds who watched is announced the joy of the light," especially since on one occasion St. Bernard compares the light of the Nativity to an immense and brilliant wax taper (*tamquam immensi et praeclari luminis cereus*).[2] In the second half of the sixteenth century (by which time the play of the Nativity and the Shepherds' play seem to have been merged) the Inn Keepers also contributed to the expenses; the tradition of matching the craft of the guild with the

81

subject of the play was thus clearly still alive. Mary laid Jesus in a manger "because there was no room for them in the inn" (*Luke* 2.7); the Inn Keepers might therefore feel equally small but happy about the play. At Beverley by 1520 the Shepherds' play was sponsored by the Vintners; their shepherds presumably came to adore the "true vine" (*John* 15.1), who can be seen at least once in a fifteenth-century carving as a lamb surrounded by vines bearing heavy bunches of grapes, and who is probably implied by the grapes and vines of the Ripon school of carvers.[3]

The York play is based on the same common original as the "Shrewsbury" (really from the Northwest) text, which preserves only the part of the Third Shepherd and his cues and which was written in the fourteenth or very early in the fifteenth century. Both elaborate the story told by St. Luke (2.8-20) of the Annunciation to the Shepherds by the angel and their visit to Bethlehem to worship the Christ Child. The Adoration of the Shepherds is a subject new to art in the fifteenth century, and there are no examples extant in York or the West Riding, although both the extant Yorkshire collections of biblical plays and the Chester collection include it, as did, apparently, the Beverley collection. The York play begins with three shepherds "keeping the night watches over their flock" (*Luke* 2.8) in the Place, which is meant to represent hilly moor land (ll. 34, 52), a Yorkshire version of St. Luke's "in the same country" (2.8), and which is probably most of the space on the Chandlers' Pageant (which they are recorded as owning).[4] The one Scaffold represents the dilapidated stable ("house," l. 91), and probably stands at one end of the Pageant. It has no door: as soon as they see the stable, the shepherds see the Christ Child lying in the manger between the ox and the ass (ll. 93-94), "Right als the aungell saide." Mary, Joseph, and (probably) angels are present but do not speak.[5] The star shines over Bethlehem (*Matt.* 2.2), the "burgh" (ll. 13, 87) of which the stable is imagined to be a part; the Chandlers perhaps light a group of candles just before Colle's words "Yone sterne to that lorde sall vs lede" (l. 81, "star") or earlier, at a point indicated on the missing leaf; but more probably the star is a painted property (see fig. 11).

The shepherds interested the York playwright, and he makes a number of points about them. They are Yorkshire shepherds and therefore address each other familiarly by the diminutive forms of their English names; the first is unnamed, the second is Hudde (or Richard), and the third is Colle (Colin or Nicholas—Tib, or Theobald, in the Shrewsbury text). With such names they must wear contemporary peasant clothing, a plain and belted full-length or knee-length gown (worn over a shirt), boots or leggings or hose with flat shoes, and hats or hoods; they may also carry equipment—crooks, tar-boxes, horns, and wallets or satchels (figs. 14-15).[6] The first refers to his hat and horn (l. 77), an ox-horn with the tip cut used for purposes of signalling.[7] In fifteenth-century art, the shepherds are normally shown as rough working men, but at the same time they are also, as was commonly understood, Israelites and so begin the play by reciting messianic prophecies as they walk together, free of care (l. 3)—prophecies from "Oure forme-fadres" (l. 5), Osee, Isaias, and Balaam. Each speaks one whole stanza. Colle, evidently somewhat uncomfortable with their talk, seems nevertheless to be reminded by it that they should take better care of their sheep, and they separate to do so, but not before he has made the oddly disinterested statement that "I haue herde say, by that same light/ The childre of Israell shulde be made free" (ll. 29-30).

A great light is very soon seen by the First Shepherd, who calls the others ("Steppe furth and stande by me," l. 40) to him in amazement. In their excitement, they share the next three stanzas, stanza 4 having as many as eight speakers. Hudde thinks the First Shepherd has gone mad (l. 38), and Colle, who has perhaps wandered furthest away, hastens to rejoin them, anxious lest he be deprived of "any feest" (l. 44). The angelic song of announcement and the shepherds' initial reaction to it are on the missing leaf. As the York text resumes, two of them certainly gape in wonder (l. 59). Amazed and open-mouthed shepherds appear on the embroidered dalmatic from Whalley Abbey in the Burrell Collection, and in a woodcut in an early sixteenth-century York Hours, where one with a beard leans on his stick, another with a beard points to the angel in the sky, and the beardless third has suddenly stopped playing his pipe, his fingers still poised over the holes.[8]

Led by the First Shepherd, who calls on the others to help him, they attempt to imitate (l. 60) the angel's song by singing a

Chapter III

"mery note"—unsuccessfully, according to Colle (l. 69). The shepherds react with incomprehension or wonder to the angelic song in all the English plays; and their attempts to interpret the meaning of *Gloria* or imitate it are first found in the early fourteenth century, in the Holkham Bible Picture Book.[9] They are indeed partly simple and unlearned men, but the First Shepherd summarizes (ll. 72-75) the angel's spoken message (*Luke* 2.10-12) and is keen to follow his instructions and find the baby: "I walde giffe hym bothe hatte and horne/ And I myght fynde that frely foode" (l. 78), he says, linking two alliterating phrases, one ("hatte and horne") not lofty (and possibly a semi-proverbial expression for things of no great worth—Whiting H175, 176) and the other ("frely foode" or "noble child") elevated and literary (*OED* freely adj. 1320 and food 6 1375, *MED* freli adj. 1a and fode n[1] la). It is Colle who says they will have no difficulty if they simply follow "Yone sterne" (l. 83, "star") and Hudde who agrees, calling on them for a second song, as they travel "With sange to seke oure savyour" (l. 85); this second song, "myrthe and melody" (l. 84), is presumably less boisterous than their first ("Ha! ha! this was a mery note," l. 65), and since the Shrewsbury version (ll. 14-37) is close to the York version (ll. 69-85) here, they possibly sing the liturgical *Transeamus usque Bethlehem* found, with plainsong music, in the earlier version, where Tib begins the song and is then joined by the others (l. 32.1). At York they walk as they sing, moving along or around the Place, almost certainly with an emphasis on "down stage," and possibly using the street. They quickly find the baby, by a fortunate chance— "happe of heele," according to Hudde (l. 90), who rejoices with some wonder, using a variation of the common "here . . . there" (*OED* here 10): "Loo, here is the house, and here is hee" (l. 91). Colle confirms that they have arrived at the right place (l. 92).

They then—in numerical order, as at the beginning of the play, and once more in whole stanzas—worship the Christ Child. The first two, stressing their poverty, present him with simple gifts (a child's brooch with a tin bell attached to it, and two hazelnuts on a string) and ask him not to forget them when he comes to power. They speak with more familiarity than reserve, and Hudde, more an extortioner than a worshipper, resorts to the proverb "bountith askis rewarde" (l. 118, Whiting B474, G74) and might deliver his last line—"Nowe watte ye what I mene" (l. 119)—with a knowing wink. The Third Shepherd, Colle, is more direct and has a better understanding, perhaps because, as he says, he is last and has not pushed himself forward (l. 121). He seems most anxious to see the Christ Child's face and perhaps crouches down to do so ("Nowe loke on me," he says, l. 120), recognizes that he is already a Prince as well as a "swete swayne" (l. 128, "boy"), presents no demands, and gives no hints. His gift, however, is noticeably awkward: a spoon made of horn and capable of holding forty peas (a hundred in the Shrewsbury version), an oversized gift and an odd nutrient for a baby.

Colle remembers to bid the Christ Child farewell and, praying "God graunte vs levynge lange" (l. 131), avoids what seems to be the terrible irony of the Shrewsbury version ("God graunt the lifyng lang," says Tib, l. 48, "thee") and thus also includes the audience in the scope of his prayer. As is appropriate for one who has shown greater perception than the others, he is now in charge, and concludes the play by leading the other two shepherds back "hame agayne," singing (ll. 130-31), as in St. Luke's Gospel ("the shepherds returned, glorifying and praising God," 2.20). The shepherds have sung three songs, led, in turn, by the unnamed First Shepherd, then Hudde, and finally Colle; their third song and probably their second are holier than their first. They return to the center of the Pageant while the angels remain at the Scaffold, whence, according to the *Meditations on the Life of Christ*,[10] one came to deliver the announcement to them. (The angels may have arrived at the stable during the play of the Nativity, at line 56, in accordance with *Pseudo-Matthew* (13), then the *Meditations on the Life of Christ*, and then St. Bridget's version, but there is no hint of them in the extant version of that play; the lost and clearly less simple revised version included an angel in the cast.[11]) The Shepherds' play thus ends as it began, with all the players back in their places on the Pageant; but there has been movement even in this short (about fifteen minutes) presentation.

Despite the missing leaf, it seems clear that the York playwright has tried to take account of the many-sided nature of his shepherds, both Yorkshiremen and Israelites, ignorant—even cunning—and perceptive, unredeemed and redeemed, serious-minded and foolish, squabblesome but comradely, willing to sing both convivial and religious songs, and capable of movement both literal and spiritual not only as a group but as individuals. St. Luke's story, at least at the beginning and the end, is closely followed (except for the star, borrowed from the story of the Magi), and the craft which financed the play is not forgotten. The focus of attention is on the shepherds, who make progress, and in the end all is subsumed in the straightforward conclusion: the shepherds have found, literally if not in all cases too intelligently, their "savyour" (l. 85).

If the shepherds interested the York playwright, they fascinated the Wakefield Master; points briefly made by the former (many on the evidence of the Shrewsbury version and analogous writings and art, not original) are fully exploited by the latter, who in the First Shepherds' play[12] allows himself more room to explore the shepherds and tries to integrate into each of them the many-sidedness only briefly exploited in the York play. He keeps to the basic outline of the York play. Both plays begin with the shepherds speaking whole stanzas, in both they sing a total of three songs, and in both they make progress, but the Wakefield Master introduces much more material and as a result produces a work far more substantial, orderly, complex (and amusing) than the York play but, nevertheless, one which, like the York play, is devoted mostly to the shepherds, of whom there were many in the West Riding, and whom God chose to honor first.

The York (and N-town and, apparently, the Shrewsbury) Shepherds' plays launch into the subject of the Annunciation to the Shepherds directly, but the Wakefield Master's two Shepherds' plays (and likewise the Chester and Coventry plays) devote their first episodes to humorous activities which are cut short only by the exhaustion of the shepherds and the appearance of the angel. The meaning of the Nativity is shown by the fully exemplified progression of the shepherds in the case of the First Shepherds' play from foolishness and insecurity to understanding and stability, from their foolish activities, which are dimly related to the Nativity, to their adoration of the Christ Child, which goes beyond the Nativity to the Eucharist.

The subject of the play is not only the Nativity but also the Incarnation itself. The playwright follows the main events of the story, but significantly diverges from it as at the beginning of the annunciation and at the end of the play, which follows *Luke* 2.8-17 rather than 2.8-20. His new material comes from the Old Testament, particularly the book of *Isaias*, which, like St. Augustine, he probably regarded as a fifth Gospel, and the book of *Wisdom*, to which he seems to point deliberately (ll. 161, 178—his own uses of the word "wisdom"); various interpretations of the Incarnation, especially St. John's, episodes and metaphors from whose Gospel he chooses to have his players enact; two popular tales; and, as always, contemporary life and language. The play requires a speaking cast of six, three (the shepherds) with major parts, and three (Jack, the angel, and Mary) with extremely small parts. Most of the action occurs in the Place, which contains a table ("borde," l. 196) with a large basket handy ("panyer," l. 281) and elsewhere a stone for Slowpace to lean his head and shoulders against (l. 325) and into which he rides or leads his horse (l. 264); the Place is much used, and a Pageant is not indicated, although the play can be presented on one, provided the area in front of it is used at least for the horse. The holy family occupies a Scaffold representing the stable, and the angel probably stands on a second, smaller Scaffold. What happens in the Place is, until the angel sings, ludicrous; on or in the Scaffolds, comic, turning the play into a divine comedy, like the York play of the Nativity and the York Shepherds' play. Like all the Wakefield Master's plays (except the Second Shepherds' play), the First Shepherds' takes about three-quarters of an hour to present. It consists of 504 lines[13] (divided into 56 stanzas) and some time-consuming business.

The play is plotted numerically, the fifty-six stanzas being divided into seven groups of eight stanzas each. The chief division, marked by a song (l. 430), is between the first six-sevenths and the final seventh, at the beginning of which (stanza 49) the shepherds decide to go to Bethlehem.[14] Their antics are not entirely over until this point, the final seventh, in the play is reached, although the end of their extreme foolishness (their drunken feast) exactly coincides with the last line of stanza 32, the precise conclusion of the first four-sevenths of the play. In stanza 33, the beginning of the fifth seventh, Slowpace makes the sign of the cross, in symbolic reference, perhaps, to Christ's human life span (like Sir Gawain, who, in stanza 33 of *Sir Gawain and the Green Knight*, crosses himself for the third time). The progress of the shepherds is thus measured in sevens, and the playwright announces this: at the beginning of the play Gib's salvation, he thinks, depends on his throwing a seven at dice (l. 38); by the end of the play, the shepherds have found salvation by the grace of him who made the world in seven days (l. 487). The two phrases are characteristically pointed, even reversed: Gib hopes "to cast the warld in seuen," while Mary invokes on the shepherds the blessing of God who "sett all on seuen." Both "set" and "seuen" fit easily into either context (*OED* set III 11 and 14b, and seven B 1b and 3b).

The number 7 has many religious associations. In this play it probably chiefly represents, as Mary implies, the power of God, which, of course, is the force behind the Nativity, although the number is sometimes more specifically associated with the Nativity. Mary's words "Tell furth of this case" (l. 491) might have linked, in the playwright's mind, the four Evangelists with the Trinity; or he might have had in mind the idea that the Nativity took place for us "for seven profits"—so the *Golden Legend*[15] counts the benefits listed in *Isaias* 61.1-7 as quoted by St. Luke 4.18-19. In any case, by allowing himself six sevenths of the play he is amply able to explore the shepherds who so fascinated him.

The play begins with Gib, the oldest of the three shepherds, walking into the Place, supposed to be a meadow or pasture-land (l. 316), or, rather, dragging himself along with the help of his crook, since he is so mournful. He wears a gown (either tattered and patched or possibly rich, ll. 89-90) and a hood (l. 136), and carries a wallet (l. 224) for his provisions over his shoulder as well as a pair of dice in a box (*OED* cast I 1e) in one hand. Like funny men throughout the ages he stays himself while delivering his serio-comic monologue to the audience; he amuses them with both what he says and how he says it, and distributes his favors equally by speaking directly to now this part of the audience and now that. He nods knowingly to them (l. 19) and puts sudden grandeur and sonority into his voice when he speaks of the rich "Iak Cope" (l. 17, "Jack Plenty") and extreme thinness when he speaks in the voice (l. 35) of Plenty's antithesis, "Purs Penneles" (l. 33, "Purse Pennyless"). The timing of the delivery is important and, helped by the many end-stopped rhyming lines, provides natural places for laughter. The playwright finds a beginning for his play in Gib's mournfulness so that he can proceed to reveal by gradual stages the joyful answer to it. What Gib says is, like the entire play, a mosaic of biblical, philosophical, literary, proverbial, and contemporary social themes expressed in widely allusive language. That God chose to show himself first to poor, humble laboring men is an observation of the Fathers, and in the later Middle Ages writers also frequently noted, in the words of the *Speculum Sacerdotale*, that the "pes and blissid birthe ne was noght shewid vn-to hye kynges, ne yit to the proude princes of the world, but to the pore hyrdes of the peple."[16] Gib is mournful for several reasons. He is a West Riding farmer not so much poor as suddenly impoverished, and he is unredeemed, both personally and as an Israelite. The theme of the lamentation of the Israelites, "The voice of the howling of the shepherds" (*Zach.* 11.3, *vox ululatus pastorum*), and the neighboring nations for their sins and sufferings runs throughout the Old Testament. Just before his prophecy of the birth of Christ, which is quoted in the play (*Isa.* 7.14 and ll. 396-97), Isaias says that the Israelites shall not be saved until their "cities be wasted without inhabitant . . . and the land shall be left desolate" (6.11). In direct contrast to the York play, the First Shepherds' play begins with what the playwright takes to be a fifteenth-century version of the "howling"—the complaint, Gib's first line, is an energetic and arresting expression of the common *contemptus mundi* theme, "Lord, what thay ar weyll that hens ar past!" He promptly proceeds, in richly proverbial language (Whiting N179), to a second common theme, the unpredictable vicissitudes of life[17] which always stand in contrast to the common idea of the invariability of God. His second stanza centers on the image of the proud, rich man, Jack Plenty, suddenly cast down, which recalls numerous biblical passages about the deposition of the mighty, including the enemies of Israel—e.g., the messianic "I will make the pride of the infidels to cease, and will bring down the arrogancy of the mighty" (*Isa.* 13.11), the more colorful (and perhaps more relevant, given the direction John Horne's monologue will take) "they that were brought up in scarlet have embraced the dung" (*Lam.* 4.5), Balaam's messianic prophecies, which are recited in the Anglo-Norman play of *Adam* (ll. 820-21), and the *Magnificat.* Jack Plenty is also at least partly proverbial and literary (*OED* Jack 1 and 35), analogous to "Jack Juggler" or "Jack Reckless."[18] In his third stanza Gib utters a common[19] but non-Boethian and not very Christian consolation—he is so low that he cannot sink lower—but is hardly consoled by it since he says that his cares are so heavy that whenever he sleeps he weeps. He then explains the immediate cause of his troubles: he has lost all his sheep to the rot, a common ovine liver disease, and is destitute; as a preliminary sign of the coming of Christ, "the flocks of sheep are perished" (*Joel* 1.18). "Now beg I and borow," says Gib (l. 27), in a literary collocation of the kind favored by the playwright, since it is simple, alliterative, and sounds proverbial.[20] Further, as he goes on in an extremity of mournfulness to explain in the next stanza, his rents or taxes are coming due and he cannot of course pay them. He is now like Purse Pennyless, perhaps also a literary or proverbial figure or a literary phrase turned into one for the nonce,[21] and his purse is weak but his heart heavy, a proverb he half utters (Whiting P444) and also a Chaucerian pun ("The Complaint of Chaucer to his Purse," ll. 3-4—heaviness of purse will banish heaviness of heart). He wrings his hands, like Adam and Eve at the end of the York play of the Fall of Man, because there is "no helpyng" (ll. 28, 36), and he has no alternative but to leave the district, a reflection of both the current problem of depopulation and abandonment of farms by tenant farmers[22] and of the desolation of the land of the Hebrews and the scattering of the inhabitants (*Isa.* 6.11, 24.1). Purse Pennyless' stage-whisper, "Wo is me this dystres!" (l. 35), recalls *Isaias* 8.22, "they cannot fly away from their distress," *angustia.* There is one vague chance, which Gib mentions but takes no notice of; his conditional "Bot if good will spryng"

(1. 29) is suggestive of Isaias' reference to Christ's kingdom: "It shall bud forth and blossom," *germinans germinabit* (35.2). Gib is now as unhappy as the Israelites and is one of the miserable, needy, and groaning poor for whom Christ comes.[23]

In the fifth and final stanza of his monologue, Gib brightens up considerably, but for foolish reasons and hardly as a fervent believer. He depends on his mistaking intelligence for chance and chance for grace, a confusion more remarkably confounded than Hudde's belief in chance. Gib will use his wit to discover how to throw a seven at dice, and if he has bad luck (that is, even if his sheep are all dead, or, alternatively, if he fails to throw a seven) then may God send grace from heaven (ll. 38-41). One way or another he will buy sheep at the fair. A seven, especially in the form of a six and a one, might well turn all England into a paradise,[24] but the Wakefield Master disapproved of dicing; he has given the three torturers a stanza each at the conclusion of the play of the Dice (a play once, in some form, a York play[25]) in which they forswear the dice and list the evils that come from dicing. Fortune will cast the rich man (like Jack Plenty) into the proverbial ditch (Play of the Dice, l. 385), to join the shepherds in the First Shepherds' play and cause only loss and then crime. Tutivillus also welcomes "hasardars and dysars" (Towneley Last Judgment, l. 364). In any case, dicing, frequently denounced by preachers, was contrary to the law in Wakefield by 1450.[26] Psalm 30, one of the sources of the play of the Dice, is relevant to Gib's muddled head; "My lots are in thy hands" (30.16) alludes, according to St. Augustine, quoted in the *Glossa Ordinaria*, not to chance but to the just and hidden will of God. It is not Lady Fortune but God's grace, as yet an afterthought and last resort in Gib's head, which will eventually bring salvation. As he sets off across the Place to go to the fair, he is rather abstracted and not looking where he is going.

The Second Shepherd, John Horne, tall (Second Shepherds' play, l. 565) and also old, enters the Place and stands at the spot whither Gib is slowly walking so that throughout his monologue it seems clear to the audience, but not to John or Gib, that the latter is bound sooner or later to bump into the former. John is more satirical than Gib. He begins by accosting the audience with a

Chapter III

Benedicite, a common form of greeting not always meant seriously, at the opening of the sixth stanza, whose bob, "Cryst sane vs" (l. 50, "protect"), nevertheless contains the first reference to Christ in the play. It is far too soon for any light to dawn, however, and the objects of his rather jovial satire are the boasting, violent, relentless, and overdressed servants of the steward of the Lord of the Manor who are not satisfied even with taking your plough and wagon, and also purveyors for good lords who arbitrarily seize provisions—perhaps one such retainer in particular who, sailing around the district with long unkempt hair (fashionable in the mid-fifteenth century[27]) and a loud voice, wears his lord's badge and outdoes his master in arrogance. John's language, like Gib's, consists of both literary ("bosters and bragers," l. 55, "galy in gere/ As he glydes," ll. 67-68) and perhaps invented ("wryers and wragers," l. 58, "wranglers and quarrelers"—also among the sinners in the play of the Last Judgment, l. 143) alliterative phrases, and he concludes with a prayer for the oppressors of the poor farmers—but not in a good spirit since, in a proverbial phrase, "good mendyng/ With a short endyng" (ll. 78-79, Whiting M500), he appears to mean he wishes they were dead. At the same time, he also evokes the words and spirit of Isaias; for their sins the country is being devoured by strangers before their very faces (1.7), and the wicked "grind the faces of the poor" (3.15, *quare . . . facies pauperum commolitis?*—"if hap will grynde," says Gib). John's conclusion is the same as the prophet's: "Woe to them that make wicked laws: and . . . oppress the poor in judgment, and do violence to the cause of the humble of my people" (*Isa.* 10.1-2). It is also the same as that expressed by the preachers, who condemned the bragging and boasting of those proud of their office, lordship, and "maintenance."[28]

Gib approaches very close and is cheerfully awakened from his daydream with "How, Gyb, goode morne! Wheder goys thou?" (l. 82), and then is rebuked with some curiosity, "Thou goys ouer the corne! Gyb, I say, how!" (l. 83, "Thou walkest . . . Oh!"). The reason for their quarrel, which is based on one of the many disputes over the use of common land—for tillage or pasturage, arising out of the tension between the profitability of raising sheep and the need to farm self-sufficiently or at subsistence level—is thus introduced, although they first commiserate with each other in a series of proverbial sayings mixed with biblical phrases turned into comfortless words: "Poor men ar in the dyke" (l. 93, Whiting D247), and "helpars/ Is none here" (ll. 94-95, also l. 36, and Whiting H338, and *Ps.* 71.12, "He shall deliver the poor from the mighty: and the needy that had no helper," *adiutor*—a particularly messianic Psalm).

Uncertainty now certainty in his head, Gib says that he is going to buy sheep. "Here shall thou none kepe" (l. 103), replies John. I'll pasture them wherever I like, responds Gib, indignantly urging on the leader of his flock of one hundred sheep, his pride and anger having turned what has not yet been purchased, with an empty purse, into a present reality—a hundred sheep form a very large but not impossibly enormous flock for a peasant. John waves the leading sheep back (l. 113), Gib on (ll. 114-15), John back (ll. 116-17), perhaps now flapping his gown and gesturing with his crook; Gib, conceding temporary defeat, yet tells the sheep to keep trying, "Whop!" (l. 119, "turn"), and John tells them to stop. Perhaps these two performers stick their tongues out at each other, "feigning foolish countenances," as they prance back and forth and sideways. Gib then calls John a rogue, tells him to leave, and threatens to strike him over the head, raising his crook to do so, "lo." "I say gyf the shepe space" (l. 123), he concludes with determination, when John, noticing that Slowpace is approaching from the corn mill, calls a truce.

The first part of one of the tales of the *Mad Men of Gotham* is thus vigorously acted out. The basic situation, the "hundred" sheep, some of the jargon ("tyr," ll. 113-14), the fact that it is the antagonist's objection (l. 103) that turns the protagonist's imaginary sheep into real ones, and (if it is in the play) the spirited vulgarity all come from the tale; but the bridge where the confrontation takes place in the tale has become common land and the quarrel thus better motivated. The tale has been made to reflect real agricultural problems; it also in several ways has become an image of the unredeemed. Gib and John "rush one upon another, . . . every man against his neighbour" (*Isa.* 3.5). John answers "a fool according to his folly" (*Prov.* 26.4), and particularly in their absence of wisdom they are idolators worshipping "worthless beasts" (*Wisdom* 11.16, *bestias supervacuas*), a phrase perhaps thought of literally by the playwright, who may also have had similar passages from *Wisdom* in mind (12.23-27; 15.4, 15). The need for true wisdom is a common Old Testament theme. Jesus refers to the stubbornness of the Israelites who refuse to "*see with their eyes, and hear with their ears*" (*Matt.* 13.15; cf. *Isa.* 9.10); at the same time, Gib and John's foolish looking at invisible, because non-existent, physical things, especially the "tup" (l. 117, "male sheep," probably the bell-wether, l. 112), is a ridiculous shadow of divine mysteries to come, "For the things that are seen are temporal, but the things that are not seen are eternal" (*2 Cor.* 4.18), and also perhaps an ignorant version of the doctrine of the Real Presence, much explored in the late Middle Ages (although not promulgated formally until 1551) and disputed by the Lollards, whom the Wakefield Master thought of as devils (Last Judgment, l. 213).

Slowpace, younger than Gib or John and their servant, enters the Place, presumably from a third direction (on the analogy of the three Magi, as in the Towneley play of the Offering of the Magi, ll. 85-158); he is leading a mare with a sack of meal on its back or perhaps riding on the sack.[29] In response to his very cheerful greeting and query (ll. 127-28), Gib, now so thoroughly caught up in his indignation that his fantasy continues to develop or change, replies that he was driving his sheep before him on his way to buy provisions when John refused to let him pass; his wheel, born of stupidity, is magnificent:

> I was bowne to by store   *bound buy*
> Drofe my shepe me before;
> He says not oone hore   *one hair*
> Shall pas by this way;
>
>   (ll. 130-33)

and the climax of his outrage, "not one hair," a perfect misappropriation of a common expression ("not worth a hair," Whiting H25-31 and *OED* hair sb 5) to sheep, in whose woolly hair, the finer the better, resided their chief value. It being plain that there are no sheep, John immediately repudiates the farce. Slowpace ridicules them with a series of proverbs, half-told tales, and semi-biblical references, turning one of his stanzas into a comic monologue, which he begins with a pun, "It is wonder to wyt where wytt shuld be fownde" (l. 143). They are like Moll, he says, adapting her story to fit the occasion. In the tale, daydreaming of the wealth which will accrue from her one possession, her pitcher of milk, she breaks it;[30] in Slowpace's unique version, she also owns one "shepe," and daydreaming of a whole flock, she drops her pitcher of milk, which breaks into fragments (l. 160). "'Ho, God!' she sayde," says Slowpace, also a performer, putting on a voice. "The heart of a fool is like broken vessel, and no wisdom at all shall it hold" (*Ecclus*. 21.17). The milk could easily have been understood to be sheep's milk, which was regularly used for human consumption; Jesus feeds us with the milk of his wisdom purchased without money (*Isa*. 55.1), and like babies we grow to salvation on milk (*1 Pet*. 2.2)—provided we do not spill it—but Gib and John, like Moll (a name with some sluttish connotations), "ar bare of wysdom to knowe" (l. 161).

For his next demonstration of their folly, Slowpace resumes the action of the tale of the *Mad Men of Gotham*. He tells one, probably Gib, politely, to hold his mare (l. 164) and the other, John, familiarly, to throw the sack "On my bak,/ Whylst I, with my hand,/ Lawse the sek-band" (ll. 165-67); he then empties out the sack over his shoulder. The tale reports that

> another man of Gotam dyd come from the market wyth a sacke of meale vppon an horse. And seyng and hearing his neyghboures at stryfe, for sheepe, and none betwixt them said a fooles will you neuer learne wyt. Helpe me saide hee that had the meale, and laye my sacke vppon my shulder, they dyd so. And he went to the one side of the bridge, and vnlosed the mouth of the sacke, and did shake oute all hys meale into the ryuer, now neyghbour sayde this man, howe much meale is theare in my sacke nowe, marye theare is none at all sayde they. Now by my faythe sayd he euen as muche witte is in youre twoo headdes, to stryue for that thyng which ye have not.[31]

"Is not all shakyn owte, and no meyll is therin?" asks Slowpace, demonstrating that "So is youre wyttys thyn" (ll. 170-71). He improves on the simple moral of the tale (the sack is as empty as their heads) by varying a proverb to produce "So gose youre wyttys owte, evyn as it com in" (l. 173, Whiting W413) and concludes with the impossible injunction: "Geder vp/ And seke it agane!" (ll. 174-75, "Gather it up and put it back in the sack"). John correctly concludes that Slowpace has plainly told them "Wysdom to sup" (l. 178) but is not intelligent enough to see Slowpace's own folly—an observation left to "Iak Garcio" (l. 179, "Jack Servingman"),[32] their boy, who has been watching their livestock and who now appears in the Place for the purpose of declaring that all three of them have behaved like the "foles of Gotham" (l. 180). He thus answers in the only way possible the conundrum posed at the end of the tale: "Which was the wisest of al these three persons? Iudge you." He also announces that their livestock are now "gryssed to the kne" (l. 188, "sunk in grass to their knees") or ruminating; real place and season, of course, overlay Palestine and winter, and so his comment is primarily an indication of the time of day (mid-day) and only secondarily, if at all, a hint at miraculous fecundity. In the same way, his "youre bestes ye ken" (l. 190) is a rather surly comment on their natural or expected abilities as shepherds and farmers and not a contradiction of their folly, which is mainly spiritual. Jack, nipping off as quickly as he arrives, perhaps takes with him the mare, which would otherwise be in the way for the rest of the play.

The children of Israel in darkness (ll. 29-30), the unnamed First Shepherd who "maddes all out of myght" (l. 38, "behaves madly"), and Hudde's notion that "happe" (l. 90, "luck") has led the shepherds to salvation—perhaps these undeveloped snippets of the York Shepherds' play triggered the Wakefield Master's imagination. If so, what has he not wrought of Hudde's "feest" (l. 44, "revelry," or "bountiful food") and the "frely foode" (l. 78)! This well-established alliterating phrase, which means "noble child" in the York play (and in the Second Shepherds' play, l. 720, as well as the Towneley play of John the Baptist, ll. 39, 164), can equally well mean "profuse food" (*MED* fode n[1] and n[2], freli adj. 1a and 2a). The wasting of the flour over Slowpace's shoulder at the

end of the Mad Men of Gotham episode—itself also possibly suggestive of the common metaphor for Christ, as in the York
Joseph's "Hayle blessid floure" (Nativity, 1. 112, "flour" and
"flower" are the same word)—suggests that Gib, John, and Slowpace are not yet ready for the "true bread . . . which cometh down
from heaven, and giveth life to the world" (*John* 6.32-33). They
are not yet close to Bethlehem, "the house of bread,"[33] or to
Christ, "true bread from heaven" which "giveth life to the world"
(*John* 6.31-38), or to the Eucharistic host.

They are, however, ready to eat, drink, and rest. At mid-day
Slowpace is entitled by long custom, and by law by 1495, to eat
and rest.[34] He churlishly demands his rights, complains of his
usual spare rations at their "mangere" (1. 201), and says "sett vs a
borde" (1. 196). John is not ready, but, with an insult, Gib decides
it is better not to challenge Slowpace and agrees, saying "go we
to mete" (1. 202). Slowpace politely but sarcastically, or possibly
seriously, replies, "Now in fayth, if I durst, ye ar euen my broder"
(1. 207, "my brother in comradeship" or "my equal in refrac-
toriness"). John is now ready to "cryb" (1. 208), also for the sake
of peace and quiet, and says, "let vs go foder/ Oure mompyns," or
"teeth," verbs more appropriately (like the noun "mangere") used
of animals than of men.

At their table, John produces some boar's meat from his bag.
Then each in turn produces a large quantity of whole cooked foods,
many requiring plates or bowls, from their bags. The twenty-one
dishes (not counting the mustard) are sometimes assumed to be
imaginary, on the analogy of the sheep, but are more likely to be
property food (perhaps made, like masks, of cloth stiffened with
plaster of paris and painted) accompanied by small pieces of real
food, which can be eaten.[35] The bags seem to be inexhaustible
and bottomless, and are either unusually large cloth bags in which
the shepherds fish around for their next surprise or (more likely)
modestly sized leather satchels. A "juggling"—that is, a conjuring
trick—is suggested by the speed with which the foods sitting on
their plates are produced, and is accomplishable if the wallets
have false bottoms and the table a false top, perhaps also with the
assistance of the sleeves of the shepherds' gowns, like the sleeve
worn by Chaucer's Canon.[36] Gib's sarcastic comment, addressed

Chapter III

to Slowpace or John, "Cowth ye by youre gramery reche vs a drinke" (l. 242), which results in the immediate production of the first bottle, suggests that the profusion is the result of either great learning, of which they are bare, or of false learning, the occult sciences reduced to minstrelish magic (*OED* gramarye 2). The performers are not only "jugglers," but like clowns and fools throughout history the shepherds are gluttons (l. 222), and the production of the dishes from bags surely too small to contain them all is a source of wonder and delight. The shepherds eat with a will, using their fingers (l. 231). All the dishes are a recognizable part of the cuisine of the fifteenth century and are either simple and plebeian (blood pudding) or elaborate and aristocratic (calf-liver infused with apple-juice), and kosher (glazed chicken) or forbidden (the hare).[37] The destitute Gib has plebeian dishes and takes advantage of the death of his sheep to eat the meat of one of them, putting a reference to it between the two halves of a proverb to form a joyful wheel (Whiting M813, "Mutton is good meat for a glutton"):

> Both befe, and moton
> Of an ewe that was roton   *rotten, dead of the rot*
> (God mete for a gloton).
>
>   (ll. 220-22)

It is Slowpace who has most of the gourmet food; he is learned in it, notes Gib sarcastically (ll. 240-42).

It is John who has the drink; he produces "good ayll of Hely" (l. 244). Gib (the leader) takes a drink from the cup they share; Slowpace demands his turn, which he gets, but John, impatient, prematurely snatches the cup from him, addresses the contents, and, to the consternation of the others, empties it. He produces a second bottle, however, and they are ready to begin again. Before they do so, Slowpace says they must kiss; he is either speaking half a proverb (the second half being acted out, Whiting C629, "To kiss the cup") or expressing brotherly and Christian sentiments, not now much in evidence, or both. They sing, and then drink once more, but Slowpace is confronted with an empty cup; frustrated again, he calls Gib and John "knafys" (l. 277), and

The York Shepherds' Play and the First Shepherds' Play

Gib, beginning a new stanza, replies, with some self-satisfied scorn, that they are indeed all "knaues" (l. 273), presumably meaning "humble men," an example of concatenation with a twist in the meaning of the word.

The feast is appropriate to the Christmas season but also here recalls the bounty promised to God's people and the great benefits he bestows on them by supernatural power despite their ingratitude, to which there are many references in the Old Testament: "I will give thee hidden treasures, and the concealed riches of secret places" (*Isa.* 45.3); "they spoke ill of God: they said: Can God furnish a table [*mensam*] in the wilderness? . . . he rained down manna upon them to eat . . . he sent them provisions in abundance . . . he rained upon them flesh . . . they did eat, and were filled exceeding" (*Ps.* 77.19, 24-25, 27, 29); "thou gavest them their desire of delicious food, of a new taste, preparing for them quails for their meat" (*Wisdom* 16.2). On the other hand, such bounty can be a prelude to God's vengeance (*Ps.* 77.30-31), which the shepherds are spared by the imminence of God's grace. They do not yet know that it is the riches of God's grace which have "superabounded in us" (*Eph.* 1.8) and whose mysteries are unfathomable, or that the old rites of eating and drinking at a festival, *in parte diei festi*, are but "a shadow of things to come, but the substance is of Christ" (*Col.* 2.16-17, *corpus autem Christi*), and that it is by the "blood of Christ," not by the "blood of goats or of calves," that salvation is obtained (*Heb.* 9.12-14), and "with grace, not with meats" that the heart is made steadfast (*Heb.* 13.9).

The feast is thus a gluttonous (preachers frequently inveighed against the sin of gluttony) and distorted shadow of the body of Christ and of grace abounding. St. Paul refers to the laws of the Israelites concerning food, and the shepherds' merry and rather blatant lack of concern for them is probably a sign that they are moving closer to salvation though they have not yet arrived since they take the meaning of the Incarnation altogether too literally. In the *Meditations on the Life of Christ*, in the section describing the Nativity, Jesus is said to have "even left Himself as food" for sinners, for us.[38] Ludolphus' chain of more complex thought is also reflected in the properties and diction of the play. He emphasizes that the Word was made flesh (*John* 1.14, *caro*, both modern English "human flesh" and "meat"), and with the exception of the mustard and possibly the pie and the tart the shepherds' food is all meat. By referring *John* 1.14 to *Isaias* 40.6, "All flesh is grass," *omnis caro faenum*, or "hay," and by identifying us sinners with beasts (*Ps.* 72.23) he can declare that the Christ Child was placed in the manger as food for the ox and the ass, who are all of us, both Jews (the ox) and gentiles (the ass).[39] It is perhaps for this reason that in the Nativity in the Bolton Hours (fig. 13) the ox is licking him with his tongue; it is certainly (I think) the reason—united with an age-old habit of speaking in jocular metaphors derived from one's work and also the common habit of speaking, with appreciation, slightingly of food ("grub")—why the shepherds speak of "crib," "manger," and "fodder" as they prepare to eat, and why John calls Gib one of the "old store" (l. 456, "old livestock").

There are equally deliberate hints of the Eucharistic form taken by this "food," even though bread is missing from the feast. The Yorkshireman Aelred of Rievaulx (d. 1167) preached that "Bethlehem, the house of bread, is the holy church in which the body of Christ is administered, that is, the true bread. The manger in Bethlehem is the altar in the church. There the animals of Christ are fed . . . in this manger in the species of bread and wine is the true body and blood of Christ."[40] The shepherds' "board," or table, is a common synonym for "altar" (*MED* bord n 3f and 4a). The food, including blood pudding and sheeps' meat, is consumed before the drink. The drink is "boyte of oure bayll" (l. 247, "cure of our distress"), an alliterative phrase commonly applied to Christ, as in the Wakefield Master's play of Noah (l. 311) and elsewhere in the Towneley plays. It is also from Hely, very likely the place of that name, but also probably Elias, commonly considered to be a type of Christ.[41]

The feast is amusing and merry but quarrelsome, especially after the first bottle, and contains sufficient hints to indicate that it is not the true feast of a Christian, neither in substance nor in decorum. In their darkness and folly, the shepherds have mistaken the meaning of "food." In the first four-sevenths of the play, vainly skirting the meaning of the Incarnation, they have gone from one extreme to the other, first mistaking the fantastic for the invisible and now the invisible for the edible. They are now blithe and satiated, and between their first and second bottles they sing, led by Gib, who starts them off on what is probably a jolly Three-Men's Song, if he sings tenor. These convivial songs were very popular in the fifteenth and sixteenth centuries and are mentioned in the *Castle of Perseverance*.[42]

The first four-sevenths of the play are now approaching their conclusion, but do not reach it without some sign of spiritual progress on the part of the shepherds, at least Slowpace. Gib's smart but true riposte, "Nay, we knaues all" (l. 278, "are all humble men"), leads John to say they will not brawl any more. Slowpace does even better, since in response to Gib's leader-like statement that they should decide who will clean up the remains of their feast and put them in the "panyere" (l. 281, "large basket") he says: "Syrs, herys!/ For oure saules lett vs do/ Poor men gyf it to" (ll. 282-84), only to have his charitable thought, a hint of the early Church—although they have not unqualifiedly taken "their meat with gladness and simplicity of heart" (*Acts* 2.45-46)—somewhat undercut by Gib, who agrees with him but only with the surly, "Geder up, lo, lo/ Ye hungré begers, frerys!" (ll. 285-86). "Lo, lo" is a call for attention, and he possibly throws a few of the larger pieces to members of the audience (the more valuable property pieces to a stage-hand standing by or perhaps Jack). (His reference to the friars does not, given the playwright's sense of humor, seem to rule out the possibility that he was one himself.) A pannier, more capacious than their three wallets combined, might well, as shown in figure 16, be used for the distribution of food to the hungry.

The shepherds have spent the afternoon in heedless merriment, and Gib says that it is growing dark and time to rest. It is again Slowpace who reveals more Christianity in him, making the sign of the cross and reciting a short (and intelligible) Latin prayer, concluding, appropriately enough, given his name, "God be oure spede!" (l. 295, "help," also "speed"). He has come so far that while the shepherds sleep it is possible for the angel to appear, even though the shepherds are decidedly not vigilant, not "keep-

Chapter III

ing the night watches over their flock" (*Luke* 2.8). Angels wearing what seem clearly to be costumes are very common in English art. Their human feet, hands, necks, and faces stick out from what are plainly garments, including tights, covered with feathers (fig. 17); a row of eight of them crowns the fifteenth-century east window of the south chapel in St. Oswald's, Methley, a parish next to the parish of Wakefield. Others wear a plain alb and amice, sometimes with a cross-diadem, but the players would have sought to costume their shining angel splendidly to contrast with the nondescript shepherds' costumes, and John's comment, that the angel spoke like a man but shone like an angel (ll. 315-17), seems decisive. In the play, one angel, representing the heavenly host, sings the *Gloria* (*Luke* 2.13-14), and the same angel, contrary to *Luke* (presumably for reasons of economy), speaks to the shepherds. As at York, he probably came from the stable, but he does not seem to have "stood by" (*Luke* 2.9) the shepherds, since Gib compares him to a cloud and Slowpace was looking upward when he saw him. The angel perhaps mounts a small but tall Scaffold to sing his song, which represents a small corner of the harmony which constantly prevails in heaven and which is, as the shepherds comment, high-pitched, melodious, and rhythmically complex,[43] in contrast to their own earth-bound effort.

In the mostly elevated diction of the frons of his one stanza the angel speaks of God's might and his present determination to save the shepherds; he stresses the simple but crucial bob to reinforce this message, and continues in the entirely plain and simple wheel to explain ("this shall be a sign unto you," *Luke* 2.12) how the imperial plan has been put into operation. The promise is from *Galatians* 4.28—"Now we, brethren, . . . are the children of promise"— or from similar passages in the Epistles, God's Old Testament promises now taking on a spiritual non-worldly meaning, indicated by the lowliness of their execution. The prosody and diction produce an authoritative and lovely elaboration of *Luke* 2.10-12:

> Herkyn, hyrdes! Awake! Gyf louyng ye shall; *give praise*
> He is borne for youre sake, lorde perpetuall.
> He is comen to take and rawnson you all;
> Youre sorowe to slake, kyng emperiall,

The York Shepherds' Play and the First Shepherds' Play

He behestys.	*promises*
That chyld is borne	
At Bethelem this morne;	
Ye shall fynde hym beforne	*ahead of you*
Betwix two bestys.	

(ll. 296-304)

Gib responds with amazement and fear; although he is perhaps too interested to fear "with a great fear" (*Luke* 2.9), and although his stanza has touches of the comic monologue about it, he nevertheless calls on God five times. John, his heart shaken by the light gleaming from the angel, disagrees with Gib's assumption that what they saw was a cloud and states confidently that their heavenly visitor was an angel speaking like a man, that they should seek the baby of whom he spoke and who is signified by "yond starne/ That standys yonder owte" (ll. 321-22), which is probably a painted star attached to the top of the Scaffold representing the stable (fig. 11), and to which he presumably points. Slowpace adds that he would have thought the brightness thunderous lightning, unless he was dreaming the angel said they should go to Bethlehem. (Perhaps the "stone" he was leaning against, l. 325, was the rejected stone which became the cornerstone, Christ—*Ps.* 117.22, *Isa.* 28.16, *Mark* 12.10.) They have, in contrast to their shared and broken stanzas preceding the angel's song, now spoken one whole stanza each. Shocked into orderliness and sobriety, they behave (unknown to them) as if the Passion, the "rawnson" ("ransom"), is as imminent as it is now inevitable by acting out an episode (ll. 332-94) from St. John's Gospel: before the Passion, Jesus said "'Father, glorify thy name!' A voice therefore came from heaven: 'I have both glorified it, and will glorify it again.' The multitude that stood and heard, said that it thundered [*tonitruum factum esse*]. Others said: 'An angel spoke to him.' Jesus answered, and said, 'This voice came not because of me, but for your sakes'" (*John* 12.28-30).

The shepherds, now in, or almost in, the New Testament, "walk," while for a little time the light is among them and they "have the light" (*John* 12.35, *ambulate*). Some did not believe, continues St. John (12.37), and so the shepherds tackle this incredulity of the Jews by presenting their own version of that part of the Augustinian *Sermo contra Judaeos, Paganos, et Arianos* which is concerned with providing the Jews with evidence for Christ. They "walk" to and fro while they talk, quickly turning to face each other at points of disagreement, or when a quick come-back is required, or when one is compelled scornfully to show knowledge to be superior to that of the others. The thirteen witnesses named by them, beginning with Isaias and concluding with Virgil, are all from the Augustinian sermon, except that the order is very different and that John, possibly still under the influence of the "ayll of Hely" of which he drank most, substitutes "Ely" (l. 377, "Elias") for Simeon. The shepherds are now speaking in their allegorical role of pastors or teachers, but imperfectly, since they lack the necessary solemnity and remain ill-mannered churls. They conclude when John decisively rejects as friarly and too subtle Virgil's Messianic Eclogue, recited by Gib (this time it is he who is possessed of "gramere") who responds by calling John and Slowpace fools, by claiming that he knows best, and by translating the two Latin lines and summarizing the Eclogue (Christianized by, among others, St. Augustine) in a way which recalls some of the foolish mistakes of the earlier part of the play so that it resembles a fool's paradise (Whiting F411) mixed with more Christian hopes:[44]

> And yit more to neuen, that Saturne shall bend
> Vnto us
> With peasse and plenté,
> With ryches and menee,   *servants*
> Good luf and charyté
> Blendyd amanges vs.
>   (ll. 398-403)

It is Slowpace, as might by now be expected, who has the best and simplest summary: "And I hold it trew, for ther shuld be,/ When that kyng commys new, peasse by land and se" (ll. 404-05), although this is still not exactly the same as "on earth peace to men of good will" (*Luke* 2.14). Simplicity is now becoming a virtue. Perfect love is casting out fear. A distinct but encumbered advance has been made.

John now says that he wishes they had understood the angel's

The York Shepherds' Play and the First Shepherds' Play

song. Slowpace wishes that they could sing it and claims, with youthful confidence, that he knows all the notes. Gib promptly challenges him to sing as high up the scale as the angel, and amidst this proverbial teasing and skepticism Slowpace promptly invents a cold in the nose which makes a solo performance impossible. He then leads the way into their second song, presumably another Three-Men's Song, in this instance religious but no match in loveliness or skill for the angel's. When their song is over, Gib, with what sounds like an announcement to the audience, says, "Now an ende haue we doyn of oure song this tyde" (l. 431), and John congratulates Slowpace: "Fayr fall thi growne!" (l. 432, "snout"), or "Good luck to you!"—a well-chosen phrase for one who alleges he has a cold in the nose. The preacher has not yet governed the comedian nor the Christian the recalcitrant sinner.

It is now pitch dark and therefore time for the shepherds, and for everyone, to make a decisive move. "I am come a light into the world; that whoever believeth in me, may not remain in the darkness" (*John* 12.46). It is Slowpace, now happily capable of belying his name, who suggests that they "ron" (l. 433, "run") to Bethlehem ("And they came with haste," *Luke* 2.16), a speed suggestive of spiritual ardor. They talk while they are walking and running, looking forward to seeing (*Luke* 2.15) "this yong bab" (l. 440) which no prophets or saints (ll. 445-46) have yet been able to see, a sight withheld from the Israelites, as Isaias, quoted by St. John (12.37-41), says since "Yit closyd ar thare eene" (l. 448) by the Lord (*Isa.* 6.9-10). Old Gib, no doubt winded, has to call a halt just before they reach the stable, but not before he sees the star, which, he says, seems to be rushing towards them. John urges them on to complete the final stretch, and declares, "Here he is!" (l. 453, another stressed bob). John sees him before they enter the stable, which is, as usual, represented as falling down and defenseless. John, probably out of deference to his elders, restrains his own eagerness, and asks who should "go in" first (l. 454). Gib, the oldest, is very casual: "I ne rek, by my hore" (l. 455, "It makes no difference to me, by my hair"); he is either shy or does not share Slowpace's eagerness, or both. He must be jostled in first by John, perhaps with a shove from behind by Slowpace, their servant.

Chapter III

Gib, John, and Slowpace then in turn worship the Christ Child, who is lying in the manger between the two animals, and present him with a gift; each speaks one whole stanza. Gib separates his elevated from his simple diction, confining the former to the frons. John and Slowpace are warmer, immediately mingling the two kinds of phrases and recognizing him as both God and tiny baby in the first lines of their speeches. Gib presents him with a "lytyll spruce cofer" (l. 466, "small box made of pine wood"), perhaps his dice-box, now that he no longer needs it. John gives him a ball (l. 471) to play with. Slowpace is the most enthusiastic; his buoyancy and excitement are very touching and his lack of tact forgivable in a youth:

> Hayll, maker of man! Hayll, swetyng!
> Hayll, so as I can! Hayll, praty mytyng!　　　*as best I know how*
> I cowche to the then, for fayn nere gretyng.
> Hayll, Lord! Here I ordan, now at oure metyng,　　　*give*
> This botell—
> It is an old byworde,
> "It is good bowrde
> For to drynke of a gowrde"—
> It holdys a mett potell.
>
> 　　　　　　　(ll. 476-84)

Unlike Gib and John, he cannot refrain from referring to himself in the frons; the most limber, he bows down for a "nearer" greeting, having a limited stock of epithets, and so that he can see God even more closely "in the face" (like Colle). His present, a bottle capable of holding two quarts, is ridiculously large for a baby, but perhaps Slowpace thinks of it as magnificent. His proverb (Whiting B475), however out of place, surely shows that he only wishes to share his new-found joy. The delight and informality of all three humble men reflect the pleasure the sight of a baby brings to all but the sourest. Their gifts are not only the gifts of the poor and awkward, more or less suitable for a baby, like the gifts of the York shepherds, but also makeshift and clumsy suggestions of the true nature of the birthday Child. The suggestions are therefore unclear and provocative. The ball might be a humble version of the orb of Kingship, the box ("cofer" or coffin) a sign of Christ's sacrifice, and the bottle an indication of the gift of wisdom, which makes one drunk with holy love.[45] The shepherds have, however, recognized their Savior with clarity, and so have almost reached the end of their journey.

They, on behalf of the audience, have now only to recognize him in the Eucharist, which their gifts have also been held to symbolize—the box for the Host, the bottle for the wine, and the ball for the Ruler of the World present in them.[46] (The gifts of the York Shepherds—and therefore of the Shrewsbury shepherds—might also be held by some to be symbolic and thus, like the gifts of the Towneley Shepherds, cleverly to combine homeliness and spiritual significance, gifts for a real baby and tributes to, in this case also, the Word Incarnate.) The little ball might also recall the bell rung at the Elevation of the Host. The two hazelnuts recall the analogy used by Ludolphus and others: inside the shell of the flesh is the sweetness of divinity, and inside the shell of literalism lies the word of the Bible—two nuts, one for the Old and one for the New Testament. Although Colle does not, apparently, give peas, only measuring the capacity of his gift of a spoon by them, peas are a fine gift for a sheep in winter, since on a well-managed farm peas were a part of the sheep's winter diet. These gifts are certainly sufficiently provoking, as are some of the gifts seen in art, to have set the Wakefield Master thinking. In the Adoration in Church of St. Peter and St. Paul, East Harling, one of the shepherds is holding a lamb, ready to present it to the Christ Child.[47] The solemn parts of the shepherds' stanzas in the First Shepherds' play are related to Levation Prayers, or short English prayers which literate worshippers at the Mass were advised to recite softly to themselves during the Elevation of the Host.[48] The Yorkshire text of the *Lay Folks Mass Book*, written just before the middle of the fifteenth century for the Abbey of Rievaulx, says:

> Kneland halde vp thy handes,
> And with inclinacyon
> Behalde the Eleuacyon.
> Swylke prayere than thou take,   *then give*
> As the likes best forto make.   *thee*
>
> (C text, ll. 224-28)

Chapter III

And for those unprovided with a prayer, the following is suggested:

> Welcome, lorde, in fourme of brede
> For me thou sufferde herd deede;
> Als thou bare the crowne of thorne
> Thou suffer me noghte be forlorne.
> (ll. 237-40)

As

The extant Levation prayers (Gib's frons has some similarities in phrasing to one[49]) are lofty and plain, and necessarily lack the warm humanity of the speeches of the men in the play and of such works as the *Meditations on the Life of Christ*, which also, however, allows for restraint: "kneel and adore your Lord God, and then His mother, and reverently greet the saintly old Joseph."[50]

Joseph is a silent "extra" in the play, but Mary, who, as usual in art, possesses a crown or diadem, and is seated (fig. 11), and may also wear gloves,[51] responds in one stanza. She prays that God, "my son" who "sett all on seuen" (ll. 486-87), may reward them and grant them eternal bliss. With authority, she instructs them to "tell furth of this case" (l. 491), bestowing on them the role of pastors hitherto only metaphorically and very imperfectly theirs. She is demure, but since, as some of her miracles suggest, she is capable on occasion of slyly rescuing sinners from the worldly consequences of their folly, she might look Slowpace in the eye as she further prays that God "spede youre pase" (l. 493)—although his name has been mentioned once only—and she might look at John and stress the pronoun when she adds, "And graunt you good endyng" (l. 493), recalling his proverb (ll. 78-81).

Gib for the first time now acknowledges her presence as he says farewell. John, in response to her wish, promises to testify to what they have seen. Slowpace recognizes that they "mon all be restorde" (l. 496, "shall be renewed")—by a "restorité" superior to "Good sawse" (ll. 237-38, "sauce") Gib calls on them to sing "all sam" (l. 499, "all together," perhaps "in unison," in contrast to the discanting Three-Men's Songs) with "myrth and gam" (l. 500, "joy and delight") in praise of "this lam" (l. 501, "lamb"). They must sing a devout and lovely song, as at the end of the York play—a song the Church has provided in her wisdom to substitute for earthly and vile songs.[52] They are "glorifying and praising God for all the things they had heard and seen" (*Luke* 2.20) for "this case" (l. 491); nevertheless, contrary to the York play and to *Luke* 2.20, they do not return home as they sing, but sing "in syght" (l. 502), standing gathered around the manger in which the Christ Child lies, singing his praises in his presence, gazing on him. This play thus concludes in obediance to Isaias: "Sing ye to the Lord. . . . Rejoice and praise, O thou habitation of Sion: for great is he that is in the midst of thee, the Holy One of Israel" (12.5-6, *in medio*).

The merriment and joy appropriate to Christmas have been transferred in abundance and with equal propriety to this amusing play about the Incarnation. The laughter is provoked by what is essentially a series of unsuccessful attempts to understand the statement that the Word was made flesh. As the first action unfolds, the whole tale of the *Mad Men of Gotham* is revealed—a source of satisfaction to those members of the audience who have already recognized it. The significance of the failure of Gib and John to substantiate their words is less readily apparent and is perhaps only clear, if then, when in their gluttony they commit the opposite error of making the Word altogether too material and fleshly. The sleep into which they fall as the natural result of their ludicrous self-indulgence is also the stupor from which the chosen are awakened, described by Isaias and explained by Jesus (*Matt.* 13.14-16). They are not keeping watch over their flock by night, and it is therefore necessary to add one crucial word to St. Luke's story (2.8-10): "Awake!" says the angel (l. 296), an exhortation to embrace the salvation accompanying the Nativity. St. Bernard begins a sermon with this appeal, "Awake and praise,"[53] and one of James Ryman's carols of the Nativity begins, "Oute of youre slepe arryse and wake."[54] Awakened, literally and morally, they are able, if only unsteadily, to recite the witnesses to Christ. They move by grace from their original misery and empty consolations to happiness and salvation. They progress, as is surely generally clear, from misunderstanding and instability to enlightenment and serenity. The playwright thus chooses, with some help from Isaias, to curtail St. Luke's story at 2.17: "When they

Chapter III

had seen, they understood," whereupon the final seventh of the play leads into the song with a demonstration of the kind of prayer appropriate at the Eucharist and the kind of meditation encouraged by St. Bernard and the *Meditations on the Life of Christ*, which can hardly have failed to bring the audience together, their laughter conquered by the loveliness: "Gaze on His face with devotion and reverently kiss Him and delight in Him."[55]

The play is barely capable of being understood only literally since so interwoven are its points and so thoroughly is St. Luke's story, a strong peg for a happy and religious disquisition on the Incarnation, taken out of its original time and place. The playwright has deftly crammed his work to the full and can hardly have expected it to be understood completely; it is thus a work for all members of the audience, each understanding parts of it in his or her own way. The sources of the material the playwright takes for his play from Isaias, St. John, and other parts of the Old and New Testaments were—no more than his hidden numerical plotting, which he must have used mainly to keep himself in order—not necessarily meant to be recognized by the audience; these sources are chiefly the playwright's authorities, but since Old Testament texts are frequently used for sermons on the Nativity he could also expect that some of his biblical sources would be recognized by some members of the audience. If the shepherds are fifteenth-century tenant farmers, leasing some land in common in the West Riding, they also represent the Israelites, so similar are their problems and so apparent is their need for a messiah; of the Incarnation Ludolphus concludes that all the prophecies become clear, "the mysteries which were earlier only indicated and lightly sketched are now accounted for and accomplished."[56] The shepherds also represent all sinners and doubters who have not yet, in Ronald Duncan's fine phrase, found Christ "like a green leaf in an old book"; the members of the audience are all shepherds or farmers or closely associated with these workers, and although the playwright has rather pushed "simple" in the direction of "simple-minded," the members of the audience are certainly meant to see themselves in the shepherds. The sketches, mysteries, and hidden allusions which possessed the Israelites are merged with the miseries, folly, and weakness of understanding with which we are besotted; they are both a source of rich comedy and an ample demonstration of what St. Bernard says we should, like the shepherds, move forward from: "the shackles of necessity, curiosity, vanity, and voluptuousness."[57] Each day our Lord comes if we feel him in our hearts and amend our lives.[58] We are all in charge of a little flock of our own deeds and thoughts, some already diseased and many of them dead, which we must try to maintain with "heavenly food," says Ludolphus,[59] and resisting temporal things we can find Christ, who, if we are people of good will, will give us peace on earth, that is, an interior peace and content, he says. Under Christ's flesh is hidden the supreme sweetness of divinity.[60] The solutions the playwright offers to the problems and hardships of life in the West Riding are thus moral and spiritual. Insignificant (in the worldly sense) Bethlehem is the only way to the heavenly city, and one day, like the shepherds, we will obtain a full view of God's perfect countenance.[61]

We can now feed our souls on the food of the divine word, says St. Bernard, and for clerics in the audience there is a rather specialized form of allegory but one certainly relevant because of the common understanding that clerics are pastors who, like the shepherds at the end of the play, must proclaim Christ and who, not entirely unlike the shepherds at the end of their feast, must distribute "spiritual nourishment," says Ludolphus, quoting Bede.[62]

St. Luke says that "Mary kept [in mind] all these words, pondering them in her heart" (2.19, *omnia verba haec*). It is not entirely clear what all these things, or words, are, but it is clear in the presentation of the play, if it can be assumed, as seems reasonable, that she is seated in her Scaffold throughout. She has watched her baby, but she has also seen the shepherds gradually approaching him, both spiritually and literally. She has seen their muddle-headed confusion, their obtuseness which the playwright enlarged upon by turning them into foolish performers in the Place, the fullest use of it being made for wandering to and fro, for doing skits adapted from tales (for which the only precedents belong to the minstrel repertoire), for prancing and feasting, for doing tricks at a table, for riding a horse, for dumping flour onto the grass, for accosting the audience with their miseries and gastronomical joys, for marching and singing, and finally for tumbling into the Scaffold that represents the stable where they are suddenly still and serene, in possession of the stability which has hitherto eluded them—explicitly so at the beginning of the play. Working literally, the playwright has taken spiritual madness to justify his representation of earthly folly and, desiring to entertain, taken earthly folly to be best represented by comedians. The play makes extraordinary demands on the three chief players; it calls for an unremitting series of "turns," each requiring proven ability to hold the attention of the audience. The Scaffold where the action of the play concludes must face the audience, who must all be able to focus their attention on it. The Place is as large an area as feasible in front of it. The angel's Scaffold is in the Place, nearer the area where the shepherds fall asleep, probably very close to the audience and to one side, to avoid blocking the view of the stable, which the angel tells the shepherds is "ahead" of them and which contains the interior peace they have long fumblingly sought. The playwright has given an extra dimension to Mary's joyful smile, by which the audience may be guided.

Chapter IV

The Second Shepherds' Play

We have conceived, and been as it were in labour, and have brought forth wind.—Isaias 26.18

The leaking roof and the sight of the demure Virgin Mary glowing with motherhood in the York play of the Nativity may have reminded the Wakefield Master of the Old Testament proverb, "A wrangling wife is like a roof continually dropping through" (*Prov.* 19.13, "dripping"), or the winter version of the same, "Roofs dropping through in a cold day, and a contentious woman are alike" (*Prov.* 27.15). And so he might have been led to conceive of Mak's wife, Jill, who is nothing if not contentious, and whose disgusting person conveniently forms a contrast, the furthest imaginable, to Mary's. This contrast is part of the plot of the Second Shepherds' play, which again consists of the playing of biblical imagery, a popular tale, popular songs, proverbial lore, and facets of contemporary rural life; these are so fused together that the dependence on French farce frequently posited[1] seems to be out of the question. If the unifying factor of the First Shepherds' play is the phrase "freely food," from which all else seems to ramify, the governing idea of the Second is the confusion of the worldly value of a real sheep, a fat ram, with the ineffable value of the figurative Lamb mentioned at the very end of the First Shepherds' play, almost as an introduction to the Second—a fully exploited pun, some of whose implications were first noticed in modern times by William Empson.[2] "Food" is almost as common a metaphor for Christ as "Lamb" in fifteenth-century English

113

religious writing. The themes of the two plays—the historical and personal discovery of salvation—are essentially the same, but different in emphasis. In the First, the shepherds gradually learn sense, losing their folly and misunderstanding; in the Second, they slowly learn the meaning of love, losing their despair and overcoming outright wickedness. It has been suggested that the playwright, not only a contriver but also a philosopher, is here reflecting the scholastic debate between those who thought fallen man to be stubborn in his mind, and those who thought him stubborn in his heart—the "intellectualist" and "voluntarist" theories.[3] A related distinction is made by the *Golden Legend*, which declares that Christ came because man had been conquered by both ignorance and powerlessness.[4]

The play requires a speaking cast of seven, consisting of four major parts, a secondary part (Jill), and two minor parts (the Angel and Mary). The playwright has reverted to the usual number of shepherds, three, melding Jack's function with Slowpace's, to produce the very special Third Shepherd, Daw, and he has introduced the non-biblical Mak and Jill. The Place at the beginning of the play is meant to be arable land near a strip of pasture. One of the two main Scaffolds represents Mak's cottage, the other the stable at Bethlehem; there is also probably a smaller third Scaffold, a high platform (l. 649) from which, as in the First Shepherds' play, the angel sings. The First Shepherds' play makes the fullest and most adventurous use of the Place, the Second the cleverest and most pointed use of the Scaffolds—beginning, however, with a unique use of the Place. The grim humor occurs in the Place, the ludicrous hilarity in Mak's cottage, and the comedy in the stable. The play, which is perhaps easier to understand than the First Shepherds' play, is the Wakefield Master's *chef-d'oeuvre* and by far the longest of his five plays. The 754 (or 756, if the absence of two lines from the frons of stanza 30 is not deliberate) lines, divided into eighty-four stanzas, probably took, with all the "pandemonium" and five songs, about an hour to present.

Numbers again control the plot, and prevent the preliminary part, the human and inchoate version of salvation, from swelling out of all proportion. The eighty-four stanzas are divisible by 2,

3, 4, 6, and 7, as is the number 756. It is not until the final sixth part of the play, which begins at line 629, that the shepherds lie down to sleep, the angel appears (*Luke* 2.8-10), and the action moves to Bethlehem. The new denominator is therefore 6, the first perfect number;[5] it perhaps serves to indicate the pythagorean and Christian perfection of the divine plan just as what amounts to a pun on the virtue of the number 7 frames the First Shepherds' play. The number 84 is perhaps meant to point to the next episode recorded by St. Luke, the Presentation in the Temple (2.21-39), at which Anna, the prophetess and widow, is present. She is eighty-four years old, acknowledges the infant Savior, and speaks of him "to all that looked for the redemption of Jerusalem" (2.36-38), as the shepherds set out to do at the end of the play. If her age is responsible for the number 84, each sixth must—as is the case—consist of fourteen stanzas. The number 14 occurs in a number of relevant biblical passages, listed by St. Isidore,[6] who also points out that 14 is made up of two 7's. The Israelites, for example, were to eat the paschal lamb, a notion central to this play, on the fourteenth day of the month (*Num.* 9.2-5). David, who was thirty years old when he began to reign, reigned for forty years—totaling 70—and thus leaves room in the play, as it were, for fourteen stanzas for the age of Christ, his Son. This complex of 6, 14, and 84 is handled with considerable dexterity, since 6 is not only symbolic but also serves as a principle of organization throughout the play, bestowing on it a comprehensiveness by aligning its progress with the first six ages of the world (the ages of Adam, Noah, Abraham, Moses, David, and Christ) as described, for example, in the *Golden Legend*,[7] a common way of looking at history which St. Matthew, who counts fourteen generations between key figures and events before the birth of Christ (1.17), encourages and which was formulated by St. Augustine and popularized by St. Isidore.[8]

The numerology is again a private guide to the playwright. Somewhat more public is his interest in the sequence of the shepherds' speeches. At the beginning and ending of the York Shepherds' play, the shepherds speak in numerical order, as do the four knights in the York play of the Crucifixion; in the middle sections of these two plays, however, the orderly rotation is interrupted. The Wakefield Master is interested in the rotation of the speeches of Noah's sons and daughters-in-law (unlike the playwright in the York play of the Flood) and of the three knights in the play of Herod, but has no interest in this kind of patterning in the First Shepherds' play. In the Second Shepherds' play, however, the system is (with five explicable exceptions[9]) complete. Gib speaks after Coll, and Daw after Gib; and when they are all present, all three always speak. As a consequence of this constant rotation of speeches, Coll begins the play, and Daw (like Colle in the York Shepherds' play, and with a more fully developed rationale) ends it. The same number of whole stanzas is allotted to each of the three shepherds.

The play, like the First Shepherds' play and for the same reasons, begins with plaintive and satirical monologues from the shepherds (this time from all three) which are, like the whole play, again fully embroidered out of Old and New Testament messianic imagery and references to contemporary social and personal crises and conflicts, a combination found also in sermons, where extortioners and wrongful oppressors of the people are compared to Pharaoh and where the prayers of the downtrodden will, it is said, be heard by God just as were the prayers of the Israelites.[10] The shepherds are more distinct from each other than in the First Shepherds' play, have two sides to their personalities, and are perhaps less clearly entertainers—roles now fully assumed by Mak and Jill.

As the play begins, Coll, an old man and a small tenant farmer, with a share of the arable land and rights to the common pasturage and a flock of sheep (partly represented by the one ewe, one ram, and fifteen young sheep who have wandered as far as Horbury, ll. 451-57) owned jointly with Gib, is alone in the Place and fast asleep on the ground. His first words, spoken as he struggles to his feet, indicate as much:

> Lord, what these weders ar cold! And I am yll happyd.
> I am nerehand dold, so long haue I nappyd;
> My legys thay fold. . . .
>
> (ll. 1-3)

The Second Shepherds' Play

No other extant medieval play begins with such Chekovian silence. The playwrights can be seen avoiding it, as in the case of the Towneley play of Jacob. Dispensing here with the more usual flamboyant opening, at providing which he is expert, the Wakefield Master yet expects his audience to pay attention from the very start (or knows that they will) even while so far nothing is happening. At his core Coll is a sleepy and muddy but also a courteous old man, the former qualities signs and causes of his downfall, his loss, and the latter quality a sign and cause of his rescue, his salvation. He yearns for a good sleep, which he never gets because, in contrast to his companion, the second shepherd Gib who is a very good sleeper (l. 355), he sleeps awkwardly. He is tired when he wakes up. His legs are weak. Next time it will be pins-and-needles in his foot. He refuses point blank, because he is too tired, to keep watch over his sheep ("Wake thou!" l. 257, the bob) and evidently deserves the cheerful sarcasm with which young Daw (characteristically speaking out of turn) greets him when they meet at the crooked thorn: "A, Coll, goode morne: Why slepys thou nott?" (l. 449). Helping to toss Mak in the canvas sheet wears Coll out completely, and his ever-present need for a good rest rapidly resurfaces; even so, he thinks his worry or anger about Mak and Jill will prevent him from falling asleep. He sleeps nevertheless, with his two companions, at this point, and the same adjustment to the angel's speech required in the First Shepherds' play is needed here also. By night Coll gets no sleep, and by day no rest—such is his consistent chain of thought. The script thus calls for wit in the performance. The actor must half-collapse on his old legs, only held up by his crook, at well-timed intervals, and yawn now and again. As he delivers his gloomy monologue he walks or hobbles here and there in the Place and addresses now this part of the audience and now that. Each stanza begins a slightly new thought, and the effect is as if he is saying, "And another thing . . ."; but his monologue is more a cry from the heart than a comic address, delivered to an audience who will feel more sympathy for his plight than amusement at the way he expresses himself.

The sorrows of the Old Testament world are evoked by the first thing the audience sees, an old man rising up out of the mud (it has been raining, ll. 127-28). "The Lord God formed man of the slime of the earth" (*Gen.* 2.7, *de limo terrae*), an episode shown in all three northern collections of biblical plays and also recorded at Beverley. The age of Adam has begun, and, perhaps more to the point, the life of this poor farmer, Coll, is made to contain within itself, as a result of the meaning commonly attached to the images of mud and mire, those very problems of the world of which he complains. He suffers from "worldly muck" (*MED* muk n [b], mire n[1] 3 [a]). Combining some of the points made by Gib and John in the First Shepherds' play and adding to them, he complains of excessive taxation, of the lying and arrogant maintained men who wear the badges of their lords (l. 28, possibly without justification—a common abuse[11]) and seize provisions, of general oppression and extortion, and, it seems, of the practice of enclosing land for pasturage which leads to depopulation—"the tylthe," or arable part, "of oure landys lyys falow," he says knowingly "As ye ken" (ll. 13-14), and the plough has been hindered by the lords' men who claim to know that what they are doing is for the best. Ploughs "put down" or "laid down" were common terms for enclosing. These problems appear to have occurred with some frequency in the Wakefield area, where all the land was leased out by the Lord of the Manor, in the fifteenth century, and with such severity (at least according to Coll) that he, a mere "husband" or farmer, less prosperous than the aggressive yeomen,[12] fears for his very life, as he stresses in his bob: "Thus ar husbandys opprest, in ponte to myscary/ On lyfe" (ll. 22-23). These worldly concerns are mirey, and Coll is, besides being literally muddy, as excessively concerned with the things of this world as are those who oppress him. The metaphor is biblical (*Isa.* 10.6, *Hab.* 2.6, for example) and common. We are stuck in an impure lake of wretchedness, says St. Bernard, and, earth-born, our bodies are as low as the soil.[13] The *Golden Legend*, explaining the sixth anthem sung during Advent, says that Christ came to save man from the "slyme of the erthe."[14] "In the mire" is also a common proverbial expression (Whiting M573) for "in trouble," and not only Coll but also Gib and Daw "run in the mire" (ll. 160, 256, 494). They are thus farmers, sons of Adam, unredeemed, and beset with worldly problems.

"My legs they fold" appears to be a rather ordinary fifteenth-century expression (*OED* fold v^1 4b and 5) but in the context of this play is also not without biblical authority. Coll does not yet realize that Christ will come (and comes) to strengthen "the weak knees" (*Isa.* 35.3) prevalent before his coming (*Ezech.* 7.17). If Coll is oppressed and in need of "rest" (ll. 8, 15-16, 19), he needs Christ, who said, "Come to me, all you that labour, and are burdened, and I will refresh you" (*Matt.* 11.28, *reficiam vos*, "give you rest"). Coll's immediate and characteristic solution, however, is to think about having a good sit-down while he waits for the other two shepherds.

In his desperate and muddy unrest and, despite some sarcasm, Coll generally maintains his sense of propriety and is gloomy to the point of self-effacement and timidity. Even in times of merciless oppression he does his best to remember his manners, not failing to enquire after Mak's wife, to remember that a gift for her new baby would be appropriate, to trust Mak and Jill, to be unwilling, tactfully and then rather obtusely, to intrude on what he takes to be their private grief (his mind is on an ovine proverb, ll. 586, 591-92, Whiting K34), to greet Mary, a gesture unique among all the shepherds in English medieval plays, before adoring her Child, and to bid her farewell before her Son, as he and his fellows leave the stable. The poor, like himself, he says, are generally meek, as meek as pets, another proverbial thought (Whiting B125, 295, D359, H560, L31, S204, S548, T540). This attitude has both an Old Testament and a New Testament side to it. "I am yll happyd" (l. 1) and "My foytt slepys" (l. 352) are rather common expressions (*OED* sleep v B 3a), but again, in this context, a piece of Old Testament proverbial wisdom is probably behind them: "To trust to an unfaithful man in the time of trouble is like a . . . weary foot, And one that looseth his garment in cold weather" (*Prov.* 25.19-20); it is the shackles of the world which hold back our "feet" from running to God, according to St. Bernard.[15] On the other hand, Coll's meekness and courtesy will lead to his salvation, as Jesus said (*Matt.* 5.4).

The playwright seems also to acknowledge the literary genre, the complaint ("mone") he puts into Coll's mouth, and also to provide him with a little comfort at the same time as he recog-

nizes (uniquely) the nature of a monologue in a play[16]—"It dos
me good, as I walk thus by myn oone,/ Of this warld for to talk in
maner of mone" (ll. 46-47). Gib, also older than Daw, now enters
the Place, and the joke, which hangs on the convention of the
Place, in the First Shepherds' play is repeated (an indication, presumably, of its success) more fully: Gib does not notice Coll, and
launches into his complaint, first blessing the audience, again as
in the First Shepherds' play. Gib's sufferings introduce a new
note into the complaints, since it is as a married man that he is
miserable. He is almost but not quite resigned to his fate; he thus
sleeps well, but is also, in his torment, more sensitive to insults,
prouder, crueller, and more suspicious than Coll. He challenges the
audience with "Why fares this warld thus?" (l. 56). The weather
bothers him (he is wearing shoes rather than boots, l. 62), he says
in his first stanza, proverbial and alliterating; his remaining five
stanzas he devotes to the suffering of married men. He is, unfortunately, at one with "We sely wedmen" (l. 65), echoing Coll's
"we sely husbandys" (l. 10); the "we" includes members of the
audience. His many children cause him trouble, his wife, like
most, is domineering, but, as the proverb (Whiting W245) says,
she must be endured; it breaks his heart to see the destiny of men
driven by fate to marry. In words reminiscent of popular and humorous songs,[17] he admonishes the young men in the audience to
think twice before marrying and, providing a preview of Jill, describes his own wife, a cackling hen, again in proverbial and
alliterating phrases: "She is as greatt as a whall,/ She has a galon
of gall" (ll. 105-06, "whale," Whiting W200-01). She has a common hen's name and is his Eve. His hyperbole is calculated to
keep the audience laughing, but he finally goes into a daze, just as
he has wandered over to where Coll is sitting; a dangerous idea
crosses Gib's mind, and, meditating flight from his impossible
wife, he lingers over his last line, which is twice as long as usual,
containing ten syllables instead of the usual four to six: "I wald I
had ryn to I had lost hir!" (l. 108). If the player keeps the usual
two stresses (on "run" and "lost"), Gib speaks in a rush, ashamed,
perhaps almost throwing the line away, so resigned and helpless
is he, gazing off into space. The only other long last line in the
play is also spoken by Gib; it comes at the end of his reference to

Isaias' prophesy of the birth of Christ (7.14) and so marks the arrival of, among other things, the perfect birth—and the arrival of the solution to all personal troubles and pains: "*Concipiet* a chylde that is nakyd" (l. 683). Gib's attitude towards children is certainly not Christ-like (*Matt.* 19.14).

Tired of waiting, Coll jumps in with his own blessing, perhaps loudly into Gib's ear from behind, or perhaps snapping his cold fingers in front of Gib's face, since he adds, "Full defly ye stand" (l. 109). They discuss the whereabouts of the Third Shepherd, Daw—Coll has heard his horn signalling from the pasture—and the ever-suspicious Gib remarks that they must beware of Daw's lies. Daw's monologue (also six stanzas long, although the fourth is an exchange with his two angry seniors) is about the instability of the world, the weather, the dangers of the night, and the plight of such servants as himself. The first line of his stanza about the weather begins the second sixth of the play. "Was neuer syn Noe floode sich floodys seyn" (l. 127), he says, continuing one of Coll's themes. "The day of Adam, day of sin. . . . For we were all born then . . . on that day, day of clouds and of fog, day of shadows and of whirlwinds, which Adam made for us," says St. Bernard,[18] and Daw suitably follows Coll by ushering in the second age of the world, the age of Noah, which Noah himself proclaims in the N-town play (l. 14). If the age of Adam in the play (ll. 1-126) is characterized by the social and personal desolation and sufferings of the old, as well as bitter weather, the age of Noah in the play (see l. 127) is marked by the arrival of blatant sin and evil in the person of Mak. Sin is now everywhere, says Noah in the Wakefield Master's play of Noah (ll. 48-54).

"Daw" is a name mentioned only once in the play by Gib (l. 111), and so if the audience is to make much of the name alone it must be spoken with emphasis. It is a pet-name for "David" and also means "simpleton" (*MED* daue n), as in the play of Noah (l. 247). As a youthful servant, Daw bears a family likeness to the traditional "cheeky boy"; as a simpleton, he is divinely *gauche*, like Jesus; and as David he will directly lead Coll and Gib out of their oppression (*Jer.* 21.12). As David, he is first heard of in the pasture (l. 111, *1 Kings* 16.19), with his horn, an ordinary part of the everyday equipment of a shepherd, but also, since it is in

Daw's hands, perhaps an earthly sign of the Lord's promise of salvation (*Ps.* 131.17, recalled in *Luke* 1.68-69) and from this point of view more appropriately attached to Daw than to the unnamed First Shepherd of the York play, or to John, whose full name is John Horne. Daw is the young one who is keeping the sheep, feeding "his father's flock at Bethlehem" (*1 Kings* 16.11, 17.15), and Gib's hired hand. In his psalm he says that he should "not be afraid . . . of the business that walketh about in the dark" (*Ps.* 90.5-6), but in the play he almost runs away when he sees Coll and Gib, for he temporarily confuses them with monsters of the night; he does an agile stumble to correct himself and also to activate Jesus' words, "if he walk in the night, he stumbleth, because the light is not in him" (*John* 11.10); Coll and Gib, however, like the Israelites (*Isa.* 8.22), are more in the dark than he is, and by the end of the play he has overtaken them.

Meanwhile, he demands (like Slowpace) his food and drink. In response Gib is especially critical and selfish, prompting Daw to pursue his monologue, now complaining about masters, their slowness to pay one's wages being one of the miseries of life, a simile used in *Job* 7.2 and here acted out, and also best answered by the New Testament ("the laborer is worthy of his reward," *1 Tim.* 5.18, *Matt.* 10.10) rather than by the insolent proverb with which Daw teases Gib (ll. 170-71). He is noticeably more energetic than Coll and Gib; his leaping contrasts with the former's inertia, and his playfulness with the latter's grim resignation. He is, as befits a youth, amorous, and despite Coll's skepticism may well one day be "glorious" to handmaidens (*2 Kings* 6.22). He is as skillful and guileless as his psalm says he is (*Ps.* 77.70-72) and so has a way of going straight to the point, of seeing the truth without hedging. It is he who announces that Mak is a thief, removes Mak's disguise, tries to take precautions against Mak's approaching the sheep, has a nightmare about Mak as a wolf, and, directly accusing him of the theft, speaks out of turn to do so. When Coll pauses outside the door of Mak's cottage and, gloomily aware as usual of what is proper, asks both ("ye") Gib and Daw if they gave the child anything, Gib is as surly as ever ("I trow not oone farthyng," l. 572, "I hope"), but the impetuous Daw flings himself back inside to the cradle and produces a truly

The Second Shepherds' Play

munificent and heartfelt gift, more than a whole day's wages to him,[19] of "Bot vj pence" (l. 579, the bob). To the Israelites in captivity the Lord promised that "You shall . . . find me when you shall seek me with all your heart" (*Jer.* 29.13), and it is Daw's wish to follow up his gift with a natural, Christian (*1 Cor.* 16.20), and liturgical kiss that reveals the "frawde" (l. 594), the stolen ram; even while the priest kisses the Pax, the *Lay Folks Mass Book* tells the worshipper, one should pray to "Goddes lambe."[20]

Daw takes on a new authority now[21] and becomes, like David, "a witness to the people, . . . a leader," as God promised (*Isa.* 55.4). He conclusively and sensibly identifies the sheep by the ear-mark (l. 611)—the normal method of marking ownership of a flock was to punch a distinctive hole in the sheep's ears[22]—to remove all doubt, and then respectfully speaks out of turn to suggest a suitably belittling but merciful and playful punishment for Mak. The three shepherds accordingly toss Mak in a canvas sheet— a difficult piece of business, but they do it, or half do it, presumably with a large triangular piece of canvas at hand in the cottage, perhaps giving Mak a chance to exhibit some of his *lazzi*-like tumbling or collapsing skills (copied from minstrels) and also providing a climax for the worldly episodes of the play which show, following St. Augustine, a humanity that is deeply curious with the effect of tempestuously living in a world in which there is much tumbling down and up.[23] Daw, now sounding like Jesus ("This is my commandment," *John* 15.12), persuades his two elders to sleep on the ground and again speaks out of turn to soothe Coll's fears away. He knows that—in contrast to their attempt, which he opposes, to imitate the angel's song—their true song now will be everlasting and quiet joy. The Lord has revealed the truth to the little one (*Matt.* 11.25), as in the First Shepherds' play he revealed it to Jack. Daw, like Slowpace, is particularly ready to go to Bethlehem, and also has the wit to pray for God's help lest they approach the Christ Child speechless or empty-handed. He is the first to declare his keenness to kneel to him (perhaps thus providing some guidance to the others, for Gib also will kneel) and does so, waiting his turn. They adore the Child in one whole stanza each. Coll and Gib speak with lofty words in the

frons and with plain delight in the wheel; Coll's turning point, the
bob, is especially pleasant, and requires good timing and emphasis: "Lo, he merys" (l. 714). Like Slowpace's stanza, Daw's is altogether more personal and ostensibly disorganized. He has ab-
sorbed the spirit of meditation, and pities the poorly clad child who
has already taken Coll's sufferings on himself. Daw's need is so
pressing, sympathy so heartfelt, and youth so irrepressible that he
almost loses control of himself, and at first seems to dispense
with his "Hail" in one line (he finally manages to utter three, of
the Trinity) to come to the point immediately: "I pray the be nere
when that I haue nede," he says, in obedience to Isaias, who says
"Seek ye the Lord, while he may be found: call upon him while
he is near" (55.6).

Their gifts appear to symbolize the Trinity and are also perhaps interwoven with the riddle song.[24] They again combine the
simple and quotidian with the eternal. Coll, giving a bob of
cherries, recalls the wounded Christ; Gib, a bird (presumably in a
cage), recalls the Holy Ghost; and Daw "bot a ball," only a ball,
recalls the sovereignty represented by the orb held by God the
Father.[25] These would be miraculous gifts if it were Christmas
time, which, of course, in a sense it is, though the play is presumably being presented in summertime, and the real miracle is how
Coll just happens to have some cherries in his satchel and how
Gib is able to carry a bird in a cage in his. The athletic and delin-
quent Daw can be expected to carry a ball in his, especially since
it is a tennis ball—tennis, among other games, was specifically
forbidden in Wakefield in 1450.[26] Again these presents are a sign
of the good intentions of the shepherds, which they are able to express only in a slightly inappropriate manner, since such gifts
(like the gifts of the York Colle, John, and Slowpace) are suitable
for a young boy but not for a new-born baby. Or, as in the Dijon
Nativity (fig. 1), time may have been mystically collapsed so that
the childhood of Jesus as well as his babyhood and the Trinity are
simultaneously recognized (as in the glass painting in St. Peter
and St. Paul's, East Harling, Norfolk[27]).

Daw, concluding the play, leads Coll and Gib in their third
song (like Colle in the York Shepherds' play). In contrast to the
First Shepherds' play, they leave the stable as they sing, and it is

difficult not to imagine that they continue to sing while they cross
the Place, returning to glorify God (*Luke* 2.20), the happy and
clumsy adolescent leading the way. Old and young are heard and
seen praising "the name of the Lord" (*Ps.* 148.12). The mono-
syllabic simplicity of the final stanza is, however lovely, as carefully wrought as the numerical perfection of the number of
speakers (there are six) in it. Fourteen seems to be about the right
age for Daw; it takes fourteen years to grow up, says St. Isidore,[28]
and this was widely accepted as the age at which one passed out
of childhood into youth.

At the end of their complaints, and after Daw has teased Coll
and Gib by telling them he has left the sheep in the corn, and
while they are blithely singing their first song (Coll appears to
lead, as tenor voice, and so this is again perhaps a jolly Three-
Men's song), Mak enters the Place. He is a very small and unsuccessful cottager, who owns no sheep and is supported mainly by
his wife's spinning and his own larceny; he appears to live from
hand to mouth. His name is mentioned no fewer than twenty-one
times in the play, and (unlike the names possessed by all the other
shepherds and farmers in the York and Towneley plays) is not an
English Christian name. "Mak" is, of course, a common Gaelic
prefix for a surname (and also itself a Lowland Scottish surname)
and suggests a pet form or dimunitive of a Scottish name parallel
to "Coll" or "Gib." lt also means a "rival" and a "married man"
(*MED* make n[1] 1a and 2c). The fourteenth-century Scottish in-
vasions must have lingered in the memory of Yorkshiremen, and
the turbulent fifteenth century saw the Earl of Northumberland
leading Scottish soldiers to Thirsk and Tadcaster, where they were
defeated in 1408. Scottish mercenaries were used to keep order at
Ripon in 1441, and the truce with the Scots signed at York in 1463
by Edward IV can hardly have immediately endeared the Scots to
the people of Yorkshire.[29] Mak, as David's antagonist, is surely
one of the people who "cometh from the land of the north," threatening Jerusalem (*Jer.* 6.22). Most things about Mak are inept and
derivative. He is not Christ-like, but comes like Christ as "a thief
in the night" (*1 Thess.* 5.2; cf. *Apoc.* 16.15). He wears a short
cloak or shoulder cape over his gown (l. 189.1), a suspicious-

looking and none too usual garment (it is not worn by the shepherds) which is rather promptly removed and probably inspected by Daw; it is an extravagant garment, not needed by honest laborers or true disciples (*Matt.* 10.10, *Mark* 6.8-9) such as Daw, who has already alluded in vain to these instructions given by Jesus. Such false disciples, overloaded with provisions, appear as foxes in carvings at Beverley, and in a carving at Ripon a fox carries away a very fat goose—a scene with similar meaning (fig. 18). Mak's first words are borrowed from David's psalms (*Ps.* 8.4) and also from Gib's complaint, to which Mak gives proverbial form (Whiting C223); they constitute a small complaint of their own which is probably meant to be overheard by the three shepherds since Mak wishes to insinuate himself into their company and play on their sense of pity with his pathetic whimpering while at the same time concealing his identity from them, his reputation being what it is. Unmasked in a flash, he immediately tries to keep to his plan by pretending to be an officer of the king from the south, a pretense no more original than his complaint, since he seems to turn himself into one of the flunkies of the lords of bastard feudalism, to whom Coll has already drawn attention. The player puts on a southern accent, probably a poor and exaggerated one, and this pretense is as transparent as the moaning. Even Mak's bob, by a stroke of genius, is completely lame and unconvincing:

> What! ich be a yoman, I tell you, of the kyng,
> The self and the some, sond from a greatt lordyng,
> And sich.
>
> (ll. 201-03)

He characteristically maintains his lie long after it has been easily penetrated, as he will do later. Himself again, he complains (copying Gib once more) of having too many mouths to feed. He melodramatically and unnecessarily (since they are already soundly asleep) casts a spell over the shepherds and—vainly imitating the Lord, who said of his judgment of Israel, "I shall make a circle round about thee" (*Isa.* 29.3)—draws a circle around them (l. 278). When he pretends to wake up with the shepherds, his pretense is as inept as ever: if Coll's foot fell asleep, Mak's neck caught a

The Second Shepherds' Play

crick; if Daw's nightmare made his heart leap out of his skin, so did Mak's. He tells them, not avoiding a Freudian slip of some magnitude, that Jill gave birth very early that morning "to mend oure flok" (l. 388). Protesting his innocence even before any crime has been discovered, he invites them to look in the sleeve of his gown to make sure that he has not stolen anything; his sleeve is, as was common throughout the fifteenth century, probably a hanging sleeve, capacious, closed at the end and slit in the middle,[30] and a proverbial place to hide something (Whiting S381). Mak is treading on thin ice. "To stuff one's sleeve with fleece" means to deceive (Whiting S383), and false prophets wear such luxurious sleeves (*Ezech.* 13.18); perhaps even more to the point, "The friar preached against stealing and had a goose in his sleeve" (Tilley F675, by 1525). Off home, he is advised by Jill to sing a lullaby to lend color to their deceit and also to serve as a look-out signal; putty in her hands, he takes the opportunity to make a fool of himself again since he is incapable (unlike his three victims) of holding a note. His final attempt to keep up the lie about the ram being a baby is outlandish and his collapse, which is both psychological and physical, is pathetic. In short, he is a chronic liar and a wicked thief and is distant from God; he commends himself to Pontius Pilate. He is thus very reminiscent of the Devil, the father of lies (*John* 8.44) and the great deceiver. Mak's transparently bad acting, including his disguise and his instant changes of personality (blundering acting became a metaphor for dissembling[31]), and his unoriginality and casting of spells also give him an air of Antichrist who, says the *Golden Legend*, precedes the Last Judgment with malice and deceit[32] and to whom the *Cursor Mundi* refers as nourished by "iogelours."[33] What happens in his cottage, however, demonstrates that he is chiefly the Devil's minion. He is proud, angry, envious, and in the end powerless.

Mak has a cottage because the "house of Israel" (*domus Israhel, Ezech.* 12.9) is a common Old Testament synecdoche for the nation of Israel. Like the house of Israel, his cottage is "full of deceit" (*Jer.* 5.27), and the Scaffold representing it answers some unusually complicated purposes. A number of medieval biblical plays require "domestic interiors," but the awkward surface things about them—such as lockable doors—that belong to farce are rare.

This is a well-constructed although not necessarily very large Scaffold, whose design requires some thought. Unless it is on a Pageant, of which there is no sign, it is probably not easily portable. A conversation taking place on both sides of a door is not easy to stage, although the York Realist, for reasons not unrelated to the kind of thinking behind the play, wrote four such episodes.[34] Since Jill speaks to the audience from the cottage while the door to the street is shut, it seems reasonable to suppose that here she delivers her monologue from a window. When the street-door is open, what goes on in the cottage is fully visible and audible. The street-door can be unusually wide so that when it is swung open all the way outwards (the shepherds can pull it open wide at l. 483) to the right of the audience the inside of the cottage is completely revealed. Some of the action associated with it, notably the tossing of Mak in the canvas sheet, can overflow into the Place, which becomes the street, but other, equally important action, especially the discovery of the ram, must take place inside it, presumably to the forefront. What is behind the inner door need not be seen, and probably is not, although the shepherds should search there.[35]

Only Mak's cottage requires two doors, the "gaytt-doore" (l. 328, the "door to the street or path") and the "hek" (l. 305, or lower half of an inner door, or a small door, *MED* hacche n 1 [a]). Holding in his arms the stolen ram, gathered up in the folds of his gown, Mak moves swiftly from the Place to his cottage, shoulders his way in through the street-door which is standing slightly ajar, and speaks in a loud whisper, "How, Gyll, art thou in? Gett vs som lyght" (l. 296). She ignores him, having just settled down to her spinning. His hands are full, however, and he needs her to unlatch the lower half of the inner divided door (animals, not unusually sheltered in the same houses as peasants, were kept in the rear, behind such a barrier, the ground sloping towards the back to carry away the run-off) for him so that he can deposit the ram in the back:[36] "Good wyff, open the hek! Seys thou not what I bryng?" (l. 305, "see"), he says. She does so, but only after keeping him waiting, rebuking him with a sharp internal rhyme, and then changing her tune in mid-line when she sees the treasure in his arms. Just as he had impatiently hoped, his "secret present

quencheth anger: and a gift in the bosom the greatest wrath"
(*Prov.* 21.14), a biblical (but not, apparently, an English) proverb
now acted out. He tells her to bar the street-door, a necessary pre-
caution, when he returns to the Place to rejoin the sleeping shepherds whom, he pretends, he has never left. He shortly leaves
them again, as they prepare to count their sheep, and returns once
more to his cottage. This time, of course, he cannot open the
street-door even with two hands free, since, at his own suggestion, Jill has barred it. Pounding on the door in vain, he shouts in
anger and embarrassment, "Vndo this doore! Who is here? How
long shall I stand?" (l. 404). Jill, perhaps thinking that the con-
stable has arrived, and being in any case preoccupied with her
spinning, does not stir. Mak is reduced first to exasperation and
then to pleading pathetically to be let in: "A, Gyll, what chere? It
is, I, Mak, youre husbande" (l. 406), he says, the last three sub-
stantives becoming increasingly weaker. The deceiver himself has
managed to get himself locked out of his own house. "Syr Gyle!"
Jill calls him with contempt (l. 408, the bob)—the "Sir" is sarcastic (*OED* Sir II 6b). The common proverb, "the guiler is be-
guiled" (Whiting G491), which has an Old Testament resonance
(*Isa.* 33.1), has thus been demonstrated in farcical action, and
Mak is once more associated with the Devil, to whom Coll refers
as he worships the Christ Child: "The fals gyler of teyn, now goys
he begylde" (l. 713, "of teyn" means "malevolent"). Christ so
treats the Devil, says Langland.[37] Jill also welcomes Mak with
"Then may we se here the dewill in a bande" (l. 407), an even
more explicit reference to the Devil (*Matt.* 12.29). (She is unwittingly anticipating the power of God, who comes to bring us out
of thralldom, a theme central to the play of Herod the Great and a
common religious expression.)

Once Mak is again inside his cottage, he and Jill bar the
street-door and are like the would-be oppressors of Israel who are
"shut up in their houses . . . exiled from the eternal providence"
(*Wisdom* 17.2), where, however, adds the *Glossa Ordinaria*,[38]
they will not be secure, as the play immediately demonstrates,
since Gib is already knocking at the door (l. 478), while Mak
looks out of the window singing in an extraordinarily loud voice.
Perhaps, like the Scottish fool named "Swagger," Mak is at first

Chapter IV

brazen; the bolder and more extravagant his lies the more he confidently expects to be believed. The final lie about an elf is no more effective than the others (the "delusions of their magic art were put down," *Wisdom* 17.7), and Mak's collapse is very sudden and pathetic. The "little ones of the flocks" have brought the proud one low, as Jeremias says (50.32, 45), and the shepherds are now making sterling progress. Perhaps the playwright is also taking literally Job's view of the wicked: "They are lifted up for a little while and shall not stand, and shall be brought down as all things" (24.24).

The third sixth of the play (ll. 253-76) centers on Mak's theft of the shepherds' ram and Jill's suggestion that they substitute it for a non-existent baby boy, a sudden and foolish suggestion which denies the truth of the proverb, "Women are wise in short advisement" (Whiting W531). The third age of the world, the age of Abraham, in place of whose son (a common type of Christ) God substituted a ram (*Gen.* 22.13)—an episode which forms part of the Towneley collection of plays—is thus perhaps wickedly echoed.

Characters like Noah's wife (also called Jill) and Jill are rare in the religious plays but not in proverbial lore. She is comic, especially if she is played by a female impersonator as it is reasonable to assume, but the playwright has taken pains to make her a credible woman. The player is perhaps a cross between the pantomime dame and the modern drag artist skilled at womanly mannerisms. Coll, ever mindful of the social amenities, makes a friendly overture (no wonder his foot sleeps) to Mak; "How farys thi wyff?" he asks. Mak replies that she

> Lyys walteryng—by the roode—by the fyere, lo!   *sprawling*
> And a howse full of brude. She drynkys well, to;
> Yll spede othere good that she wyll do!
> Bot sho
> Etys as fast as she can,
> And ilk yere that commys to man
> She bryngys furth a lakan—   *baby*
> And, som yeres, two.
>
> (ll. 236-43)

She has a different view of the matter. A working woman, she is proud of her resourcefulness, made all the more necessary by the inability of her incompetent buffoon of a lying husband to support his family. Her work is never done, and she can ill afford to be constantly getting up to answer the door. Some families bought fleece each week, spun it, returned to the clothier each week to sell it, and used the income to buy fleece for the next week's work.[39] Too much responsibility of this kind has made her truculent, volatile, and quick to change her tone. She rightly assumes that her "Mak" has failed to think through the details of his crime, seizes with self-satisfaction the opportunity to devise a way of (literally) covering it up, and gratuitously and proverbially ("Women can rede to help men at need," Whiting W536) remarks that she is always ready with good suggestions (l. 342), even when, she later innocently adds as she stretches the proverb, they are not necessary (l. 433). At Wakefield, common scolds were fetched before the Manor Court,[40] and Jill, who has an ordinary English name, is a recognizable kind of wife for whom it is possible to find some sympathy.

She is also the proverbial domineering woman, like her cousins in Lydgate's Christmas Mumming (about 1430), Cicely Sourcheer and Beatrice Bittersweet, who beat their husbands black and blue with their distaves and scowl at them over the ale pot when they come home from work (at least they have regular employment) for dinner. Harry Bailey's wife, "byg in armes," is as bad.[41] Jill may not hit her husband with her distaff (or pin him down by squatting on him) like Noah's wife, or like the many irate women, who frequently wield distaves, carved on misericords, including those of the Ripon school, but she is well acquainted with the ale pot and certainly dominates him. The carols about marriage present no prettier picture.[42] Lydgate associates his domineering wives with the Old Testament.

The playwright stops short of giving Jill much resemblance to such impossibly powerful monsters of depravity as the wives in Sir David Lindsay's satirical play (1552), who when they break wind frighten the horses and when they cough shoot phlegm onto the walls.[43] Jill is disgusting enough as it is (according to Mak), and her bottom, to which she herself draws attention (and which was stuffed, no doubt, with wool or fleece)—"Behynde!" she cries, the preposition, but also inevitably the noun here (MED bi-hinde)—must be large enough to cause hysterical laughter but not so enormous as to defy belief altogether. The Wife of Bath, who is also occupied with the woolen industry and possessed of a common name, has wide hips, and Morgan the Fay gives herself "buttokez balȝ and brode" ("bulging and broad") when she becomes the forbidding hag in *Sir Gawain and the Green Knight*.[44] Jill (her name is mentioned nine times in the play) is not only a rather contemptuous name for a woman but also a name for a mare (*MED* gil n[2] b).

Like Tib in the farce of *Johan Johan* (c.1529), she is so closely associated with laziness, gluttony, sexual activity, and windiness that her ample and intractable self may fairly be taken as a representation of the Flesh itself. The metaphorical or allegorical association of woman with the Flesh is a medieval commonplace. Langland says that an unkind wife is our stubborn flesh,[45] and in the fifteenth-century morality play *Mankind*, Mankind says that it is "a lamentable story/ To se my flesch of my soull to have gouernance./ Wher the goodewyff ys master, the goodeman may be sory."[46] At Shibden Hall, a glass panel in the same window as the punning devil but painted in the sixteenth century shows a woman who holds her distaff, fleece, wool, and spindle and who beneath the waist (or girdle, as King Lear would say) is a beast—a spotted leopard or lion.[47] Jill is thus married to a suitable husband, for "Woman has an art more than the Devil" (Whiting W508)—yet another proverb shown in action in this play—and their cottage is thus inhabited by the Devil and the Flesh.

In the fourth sixth of the play (ll. 377-502) the shepherds search unsuccessfully for their ram. They come, as in the age of Moses, the fourth age of the world, out of the wilderness, the scrubby and thorny area around Horbury, but only within sight of the promised land (*Deut.* 4.22, 32.52, 34.4). They are trapped by their own worldly concerns and by the machinations of Mak and Jill until Daw leads them to the truth in the fifth sixth (ll. 503-628), the age of David.

"Here shall we hym hyde . . ./ In my credyll," says Jill, and "I shall lyg besyde in chylbed, and grone" (ll. 333-35). A common

Old Testament simile for pain and fear is "as a woman groaning in the bringing forth of a child." The pain and fear felt by the Babylonians and other enemies of the Lord are so described by Isaias (13.8, 21.3) and Jeremias (48.41, 49.22-24); more particularly, Isaias and David associate the simile with the establishment of the Church and the coming of Christ. When the city of God was established "There were pains as of a woman in labour" among the wicked, like Mak and Jill (*Ps.* 47.7); and the emptiness of Jill's child-bearing reflects the helplessness and uncertainty of the Israelites before the coming of the Lord: "As a woman with child, when she draweth near the time of her delivery, is in pain, and crieth out in her pangs: so are we become in thy presence, O Lord. We have conceived, and been as it were in labour, and have brought forth wind," or odor (*Isa.* 26.17-18 *peperimus spiritum*), not an inappropriate activity for Jill, given her pedigree. Thus the false delivery in the play indicates the imminent downfall of the wicked and precedes the discovery of the true Christ Child. The windiness of the Flesh, often humorously exaggerated, and popular tales about stolen sheep hidden in childbeds (never, however, recovered) are thus dove-tailed with a particular form of messianic imagery, which, in view of the subject of the play, must be regarded as the chief source of this part of the plot, the farcical high point, although not the highlight, of the play.

The contrasts between Jill and the ram and Mary and the Christ Child are plentiful but only easily apparent if what happens inside the cottage is plainly visible. Jill is seen tying the sheep's four feet together, putting it in her cradle, and covering it up. Mak must help her, for this is no easy business although an analogue from real life in the Yorkshire Pennines shows that it is possible.[48] The sheep is thus bound tightly, like the new-born Christ Child. With any luck, it will bleat, a sound not too far removed from a baby's cry—a point most amusingly made in the version directed by Howard Sackler.[49] Jill then gets into bed and lies, like Mary in one common iconographic tradition, as in the Bolton Hours (fig. 13), and perhaps the Coventry play (l. 698*sd*, "*jesen*" or childbed), next to her "son." It is a foul smelling beast, unlike the Christ Child, who is most sweet smelling. Mak intends to eat this ram (a foolish economy, since its chief value lies in its ability to tup the ewe, l. 457, and in its fleece) and a burnt Old Testament "ram" might produce a "most sweet savour" for the Lord (*Exodus* 29.18), but Christ the Lamb will deliver "himself up for us, an oblation and a sacrifice to God for an odour of sweetness" (*Eph.* 5.2). For the wicked and unredeemed Israelite woman "instead of a sweet smell there shall be a stench" (*Isa.* 3.24); Jill is used to it, but there is plenty of opportunity later for some comic nose-holding by the shepherds. When the Lord comes, he will remove far off from us "the northern enemy . . . into a land impassable, and desert, with his face towards the east sea, and his hinder part towards the utmost sea: and his stench shall ascend, and his rottenness shall go up, because he hath done proudly" (*Joel* 2.20), and so when Jill tells Mak to cover up well her and her bottom ("Behynde!" l. 435, the bob), she perhaps sticks it up, one sign of the evil anger and contortions to which the Devil and the Flesh put us. Jill prepares to groan in agony when she hears the look-out signal. Unlike Mary, Jill is bossy, untidy, dirty, fecund, given to sprawling around, scratching her toes, drinking, and complaining. Mary is obedient, neat, clean, virginal, and modestly busy. With her distaff, her spinning, and her groaning, Jill is much like Eve the sinner, who is banished from paradise to a life of spinning and toiling (the angel gives her a distaff in the York play of the Expulsion[50]) and to sorrow in childbirth (*Gen.* 3.16), pains also mentioned in the York play and spared Mary, the woman who came to right the wrongs caused by Eve and who often embroiders delicately rather than spins; again, the divine plan is made specifically relevant to the hard life of the industrial West Riding.

The shepherds arrive, all covered in mire, and so in a sense mankind, his own worst enemy, is now all assembled in this cottage in the form of the World and the Flesh, aided and deceived by Mak, the Devil and the door-keeper (l. 479). These are the three things, in this play almost completely persons rather than abstractions, from which Christ comes to save us, as the morality plays demonstrate. He will take the "mire" (*Ps.* 68.3) of the World on himself, mortify the Flesh, and defeat the Devil. He substitutes himself for our own smelly obsessions to which we cling long after their emptiness is revealed. Jill moans and snorts and tells the shepherds to leave. When they come nearer to her, she puts more power into her act, groaning loudly and, like a true mother, defensively. The sense and phrasing of Mak's entirely thoughtless or foolishly bold asseveration, spoken with an emphasis on "this" as he points to the cradle—"As I am true and lele, to God here I pray/ That this be the fyrst mele that I shall ete this day" (ll. 521-22, "lele" means "honest")—are promptly repeated by Jill, whose determined lies ring, at the instigation of the Devil, throughout her bob and wheel:

> A, my medyll! *middle*
> I pray to God so mylde,
> If euer I you begyld,
> That I ete this chylde
> That lygys in this credyll *lies*
>
> (ll. 534-38)

There are here shades of the "freely food" which has been on not only Mak's mind from the beginning (ll. 323-24) but also, more obscurely, on Coll's, who, when he awakens for the first time, cries, *"Resurrex a mortruus"* (l. 350), a piece of the Creed which, if only he had got it right (*resurrexit a mortuis*), would have helped him, but which sounds more like *resurrectio a mortreuus* or a rising to meat stew or broth, a dish Chaucer's cook was good at making (I.384), most comforting for a cold and wet outdoorsman, and a common word (*OED* mortress). Coll has had a warning as well as a pleasant dream, and messianic imagery is again put to work. Jeremias (*Lam.* 4.10) and the prophets bewail the fate of Jerusalem awaiting salvation under the law of Moses in similar terms: "The hands of the pitiful women have sodden their own children: they were their meat," he cries (cf. *Lev.* 26.29, *Deut.* 28.57, *Bar.* 2.3, *Ezech.* 5.10). Your "hartys" should melt at such a sight if you knew how she had "farne" (ll. 531-33, "farrowed"), says Mak to the shepherds—echoing the melting hearts and labor pains predicted by Isaias for the enemies of God (*Isa.* 13.7-8).

When the sheep is discovered by Daw, Mak and Jill, true to their incorrigibly lying nature, vainly keep up the pretense. Jill even hoists the sheep out of the cradle and vigorously dangles it on her knee (no mean task)—a significant move, for Mary does the same with the Christ Child: the angel announces (following *Luke* 2.12) that he "lygys . . ./ In a cryb" (ll. 644-45 "lies," and 689), but at some point, perhaps as the shepherds approach, and contrary to *Luke* (2.16), Mary takes him out of the crib and holds him on her knee (l. 747), which is in art the common position for him when the shepherds adore him, but which is not indicated in the First Shepherds' play. Jill's desperate lullaby

> A pratty child is he
> As syttys on a wamans kne;
> A dyllydowne, perdé,
> To gar a man laghe   *cause*
>
> (ll. 607-10)

is not, of course, echoed by the demure and straightforward Virgin Mary, but she does in her one stanza (in contrast to her one stanza in the First Shepherds' play) describe the Annunciation and the supernatural conception as being part of God's power and plan (ll. 737-40). And old Coll's reaction to the Christ Child, with whom he certainly smiles and probably laughs, is the Gospel truth of the last line of Jill's jingle (l. 610), which is true only in a ridiculous sense.

After Mak is felled, the shepherds return to the Place, presumably taking with them the ram, which they could then release to a waiting stage-hand—he who is also needed in the First Shepherds' play. Mak and Jill are heard no more, nor, probably, seen; shut up in their home, they are exiled (*Wisdom* 17.2) for ever, and Mak probably slinks back inside, just before he and Jill bar the street door behind them.[51] The shepherds have tamed or banished the wolf.

The angel's song is again skillfully rhythmical (ll. 656-59). His annunciation to the shepherds is especially courteous. Coll, Gib, and Daw have perhaps never previously been addressed so politely in their lives, and God's messenger is the answer to all arrogant maintained men, Mak being no adequate rival (ll. 386-98) to the angel—generally having the opposite effect, indeed, since Mak's message is false, he causes the shepherds nothing but

The Second Shepherds' Play

trouble, and he thinks he is putting them to sleep rather than awakening them. The effect of the wonderful bob and wheel of the angel's one stanza is borrowed from the First Shepherds' play, but the emphasis in the frons is different. The playwright has selected from the commentaries the words of the angel, who specifically states that God is "now" born to take back from the Fiend what Adam had lost—that is, the souls of his creatures—and to destroy the Devil. The angels will be led by the "now" born King in battle against the powers of Hell, says Ludolphus in this context.[52] The fourth line is warmer. "God is made youre freynd" (l. 641) echoes the idea of God's friendship, which is ultimately based on Jesus' words which foretell the Passion: "Greater love than this no man hath, that a man lay down his life for his friends" (*John* 15.13-15). These words run throughout the York and Towneley plays, and their connotations are strong because of the high value placed on friendship—pure and unique—during the Middle Ages.

The reaction of the shepherds to the angel's song is in keeping with their personalities. Poor Coll says they must not forget to go to Bethlehem even if they are "wete and wery" (l. 671, "wet and weary," an ordinary rather than literary alliterating phrase); child-ridden Gib, disagreeably cutting off Coll's protracted attempt to sing the angel's song, speaks of childbirth and gives Isaias' prophecy (*Isa.* 7.14); Daw, having corrected Coll about the nature of mirth, speaks only of his feelings, his youthful sympathy for the Child "poorly arayd,/ Both mener and mylde" (ll. 690-91, "meaner") and also reflects Simeon's peaceful words (*Luke* 2.23-30). Simeon set an example of devotion—we should, like him, embrace the holy infant, says St. Bernard.[53] Coll, shy of believing such unheard of news after a lifetime of rejection, is given the words with which to expand on the angel's explanation, "this shall be a sign unto you" (*Luke* 2.12), which is not spoken in the play but which, together with Bede's interpretation that the angel offered evidence to the shepherds because the Israelites were accustomed to signs and tokens,[54] is the source of Coll's comment,

> We shall se hym, I weyn, or it be morne,   *see eve*
> To tokyn.   *as a sign*

When I se hym and fele,
Then wote I full weyll
It is true as steyll
That prophetys haue spokyn:
(ll. 695-700)

in which the learning is perhaps buried by the proverbial comparison "true as steel" (Whiting S709) used earlier, and of course falsely by Mak (l. 226), and also in the Noah play with gratification by God of Noah (l. 120). The bob here is again of great significance.

It is sometimes suggested that, in order to underline the connection between the two nativities in this play, one Scaffold served to represent both Mak's cottage and the stable at Bethlehem. This arrangement is very unlikely to have been in the playwright's mind. It is contrary to the nature of Scaffolds, which spatially represent distinct and often (as here) antagonistic places. In this play, the tumble-down (there is no question of gaining admittance) stable stands in direct contrast to Mak's tightly shut cottage. The stable is, in the worldly sense, defenseless, and like the Church it is open to all comers: "thy gates shall be open continually: they shall not be shut day nor night," says Isaias (60.11), in a prophecy fulfilled by the coming of the Magi, and St. John reports the Lord as saying, "Behold, I have given before thee a door opened, which no man can shut" (*Apoc.* 3.8).

Since characters in medieval English plays do not, once the play has begun, normally enter the Place or walk to their Scaffolds without saying anything, without announcing their arrival, it is reasonable to suppose that in the First Shepherds' play Mary, Joseph (who again says nothing), the Christ Child, and the ox and the ass have been present in or on their Scaffold throughout the play waiting serenely and in full view for the tumult and falsehood to cease.[55] From the beginning, the sight of the Holy Family has represented the open door towards which old Coll, ever since he has risen up out of the mud, must with his companions make his way. The two main Scaffolds can stand in front of the audience, not far apart, and the angels can conveniently and symbolically separate them, representing the vanguard of our defense. A modern director will feel compelled, since most of the action takes place there, to put Mak's cottage in the center, but it is probably more important to the playwright that it should stand somewhat to the audience's right and the stable somewhat to their left so that the Christ Child can be at God's right hand (as is Christ in the Trinity, fig. 24). Both Scaffolds represent very poor dwellings belonging to very poor people, and both are in a small town. In both a partition separates the human inhabitants from the livestock, and the manger in the one parallels the crib in the other. But one is locked up, the other impossible to close: Christ came "to preach the opening of what is closed," says St. Bernard, "so that with the joy of salvation we may receive the crown of our little King."[56]

The main direction of the play is not hard to grasp. The shepherds, in whom the members of the audience are again invited to see themselves, must progress from their Israelitish and contemporary sloth, bitterness, and disorderly conduct—and their general muddy obsession with the things of this world—and must overcome the Flesh and also the Devil in order to reach their Savior. Their struggle to do so is expressed in the prosody. The bobs in this play, normally end-stopped and frequently strong, capture oaths ("Do way!" "Bot hatters!"), commands ("Wake thou!" "Be styll," "Gett wepyn!"), ejaculations ("A, my heede!" "I swelt!"), insults ("Syr Gyle!"), and climaxes ("Ich fote that ye trede goys thorow my nese/ So hee," ll. 488-89, "so high"), and anticlimaxes ("We haue mayde it," l. 149, "eaten it"). Similarly, the number of broken stanzas far exceeds the number of one-speaker stanzas; the former come especially thick and fast from the age of Noah to the age of David as the tumult and confusion of this world is expressed. At the beginning of the play there is loneliness in the monologues, at the end fellowship and harmony.

More clearly than in the First Shepherds' play, a little bit of courtesy on the part of Coll, enthusiastically seized on by Daw, means that they are ready for the appearance of the angel. Love in themselves enables them to overcome the Devil and not be deceived by him. He would have them run to the wrong house through the "myre" (l. 494), focus their attention on this world,

Chapter IV

and believe that a ram and not a Lamb is what they should seek. But not even a valuable ram pasturing in the West Riding, not even one with red marks on his back (from reddle[57]) or clipped possessively in the ear, is nearly as precious as the "lamb unspotted and undefiled" (*1 Pet.* 1.19), the image of God familiar in ecclesiastical art, including local art (fig. 19)—not even if it is bound in swaddling clothes. Both are referred to in the play as a "lytyll day-starne" (ll. 577, 727), the morning light and day star of messianic imagery confirmed in the New Testament (*Isa.* 8.20, 58.8, *2 Pet.* 1.19, *Apoc.* 22.16). Daw follows St. Peter's epistle, for the morning star certainly rises in his heart. It is a true proverb that a lamb will die as soon as a ram (Whiting S209), but one might, in any case, to be able to tell the difference between them—an exercise surely no harder than telling a goose from a swan, a falcon from a crow, or (l. 368) a wolf from a lamb (Whiting F34, W445-46)—that is, a good shepherd from a thief (*Matt.* 7.15). The shepherds are, of course, helped by the power of God, which is stressed in the final part of the play by the angel, Coll (ll. 712-13), and Mary (ll. 737-40), whose first words echo Mak's (l. 190)—a power expressed paradoxically, as always, in lowly and defenseless form. In the play of John the Baptist in the Towneley manuscript, Jesus (uniquely among extant English plays) gives John a lamb as a sign of himself (l. 210.1), and this collection is notable not only for the absence of plays about Christ's ministry but also, as has been pointed out, for the constant Eucharistic references in the plays concerning the life of Christ.[58] The Wakefield Master appears to have built on this emphasis,[59] first with a play about the meaning of the Incarnation and next with a play about the defeat of the arrogant World, the intractable Flesh, and the lying Devil, the familiar division of the deadly sins, which were, as in this play, made more like lively people and more interwoven with each other as the medieval period drew to a close.[60] These are the many enemies from which Christ saves us and from which we go forth (l. 704): "the flesh, than which no enemy can be closer; this worthless age, which from all sides surrounds you; the princes of darkness, who brought together in the air, obstruct your path. However, do not fear tomorrow, that is, soon you shall go forth," says St.

Bernard.[61] They are avoided, defeated, and visibly gone forth with the aid of the power of God's love captured in the form of a gentle lamb—"as gentle as a lamb" and its variations is one of the most common proverbial comparisons (Whiting L25-36) and occurs in the Towneley play of the Pilgrims (l. 52) which the Wakefield Master knew. The play shows the laying aside of "all malice, and all guile, and dissimulations, and envies, and all detractions," or slander (*1 Pet.* 2.1).

The play is, however, gloriously unamenable to a single interpretation; it is more suggestive than schematic just as its people, especially the shepherds, whose sins (mentioned only once, l. 677) seem rather ordinary, are more credible as persons than analyzable as vices. Various lines of thought and turns of sympathy are possible. Some members of the audience may have seen themselves as lost sheep, the sinners Christ was and is sent to find (*Matt.* 15.24, *Luke* 15.6), and felt that Coll, Gib, and Daw are certainly on the right lines as they make a determined effort to find their sheep in order to save him from the wolf (*John* 10.10-14)—and noticed that they find it by the exercise of love. True sheep know their Lord, and, looking at Mak's closed cottage and then at the open stable, some may have thought of Jesus' words, "I am the door of the sheep" (*John* 10.7)—that is, according to the *Glossa Ordinaria*,[62] Christ who opens himself to all who follow him. Others may have been more impressed with Mak as Antichrist—the one who puts on a false show before the third coming of the Lord.[63] Not many, if any, will have understood Mak's name to be a cunning reversal of "Cam" or "Cain," but more might have known that at the third coming the Lord will come as a thief in the night; "then shall sudden destruction come upon them, as the pains upon her that is with child" (*1 Thess.* 5.3). Both the Devil and Antichrist are archdeceivers, and Jill, like the whore of Babylon, does give birth to a "hornyd lad" (l. 601, *Apoc.* 12.2-3, 17.1-6). The sifting of souls at the Last Judgment is also possibly falsely imitated by the canvas in which Mak is tossed; childbirth and still-born birth might be aided in this way by midwives, but a canvas might also be used to sift wheat from chaff;[64] the Lord God is perhaps doing this as souls are gathered up to him in a cloth (angels frequently take souls to him, as on a boss at St.

Chapter IV

Mary's, Beverley).[65] These hints both of Christ as the good shepherd and of Antichrist and the third coming are certainly present in the play for those who would puzzle over them.

Because of the way in which the play begins and ends, however, the overall impression is, I think, of the contrast between Coll, powerfully representing the "heavy yoke which is on all sons of Adam,"[66] and Daw. Between them, they come to see the first coming, the Nativity, and the second coming, the coming of Christ into the individual heart, and the emphasis of the play is on both, especially the latter. Like examples in art where one of the shepherds is shown as beardless, they are distinguished, as in the First Shepherds' play, by their ages; and the younger learns decorum from the older, and the older love and wakefulness from the younger. St. Paul provides the ever pressing interpretation of the Old Testament warnings against sleepiness. "Rise thou that sleepest, and arise from the dead: and Christ shall enlighten thee," he says (*Eph.* 5.14), referring to Isaias' words, "awake, and give praise, ye that dwell in the dust," and "Arise, be enlightened, O Jerusalem: for thy light is come, and the glory of the Lord is risen upon thee" (26.19, 60.1). "Ryse," says the angel (l. 638). Old Joseph and Gib and John of the First Shepherds' play heed these words. Joseph sees the light that is come. Colle in the York Shepherds' play and Jack and Slowpace of the First Shepherds' play have much of Daw in them. They all at first unfortunately lack the "spirit of meekness" (*Gal.* 6.1) requisite in good pastors (in the metaphorical sense[67]), but it becomes clear that in contrast to the old shepherds they are "new" (*Eph.* 4.24, *Col.* 3.10). These metaphors are enacted. The sprightly Daw, particularly, has set himself "free from the law" relative to servitude, not to mention the by-law relative to tennis-playing, about which he shows perhaps not so much "conscious humour"[68] as conscious good humor so that he may now "serve in newness of spirit" (*Rom.* 7.6) and lead his elders to Christ and fresh-heartedly accept him, both as he is born and now. The cheeky servant comes to represent divine simplicity and thus wins over his benighted masters. Daw has the sympathy of the audience from the beginning when he scoffs at Coll and Gib, and he keeps it throughout the play. His part is slightly longer than theirs.

The Second Shepherds' Play

The smiles he inspires come from a sense of his youthfulness turning into rightness and from showing the power of love. The hilarity is caused by the opposite—the transparent and ridiculous deceptions of Mak and Jill about whom, as about Daw, there is (rightly) a sense of reality, but whose excessive and ridiculous contrivances are not only plainly wicked but also swiftly penetrated by Daw's simplicity in what must be one of the best arranged climaxes (ll. 575-623) in all of playwriting—comparable to the climax in the play of Noah when Noah's wife is persuaded bit by bit by a mixture of diplomacy, threats, and fear to board the Ark (ll. 352-73). This episode in the Second Shepherds' play so fully expresses the characters of the participants that it is far from being farce. The play is marked indeed by "rollicking" laughter, smiles, touches of rapt devotion (especially on the part of Daw) of the kind encouraged by the meditative tradition and also by a sense of fullness—the whole of history seems present—which is certainly meant to set the audience wondering. A good play will cause the audience to think, and a good biblical play to worship. The Second Shepherds' play does both. Once again, they (especially any clerics present) are left to "avoid foolish and old wives' fables" and to "Meditate upon these things" (*1 Tim.* 4.7, 15) and to be no longer "a spectacle not only to this world but before both angels and men," as St. Bernard puts it.[69] At the same time, there is no better excuse for some fun than the defeat of the Devil and of whatever of Mak and Jill there is in the shepherds and in us, followed by the consequent salvation of mankind. No better reason "To gar a man laghe" (l. 610, "make a man laugh").

Chapter V

The York Play of the Slaughter of the Innocents
and the Play of Herod the Great

God hath overturned the thrones of proud princes.
—*Ecclesiasticus* 10.17

The extant text of the York play of the Slaughter of the Innocents is, presumably, the text of that play as it was presented at the time the manuscript was written (1463-77) and for some years earlier; however, in the sixteenth century when John Clerke was at work checking the texts of the plays, it had been discarded in favor of a different version, now lost.[1] Throughout the life of the York plays, the play of the Slaughter of the Innocents was the responsibility of the Girdlers, who were assisted by the Nail Makers and sometimes by the Purse Makers and Timber Sawyers. The Girdlers manufactured studded belts, book clasps, dog collars, mountings and ornamental metal work for sword and dagger sheaths, buckles, and other small metal objects.[2] Their connection with the subject of the play lies chiefly in the costumes and hand properties of the knights who kill the children. A notable feature of fifteenth-century armor is the ornamental belt or girdle surrounding the thighs (fig. 20), which the knights in this play surely wear since in 1446 William Revetour, a priest and deputy civic clerk who had a strong interest in plays, bequeathed "to the Girdlers of the city of York for their play on the feast of Corpus Christi one gilded brazen crown and one girdle with gilded and enamelled bosses."[3] One knight draws a short sword (l. 212, "knyffe") with which to stab a child; Herod's evil counselors

144

carry large books which might have prominent clasps; and Herod may have worn a purse with a metal knob on his belt from which to reward his knights (l. 254)—perhaps he jingles it when he promises to be their "frende" (l. 165, "friend"). To be so closely associated with this play, which is the last in the sequence of the Nativity plays and which, following St. Bridget of Sweden and others, verbally, visually, and thematically looks strongly towards the Passion, was a painful honor.

The York and Towneley plays are the only extant English plays devoted exclusively to the subject of the Slaughter of the Innocents, the four other English plays and most of the liturgical plays[4] intermingling it with the stories of the three Magi and the Flight to Egypt, as does the Gospel (*Matt.* 2.1-18), which is followed in some English art.[5] A lost play presented at Beverley by about 1515 and perhaps related to the York play apparently also dealt with this subject only,[6] as do three extant liturgical plays and many paintings throughout the Middle Ages.[7] By isolating the story to make a play out of it, the York playwright or his sponsors set an example for the Wakefield Master, who knew the York play and developed its potential.[8] The York play concentrates on the character of Herod and his court, which, largely by implication, forms a contrast to the earthly character of Jesus, the other King of the Jews (a contrast shown in art by juxtaposition[9]), and the kingdom of heaven.

Herod dominates the cast although he speaks considerably fewer than half the lines. It is clear that the one Scaffold on the Girdlers' Pageant represents Herod's court, and it is extremely likely that throughout the play he is seated on his customary throne, which in art is more often than not shown at the left.[10] The messenger or herald (*nuncius*) approaches the throne from the Place and is told to "come nere" (l. 75). The knights are at hand on the Scaffold with the counselors, and they depart (ll. 192-93) to carry out the massacre in the Place, perhaps at ground level, and return (l. 234) to the Scaffold to report. Herod presumably wears the property ("gilded brazen") crown bequeathed to the Girdlers in 1446, and it would be unusual if he did not also carry the sword frequently alluded to in connection with such tyrannical characters. With his alternating moods, it is unlikely

Chapter V

that he sits still. His agitation is represented by his crossed legs in two glass paintings, about 1350 and 1375, of the Slaughter of the Innocents in York Minster which show him on his throne, watching or directing the massacre.[11]

He begins the play, like many such characters, by calling for order and proclaiming his own greatness. He is, he blasphemously says to the audience, their "louely lord" and the lordliest "kyng" alive (ll. 8, 11-12), and his god is Mahounde to whom all ought to be allied. He is perhaps to be understood as testing his counselors' loyalty; "herto what can ye tell" (l. 24) is not otherwise well motivated. He announces that he is concerned about the child of whom the three kings spoke and with whom he shows his annoyance and ferocious anger throughout the play by the use of characteristic abusive epithets: "gadlyng," "lad," "faitor," "brothell," and others, including the possibly more pointed "fandelyng" (l. 157, "illegitimate child," and "little rascal"—*MED* "fondling" n). The two adjectives used in the Gospel to describe Herod's state of mind, *turbatus* and *iratus* (*Matt.* 2.3, 16), follow the sequence of the story, but in this play, as in others, Herod is made to swing between these moods throughout the play. He begins angrily, then expresses his distress and, having been looking forward (like King Arthur) to hearing "tydyngis" of "meruayles" (ll. 77, 81), reacts to the news his messenger brings of the departure of the three kings with a mixture of anger, despair, and disbelief. "A, dogges, the deuell you spede" (l. 106) comes at the moment in the Gospel when he is said to be *iratus*, and he might at this point stand up as he vainly shouts at the three kings in their absence. He foolishly banishes the messenger—a characteristic sign of tyranny[12]—and declares that if he can catch the Christ Child, "that faitoure" (l. 128, "liar"), he will have both him and (contradicting himself) the messenger, who makes the expected speedy departure, hanged. This outburst of anger is followed by more despair. While the massacre is taking place, Herod might even doze off (although there is no sign of the wine with which such tyrants often fortify themselves)—at least it seems that he has to be prodded into paying attention by one of the counselors when the knights return. On learning that they cannot be certain that they have killed the one child in which he is interested, he is at first impatient or even petulant ("I aske but aftir oone," l. 260) and then, realizing that he may have fled, so angry that he declares he will never "byde in bedde" (l. 273, an ordinary-sounding phrase but one which might have caught the York Realist's attention) until he is captured. Rising from his throne with a battle cry, he charges off followed by his sycophants and pauses only to conclude the play by inviting everyone in the audience who adheres to the faith of Mahounde to follow him. It is clear that he does not leave his throne or his Scaffold until the very end of the play.

This volatile and insecure tyrant is accompanied by evil counselors. Their only function, they say, is to protect him by force and to keep him full of joy, notions which almost recall the purpose of the angels as expressed in the first five York plays. In blatant contrast to the chief priests and scribes of the story (*Matt.* 2.4-6), they reassure Herod that there is no truth to the information provided by the three kings. They are both termed *consolator* and perhaps aptly so since the word might mean "flatterer."[13] They cure Herod's despair temporarily by advising him to summon his knights immediately and to order them to kill all the boys under the age of two in and around Bethlehem, as in the story (*Matt.* 2.16); in the play, his distress has deprived him for the moment of his wits. It is at the prompting of one of his counselors, who has yet more foolish and wicked advice to give, that Herod leaves his throne at the end of the play to give chase. Such flatterers and advisors inevitably accompany tyrants, said the social critics,[14] and Herod was no exception, says Ludolphus in this connection, following the *Glossa Ordinaria* (referring to *Prov.* 29.12): *Rex injustus omnes ministros impios habet.*[15]

The two knights are "curtayse and hende" (l. 163, "noble and gracious"), according to Herod, and the play ridicules dishonorable and cowardly members of the knighthood, who fail to protect the innocent. The two women put up some resistance, and the knights appear about to fail, until the first gives a battle cry, "Asarmes" (l. 207); they also appear to flee as quickly as possible from the grief-stricken and enraged women but are proud of the sharp combat in which they have engaged. The women appear to have nothing but their fists with which to defend their children,

Chapter V

and the self-satisfaction of the well-equipped and solidly armored knights is ludicrous.

This is a short play (281 lines[16]) with eight speaking parts, all of them important, which must have taken about twenty minutes to present. Nothing can be known of the playwright, whose stanza, used consistently throughout the play, occurs in no other York plays. The diction, which frequently alliterates, is either mock-heroic or low, as befits this court. The sources of the play, other than the Gospel, are the pagan tyrants found in earlier plays, including liturgical plays, in which Herod's pomposity and rage are emphasized and in which he has a messenger,[17] and the common assumption that the motive for Herod's behavior is jealousy for his kingship, a motive not made clear in the Gospel but easily and commonly inferred. The overall impression is of the weakness and cruelty of Herod, the wickedness of his counselors, and the lack of honor of his knights. The playwright shapes the play so that it begins with Herod's pride and ends with his desperation, and is not shy of introducing the ludicrous since he knows that he is writing a comedy. The innocents are the first martyrs and are crowned in glory; they die in place of Christ, as indicated by the short title given to the play in 1415, *Occisio innocentum pro christo*,[18] and as explained by the *Glossa Ordinaria*, Ludolphus, and many others. The failure of the enemies of Christ is made explicit in the play; the second mother concludes that the knights have worked in vain, for they will never find the one they have sought. The disillusion of Herod at the end of the play may well be cause for laughter. The play is well organized but makes its points briefly. The nature of Herod and his court is clearly shown but not elaborated. The Wakefield Master has taken this play (together, perhaps, with the Towneley play of the Offering of the Magi, in which Herod is similarly angry but helpless) as a starting point only, developing its general tone and radically changing some of its points (and its staging) to produce a much more powerful, substantial, and authoritative play.

The Wakefield Master moves the *Nuncius*, more clearly a herald than in the York play, to the beginning of his play in order to prepare the way for an absurdly unstable Herod; and he concludes the play, uniquely and in direct contradiction to the York play, by showing Herod's exultation at the success (as he thinks) of the massacre, a point the playwright could have copied from Ludolphus. The plot is not arranged numerologically, although number symbolism contributes to the meaning of the play, first, perhaps, because this is the only one of the Wakefield Master's five plays having an odd number of lines (513) and stanzas (57); the general horror or suspicion of odd numbers—Lucifer reduced the ten orders of angels to nine, as the play of Noah points out—perhaps led the playwright to stop at an uneven point, since his play ends with horror still abroad. The rivalry of the two kings again constitutes the theme, which is made more explicit and fastened onto the matter of the "name" of Jesus, in which there was much current interest. The ludicrous and cruel nature of Herod and his court is again demonstrated but with far more contemporary, proverbial, and biblical resonance than in the York play—and taken to amazing but well-grounded extremes so that the result is both exciting and horrifying. Herod, whom commentators, both medieval and modern, often see either as representing Satan or Antichrist,[19] again dominates the play, this time speaking almost half the lines. His tongue is eloquent indeed but without "wisdom," and he is thus not fit to be king in Jerusalem where, by contrast, "the Lord is our king" (*Isa.* 33.19-21). He gives his name to the play, which in the manuscript is entitled *magnus herodes*, a title unique (among plays), characteristically correct, and ironic. Josephus refers to Herod as "great" to distinguish him from his sons and grandsons, and this Herod has been since late antiquity normally referred to as Herod the Great.[20] Some passages in the play suggest that the Wakefield Master had some knowledge of material derived from Josephus, perhaps that in Peter Comestor's *Historia Scholastica.* Herod's court is fuller than in the York play, and among the Wakefield Master's plays this has the largest cast of speakers, requiring ten. He provides three women, perhaps aware that three, representing the first three mothers of Israel, of whom Rachel was one, normally appear in art.[21] In his quest for symmetry, he has provided three knights to confront them in turn—a number and balance found in none of the other English plays, which provide groupings of two and two, four and four, and two and three. Perhaps the parts of the three women were originally played by the same men who took the parts of the three women in the play of Noah. As at York, Herod has two counselors, whose parts, however, are longer, and who are more accurately related both to other chief priests and scribes of the story (*Matt.* 2.4-6) and to contemporary court practice. He also has a page, who says nothing but who is needed to carry the wine. The holiness of the comedy again licenses the farce, which the Wakefield Master has managed by a logical but original and imaginative contrivance: removing altogether Herod's traditional Scaffold, his usual throne, he has thus left him, in his grandeur and anguish, with nowhere to sit. He therefore has created a play by taking literally the words of *Ecclesiasticus*—"God hath overturned the thrones of proud princes, and hath set up the meek in their stead" (10.17, *destruxit*: "subverted" or "destroyed")—and the many similar passages in the Old and New Testaments, especially the words from the *Magnificat* which are recited in the sequence of Nativity plays in the Towneley collection (Salutation of Elizabeth, ll. 49-78) and sung at York in the Annunciation and Visitation play (l. 240*sd*): "He hath put down the mighty from their seat") (*Luke* 1.52, *deposuit*). The playwright comes very close to making slapstick or furniture jokes out of these expressions. The entire play, which probably took about forty minutes to perform, appears to have been presented in the Place, about which Herod lurches in fits and starts like the wind, confronting the audience with some outrageous threats and offers. As usual, the playwright leaves a number of things deliberately unspoken, trusting his audience to draw the necessary conclusions.

In pointed contrast to the opening of the Second Shepherds' play, the play of Herod the Great begins loudly and boldly. The herald stalks into the Place and, after blessing the audience with a heavily alliterating and blasphemous sentence—"Most myghty Mahowne meng you with myrth," which stands in stark contradiction to many more comforting and familiar greetings, such as "Grace be to you and peace from God our Father" (*Col.* 1.3)—he then proceeds to deliver a proclamation from a scroll. The play-

The York Play of the Slaughter of the Innocents and the Play of Herod the Great

wright's first joke is thus achieved by reverting to an old practice. The oldest English vernacular plays begin in this way. In the English version of the thirteenth-century prologue to a play,[22] the speaker tells the audience to sit still and not "to lette hure game" (1. 8, "hinder our play") and goes on to announce that the Emperor has ordered that anyone who fails to do so will be hanged promptly—except for children and imbeciles, who will be thrashed instead. As ever he hopes to see Mahound, so shall it be. In the Anglo-Norman version of the same prologue, the speaker is more clearly a herald delivering a proclamation. The pretense is always that the audience, allegedly murmuring and milling around, are the subjects of an evil character. This pretense, the circumstantial elaboration of the threat which is normally accompanied by great boasting, as in the play of Herod, and the blasphemous references to Mahound, all become standard features of medieval English plays, although most plays dispense with the herald and thus leave the threat and the boast to the protagonist himself, as in the York play of the Slaughter of the Innocents, the Towneley plays of Pharoah, Caesar Augustus, the Offering of the Magi, the Scourging (ll. 24-27, with four lines borrowed from the Wakefield Master's addition to the Conspiracy, ll. 23-26), the Crucifixion, and the Resurrection, and also the beginnings provided by the Wakefield Master himself to the plays of the Conspiracy and the Dice. Some forty medieval English plays begin in this way.[23] These speeches are usually connected only in the most general way with what follows, as, for example, in the Towneley play of the Offering of the Magi; the speakers only loosely resemble, in their pride and ferocity, the enemies of Christ as described in the Bible; and they are also not particularly recognizable as English aristocrats. They are more like the pagan tyrants of English romances and saints' legends.[24]

The Wakefield Master is interested in sharpening the relevance of these speeches to the plays and to contemporary society while at the same time enlivening the pretense. For example, his herald's offer of Herod's "grith" (1. 4, "protection") to the audience in return for their praise and obedience (and for listening, or at least for speaking only in whispers) is clearly meant to be the act of a medieval monarch[25] or magnate and is the first of a number of detailed satirical comments on members of the first estate which bring the play closer to home than the York play of the Slaughter of the Innocents. The herald presents Herod's writ with some dignity, addressing the degrees of the kingdom in a way parallel to fifteenth-century proclamations: "Henry by the Grace of God Kyng of Englond and of Fraunce, and Lorde of Ireland, to all Archebisshoppes, Bisshoppes, Dukes, Marquesses, Erles, Barons, Knyghts, Squiers, and all other our true and lovyng subjectes of this our Reame of Englond . . . gretyng."[26] More in sorrow and shock than in anger he next makes the main point of the story: Herod is "Selcouthly sory:/ For a boy that is borne herby/ Standys he abast" (ll. 25-27, *Matt.* 2.3). He devotes most of his speech to introducing the theme of the play: it is Herod who is "kyng—by grace of Mahowne—/ Of Iury" (ll. 10-11), and he will not tolerate the thought that this "boy" ("scoundrel") "of Iury mythtyus kyng shal be ay" (l. 220), as one of the counselors later expresses it, paraphrasing *Isaias* 9.17. "A kyng thay hym call, and that we deny," the herald plainly says (l. 28). Herod "stands" abashed or discomfited, and is often so conceived, mockingly, in lyrics: "alas! and welaway,/ for I am shente;/ this chyld he wyll my kyndam hente." The tone is the same at the beginning of the hymn *Hostis Herodes*, sung at Vespers on the Vigil of the Epiphany, according to the York use.[27] Ludolphus, paralleling the thinking of the *Golden Legend* and following the same thought as the *Glossa Ordinaria* (on *Matt.* 2.3), writes authoritatively that Herod is perturbed, "fearing lest he should reign in his stead, and he himself dispossessed as if he were a foreigner."[28] It is because Herod fears for his kingdom and for the legitimacy of his rule that the herald puts such stress on Herod's power and kingship and on the necessity of the audience's allegiance to him. The usual call for order has thus been directly integrated into the plot of the play as well as related to contemporary forms of official proclamations.

The herald unwittingly points to the absurdity of Herod's claims by praising him in inapplicable biblical terms,[29] so much so that one is reminded that Christ himself shall have a messenger "who shall prepare the way" (*Mark* 1.2); this is probably the Wakefield Master's authority for moving the herald to the beginning of the play. The whole speech (ll. 1-72) is framed by perversions of the words of the prophet (*Isa.* 9.6-7, 45.22-25), and, as usual, biblical phrases are intermingled with current everyday or literary language, especially alliterating and proverbial or semi-proverbial phrases, expressing the admixture of the historical Herod, the enemies of Christ, and the contemporary tyrant. When, for example, the herald proclaims that anyone thinking of rebellion, "Be he neuer so bold, byes he that bargan" (l. 21), he is uttering a common phrase that happens to alliterate (*OED* bold a. 3, *MED* bold adj 3) and linking it to an alliterating proverbial expression (Whiting B42).[30] Or "busk to youre beyldyng,/ Youre heedys for to hyde" (ll. 35-36), he suggests with a sneer, now linking an ordinary phrase (*OED* hide v[1] 1 d, *MED* v[5]) with a biblical thought and saying more than he knows, for in the presence of the enemy the Lord "hath hidden me in his tabernacle . . . hath protected me" (*Ps.* 26.5); "beyldyng" might be a fair translation of "tabernacle." Herod is "Kyng of kyngys . . ./ Chefe lord of lordyngys" (ll. 36-37), a clearer parallel to the true King, who is "the Lamb" who "shall overcome them, because he is the Lord of lords and King of kings" (*Apoc.* 17.14; cf. *1 Tim.* 6.15). Again, "Ther watys on his wyngys that bold bost wyll blaw" (l. 39) joins together a blasphemous echo of the comfort provided by the Lord ("I will rejoice under the covert of thy wings," *Ps.* 62.8), half a belittling proverb ("Make great boast and do little," Whiting B417) and a common alliterating phrase (*OED* blow v[1] I 11, *MED* blouen v[1] 7[c]).

The herald next provides an alliterating list of Herod's kingdoms (not forgetting Kemptowne). This list is well-motivated, since it is meant to counter the claims of the new King. It is a jocular and hyperbolic version of the *exordia* of real proclamations and an expansion of the more usual general statements such as those uttered by Herod in the York play of the Slaughter of the Innocents who says he "hase this worlde in welde" (l. 20, "in his power") and in the Towneley play of the Offering of the Magi, where he says, "Lord am I of euery land,/ Of towre and towne, of se and sand" (ll. 7-8). Long alliterating topographical lists also occur earlier; the first appears in the *Castle of Perseverance* (ll. 170-78), and here the claim is true, however re-

grettably, for the World (the speaker) is indeed present everywhere; and insofar as the Wakefield Master's Herod is an
allegorical figure, his claim is also, unfortunately, true, for the
Devil and the enemies of Christ are indeed to be found in all the
places the herald mentions, even Paradise. Herod represents all
the persecutors of Christ, says the *Glossa Ordinaria* (on *Matt.*
2.16). It is probably no coincidence that the herald names seventeen places, since seventeen kings will "fight with the Lamb"
(*Apoc.* 17.3-14).[31]

"He is the worthyest of all barnes that are borne" (l. 55, "most
deserving," "most worshipful"), the herald logically continues—a
direct answer, in which the "He" must be stressed, to the "boy
that is borne herby" (l. 26), an argumentative and desperate claim
brought on by the common understanding that says, "When the
king of heaven is born, the king of the earth is perturbed" (*Glossa
Ordinaria*, on *Matt.* 2.3). In the next line, the herald's statement
that "Fre men ar his thrall" (l. 56) is not only not paradoxical (in
a violent society in which nominally free men might become
bound to a lord) but also a declaration of a method of ruling
directly opposed to that of the King of Heaven, who is born to set
men free rather than, like the Devil, to hold them in thralldom.
This is a common biblical metaphor (*Ps.* 106.14, for example, or
Luke 13.16, *Acts* 7.6) as well as a favorite statement of St.
Bernard, a frequent metaphor in religious poetry, and a thought
that might well be evoked by the sight of the Nativity and the
swaddling clothes. The herald, having initially offered "gracyus"
greetings, now introduces—no doubt speaking sweetly—some
more specific information about Herod's worthiness: he can
"brall" (l. 57), that is, fight without rules, and also "byrkyn many
bonys" (l. 63, "break many bones").

"Downe dyng of youre knees," cries the herald (l. 60, "Fall
down on your knees"), thus pointing to the prophecy of Isaias of
which much of this proclamation—including the three references
to the might and grace of Mahowne (the herald is never so explicit as the York counselor who opines that "Mahounde is God
werraye," l. 35, "true"), the demand for allegiance (l. 15), and the
reference to Herod's far-flung empire—is a perversion: "Be con-
verted to me, and you shall be saved, all ye ends of the earth: for

The York Play of the Slaughter of the Innocents and the Play of Herod the Great

I am God, and there is no other. . . . For every knee shall be bowed to me, and every tongue shall swear. . . . In the Lord are my justices and empire" (*Isa.* 45.22-25). This passage is applied to Jesus by St. Paul, who says that at "the name of Jesus every knee should bow . . . [and] every tongue should confess that the Lord Jesus Christ is in the glory of God the Father" (*Phil.* 2.10-11), and is also directly quoted by him (*Rom.* 14.11). The herald's idea is not only blasphemous but also contrary to the custom of the English, who knelt on only one knee to man, reserving two knees for God.[32] Speedily going into a paroxysm of awe and glee, the herald announces the imminent arrival of his king and, kneeling down, hopes, unsuccessfully, to set an example for the audience as Herod enters the Place accompanied by his entourage.

For a playwright with the Wakefield Master's sense of humor, such an extraordinarily enthusiastic introduction might well mean that the Herod who arrives is remarkably unimpressive and chronically ineffective.[33] He might well also be short in stature; he sometimes appears to be so in art. Herod wears a crown, carries a sword, and is also encumbered with a spear. His sword, as in other such episodes, is perhaps a large property sword (too large for him to wield safely) and is a visualization of the common Old Testament image: the Lord redeems us from the "malicious sword" (*Ps.* 143.10), and the Lord himself wields a mighty sword (*Deut.* 32.41). Herod wears a gown or demi-gown or a doublet (possibly too large for him), and his "wyngys" (l. 39) might refer to its ample hanging sleeves.[34] He is accompanied by his two counselors carrying their books and by a page boy.

Whom has the herald been addressing—that is, whom has he assumed the audience to represent? And, consequently, whom is Herod on his way to visit? The Gospel reports that not only Herod but "all Jerusalem with him" (*Matt.* 2.3) were troubled. The *Golden Legend* explains that the citizens of Jerusalem fear Herod because his reaction to bad news is unpredictable.[35] Their fears are justified in the play, and so are his, the former by his reign of terror, and the latter by the birth of Christ. As the play opens, a potential rebellion is thus being quelled, and the herald is addressing the people of Jerusalem. In his impatience, Herod has impetuously issued forth from his palace to see for himself the state of mind of the citizenry whom he does not trust, as Ludolphus says,[36] and also to meet his knights, half way, in the Place, whom, as in the *Cursor Mundi*,[37] he has previously sent out as spies, or thinks he has, to trace the three kings. He fears the worst and is especially anxious to question them. The knights have thus performed the errand allotted to the messenger in the York play, where, however, it is undertaken as if by chance, and by implication in some of the liturgical plays by Herod's messenger as armed attendant;[38] the Wakefield Master's herald, freed of this task, is available to expand the context of the play.[39]

The herald reports to Herod that the audience still constantly "carp of a kyng" (l. 78) and that loud "romoure is rasyd" (l. 76) of the new King, contrary to Herod's express orders. Herod's motivation is again made clear in this repetition of the player's game. After listening calmly to the herald's report, Herod realizes that his first task is to reassert his authority over the populace—easily done, he thinks. His speeches are not merely bombastic, for he is clearly presented as a manic-depressive with bouts of lucidity, a volatility already suggested by the York play and found, in little, in the Towneley play of the Offering of the Magi. His diction and prosody follow his changing moods. His violent anger is punctuated by moments of politeness, self-doubt, self-satisfaction, deep despair, sarcasm, and action; the stanzaic form carries his meaning—his bobs and his last lines are both usually very strong. This is no mere part to tear a cat in. Once ₒettled down, he is at once set off into a rage again; a sense of timing in his delivery is needed so that the ludicrous nature of his rages (here he goes again) will be apparent.

He turns on the audience in fury, and for six stanzas (ll. 82-135) abuses them, once or twice quietening down to appeal to their sense of pity. In language far more coarse and savage than his more formal herald's he calls for silence simply by threatening to butcher them. He will break their bones, skin them, and inflict other tortures (unmentioned because in his fury he cannot, like King Lear, pause to think of them). He has the authority to do so, he claims, since all might is in him and in him stand life and death, a claim common to pagan tyrants in romances and saints' lives, including the Second Nun's Tale.[40] The threat of skinning also occurs in the Towneley play of the Offering of the Magi (l. 61). Herod concludes by threatening to cut the members of the audience up into stewing meat if they so much as move. This outburst is well-designed. The playwright presents Herod in such a way as to make the massacre, or the butchering to pieces of the innocents, *trucidatio*, as Ludolphus and others call it, a logical result of his state of mind. Further, while capital punishment aggravated by torture was common in the late Middle Ages, the authority or source for these two stanzas (ll. 82-99) is a prophetic passage from the Old Testament. Herod is behaving precisely like the perverse rulers of Jerusalem "that hate good, and love evil: that violently pluck off their skins from them, and their flesh from their bones. . . . Who have eaten the flesh of my people, and have flayed their skin from off them: and have broken, and chopped their bones as for the kettle, and as flesh in the midst of the pot" (*Mich.* 3.2-3: *qui odio habetis bonum, et diligitis malum; qui violenter tollitis pelles eorum desuper eos, et carnem eorum desuper ossibus eorum? qui comederunt carnem populi mei, et pellem eorum desuper excoriaverunt, et ossa eorum confregerunt, et conciderunt sicut in lebete, et quasi carnem in medio ollae*), a description possibly joined in the playwright's mind with the prophetic parable of the boiling pot (*Ezech.* 24). More generally, wicked princes, the enemies of Christ, for whom the innocents stand, are often compared to savage animals in the Old Testament and several times are said to devour and eat the faithful (*Jer.* 50.7, *Ps.* 13.4, 26.2); they "eat up my people as they eat bread" (*Ps.* 52.5). "They have opened their mouths against me, as a lion ravening and roaring"—a passage from a Passion psalm (21.14)—is specifically referred to Herod (Herod Antipas) by the commentators.[41] The Sanhedrin also "gnashed their teeth" at St. Stephen (*Acts* 7.54: *stridebant dentibus*), who had been preaching freedom from oppression. At the same time, Herod is also again ridiculously imitating the Lord who promised to "break into pieces" the unfaithful and the enemies of the faithful (*Ezech.* 5.11: *confringam*; 25.7: *conteram*). Again, Herod's threat to "clefe/ You small as flesh to pott" (ll. 98-99) is also a proverbial expres-

Chapter V

sion not rare to tyrants (Whiting F270, Tilley F361)—and which, it is perhaps appropriate to add, has found its way, possibly from some late medieval play, into the English folk play, in which "flesh" (to the confusion of folklorists) has by oral transmission become "flies"; thus the protagonist is given such lines as "I'll cut him. I'll slash him as small as flies/ And send him to the cookshop. . . ."[42] The Wakefield Master is the first to use this expression in a play, and he does so because it blends with the biblical image of devouring. When Herod cries, "Peasse, both yong and old, at my bydyng" (l. 91), only to follow this injunction with this gruesome threat, he is implicitly answered by Jesus, who said, "My Peace I give unto you; not as the world giveth do I give unto you. Let not your heart be troubled, nor let it be afraid" (*John* 14.27).

Herod quietens down to explain his plight. No longer certain of himself, he is both terrified and angry that the new king will seize his crown. "My myrthes ar turned to teyn" (l. 100, "sorrow"), he says, desperately inverting the words of the Lord, "I will turn their mourning into joy" (*Jer.* 31.13), spoken immediately before the prophecy fulfilled by the massacre (*Matt.* 2.17-18, *Jer.* 31.15). Hovering in uncertainty, he fears the worst and is both frightened and angry. With his "you's" and "ye's" (ll. 83, 89-90, 95, 97-99, 122, 129) he seems to be rushing to and fro, addressing different sections of the audience before whom he pulls up short and waves his sword and spear, his boiling rage frustrated. One unfortunate player, playing the part of the Devil in a play at Tamworth, Staffordshire, in 1536, accidentally smote on the shins with an iron chain a member of the audience, the High Steward of the town; he "myght have stoude forther owt of my way," the young player complained.[43] The player taking the part of the Wakefield Master's Herod was probably better coached in whirlwindery. By his actions, he is here meant to be a ludicrous version of the "whirlwind of the Lord's indignation," a common Old Testament expression (*Jer.* 23.19, for example); the playing of this image might also have found support in the *Golden Legend*, which says on the authority of St. John Chrysostom that Herod was troubled "in suche wyse. As the bowes of the tree that ben hye ben soone moued with the wynde, soo they that ben in

The York Play of the Slaughter of the Innocents and the Play of Herod the Great

hye estate of the worlde a light renome troubleth them" ("light renome" means "low reputation" or "slighted renown").[44] The same simile (probably from the same source, although the expression is proverbial, Whiting W336) is mentioned in the Proclamation of the N-town plays where Herod is said to be "as wroth as wynde" (l. 217) and in the introduction by the Poet to the Digby play of the Killing of the Children (l. 45); but in these plays the image is not so fully turned into action. Characteristically, the Wakefield Master's method allows the image to be shown rather than spoken. It is resumed when Herod rushes about to express his anger at his knights and counselors, and, at the end of the play in a reprise, when he refers with some satisfaction to this ability to lunge unpredictably here and there.

Herod's standing is indeed being questioned—a point repeatedly made in the play. He turns to his knights to find out if the three kings have failed to return. He fears that his "sleght" (l. 121, "trick") has not worked. His words to the kings, "when you have found him, bring me word, that I too may go and worship him" (*Matt.* 2.8), were commonly (and naturally) interpreted as devious—for example, in the *Golden Legend*[45] and by Ludolphus.[46] Informed by their leader, the first knight, that the kings have, as he feared, gone "Anothere way" (l. 147, from *Matt.* 2.12), Herod, after a quiet and perhaps pitiful half line, goes on the rampage again, this time attacking his own knights: "Why, and ar thay past me by?" he says queruously, and then cries, "We! outt! for teyn I brast" (l. 148, "for pain I burst"). "Wher may I byde?" (l. 150), he expostulates. From the beginning, the playwright has imagined Herod as deprived of his throne and arranged the plot, which has had Herod leave his customary throne behind him, accordingly. He is helpless without this support. In most plays it is clear from direct references to it or from the coming and going of others to and from the tyrant that he is seated on his throne. In the Towneley play of Caesar Augustus, for example, Caesar is "Syttyng" on a throne on a Scaffold (Innocents, ll. 153-56), and at Chester Herod is "a comly kynge sittinge on hye" (l. 73); in the York play of the the Slaughter of the Innocents and the Towneley play of the Offering of the Magi, the arrival and departure of the other players imply that Herod remains in one

Chapter V

place throughout the play, and the analogues in other plays and in art show that he is seated. "Many tyrants have sat upon the throne" (*Ecclus.* 11.5), and Herod is normally one of them. In the play of Herod the Great, however, such references are conspicuous by their absence and such inferences impossible to draw, their place being taken by a number of allusions to Herod's failure to sit down or to stay put in one spot.[47] His "Where may I byde?" (l. 150) thus means both that he suffers from the fear of exile Ludolphus imputes to him[48] and also that he has nowhere to sit down—the latter meaning being the more immediate. As he, cast loose from his moorings, foolishly rushes about in the Place, his sycophantic entourage must keep up with him; his two counselors trot after him, precariously carrying their books; the page follows, bearing a goblet and jug of wine. As this impossible group twists and turns in circles, the opportunities for farcical action are abundant.

It is now that Herod becomes "exceedingly angry" (*Matt.* 2.16), and the playwright has found a way to demonstrate this, even in the face of the extremity of anger already manifested by him, by increasing his references to his health and instability. He rushes about cursing his incompetent knights. He "gnashes" his teeth at them, like the savage enemies of Christ (*Lam.* 2.16, *Ps.* 34.16, 36.12, *Acts* 7.54). He beats them, presumably with the flat of his sword "on the hinder parts," again farcically copying the indignation of the Lord (*Ps.* 77.66). At the same time, he feels extremely unwell and stops to stagger a little; his heart is giving way, as Isaias predicted (13.6-7), and God is making him "stagger like men that are drunk" (*Job* 12.25). "I wote not where I may sytt for anger and for teyn" (l. 172, "pain"), he cries. He is a sick man. His physical ailments appear to be the result of his rage, hypocrisy, and despair—a not uncommon assumption.[49] He says, "within I fare as fyre" (l. 101), as he bursts open. He pants and has difficulty breathing. He suffers from the pains of the wicked described at length in *Job*, chapter 20, probably in part the source of much of Herod's language here ("he shall burn," *Job* 20.22); and as he cries, "My guttys will outt thryng/ Bot I this lad hyng" (ll. 240-41), he perhaps fears the Lord, who is not beyond striking him with hemorrhoids, as he struck the Philistines (*1 Kings* 5.9).

These and similar punishments afflicted on God's enemies (e.g., *Deut.* 28.27-28) closely correspond to Herod's ailments, which, however, more closely resemble the historical Herod's sicknesses as described by Josephus. Towards the end of his life, when he ordered the massacre of the innocents, Herod, mentally and physically diseased, was subject to violent changes of mood. Josephus writes:

> But Herod's illness became more and more acute, for God was inflicting just punishment upon him for his lawless deeds. The fever that he had was a light one and did not so much indicate symptoms of inflammation to the touch as it produced internal damage. He also had a terrible desire to scratch himself because of this, for it was impossible not to seek relief. There was also an ulceration of the bowels and intestinal pains that were particularly terrible, and a moist, transparent suppuration of the feet. And he suffered similarly from an abdominal ailment, as well as from a gangrene of his privy parts that produced worms. His breathing was marked by extreme tension, and it was very unpleasant because of the disagreeable exhalation of his breath and his constant gasping. He also had convulsions in every limb that took on unendurable severity.[50]

Josephus also describes from time to time Herod's mental condition: "Herod's whole life became unbearable to him, so greatly was he disturbed, and because he trusted no one, he was greatly tormented by his anxiety. . . . He took on the appearance of suffering from madness and from foolishness as well."[51]

The text strongly suggests that in his first scene with his knights, once his fear has become a certainty, Herod alternately rages and collapses. In a roof boss in Norwich Cathedral (1509), he is shown as not only raging but also being held up or restrained by two assistants;[52] and at the foot of the fourteenth- or fifteenth-century font in All Saints, Aston (some twenty miles south of Wakefield), a small Herod has collapsed under the effort of wielding his sword and has twisted his shoulder in his convulsions (fig. 21). The effete but vindictive Absolon was perhaps not so badly cast to play Herod "upon a scaffold hye."[53] Herod is

Chapter V

well compared, by Sir John Paston's correspondent, to the Earl of
Suffolk, who in 1478 first ate a good dinner and then, proceeding
to pass judgment on Sir John, seized some of his lands, threatened
him in his absence (like the York Herod) with his spear, required
his heart's blood, and all the while "so feble for sekenes that hys
legges wold not bere hyme, but ther was ij men had gret payn to
kepe hym on hys fete. And ther ye were juged." Sir John's correspondent prefaces his narrative with the remark that "ther was
neuer no man that playd Herrod in Corpus Crysty play better and
more agreable to hys pageaunt then he dud."[54]

Recovering some of his dignity, Herod dismisses his knights,
who have put up a rather feeble defense; one of them, establishing his priority and allegiance, secures a vague promise of
"fauoure" (l. 192), the first of several. Herod now turns to consult
in secret "the chief priests and the scribes" (*Matt.* 2.4) or, as the
playwright has it, his "preuey counsell," (l. 196), a term probably
used in its modern sense of "Privy Council" (*MED* prive counseil
n [c]) since matters deeply affecting his royalty are at stake. He
politely asks his own counselors to look in their secular rather
than religious books for information about the Virgin and the new
King which "Oone" has privately told him about, thus calling "evil
good, and good evil" (*Isa.* 5.20). The "one" was probably meant to
be understood to be a spy reporting Simeon's words, of which
Herod was commonly assumed to have heard.[55] Disobeying his
instructions, they find Isaias' prophecy (7.14). At this second
piece of bad news Herod makes the important decision to take a
drink—thus further fulfilling the prophecy ("Woe to you that are
mighty to drink wine," *Isa.* 5.22)—and then reacts much as he has
done to the news the knights have given him—with a mixture of
insults, violent anger, and palpitations. As he cries, using a common fifteenth- and early sixteenth-century term for a "blockhead"
(*OED* Doddypol a), "Fy, dottypols, with youre bookys—/ Go kast
thaym in the brooks!" (ll. 231-32), it would be appropriate for
him to heave one or two of the heavy tomes at them, just as he
has thrown a few stones at his knights—or been about to do so. He
had thrown books and swords in liturgical plays.[56] He raves
helplessly, jerkily, and confusedly. He is furious at the cunning
and hypocrisy, as he sees it, of the deceptive base-born one who

comes like a holy man to rob him of his rights—an hypocrisy more appropriately attributed to Herod himself by the commentators quoted by Ludolphus, who follows the *Glossa Ordinaria* (on *Matt.* 2.8): again Herod promised devotion (*Matt.* 2.8), but sharpened his sword and portrayed the malice in his heart as humility.[57]

His counselors, like the York counselors and for the same reasons, are only too anxious to please him; they tell him it is easy enough to kill a one-year old. The playwright has thus adhered to the story (*Matt.* 2.4-6) by making Herod's counselors give him honest information, turned them into an English institution by calling them a Privy Council, and kept the sycophantic cruelty found in the York play. Since Herod is hardly capable of thought any longer, the first counselor assures him that the child shall "dy on a spere" (l. 252), and the two counselors confer sagely and in silence while Herod waits impatiently, either fidgeting, standing on one leg and now on the other, holding his stomach, or collapsed on the ground. The second counselor, delivering the plan, advises Herod to order his knights to kill all the boys two years old and younger within and around Bethlehem (*Matt.* 2.16). Since Herod has already said that the child is only one year old, the two years of the Gospel is here introduced as a prudent margin of safety. Prophecies of Christ's Passion which refer to evil counsels which will come to naught are echoed (such as *Ps.* 20.12), for the audience knows, even if they have not seen the previous play in the Towneley collection—the Flight into Egypt—that Christ will survive this slaughter. Herod revives on learning of the plan, which he calls a "right nobyll gyn" (l. 261, "stratagem"), and becomes so excited that his heart starts to race again. Always provided that he lives to do so, he will, he says, make the second counselor a pope; for now, he rewards them (worthlessly) with "a drope/ Of my good grace" and also with money, rents, and "powndrys" (ll. 265-67)—that is, the rights to impound (*OED* pound sb[2] I 3). This is the meaning of the term since these gifts are followed by others of castles and grounds and unlimited hunting rights through "all sees and soundys" (l. 269), a common alliterative phrase which means "everywhere" and which is joined here with a contemporary social and economic problem, the practice of emparking (enclosing) land, once leased to such people as Coll and Gib, for the purpose of lordly aggrandizement and hunting (the king transferring hunting rights from himself). This was a problem that afflicted the Wakefield district of the West Riding in the fifteenth century.[58] The enormous wealth and proprietary rights of some members of the first estate led to corruption on the part of the counselors; such corruption is also condemned in prophecies concerning the wickedness of the Israelites: "Woe to you . . . That justify the wicked for gifts" (*Isa.* 5.22-23).

The Wakefield Master has thus turned the Place into a playground for a savage weakling whom he has conceived on the basis of earlier tyrants and Herods but compounded more richly out of prophetic Old Testament passages, some knowledge (it seems) of the historical Herod, commentaries on the story related in the Gospel, and contemporary social conditions and language. He has given a playwright's thought to the simple formula commonly associated with such tyrants—"ffor wo my wytt is all away" (Towneley play of the Offering of the Magi, l. 299)—and produced, with authorization, a fully pathological figure, so ludicrous as to be terrifying yet well within the scope of the plot and meaning of the play. No other Herod throws stones—and no other English Herod throws books, for that matter.

Herod has at his command "All the flowre of knyghthede" (l. 272); in the York play they are "knyghtis kene" (l. 150), and in the Anglo-Scots paraphrase of Ludolphus' *Vita Christi* they are "men of armes bald" ("bold"),[59] all common expressions. When there is no emphasis on the corruption of knighthood, Herod's men are referred to simply as "tormentors," as in the fifteenth-century ballad of St. Stephen and Herod;[60] this word is commonly used for those assisting the pagan tyrants in the English romances and saints' lives, and sometimes for characters in the plays (now lost), including the Coventry play of the Passion and an early fourteenth-century "clerks' play."[61] The York play joins the concepts of tormenting or torturing and of knighthood, and the Wakefield Master thinks through this matter and produces as a result full and vicious satire.

The duties of the members of the great first estate of knighthood are to protect the poor, punish evil-doers, and preserve freedom, but knights are frequently said in late medieval English sermons to be decadent, lazy, fond of elegant golden armor, and, given to swearing and boasting of imaginary exploits, of roaming the country where they discourteously ravish the poor and victimize the innocent.[62] They are compared to the knights who crucified Christ and who, on the evidence of messianic passages, are often depicted as both empty-headed and animal-like; they are "senseless and foolish" (*Jer.* 10.8). They are thus often depicted in art as ugly. They may have large "Jewish" noses; they may equally well have large curved mouths and pronouncedly snub noses (fig. 22) like dogs and share the animal-like face of Chaucer's Miller, a coarse and gratuitously brutal person:

> Upon the cop right of his nose he hade
> A werte, and theron stood a toft of herys,
> Reed as the brustles of a sowes erys;
> His nosethirles blake were and wyde.
> A swerd and bokelar bar he by his syde.
> His mouth as greet was as a greet forneys.
> (*Canterbury Tales* I.554-59)

Such a face belongs to one of the knights, who has a snub nose and heavy cheeks, in a glass painting of the Slaughter of the Innocents, about 1350, at York Minster,[63] and such faces, which are probably at least sometimes literal versions of the Old Testament "dogs" (*Ps.* 21.17), are not uncommon in art.[64] In the play of Herod the Great two of the knights have noses worth mentioning. Perhaps they wear false noses. In later plays the wicked often sport great and ugly noses, and it is generally assumed that for this purpose the players wore masks.[65]

The herald, having been dispatched by Herod to fetch them (with a half-promise of place and favor), tells the knights to put on their "armowre full bright" (ll. 280, 292) and their "best aray" (l. 281), the "gret araie" of which, according to the critics, they are obsessively proud.[66] The art of the armorer developed during the late fourteenth century, when plate armor replaced chain mail, and throughout the fifteenth century.[67] The knights in the play, who also wear hoods and tabards—short surcoats open at the sides, short-sleeved, emblazoned with armorial bearings, and worn over plate armor on the torso (*OED* tabard 2)—are rather surprised to learn that they are required to engage in some fighting, and their first concern seems to be that their armor will be dented or lose its sheen. "What, in our best aray?" (l. 287) the first knight exclaims incredulously in response to the herald. They appear to be fashionably and brightly armored already and to feel that they ought perhaps to take their best armor off before entering any "fray" (l. 282). Their surprise and confusion form a contrast, probably deliberate, to the business-like and elaborate armoring of knights idealized in romances.

Preceded by the herald, who greets Herod with the epithet otherwise reserved by the playwright for God, "all-weldand" (l. 291), the first knight greets Herod in chivalric and romance terms, "Hayll, dughtyest of all" (l. 294), a reputation already claimed by Herod and already shown by his behavior to be very far from deserved. Herod's wits having temporarily settled, he gives the three knights their instructions, explaining his cause: his gall-bladder will burst unless he takes vengeance on the scoundrel who "shuld be kyng ryall" (ll. 300-03). He is repeating himself so that the point will be clear: he will pay handsomely, if vaguely, for vengeance. The chivalric ideal of "largesse" or prodigal generosity is perverted by Herod throughout the play not only into bribery but also into bribes promised and then withheld, just as the code of fair fighting, good manners, and courtesy is about to be broken by the knights.[68] Herod warns them of the ferocity of women. They very briefly confer (like the counselors) over the question of leadership, and the first appears to establish his preeminence by repeating his simple trick of being quickest off the mark to respond loyally to Herod. He promises that they will make a doleful "lake" (l. 322). He is probably responding to Herod's instructions, "Spare no kyns bloode,/ Lett all ryn on floode" (ll. 312-13), and is promising a river or lake (*OED* lake sb[3] and sb[4], *MED* lak[e] n[1] 2) of blood, as Herod's later satisfaction at the "flode" (l. 471) of blood indicates. The first knight might also be promising a grievous fight (*OED* lake sb[2] 2) or introducing the idea of sporting with Christ (and, here, his representatives) which runs through the plays of the Passion (*OED* lake

The York Play of the Slaughter of the Innocents and the Play of Herod the Great

sb[2] 1). Successful vengeance, says Herod, possibly unctuously, will find him "freyndly" (l. 324)—that is, he is again vaguely offering a reward and also again usurping the attributes of friendship commonly said in these plays to belong to God.

In a different part of the Place, meant to be in or near Bethlehem, and referred to both as a "strete" (l. 482) and a "flat" (l. 489, "plain"), the third knight threatens to "reyll" (l. 326, "run riot"), no doubt having modeled his behavior as a knight after his king's. The first, as the leader, rather fearfully notices three women approaching and confronts the first of them while the second and third knights lounge at their ease. Each knight in turn faces one of the women and kills her boy (apparently with a spear, l. 252), then seizing him from her breast, according to Ludolphus[69] and earlier authorities; each woman in turn puts up a defense and laments, crying out for vengeance and weeping over the bloody bodies of the children in terms which recall Mary's lamentation at the Crucifixion, thus making clear, by implication, that their sons have been killed for Christ. In the York glass paintings, mothers hold their infants to their breasts, and soldiers impale others on spears (one while his mother is still holding him); in a panel of painted glass in St. Peter Mancroft, Norwich, the infants are killed with swords, and one of the mothers seizes a knight by the neck.[70]

The three murders have been thought through with care, and they differ from each other. The first knight is sarcastic. The woman tries to flee, threatens to call for help and to punch him on the nose, and then attacks him by tearing or pulling at his hood. He then kills her child, and she laments. The second knight is more direct. The woman scratches at his head, begs for mercy, and tears at his tabard before he kills her child, and she laments, rightly calling him "No man!" (l. 356)—in opposition to Herod's perverse promise to make "men" of the knights. The third knight, well-schooled in torture, puts on a kind and gentle tone of voice (a perverse version of the chivalric "franchyse" or freedom and naturalness in manner) and coaxes the third woman to approach him; she does so, obediently but fearfully, whereupon he immediately kills her child; she punctuates her subsequent lament by striking out at him and hitting him on the "groyn" (l. 382, "snout"). At the conclusion of the first two bouts, the unengaged knights languidly applaud what they have just seen or studied with a professional eye. "Well done," says the second (l. 347), and "This is well-wroght gere," says the third (l. 370, "business"). This is churlish sarcasm, not the game later played by the Vice in the interludes. At the conclusion of the third episode the first knight threatens the three women so that they flee and then remarks to his two colleagues with some satisfaction that they have successfully routed them. To his credit and, as in the York play, the Wakefield Master has not prolonged this section of his play. The lamentations are loud and forceful but brief. (The one stanza he added to the play of the Crucifixion is for St. John, to help interrupt the Virgin Mary's lengthy grieving, ll. 373-81). The struggles, although accompanied by insulting words on both sides, are deadly serious and especially noticeable for the helplessness of fingernails against gleaming armor, an image similar to the image common in paintings and carvings of the Crucifixion in which a very thin and nearly naked Christ is no match for his fleshy and muscular opponents. The women squall and scratch helplessly, and lesser (and later) playwrights seized the opportunity to turn what at York, and even more so in the Towneley collection, is calculatedly horrifying into farce so that the effect is more like the domestic squabbles shown on misericords, one of which, in St. Mary's Church, Whalley, Lincolnshire, from the early fifteenth-century shows a warrior, his weapons abandoned, kneeling before a woman who beats him with a frying pan.[71]

The knights immediately start arguing, mainly because the first knight, insisting on his superiority, breaks for the second and last time the otherwise entirely numerical sequence of their speeches throughout the play to do so (ll. 191, 413). The second pretends to agree with him but in a comic aside to the audience immediately disagrees. They return to Herod, the first bringing him good news, gruesomely echoing the angel's words to the shepherds (*Luke* 2.10): "Full glad may ye be;/ Good tythyng we bryng" (ll. 416-17). They report the success of their expedition (hardly the testing and far-flung adventure required by the code of chivalry), and the third is mercenary enough to ask for his reward. As he has previously rewarded his counselors, Herod,

The York Play of the Slaughter of the Innocents and the Play of Herod the Great

now content, rewards his knights; he is again a fifteenth-century magnate paying off his followers, and he is also rather like the patron of a tournament to which the presence and words of the herald—heralds conducted tournaments—lend color, since Herod announces that each knight has won a lady. The gift is more lecherous than chivalric, however, and thus suitable for a follower of Mahounde.[72] Their reactions are greedy (they ask for more), skeptical, and pointedly worldly; the third goes so far as to say that their possessions now will never be exhausted, but it is, of course, God's protection which is everlasting (*Ps.* 9.8), not man's. They worship Herod with three "Hails" (ll. 455-56) and depart with his blessing, "Now Mahowne he you bryng/ Where he is lord freyndly" (ll. 458-59), a blessing only too appropriate to this court, for he is unwittingly sending them to hell.

After this full, relevant, and satirical association of Herod the Great's men with the small private armies of fifteenth-century Yorkshire, one of the most turbulent areas in the kingdom,[73] the knights leave the Place. Herod remains with his counselors, herald, and page. His concluding speech to the audience, which, like his first speech to them, consists of six stanzas (ll. 460-513), is a reprise and development of the main points of the play. He begins with what is probably a reference to the small practical difficulty that has beset him ever since his impatience led him to leave his palace—allowing for a quibble on the word "stand": "Now in peasse may I stand" (l. 460). At the end of his speech he reminds the audience that he might begin with no advance notice, as if it is his unalterable nature, "to rokyn" (l. 508), that is, to rush to and fro, shaking with rage, as they have seen him do in the first part of the play—firm evidence that he has no throne. You know me, he says. He is calm now and (the playwright inventing yet another—and novel—role for the audience) invites the members of the audience to draw near while, outrageously expanding his usual *modus operandi*, he offers them enormous bribes, only to postpone the bribes until he comes again and even then leaving the delivery of this corrupt largesse in some doubt. Like the shepherds' food, this is a foolish but tempting version of God's invisible but certain bounty. His heart is finally at ease now that he has shed so much blood, and he proclaims peace throughout his kingdom. The sight of the overflowing blood so pleases him that he gives off a great laugh, which, however, turns into a coughing fit, a reminder that his internal organs are diseased. "So light is my saull/ That all of sugar is my gall" (ll. 474-75), he says—a typical expression, being half-proverbial (there is no such proverb, but "gall" and "honey" form several) and half-messianic, identifying "bitter" as "sweet" (*Isa.* 5.20). He sets the number of dead bodies at 144,000. This king and his kingdom could not more clearly be of this world, and at the same time indicate, by contrast, the existence of a calmer king who is indeed majestic (and in constant good health); who will shed his own blood, not that of others; who will in reality come again; and in whose stable kingdom, held together by love rather than bribes, all, including those who have just been slain ("an hundred and forty-four thousand . . . of every tribe of the children of Israel," *Apoc.* 7.4), will find true "peace."

Unlike the York Herod (and the Herods in the other English plays which include the Massacre of the Innocents) our hero is now convinced that he has achieved his purpose and defeated him whom he most feared—or is now at least sufficiently convinced that he is free of care:

> And els wonder ware—and so many strayd   *were strewn*
> In the strete—
> That oone shuld be harmeles,
> And skape away hafles. . . .   *helpless*
> (ll. 481-84)

The thought is paraphrased from Ludolphus, who writes that Herod "putabat enim quod si omnes pueri occiderentur, unum, quem quaerebat, evadere non posset."[74] Ludolphus immediately adds the thought (from *Prov.* 21.30), which the playwright feels he has made so clear by implication that he can leave unspoken, that Herod did not know, unhappy man, that "non est consilia, non est sapientia, non est prudentia contra Dominum." There is irony in Herod's "els wonder ware," for "wonder" is a strong pun, meaning both "surprise" and "miracle" (*OED,* wonder sb I 1, 2).

The York Play of the Slaughter of the Innocents and the Play of Herod the Great

The unexpected, of course, has in fact already occurred by divine intervention, the angel having told Joseph to flee with Mary and Jesus, as members of the audience (or most of them) well know. Like all worldlings, Herod is thus a fool, and he is foolish enough in his triumph to clarify what has been his aim throughout. The traditional ranting has already been sharpened in this play. The boasting is more clearly motivated than usual since the possibility of a rival king makes it all the more necessary for Herod to insist on his own powers and rights as monarch. The general call for order also is further narrowed and given more point. The alleged murmuring of the audience is not (as usual) mere unspecified chatter but specifically consists of rumors about this rival king. Herod now becomes even more explicit: reminding the audience of his abilities as a butcher, he tells them that "No sufferan you sauys" (l. 499, "no sovereign saves you"), words which, of course, ring hollow to the Christian audience. His last words are: "Bot adew!—to the devyll!/ I can no more Franch." If he knew more French, even a little, he would know that "adieu—to the devil" is a self-contradictory expression, mammothly, in four little words, revealing him to be the enemy of all present. His own tongue is his foe (Whiting T376) as it has been throughout the play. His sparse French (ll. 171, 273) may also reveal some social pretensions (although why such a savage should bother is not clear) and perhaps also his alien nature.[75] He rushes off, laughing and stumbling like an idiot.

The playwright provides the audience with some repeated clues and some explicit hints and leaves them to draw their own conclusions. Perhaps the predominant unstated subject of the play is the Name of Jesus. In the York Slaughter of the Innocents, when the messenger reports that the three Magi have given presents to "that frely foode," Herod responds by groaning in despair (ll. 110-14); when the messenger further reports that they "called his name Jesus" (*Matt.* 1.25), Herod promptly calls him a liar (ll. 118-19). In the play in the Towneley collection Herod cannot bear the thought of Jesus being named or even existing. This is the concern of the proclamation with which the play begins, of Herod's initial frenzies—"My name spryngys far and nere"

Chapter V

(l. 109), and "Trow ye a kyng as I will suffre thaym to neuen" (l. 129, "to name")—and of his warnings: "No kyng ye on call/ Bot on Herode the ryall" (ll. 501-02). He cannot bring himself to name Jesus, or even, as the play concludes, to utter the word "name," for which he substitutes the pronoun "it": "For if I here it spokyn when I com agayn,/ Youre branys bese brokyn" (ll. 505-06). Bede and Isidore, followed by Ludolphus, explain that Herod's aim is not only to kill Jesus but to "expunge his name from the earth" (Bede, *In Matthaei Evangelium Expositio*, 2: "Herodes vero significat odium Judaeorum, qui nomen Christi delere et credentes in eum perdere cupiebant"; Isidore, *Allegoriae quaedam sacrae scripturae*, 143: "Herodes, qui infantibus necem intulit . . . diaboli formam expressit, vel gentium . . . cupientes exstinguere nomen Christi de mundo"). The playwright takes an ordinary phrase, *nomen Christi delere*, and makes Herod's mania depend on his neurotic obsession with what appears to be a technical detail, the name of his enemy. To the members of the audience, however, Herod's obsession is entirely understandable, for it corresponds to the increasing fifteenth-century interest in devotion to the Name of Jesus. The Name, particularly the "Sweet" Name, acquired in devotional literature sanctity and spiritual efficacy. As early as the twelfth century the hymn *Dulcis Jesu memoria* was perhaps composed by Cistercians in Yorkshire, and the Name of Jesus is central in the fourteenth century to the devotion and propaganda of the Yorkshire mystic Richard Rolle. Poems by Rolle, his followers, and others glorify the name "Jesus," often beginning each stanza with the holy name. The movement, which had an active as well as a contemplative following, was strong and in the fourteenth century led to the establishment of a votive Mass of the Holy Name that grew in popularity in the fifteenth century. At Durham, this Mass was sung every Friday before a special "Jesus altar." Eventually as a result of this widespread movement the Convocation of Canterbury established the Feast of the Name of Jesus (7 August) in 1488, and the Convocation of York took the same step in 1489, following the wishes of the Archbishop of York, Thomas Rotherham, who in his will would also provide for the establishment of a college in honor of the Name of Jesus, in Rotherham, south of

Wakefield.[76] Since the recitation of the name "Jesus" was felt to be so spiritually efficacious, threatening the audience for mentioning it—or for "calling" on this unmentionable name—lends a further and special point to Herod's relationship to the members of the audience, who can, as a result, pay even more devout attention to the Name of Jesus, even though it has not once been spoken in the play.[77]

The Wakefield Master also trusts his audience to conclude for themselves that Herod has failed—a failure evident not only from their general knowledge but also by showing Herod reaching the opposite conclusion. What is explicitly stated in the York play (ll. 231-33) is here obliquely shown. One cannot devise successful stratagems against the Lord or "make his beard" ("outwit," Whiting B116), as the third knight crudely suggests of the Magi (see l. 189), since the Lord "has searched out . . . the heart of men: and considered their crafty devices" (*Ecclus.* 42.18). The mighty enemies of Christ are bound to fail, as numerous passages in the Old Testament affirm; with the birth of Christ, the oppressor will be overcome (*Isa.* 9.4-5). Despite Herod's numerous kingdoms, Christ will eventually reign everywhere. Moreover, although he speaks of his own death as almost inconceivable ("Were I dede and rotyn," l. 494, "rotten"), Herod will die the worst kind of death in spite of the skips of joy he gives as the play ends. It was commonly understood on the ultimate authority of the apocryphal gospels that he would suffer punishment for shedding the blood of the children, retributive death also occurring elsewhere in other (and earlier) English religious plays.[78] He unwittingly alludes to his own fate by threatening the three Magi, *in absentia*, with it: "Lucyfere in hell/ Thare bonys shall all totyre" (ll. 141-44, "tear to pieces"); however, Hell has "opened her mouth," and those like Herod, the "high and glorious ones shall go down into it," says the prophet (*Isa.* 5.14). Equally relevant, given the way Herod begins the play, is the Lord's promise that "all they that devour thee, shall be devoured . . . they that waste thee shall be wasted, and all that prey upon thee will I give for a prey" (*Jer.* 30.16). When he gives their number so precisely (a reference unique among English plays) Herod also unwittingly acknowledges that his victims are martyrs. They go straight to heaven, as Ludolphus explains[79] and as the liturgy for Candlemas (2 February) indicates. The ludicrous failure of the mighty and the salvation of the children make this play a comedy, and comedy, in the Wakefield Master's mind, means farce and loud laughter.

Christ's words, "My kingdom is not of this world" (*John* 18.36), are implicitly behind the whole play since it so thoroughly presents the worst features of the first estate in the fifteenth century. The egregiously proud nobleman, his unchivalric knights and evil counselors—and the Seven Deadly Sins in which they freely indulge—are to be understood as standing in contrast to God's kingdom: "The Lord hath prepared his throne in heaven: and his kingdom shall rule over all" (*Ps.* 102.19, also *Luke* 1.31-33). Despite the verbal profundity of the text, especially the constant echoing of prophetic passages from the Old Testament, it is certainly possible that some members of the audience missed this point and relished the play as mainly a satirical version of contemporary government.[80]

The most personal application of the play is probably meant to be found in Herod's repeated insistence on and unsuccessful attempt at revenge (l. 167, a stressed bob, followed in the wheel by a feeble scrambling around on the ground for stones with which to pelt his incompetent knights). "Vengeance is mine," says the Lord (*Rom.* 12.19, referring to *Deut.* 32.35 and a number of Old Testament passages). John Mirk begins his sermon *De Innocentibus* not with his usual "Good men and woymen" but by drawing a parallel between his listeners and the Innocents: "Goddys owne blessed chyldern, that byn comen this day to holy chyrch yn the worschyp of God and the chyldern that weren yslayne for Goddys sake."[81] The people of the West Riding are children of God, and the solution to their sufferings, particularly those who have been victims of the bellicose or grasping lords, is to be left in the hands of the Lord. As the *Glossa Ordinaria* (on *Matt.* 2.16) says, representatives of Herod are still at large in the world (and so the playwright deliberately left him gleefully abroad), and the preachers saw these proud magnates as suffering (like Herod in this play) from the sin of vainglory, a species of devilish pride; in the words of Chaucer's Parson, "Veyneglorie is for to have pompe and delit in his temporeel hynesse, and glorifie hym in this worldly estaat."[82] They must repent and change their ways, or when the time comes the Lord will upset these mighty ones. Just as Herod took vengeance, so vengeance fell on him, Mirk concludes. The small as well as the great are capable of persecuting Christ by neglecting him, or swearing by parts of his body, or failing in the Corporal Acts of Mercy, and so they too can be representatives of Herod or his followers. The whole play is an oblique cry for God's mercy; the devout repetition of the word "Jesus" will help secure it. It is thus spiritual comfort and advice that the playwright provides, and he does so merrily, supplying loud laughter in the process, secure in the Lord's promise.

Chapter VI

The York Play of Christ before Annas and Caiaphas and the Wakefield Master's Play of the Buffeting of Christ

Behold their sitting down, and their rising up, I am their song.—Lamentations 3.63

The only play whose subject is shared by the York Realist and the Wakefield Master is the play of Christ before Annas and Caiaphas or, as it is called in the Towneley manuscript, the *Coliphizacio*, "Buffeting." These are also the only English medieval plays extant (or, apparently, recorded[1]) devoted exclusively to this subject, which is also not very common in English art. There are no extant representations of the Buffeting in the religious art of the West Riding and only two at York, one in painted glass in the choir of York Minster and the other a manuscript illumination in the Bolton Hours (fol. 62).[2] The two plays have, with some exceptions—notably their beginnings and endings—the same general shape and a number of verbal parallels; it is therefore not unlikely that the Wakefield Master knew the York play.[3] If so, he proceeded in his own way, ignoring those effects characteristic of the York Realist's work and seizing the opportunities which allowed him to pursue his own particular interests. From the crowded flow of events in the York play, the Wakefield Master selects a few upon which to concentrate. For example, in the York play Caiaphas, ordering that Jesus' hands be untied, sarcastically and proverbially remarks that "Itt is no burde to bete bestis that are bune" (l. 243, "no fun to beat beasts which are tied

176

up");[4] this metaphor is taken by the Wakefield Master and turned, with biblical authority, into a whole episode, which occurs at the beginning and ending of his play.

He selects from the story of Jesus before the Sanhedrin (*Matt.* 26.57-68, *Mark* 14.53-65, 15.1, *Luke* 22.63-67, *John* 18.13-28) the episodes of the arrival of Jesus, the examination, the consultation, and the buffeting. The power and legal cunning of the enemies of Christ—this time those from the second estate—their ludicrous failure, and his unassailability are stressed; and the play, as usual, is powerful enough to sustain a contemporary social interpretation (the second estate was as fully satirized in fifteenth-century England as the first) and also welcomes personal interpretations by members of the audience. In addition to the Gospels and (it seems) the York play, the sources of the Towneley play include, as usual, various passages from the Old Testament, particularly from the books of *Job, Jeremias, Isaias, Lamentations,* and *Psalms,* which provide many of the expressions that inform the language of his characters and also many of the images that, taken literally, provide much of the evidence of the play. Now that the playwright is dealing with the Passion, the books of *Job* and *Jeremias* particularly come into play since throughout the Middle Ages Job and Jeremias were normally regarded as types of Christ. St. Gregory's became the standard commentary,[5] which shows how Job's sufferings and words foretell the Passion,[6] so much so that Isidore is able to say simply that "Job in his deeds and words expresses the person of the Redeemer."[7] Isidore, like Jerome, says the same of Jeremias.[8] Much in these and other commentaries, as well as much in the *Meditations on the Life of Christ,* is to be found in Ludolphus' *Vita Christi,* which explains a central part of the story in the same way the playwright plots it and is also a guide to the ways in which the audience might be expected to react to the play. By the early sixteenth century, Ludolphus' way of thinking about the Passion had been turned into English by John Fewterer,[9] Confessor General of the Brigittine Monastery of Syon, Middlesex, in his *Myrrour or Glasse of Christes Passion* (1534); much of Fewterer's text is based loosely on Ludolphus' *Vita Christi*[10] and provides some close parallels to what happens in the play. Even though he ignores almost entirely the usual Old Testament types of Jesus' maltreatment (which include Hur spat on and Noah mocked by Ham, for example), there is thus ample reason to suppose that the Wakefield Master looked, in his characteristic way, to the Old Testament for authority even while he also looked with a critical eye at contemporary ecclesiastical lawyers.

His play requires a speaking cast of six—for the four main parts (Caiaphas, Annas, and the two knights), the "cheeky boy," and Jesus, who speaks only four lines. The one Scaffold contains seats or episcopal thrones for Caiaphas and Annas, and the relationship between the Place, which is extensively used, and the Scaffold is particularly significant; the distance between them supports much of the meaning of the play and is also calculated carefully enough to cause the climactic farce. The play consists of 450 lines and must have taken a half hour or more to present.

The play is plotted numerically, the new divisors being 9 and 3.[11] Jesus' part, as in the series of Passion plays at York (although not in the York play of Christ before Annas and Caiaphas), is mostly to suffer in silence. He speaks in the Towneley play only in response to Annas' question, "Say, art thou Godys son of heuen" (l. 249):

> So thou says by thy steuen,
> And right so I am;
> For after this shall thou se when that I do com downe
> In brightnes on he, in clowdys from abone.   *on high above*
>   (ll. 251-54)

Jesus thus begins (counting by lines, not stanzas) the final four ninths of the play. His speech is a paraphrase of *Matthew* 26.64 (and *Dan.* 7.13)—"Thou hast said it. Nevertheless I say to you, hereafter you shall see the Son of man sitting on the right hand of the power of God, and coming in the clouds of heaven"—and recalls the familiar representations of the Last Judgment, which hovers behind the play. The number 9 is appropriate to this moment in the play when Jesus asserts his authority and the authority of the Trinity. The number 4 may have meant many things to the playwright; perhaps he was thinking of the four Gospels, all of which report a buffeting. The narrative poem known as *The Northern Passion*, certainly familiar to the York Realist and perhaps to the Wakefield Master, imagines Jesus replying to the raging Caiaphas "with milde steuyn" (l. 663, "voice");[12] this is probably the tone of voice, quiet but firm, which the player playing Jesus adopts in the play.

The second third of the play concludes with Caiaphas' utter frustration and collapse and his sudden thought that he has knights who dare knock Jesus "on the pate" (l. 300). The final third of the play consists of the Buffeting, to which the rest of the drama has been made to lead. The number 3, of course, also expresses the Trinity, and at the conclusion of the second third of the play Caiaphas and Annas, ceasing their examination of the second person of the Trinity, the Son of Man, have been completely unable to shake him. That "pate" (l. 300), the final word, may have had some significance for the playwright, who later plays with the meaning of "head" and "crown."

For the Buffeting, the Wakefield Master found yet another method (again unique among extant plays) with which to open a play. As the play begins, Caiaphas and Annas are present on the Scaffold, enthroned next to each other in their episcopal seats. In the popular imagination they are contemporary bishops.[13] Throughout the play they speak and behave in a thoroughly medieval manner. Caiaphas refers to himself as a bishop seated in grandeur; his gown has a belt around it, and he wears a large episcopal ring. It would have looked odd had they not also worn mitres and held crosiers (both of which, in the fifteenth century, were much like those still in use). Medieval English bishops were well dressed and accoutered.[14] They might wear four or five rings over their gloves, and Caiaphas' and Annas' gowns are probably dalmatics worn under heavy cloaks with fur collars. Caiaphas, if not Annas, might be fat, like Chaucer's monk, who was "a lord ful fat and in good poynt";[15] *Job* says that the wicked one who has "stretched out his hand against God" is fat—"Fatness hath covered his face, and the fat hangeth down on his sides" (15.25, 27). This passage, which is relevant to what happens later in the play, is, as is to be expected, interpreted by Gregory to mean that Christ's enemies are blinded and swollen by coveting worldly things[16]—a covetousness for which Caiaphas makes no apology; the playwright, thinking of his player and how to dress him up, may well have taken the fatness literally and hence may have had in mind some bulbous padding for him.

The York Realist is content to begin his play with the familiar boastful speech addressed to the audience, this time somewhat ingratiatingly, by Caiaphas. The Wakefield Master, however, has not leaped at the obvious but has thought the matter through. The synoptic Gospels record that his captors "led" (*Matt.* 26.57) Jesus to the house of Caiaphas; *John* adds the detail that "they bound him" (18.12). Following the common understanding expressed in the *Glossa Ordinaria* (on *Isa.* 53.7), both the *Meditations on the Life of Christ* and Ludolphus (and Fewterer) refer at this point to the messianic Old Testament simile: "he shall be led as a sheep to the slaughter, and shall be dumb as a lamb before his shearer, and he shall not open his mouth" (*Isa.* 53.7; cf. *Jer.* 11.19). At the same time, in the words of the *Meditations on the Life of Christ*, they envision Jesus as both "furiously driven" and "dragged."[17] "As mild as a lamb" and "to be led like a lamb to death" are both proverbial expressions (Whiting L32, 42) and render the ferocity gratuitous. Job compares himself to an innocent but ill-treated ox or ass (6.5), and the playwright perhaps has this simile in mind, although it is the passage from *Isaias* which occurs in the liturgy for Holy Week. Asses are proverbially slow and dull (Whiting A218, 223), as are beasts generally (Whiting B125); to be beaten, chased, deprived of rest, and killed like beasts are also proverbial expressions (Whiting B135, 136, 141, and 137).

What the playwright does with the help of the proverbs is to take the Old Testament similes literally; he is also, by sympathetically imagining the effect of the buffeting, able to make the driving and dragging seem to be miserable necessities. As soon as Annas and Caiaphas are seated, two knights, entering the Place, drive Jesus forward. Jogging behind Jesus, they hold a cord or rope to which he is tied. The first clicks his tongue and makes the kind of encouraging noises (the same, "io," used for the plough team in the Towneley play of the Killing of Abel) one would make to an animal to urge it on: "Do io furth, io! and trott on apase!/ To Anna will we go and Syr Cayphas" (ll. 1-2). They thus enact the image, rather than narrating it (by contrast, in the same episode in the N-town Second Passion play, Annas tells Jesus, "as an ox or an hors · we trewly the bowth," l. 105, "bought"). The Johannine rope is here, but the "trot" reveals that it is slack. The animal is mild. The knights notice that his head is bowed down, and they attribute his attitude to exhaustion; the playwright also perhaps thought of him as fulfilling the prophecy: if I am just, "I shall not lift up my head, being filled with affliction and misery" (*Job* 10.15). The knights talk to Jesus while they are on the move, as the text makes clear, and so perhaps they trot in a half-circle around the Place (somewhat as in the N-town play in which, at "A good pas," "*thei ledyn jhesu A-bowt the place · tyl thei come to the halle*" of the high priests, ll. 244, 244*sd*, "pace," "lead") before coming to a halt, exhausted, in front of the two bishops on the Scaffold. If the players fully follow the *Meditations on the Life of Christ* or Ludolphus, they hoot at Jesus and strike him so that he staggers along; his cloak has been removed, his "garments carelessly girded up," and he is "bareheaded and bent with weariness."[18] He thus stands still in anguish and disarray in front of Annas and Caiaphas, who, at the other extreme, are seated, well-fed, and well-dressed.

Dragging is added to driving at the end of the play and is the result of what has happened to Jesus. He is now too beaten to move and can hardly lift his feet. He must be dragged along, and so the first knight says, "Com furth, old trate,/ Belyfe!/ We shall lede the a trott" (ll. 427-29, "trate" meaning "old woman"), his bob ("quickly," "look lively") being especially cruel, and his "a trott" echoing his original "apace" (l. 1). The perverse page, Froward, thinking he knows an easy task when he sees one, adds, "Then nedys me do nott/ Bot com after and dryfe" (ll. 431-32). The savage leading and driving of the devout imagination are thus accounted for and are made the logical outcome of what has happened in the play. The three drag and drive Jesus out of the Place, and, accordingly, when this sad sight reappears in the following play, the Scourging, in a passage written by the Wakefield Master, two are pulling and one driving him. This time, making their way through the audience, they insult and mock him; they now talk of spitting in his face (1. 72, from *Matt.* 26.67 and *Mark* 14.65), an action carefully separated by the playwright from the Buffeting.

In the speech-headings each knight is called *tortor* ("torturer"), but in the text of the play they are consistently referred to as knights. They carry swords and in character and (probably) appearance are close relatives of the knights in the play of Herod the Great. They are ugly in the glass painting (early fifteenth-century) of the Mocking and Buffeting in York Minster.[19] Ludolphus compares them to "ravening wolves,"[20] and the *Meditations on the Life of Christ* to dogs,[21] referring to the Passion psalm (21.17). The playwright probably saw the knights jerking and pushing Jesus as they taunted him. Their language in this first episode is compounded of inapplicable biblical terms, proverbial expressions, self-centered complaints, and accusations taken from the Gospels. In his desire for economy, the playwright gives them the role of the false witnesses of the Gospels (*Matt.* 26.59, *Mark* 14.56), and also puts into their mouths the accusations made by the Sanhedrin in the presence of Pilate (*Luke* 23.2, 5). They call out to him that he will receive not "grace" (so also in the play of the Scourging, where "of vs thre gettys thou no grace," 1. 73, is spoken in obvious ignorance of the Trinity) but "euerlasting wo" (ll. 3-4) from Annas and Caiaphas, as if it were in their power to bestow salvation and damnation. He has caused the people to forsake their laws to follow him and his "lawes new" (1. 20), and has caused a general commotion; these are the concerns of the Sanhedrin, who claim he "stirreth up the people, teaching" (*Luke* 23.5). The second knight shouts after him, "As good that thou had/ Halden still thi clater" (ll. 26-27), an insult whose tone and sense are perhaps borrowed from the *Meditations on the Life of Christ* in which, in the house of Caiaphas, Jesus is "reviled" by soldiers who say, "Do you believe yourself to be better and wiser than our chief priests? What folly! You ought not to open your mouth against them."[22] The first knight adds, "It is better syt still then rise vp and fall" (1. 28), a common proverb (Whiting S355) but one particularly applicable to what is soon to happen in this play. They both, reflecting the commonly alleged laziness of knights, complain of their own exhaustion, oblivious of Jesus.

Christ before Annas and Caiaphas

His captors deposit Jesus at a strategic spot in front of the bishops' Scaffold. The first knight's words—"Haill, syrs, as ye syt, so worthi in wonys" (l. 46, "distinguished among men")—are the first of several which are meant to indicate with certainty that Annas and Caiaphas must be seated. After a series of accusations by the torturers which come largely from the synoptic Gospels (*Matt.* 26.61, *Luke* 23.5) and the gospel of *Nicodemus* (16) and which center on his disturbance of the "law," the comic "examination" (by Caiaphas, ll. 129-80) begins. A note of anxiety is detectable behind the accusations and the officious and legalistic questions of the bishops (an anxiety mentioned in the *Meditations on the Life of Christ*, where Jesus is led along "with anxiety"[23]), but Caiaphas, losing patience with the knights, dismisses the "talkyng" by echoing that word as he begins his six stanzas (ll. 127-28). His questioning of Jesus is a complete failure, since Jesus, in fulfillment of the prophecy (*Isa.* 53.7) and as recorded in the Gospels (*Matt.* 26.62, *Mark* 14.60), says nothing.

Caiaphas makes a fool of himself in his efforts to force Jesus to talk. In the York play, Caiaphas has no sooner begun his examination than he declares that Jesus must have lost his tongue, an observation also made earlier by Annas for no apparent reason since Jesus has not yet been asked any questions or given a chance to speak. These observations are clearly not true in the York play, for Jesus is soon answering Caiaphas' question, posed as in the Gospel (ll. 291-95, from *Matt.* 26.63), and speaking fully, as in *Luke* and *John*, rather than once only as in *Matthew* and *Mark* and the Towneley play. If the Wakefield Master knew of this briefest version of a potentially humorous episode, he set to work to realize its possibilities, perhaps with the knowledge that the York Realist expanded at length on Herod's futile attempt to make Jesus talk in his play of Christ before Herod—and equally likely with the same knowledge as Ludolphus and Fewterer, who writes that "the more that our sauyoure Jesus kepte silence to them that were not worthy his answere: the more Cayphas the bisshop beynge in great furye/ prouoked Christe to answere."[24]

Caiaphas' speech is not rant. He tries a variety of tactics to force Jesus to talk. After each of his first four stanzas (that is, after ll. 135, 144, 153, and 162) he might pause to see what effect,

Chapter VI

if any, his words are having before trying again, stretching all his limited resources. He is at first scathing and indignant, especially about the claim to be King, warns Jesus of the consequences of his deeds, commands him to approach him and whisper in his ear, and says if he fails to do so he will denounce him. Jesus does not move. Caiaphas next tries mocking him, puts on a great show of pretending to be deaf, expands on his threat to denounce him by promising (rather mindlessly, since he is a prisoner) that a hue and cry will be raised after him as if he were a wolf (thus reversing the true situation since it is his enemies who are the wolves), and intensifies his insult from "harlott" (l. 129) to "Vile fature" (l. 140, "impostor," the bob). His increasing frustration is evident by his rather childishly lowering his demand from a whole answer to just "Oone word" (l. 141) as he changes his tone and pretends to have his prisoner's best interests at heart. He warns him of the legal maxim (in the form of a Latin proverb) that silence amounts to an admission of guilt. Still frustrated, he becomes fixated on his need for just one word: "Speke on oone word, right in the dwyllys name!" (l. 145, "devil's"), a demand deliberately couched in a way opposite to that recorded in the Gospels ("I adjure thee by the living God," says Caiaphas, *Matt.* 26.63) and thus certain to produce no response. Angry again, he demolishes, with heavy sarcasm, Jesus' claim to be King and mocks the absence of both the trappings of worldly power and a proper lineage. He calls him a bastard, living by theft. Caiaphas, again changing his approach, tries what pomposity will do. Swollen with worldly honors, he despises the downcast, like Job, who will nevertheless eventually be in glory (*Job* 22.29-30). Caiaphas thus boasts of his dignity and his power as an ecclesiastical lawyer whose illegal income is large, using the same proverb (ll. 161-62) as Chaucer's Friar Huberd (Whiting P438); he enjoys the "profits of priesthood," says Ludolphus.[25] He seems to hint that he will release Jesus in return for some subservience and a bribe. This approach produces no results, and, losing all his patience, Caiaphas wishes him in hell ("Weme! the dwillys durt in thi berd,/ Vyle fals tratur," ll. 170-71) and rushes on to beg desperately for any reply, abasing himself to ask Jesus merely to mumble something. He who was once certain of a confidential

whisper now screeches at Jesus for one word or even just a piece
of a word. He concludes that Jesus is not dumb but either stupid
or deaf. The playwright is putting Psalm 37, related by Fewterer
to the examination by Caiaphas,[26] into action: "they that sought
evils to me spoke vain things, and studied deceits all the day long.
But I, as a deaf man, heard not: and as a dumb man not opening his
mouth" (*Ps.* 37.13-14). When the calumnies of the Jews were of
no avail, they had recourse to the aid of shouts, says Ludolphus,[27]
and at the end of his examination Caiaphas is shouting so loudly
that Annas has to intervene. Like Job (12.4, 21.3, 30.9) and
Jeremias (20.7), Jesus has been mocked, scorned, laughed at, and
called a fool by Caiaphas, who has also in fits and starts worked
himself up into a frenzy and "gnashed with his teeth upon" him
(*Job* 16.10), a verse interpreted with reference to the adversaries
of the Church, while Job's sufferings (16.8-18) are related to this
hour of the Lord's Passion. Caiaphas' questioning has been altogether too "bustus" (l. 213, "violent") to be successful.

After his examination, the chief priests held "a consultation"
(*Mark* 15.1, *Matt.* 27.1), prefigured by *Jeremias* and *Job* 5.12,
about how to put Jesus to death. The playwright needs this consultation now. He takes it and renders it ridiculous by turning it
into a dialogue in which the calm and hypocritically fair-minded
Annas tries to soothe the agitated Caiaphas, who has now become
not only frustrated but also—in accordance with St. John, who
reports that Caiaphas tells the "council" that Jesus must die (*John*
11.49-51)—murderous. Caiaphas' anger is still swelling, and the
first mention of the buffeting comes when he says, "Bot I gif hym
a blaw my hart will brist" (l. 191). His wish to hit Jesus recurs
and is accompanied by threats and demands for the kind of
punishment of which Job and Jeremias complain. I shall thrust
out his eyes, cries Caiaphas, perhaps gesturing with his episcopal
crozier and echoing the King of Babylon (*Jer.* 39.7) and the
Philistines who put out Samson's eyes, one of the standard
"types" of the Mocking.[28] Put him in the stocks, he screams,
echoing one of Job's complaints—"He hath put my feet in the
stocks" (33.11). Annas scarcely succeeds in calming Caiaphas,
although he addresses his particular frustrations. Jesus does not
answer because he knows he is already defeated—and in any case

is not in his right mind, says Annas—and the best way to make him speak is to treat him fairly, according to the law, which is flexible enough to allow them to achieve any results they desire. Threats will not succeed in drawing him out. As for his claim to be King, the law also has a remedy, and Annas will therefore undertake the questioning. Proverbial smoothness will go far (l. 211, Whiting F17), and the old law—and fifteenth-century law—are slippery.

Annas, beginning his examination of Jesus exactly like Caiaphas, tells Jesus to "com nar" (l. 240, "come nearer"), but again, as the text makes clear, Jesus does not move. "Why standys thou so still when men thus accuse the?" (l. 246, "thee"), asks Annas. It is in answer to Annas' direct question ("art thou Godys son of heuen," l. 249) that Jesus speaks. In *Matthew* and *Mark* it is Caiaphas who asks the question—"I adjure thee by the living God that thou tell us whether thou be the Christ the Son of God" (*Matt.* 26.63)—and receives the reply. This detail is kept in the York play (ll. 291-95). Commentators imagine Jesus as now willing to reply "for the reuerence of the name of God."[29] The playwright, having conceived of Caiaphas as a blustering fool (and holding his biggest joke, which is at Caiaphas' expense, in reserve), ignores this arrangement. He is justified by *Luke*, who does not name the questioner (the question is not asked in *John*), and is probably interested in having Jesus respond to Annas, whose legal-mindedness is part of one of the themes of the Passion, which the Wakefield Master seizes on, in other plays; he also does not hesitate to reverse the order of the two examinations: according to *John*, Jesus was first led to Annas for questioning and then sent to Caiaphas. Both the Wakefield Master and the York Realist collapse the appearance before Annas and the appearance before Caiaphas into one appearance, and the York Realist keeps the Johannine order of the examinations, his Caiaphas with characteristic formality deferring to Annas. The Wakefield Master's Caiaphas is the first to speak, pushes himself forward, and does not take turns with Annas or defer to him, as he does in the York play.

Caiaphas has had the lion's share of the speeches, and his passion is much like Herod's obsession. Legal niceties are not enough to satisfy Caiaphas, just as Herod's one regret in the play of Herod the Great was that he himself had no chance to give even a single blow ("bot oone bat," l. 490) to the Christ Child, an idea which certainly links these two plays together. The player who immediately before had taken the part of Herod might easily have been assigned also the part of Caiaphas. They might be ignorant of Christ's mission, but they less excusably both forget two Old Testament injunctions: "Speak not anything rashly," and a "fool multiplieth words" (*Ecclus.* 5.1, 10.14)

Jesus has hardly spoken before Caiaphas interrupts. He is ready for action (ll. 259-60, from *Matt.* 26.65). He is ready to kill him, but Annas continues the "consultation," again urging that they let the law take its course. They must hand Jesus over to the temporal law and send him to Pilate (l. 292, from *Matt.* 27.1-2, *Mark* 15.1), the second estate having no power over life and death in Jerusalem[30] or in fifteenth-century England. Their very rapid exchange (ll. 271-79) suggests that they form the "council of the malignant" (*Ps.* 21.17) who are the enemies of Christ (says the *Glossa Ordinaria* on this passage and the *Meditations*[31]), whose stratagems are bound to fail.

Caiaphas is, of course, not so easily satisfied, and his emotional frustration needs physical expression. His heart feels so cold that he thinks he is dying, and he is suffering from so much stomach gas that his belt is about to break, naturally so, and biblically so, since the choleric prelate is an enemy of Christ, one of those whose hearts are changed and belts loosened by the Lord in his wisdom (*Job* 12.18, 24). Caiaphas has an irresistible need to thump Jesus and to keep on thumping him (ll. 283-84) "For euer," the angry bob.

The playwright now follows Ludolphus, who is following Bede, by making a great deal of play, for which his strategic "blocking" has been a preparation, derived from the simple, almost innocuous passage in *Matthew* (26.62) and *Mark* (14.60), who record that the high priest stood up. Ludolphus,[32] like Bede, gives Caiaphas a motive. He rises up in fury, they say, growing ever more angry. "The movement of his body showed the frenzy of his mind," says Ludolphus.[33] Just so the playwright makes this

movement the physical climax to Caiaphas's red-faced indignation and boiling rage. Ignoring Annas' restraining hand, fat
Caiaphas finally struggles agitatedly out of his throne. Annas
makes one more appeal, and receives only a pompous reply from
Caiaphas. What is often a mere "tag" and conventional expression
of humility ("Myself if I say it," l. 290) is here a clear and ridiculous expression of Caiaphas' self-importance (that pride which,
according to the *Glossa Ordinaria* on *Job* 12.18, has caused the
Lord to loosen his belt):

Anna.	Sir, ye ar a prelate.	
Cayphas.	So may I well seme,	
	Myself if I say it.	
Anna.	Be not to breme!	*violent*
	Sich men of astate shuld no men deme.	
	(ll. 288-92)	

It is too late. Having stood up, Caiaphas leans forward over the
edge of the Scaffold and takes a grand swipe at Jesus—only to
miss him, since he is standing just out of reach. "Say, why
standys he so far?" says the violent Caiaphas (l. 299), now suddenly made to look extremely foolish. The comic anti-climax is
made possible by one of the most imaginative and intelligent uses
of the Place and Scaffold in the whole of medieval drama.

If the "standing up" of the Gospels is filled out with a motivation from Ludolphus, the resulting slapstick farce comes from
Job. In *Job*, the Lord is said to bring "to nought the designs of the
malignant, so that their hands [*manus*] cannot accomplish what
they had begun" (5.12). The synecdoche—"hand" or "hands"—is
very common in the Vulgate; the playwright has taken it literally,
and not without some hint of the opposite, the unerring and
mighty hand and "stretched out arm" (e.g., *Deut.* 7.19) of the
Lord so frequently alluded to in the Old Testament.

A similar effect, impossible to reconstruct from the text but
apparently less pointed, forms part of the business of the play of
the Scourging in which, in the Wakefield Master's addition,
Pilate says to Jesus, "herk, felow, com nere" (l. 112), and then,
"why standys thou so far?" (l. 131).

It is clear that Caiaphas has risen from his throne, since,

tottering at the failure of his physical effort, he must be told to sit down again. Annas, still urging Caiaphas to stay within the law and to remember that he is a prelate, solves the problem of his fellow bishop's irascibility by seizing on Caiaphas' suggestion about the knights and arranging for them to beat Jesus so that his colleague's unquenchable but frustrated urge to keep on thumping him can be satisfied vicariously and the requirements of *Mark* ("the servants struck him with the palms of their hands," 14.65) met. Gregory relates what is happening here to Jesus to *Job* 2.6: "And the Lord said unto Satan: Behold he is in thine hand, but yet save his life." The chief priests are members of Satan's body, and Jesus allows himself to suffer at their hands, like Job, who is constantly smitten. Annas tells the knights to get their "equipment" ready (ll. 319-20), and they promise to do a good job of shaking, knocking, cuffing his head, and striking Jesus. Their leader, reassuringly asking Caiaphas to relax and view the buffeting in comfort, promises him a feast of a show. Caiaphas sits down with enthusiasm but withholds his blessing and promises to bless with his ring the knight who does best.

This brilliant episode is present in the York play but little is made of it: the outline is not nearly so firm, and it is almost lost in the rush of events and pieces of other stories. Caiaphas and Annas are seated together in judgment. The distinction between them—the former blustering and the latter suave—is not clear and consistent. They both wish to beat Jesus, and each restrains the other, although a case can be made for a consistently calm Caiaphas, a connoisseur of torture, and an excitable Annas. Jesus' reply to Caiaphas' question seems to galvanize him into action, and he certainly at some point stands up, and he is angry; he possibly reaches out to hit Jesus since he cries, "Heres thou not, harlott? Ille happe on thy hede" (l. 305), an expression which, however, is common (meaning "may ill fortune befall you") and probably not yet meant literally—the Towneley Caiaphas similarly says, "Harstow, harlott, of all? Of care may thou syng!" (l. 129). In the York play, Annas' reminder, "Nay sir, than blemysshe yee prelatis estate,/ ye awe to deme no man to dede for to dynge" (ll. 336-37), receives no such pompous reply as in the Towneley play. The York Caiaphas has to be told to sit down, but again no effort is made to fuss over him, to restore his sadly shattered episcopal dignity.

It appears that the buffeting occurs in the Place since Caiaphas regrets that he cannot accompany the knights; and after it is over, they return to him. It probably takes place in front of the bishops' Scaffold so that Caiaphas has the grandstand view he is promised. The arrangement in the York play is the same. Froward is sent to fetch the non-biblical but traditional stool which is needed, according to the knights, because Christ is too tall for them to reach his head without jumping up and down, "hop and dawnse/ As cokys in a croft" (ll. 354-55). He could kneel, Froward had said, objecting to the stool (he is too lazy to get it). But Light adds the reason that the stool is also "for a skawnce" (l. 353, "joke"), catching the spirit of mocking. A tall player is needed, but the exchange is not introduced by the playwright simply because the player was tall, as Christ also is in the Buffeting in the Bolton Hours (fol. 62, in, appropriately enough, the initial *D* of *Deus*) where the seated Jesus, wearing a cloak, is noticeably tall. He is also taller than the high priests in a woodcut in a York Missal printed in Paris in 1533 (STC 16224, fol. iv). Froward, whose name, as the play points out (l. 379), means "perverse," is young, slow and reluctant to go about his tasks, and resentful of the way he is treated—especially of the fact that his wages are in arrears. He wishes Jesus to suffer directly and is not sure that either of his two elders have sense enough to inflict sufficient pain on him. It is for this reason that he only reluctantly fetches a stool (Jesus would suffer more pain if he were made to kneel); he is not very interested in this game the knights are planning, and perhaps for the same reason only inadequately blindfolds Jesus, which he regards as another pointless task invented to keep him busy; the blindfolding is from the Gospel (*Luke* 22.64). The buffeting itself makes sense to him, and he first appoints himself the referee and then willingly joins in. His last words imply that he is especially cruel, eager to whip Jesus on his way while the knights drag him. The stool and the veil are called for in the York play, but there is no argument about them—there is no such character as Froward there.

Christ before Annas and Caiaphas

As a "cheeky boy" Froward is clearly related to Slowpace and Daw, but unlike them his youth does not signify that there is goodness in him. On the contrary, this time the playwright has thought to borrow this character for the purpose of representing the "perverse generation" of the Israelites. His function is to make sure that the game becomes more than a joke and to urge the knights on to harder and crueller blows and to set an example for them. The buffeting accordingly increases in savagery. The knights and Froward strike Jesus with their fists, hands, and fingernails, mainly on the head and also perhaps on his back (*Isa.* 50.6). Jesus is slumped on the stool. What happened to Job, and therefore to Christ, is thoroughly enacted: "my sorrow hath oppressed me, and all my limbs are brought to nothing. . . . [A] false speaker riseth up against my face, contradicting me. He . . . hath gnashed with his teeth upon me: my enemy hath beheld me with terrible eyes. They have opened their mouths upon me, and reproaching me they have struck me on the cheek" (*Job* 16.8-11). The Gospels do not specify that Christ was struck on the head or face. It seems likely that the passage from *Job* fuelled the playwright's imagination, the buffeting following so quickly after Caiaphas has risen. The ferocity is evident in some works of art in which Christ's assailants raise their hands up behind their shoulders, as in the Bolton Hours painting of the Scourging (fol. 57^v), so that the blows can descend at full speed, a gesture suggested by Froward's words: "I can my hand vphefe" (l. 408, "raise up"). They vie with each other, as in the Anglo-Scots paraphrase of Ludolphus, "Than but delay opoun [him] all thai schot,/ Preiffand thar pith, quha fastest couth him sair."[34] They hit hard to please the ferocious bishop, says Ludolphus.

The knights, however, make a game out of the buffeting. The biblical "Prophesy to us, O Christ! who is it that struck thee?" (*Matt.* 26.68, *Mark* 14.65, *Luke* 22.64) has been turned into a variation of the youthful slapping game known as "Hot Cockles." Some preachers point to the resemblance.[35] In the York play the knights promise to play "popse" (l. 355) with Jesus, an otherwise unrecorded word which is probably the name of a similar game, "pops," meaning "knocks" or "hard blows" (*OED* pop sb^1 1a). The buffeting is not infrequently called a bobbing in Middle

English (*OED* bob v^2, to mock by striking with the fist).
It is Caiaphas who in the Wakefield Master's play first uses
the word "game," telling Jesus during his frustrated examination
of him that he will become known as "Kyng Copyn"—or (probably) "King Littlehead" (*OED* cop sb^2 I 1c, and -ine suffix^4), an
ominous piece of mockery—"in oure game" (l. 166). Apart from
its general resemblance to Hot Cockles, other games are referred
to during the buffeting, "a new play of Yoyll" (l. 344), cock-
fighting (ll. 354-55), and nine-pins (l. 408). In the York play,
Annas says that the "game" has begun (l. 205), and the knights,
besides playing "popse" with him, tease Jesus with a drinking
game (l. 369). These games are another way of demonstrating the
sinfulness of the Israelites (and also of showing the effect of sins
committed by members of the audience).

Annas, Caiaphas, and their knights are sinners and enemies of
God. At York, Caiaphas, near the beginning of the play, tells
Annas that he has sent for Jesus "halfe for hethyng" (l. 33), that
is, partly for amusement. Later, one of his body servants ex-
citedly awakens him with the news that "layke" has arrived
(l. 190), a word with a range of meanings from "sport" to "way of
proceeding." Later, Annas says that there will be "joie" (l. 274) in
bringing Jesus down. The *Meditations on the Life of Christ* and
Ludolphus relate the actions of Annas and Caiaphas to the behavior of the sinful Israelites, who, according to *Isaias*, behave
before the coming of Christ "as conquerors rejoice after taking a
prey" (9.3). Annas and Caiaphas form the "council of the malignant" of Psalm 21 (21.17), widely understood to refer to unbe-
lievers and the enemies of Christ.[36] Jesus was arrested as a result
of a plot instigated, according to *John* (11.45-53), by Caiaphas,
and this is twice mentioned in the York play (ll. 61, 71). Both *Job*
and *Jeremias*, in the passage which seems to have triggered the
opening of the Wakefield Master's play, speak of the plans and
plots of the malignant. The rejoicing and conspiring of the Israelites are linked by the word "game," which in Middle English has
a range of meanings. "Game" certainly means "scheme," "trick,"
or "plot," and unquestionably has this meaning in two of the other
Wakefield Master's plays (Noah, l. 214; Second Shepherds' play,
l. 427) and also, as some contexts show, "ill-advised scheming to

Christ before Annas and Caiaphas

dominate."[37] In the York and Towneley plays the word is spoken with a certain evil relish, capturing the rejoicing of the Israelites. The scheme promises to be not only successful but also amusing. Caiaphas and Annas are conspirators, happy ones in the York play, violent and cunning in the Towneley play.

The "game" in the Passion plays is essentially a cruel hunting down, seizing, and torturing of the prey. "My enemies have chased me and caught me like a bird," laments Jesus in the person of Jeremias (*Lam.* 3.52), words associated with the capture of Christ.[38] The process begins with the Conspiracy and Betrayal. At the end of the York play of the Agony in the Garden and the Betrayal, the Jews and the knights seize Jesus, and one of the former exclaims, "We, haue holde this hauk in thi hende" (l. 302, "hawk" or, more probably, "auk," both birds). In this sense also Jesus is "game," a hunted creature, to his enemies (and since hunting is not infrequently regarded as a sign of sinfulness, and clerics who hunted were frequently satirized).[39]

Among their other sins, Caiaphas and Annas fail to obey the prohibition of the Lateran Council against hunting by prelates. They neglect their offices and hasten "to be partakers of the games" (*2 Mach.* 4.14).

The word "game" in Middle English also has its modern senses of "childish amusement" and "athletic contest," and thus in a way is very characteristic of the work of these two playwrights. They have produced visible puns on the primary and secondary meanings of the word "game" in these plays ("happy plot" and "hunted creature"), as it is used by Annas and Caiaphas. In this way, to show the crafty strategies of the mighty to be ineffective since the sinners of Jerusalem "shall be all proved together to be senseless and foolish," as *Jeremias* says (10.8), and the hunted one escaping to clouds of glory, the playwrights reduce the schemes and pursuits of Caiaphas and Annas to pointless and childish activities. To make themselves clear, the York Realist refers not to one but to two games and the Wakefield Master to four.

To emphasize this meaning, the Wakefield Master invents a new ending for his play. At York, Caiaphas is very satisfied, orders his knights to take Jesus to Pilate, and concludes the play (not unlike the Wakefield Master's Herod) by saying to the chief knight, "Sir, youre faire felawschippe we betake to the fende" (l. 394, "give to the fiend"), "Goose onne nowe, and daunce forth in the deuyll way" (l. 395); but in Towneley Caiaphas is suddenly struck with fear and distress, not trusting Pilate to be free of corruption. Caiaphas should know: he also is susceptible to bribes. His suspicions are, in fact, well founded, for at the beginning of the previous play, the play of the Conspiracy, Pilate, in a speech provided by the Wakefield Master, announces his own corruptibility. Projecting his doubts by means of a familiar proverb, "gyftys marres many man" (l. 439, Whiting G69), Caiaphas chases after his knights to spy on them and to "persew" or hunt Jesus to his death. "Fare well! we gang, men," he concludes (l. 450), anxiously addressing the audience. He is now not unlike the York Herod in the play of the Massacre of the Innocents.

There is much in the play of the Buffeting to remind the audience of the Crucifixion, as has been argued. This playwright is, however, more interested in making clear the failure of those who oppose Christ. He does so by subjecting them (especially Caiaphas) to ridicule; for this he finds his material and authority in the Old Testament. The loud laughter evoked by the sight of Caiaphas nearly toppling over in his effort to reach out and slap Jesus with his hand is well justified. The hand of the Lord is mightier, Christ in glory and the Last Judgment (mentioned at a key moment in the play) are bound to come, and the Church shall enter into joy, characterized by some writers in terms of laughter.

The playwright is equally interested in the law. In the Towneley plays which he certainly knew he found a Pilate who was (uniquely) characterized as a corrupt lawyer. He extends this theme, first by applying it to contemporary ecclesiastical lawyers, with whom Caiaphas identifies himself and of whom Annas is also clearly one. They speak law Latin, and they and their knights refer to contemporary law, both spiritual and temporal, not usually clearly distinguishable from the laws of the Sanhedrin to which they also refer. And the knights misunderstand the nature of the new law they accuse Christ of being intent on establishing.

Christ before Annas and Caiaphas

Throughout the play, the power of law in general and the help-lessness of the innocent once in its grip are stressed together with the necessity, according to Annas, of following the letter of the law. (By contrast the law is mentioned in the York play only in four instances, at ll. 43, 111, 160, and 387.) The playwright never makes explicit the further extension of this theme that is clearly in his mind.[40] He leaves it to the audience to remember the beati-tudes, to recall that Christ came not "to destroy but to fulfill" the law, and to remember some of the numerous commentaries on the statements in the epistles such as "the law of the spirit of the life in Christ Jesus hath delivered me from the law of sin and death" (*Rom.* 8.2). Faith, grace, and mercy override the Old Law and in some English writings, such as Love's translation of the *Medi-tations on the Life of Christ*, themselves constitute the new law.[41]

In the case of the Buffeting proper, the full meaning is also left unexpressed. The sight of it (kept mercifully and again tact-fully brief) clearly evokes pity and sadness at the stupidity of it; the meaning of it concerns all sinners. Christ is not only himself but the head of the Church. Ludolphus, following Gregory, says that all Christians who do wrong, despite confessing Christ, are aiming blows at the head of the Church. Hence, probably, the stress in the Towneley play on Christ's "head" and the pun: it is Christ's "crowne" (l. 363) which is struck, a detail missing from the Gospels (his "face" is mentioned, *Matt.* 26.57) and a pun missing from the other plays. When pondering this, the first epi-sode of Christ's sufferings, one was expected to react with com-passion, repentance, amazement, and exultation.

The crowded York play of Christ before Annas and Caiaphas, clearly identified as a bishop, includes in addition not only the related episode of the denial by Peter and the single buffet re-corded by *John* (22.64) as well as the general buffeting, but also three episodes which are not based on stories in the New Testa-ment: Caiaphas' drinking wine; Caiaphas' going to bed; and two knights with their prisoner, Jesus, parlaying their way in to see Caiaphas. These episodes occupy more than half of the play (ll. 1-201) before the actual appearance of Jesus before Annas and Caiaphas begins; they come from Old Testament images of the enemies of Christ meshed with satirical observations on the life of the well-to-do in the fifteenth century.

In Psalm 68, also a Passion psalm used in the liturgy of the Holy Week Masses, the speaker, a figure for Christ, says, "they that drank wine made me their song," or their object of mockery; and in *Isaias*, it is said that true judgment is marred by wine: "the priest and the prophet have been ignorant through drunkenness, they are swallowed up with wine, they have gone astray in drunkenness" (28.7). The *Meditations on the Life of Christ*, describing Christ's Passion in general, alludes to the first of these passages.[42] The *Glossa Ordinaria* (on *Ps.* 68.13) takes the wine to symbolize an excessive attachment to the pleasures of this world, but the playwright understands it literally and so produces a small representation of a *voidee*, the noble custom of serving wine before retiring for the night to which there is frequent allusion in fourteenth- and fifteenth-century romances (in *Sir Gawain and the Green Knight*, for example, ll. 1403, 1668, where choice wine is served). In the play, it is Annas who suggests that the time has come for this ceremony. It is long past ten o'clock, and the now agitated Caiaphas needs soothing. One of Caiaphas' two body servants fetches "wyne of the best," and, presenting it to Caiaphas, says,

> My Lorde, here is wyne that will make you to wynke,
> Itt is licoure full delicious my lorde, and you like.
> Wherfore I rede drely a draughte that ye drynke,
> For in this contré, that we knawe, iwisse there is none slyke,
> Wherfore we counsaille you this cuppe sauerly for to kisse.
>
> (ll. 76-80)

The servant is both extremely polite and very proud of the high quality of this imported wine. There is some evidence that the actors enjoyed this scene and liked to dwell on it; in performance, the actor playing the part of Caiaphas sometimes borrowed two lines from the similar episode in the following play (l. 135), as John Clerke's note against lines 75-76 in the manuscript shows. It seems reasonable to conceive of the characters as bowing and scraping to each other in elaborate politeness. Caiaphas can be well-mannered to the point of facetiousness. Prompt obsequiousness by the knights also perhaps crept into the play, as another note by Clerk indicates (l. 23*sd*). The playwright produces a satirical and humorous picture of upper-class manners (drunkenness is not far away, however, and seems to afflict Pilate in the next play). Pulpit moralists in the fifteenth century frequently feel called upon to condemn excessive drinking, especially drinking to such an extent that you have to be helped to bed by your servant, as is Pilate in the next play. There are four such *voidees* in the York Realist's plays. Christ is the "true vine" (*John* 15.1), and these scenes can hardly have failed to remind some of this central New Testament metaphor and to have appeared, therefore, as representations of behavior both blasphemous and immoral.

After drinking, Caiaphas goes to sleep. He is carefully and gently laid down on his bed and covered with bed-clothes which are neatly tucked in. It is past his bedtime, and he sleeps soundly throughout the episode of Peter's denial as well as the arrival of Jesus with his captors. His body servants shake him to wake him up, with three "My Lords" to tell him the good news, but at first he is so sleepy that he refuses to get up and then fails to understand what is going on. The beds of the well-to-do were elaborate affairs in the fifteenth century and a source of pride, especially feather-beds with canopies and embroidered covers (fig. 23). "Tenderness of flesh" is frequently inveighed against by fifteenth-century preachers, who regarded it as an epidemic. There are four such bed episodes in the York Passion plays. On the one hand, they represent the pride and luxury of the Israelites, sleeping "upon beds of ivory" (*Amos* 6.4), and on the other the sluggishness both physical and spiritual of all sinners, then and now. St. Bernard's words are relevant: "How many noble, according to the flesh, how many powerful, how many wise of these generations, rest this hour in soft pillows; and none of them was worthy to see the new light";[43] these words echo *Ezechiel*, "Woe to them that sew cushions under every elbow" (13.18). The same effect occurs also in the Towneley Play of the Dice (ll. 65-72, 183-97), and so was known to the Wakefield Master.

The York playwright is, however, also engaged in tying his sequence of plays together, for Christ, like Job, suffers on a "bed of pain," as the *Meditations on the Life of Christ* says.[44] This is a

Chapter VI

common theme of fifteenth-century religious poetry. The luxurious beds and their sybaritic occupants are recalled in the final play of the Death of Christ when Jesus says that he has nowhere to lay his head, and also when he says that his skin is "ragged and rent" (1. 120; see also fig. 24). His bed is a bed of nails. He has no soft covering or soft pillow.

When the two knights, with their captive, Jesus, his hands tied together with rope, arrive at the house of Caiaphas, they encounter some difficulty gaining entrance. They cross the courtyard where (as in *Luke*) Peter denies Jesus and suffers from his look of reproach; but when they reach what the play refers to as Caiaphas' "halle here at hande" (1. 174), they are stopped by the closed door on which they knock after making some considerable to-do about not making any noise (ll. 176-79). Caiaphas' body servants are at first adamant: "Gose abakke bewscheres, ye bothe are to blame/ To bourde whenne oure busshopp is boune to his bedde" (ll. 182-83).

Again, there are four such episodes in these plays. On three of these occasions Jesus is with his captors, once at a door and twice at a gate.[45] The privacy and seclusion of the enemies of Jesus is thus emphasized. After the settlement in Jerusalem, great gates (with porters) were established to keep clean the house of the Lord (*1 and 2 Par.*, *passim*); hence the prophets alluding to the sinful of Jerusalem refer to its gates. Psalm 68 again probably provided the trigger for the playwright: "the zeal of thy house hath eaten me up. . . . They that sat in the gate spoke against me" (ll. 10-13), especially since those who "sat in the gate" were widely understood to be the Scribes and Pharisees, as the *Glossa Ordinaria*, on Psalm 68.13, reports, adding that they lacked understanding. Job laments that the houses of the wicked are secure (21.9), and Jeremias also has enemies sitting at the "gate" and demanding his death (26.10). The playwright follows up the literal implications of these words—"house" and "gate"—and builds up his short episodes of coming and going, pictures of the awkward logistics of human and sinful endeavor, around them.

Any debate or gossip about the detailed "typological" patterns of the plots would be by no means sterile or merely intellectual. The comic episodes are accurately and religiously justified by

reference to their Old Testament starting points, but they also
have a personal meaning for all members of the audience. Sloth,
drunkenness, and a closed heart keep one away from God, as
fifteenth-century preachers never tired of insisting.

And again he has in mind the final play of the cycle. "I have
given before thee a door opened, which no man can shut," says
Jesus (*Apoc.* 3.8), and one of the most obvious things about the
cross on Calvary, often stressed by writers in the meditative
tradition, is the openness of Christ's death—unhidden and available for all to see, not to mention benefit from—a point stressed
in the play, in which Christ consistently addresses "man," that is,
everybody, in contrast to the wicked who make a great point of
social distinctions in their speeches from (in this play) "senioures"
to "churles." When the true Church is established, says Isaias, the
"gates" of Jerusalem shall be open continually; they shall not be
shut day nor night (60.11).

The theology of this sequence of plots is very clear, and is
expressed in the founding sermon of the York Corpus Christi
Guild: the Passion was and is both caused by human sin—then
and now—and was and is the answer to it. The York Realist's
plots, triggered by Old Testament types of the Passion, carry this
meaning: the wines are answered by the vinegar, the beds by the
cross, and the doors by the openness.

The York Realist's Pageant is crowded. His play has ten
speaking parts. Caiaphas has the starring role, speaking about a
third of the lines (in contrast to the Wakefield Master's play in
which, while Caiaphas has the main part, he does not overshadow
Annas so clearly). Caiaphas' Scaffold consists of his court, with a
judgment seat, a seat of Annas, and also of his bedroom, with a
bed. It has a practicable door from the Place which represents the
courtyard, in which there is a fire for Peter to warm himself at
and through which Jesus' captors lead him. Caiaphas' Scaffold
can hold seven speakers and probably some silent extras since
Caiaphas calls for his household to assemble (l. 235). Elsewhere
in the Place, the knights buffet Jesus somewhere within sight of
Caiaphas, but not on his Scaffold. Episodes follow fast on each
other, and the dialogue moves rapidly, to and fro even for Jesus,
who in this play does not remain mostly silent (*John* 19.9). The

overall effect is of a crowded, bustling, and scheming world—the same effect left in the mind of a reading of the *Meditations on the Life of Christ.*

The York play was, throughout the life of the plays, sponsored by the Bowers and Fletchers. The Bowers and Fletchers are among the earliest craft guilds recorded as maintaining "pageants," the Fletchers in 1388 and the Bowers in 1395. By 1415, they are recorded as having joined together to sponsor the play of Christ before Annas and Caiaphas, and they remained responsible for it until the plays ceased.[46] They manufactured bows and arrows, including those used in warfare, and are therefore appropriately assigned to one of the plays which shows the beginning of the final attack on Christ. More particularly, their weapons are sharp and swift, suitable metaphors both for the blows Jesus receives in this play and also (like Hamlet's dagger) for the accusations and questions hurled at him, which Gregory refers to as "missiles." Job's calamities are the result of the "arrows of the Lord" (6.4). The Bowers and Fletchers have much to answer for.

Notes

Introduction

[1]W. A. Davenport, *Fifteenth-Century English Drama* (Cambridge: D. S. Brewer, 1982), p. 131.

[2]There is no full list of revivals. The following are helpful, but not always accurate: Harold Child, "Revivals of English Dramatic Works 1919-1925," *Review of English Studies*, 2 (1926), 177-88; Harold Child, "Revivals of English Dramatic Works 1901-1918, 1926," *Review of English Studies*, 3 (1927), 169-85; John R. Elliott, Jr., "A Checklist of Modern Productions of the Medieval Mystery Cycles in England," *Research Opportunities in Renaissance Drama*, 13-14 (1970-71), 259-66; Glynne Wickham, "Calendar of Twentieth Century Revivals of English Mystery Cycles and Other Major Religious Plays of the Middle Ages," in his *The Medieval Theatre* (New York: St. Martin's Press, 1974), pp. 221-26; [see also John R. Elliott, Jr., *Playing God* (Toronto: Univ. of Toronto Press, 1989), pp. 145-48]. Major current productions are annually listed and often reviewed in *Research Opportunities in Renaissance Drama*, beginning with Vol. 17 (1974), and in *Medieval English Theatre*, beginning with Vol. 1 (1979).

[3]*Times*, 15 July 1901, p. 8; *Stage*, 18 July 1901, p. 7; *Athenaeum*, 20 July 1901, p. 103.

[4]A. F. Leach, *A History of Winchester College* (London: Duckworth, 1899), p. 484; *Era*, 20 December 1902, p. 19.

[5]F. W. Moorman, "The Wakefield Miracle Plays," *Transactions of the Yorkshire Dialect Society*, 7 (1906), 5-24. Moorman, following Charles M. Gayley, *Representative English Comedies* (New York: Macmillan, 1903), I, xxxii, gives credit to an unnamed American university for first reviving the play; the only notices among Gayley's papers in the archives at the University of California, Berkeley (I am informed by the University Archivist), refer to a performance there in 1904 of his *The Star of Bethlehem* (New York: Fox, Duffield, 1904), a work which preserves most of the text of the Second Shepherds' play but intersperses it with other plays and is thus merely the first of many adaptations to amalgamate various plays from dif-

201

Notes

ferent collections. In the version performed by the Harvard Dramatic Club on 18 and 19 December 1923, the Second Shepherds' play is cut to shreds (Donald F. Robinson, *The Harvard Dramatic Club Miracle Plays* [New York, 1927], pp. 31-68). Clarence G. Child, ed., *The Second Shepherds' Play, Everyman, and Other Early Plays* (Boston: Houghton Mifflin, 1910), p. xxx, writes that the Second Shepherds' play "within recent years (1908) has been given at four colleges with success."

[6]*The Gryphon: The Journal of the University of Leeds*, 10, No. 4 (March 1907), 50; *Yorkshire Post*, 9 February 1907, p. 8; *Leeds and Yorkshire Mercury*, 9 February 1907, p. 6.

[7]Matthew H. Peacock, "The Wakefield Mysteries: The Place of Representation," *Anglia*, 24 (1901), 508-24.

[8]*The Wakefield Express*, 9 April 1910, p. 9.

[9]Robert Speaight, *William Poel and the Elizabethan Revival* (London: Heinemann, 1954); Andrew Stephenson, *The Maddermarket Theatre Norwich* (Norwich, 1971), on Monck. [The only published account of Browne's work is contained in E. Martin Browne and Henzie Browne, *Two in One* (Cambridge: Cambridge Univ. Press, 1981); his papers relating to medieval drama are at the University of Lancaster.]

[10]H. Gollancz, "The Chester Mystery Plays," *Journal of the Chester and North Wales Architectural, Archaeological, and Historical Society*, n.s. 14 (1908), 18-28; Joseph C. Bridge, ed., *Three Chester Whitsun Plays* (Chester: Phillipson and Golder, 1906), "as produced by Nugent Monck for the English Drama Society"; *Times*, 6 December 1906, p. 14; *Athenaeum*, 8 December 1906, p. 746.

[11]Rex Pogson, *Miss Horniman and the Gaiety Theatre, Manchester* (London: Rockliff, 1952), pp. 52, 201; *Manchester Guardian*, 1 March 1910, p. 7 (signed A. N. M.). The play formed a double bill with *Youth*.

[12]W. Bridges-Adams, *The Irresistible Theatre* (New York: Collier, 1961), p. 65. Bridges-Adams writes as an eyewitness.

[13]Yeats to Tynan, in W. B. Yeats, *Letters to Katharine Tynan*, ed. R. McHugh (New York: McMullen Books, 1953), p. 113; Katharine Tynan, *Miracle Plays* (London: Lane, 1895); Allardyce Nicoll, *English Drama 1900-1930: The Beginnings of the Modern Period* (Cambridge: Cambridge Univ. Press, 1973), pp. 124, 228, and *passim*; Robert Hogan et al., *The Rise of the Realists, 1910-15*, in *The Modern Irish Drama: A Documentary History* (Dublin: Dolmen Press, 1979), IV, 170; Gordon Crosse, *The Religious Drama* (London: Mowbray, 1913), p. 164.

Notes

[14]Martial Rose, *The Wakefield Cycle of Mystery Plays*, Bretton Hall Production, Foundation Lecture ([Wakefield,] 1967).

[15]*Times*, 6 April 1961, p. 8; *Observer*, 9 April 1961, p. 27.

[16]*Times*, 29 May and 17 July 1962.

[17]John Hodgson, "The Second Production," in Rose, *Wakefield Cycle*, pp. 14-15; Martial Rose, trans., *The Wakefield Mystery Plays* (Garden City, N.Y: Doubleday, 1962).

[18]Review by Peter Happé in *Research Opportunities in Renaissance Drama*, 23 (1980), 81-82.

[19]Sarah Carpenter, "Towneley Plays at Wakefield," *Medieval English Theatre*, 2 (1980), 50-51; see also Paula Neuss, "No Room in the Ark," *Times Literary Supplement*, 4 July 1980, p. 756.

[20]Louis N. Parker, *The York Pageant. July 26th to 31st, 1909. Book of the Words* (York: Cooper and Swann, [1909]), pp. 95-99. The "play" (40 of the first 85 lines) concluded at line 85. Robert Withington gives an account of "Parkerian" Pageants in his *English Pageantry* (Cambridge: Harvard Univ. Press, 1918-20), II, 194-234.

[21]Christopher Innes, *Edward Gordon Craig* (Cambridge: Cambridge Univ. Press, 1983), pp. 72-83; Laurence Housman, *Bethlehem: A Nativity Play* (New York: Macmillan, 1902). Housman was responsible for the art nouveau design of Katharine Tynan's *Miracle Plays*.

[22]*Yorkshire Herald*, 3 January 1925, p. 4; 5 January 1925, p. 7; 6 January 1925, p. 4; *Yorkshire Gazette*, 10 January 1925, pp. 4, 6; Paul H. Wright, *The Word of God: A Miracle Play Adapted from the Medieval York Cycle* (York, 1926); Norman MacDermot, *Everymania: The History of the Everyman Theatre Hampstead 1920-1926* (1975), pp. 25, 124; J. S. Purvis, *The York Cycle of Mystery Plays: A Shorter Version* (London: SPCK, 1951).

[23]*Times*, 18 December 1959, p. 12.

[24]E. Martin Browne, *The Production of Religious Plays* (London: Allan, 1932), pp. 16-17.

[25]E. Martin Browne, "A Note on the Production at York, 1951," in Purvis, *York Cycle of Mystery Plays: A Shorter Version*, p. 14.

Notes

[26]Review by John R. Elliott, Jr., in *Research Opportunities in Renaissance Drama*, 15-16 (1972-73), 125.

[27]Production using three stations was adopted in part to refute the theory of Alan H. Nelson, "Principles of Processional Staging: York Cycle," *Modern Philology*, 67 (1970), 303-20.

[28]Jane Oakshott and Richard Rastall, "Town with Gown: The York Cycle of Mystery Plays at Leeds," in *Towards the Community University*, ed. David C. B. Teather (London: Kogan Page, 1982), pp. 223-24.

[29]J. S. Purvis, *The York Cycle of Mystery Plays: A Complete Version* (London: SPCK, 1957); A. C. Cawley, *Times Literary Supplement*, 9 May 1975, p. 510; Oakshott and Rastall, "Town with Gown," pp. 213-29; David Parry, "The York Cycle at the University of Toronto," *REED Newsletter*, [2, No. 1] (1977), 18-19; K. Reed Needles and Steven Putzel, "Toronto: The Pageant Wagons," *Medieval English Theatre*, 1 (1979), 32-33; David Bevington *et al.*, "The York Cycle at Toronto: October 1 and 2, 1977," *Research Opportunities in Renaissance Drama*, 20 (1977), 107-22; Alexandra F. Johnston, "The York Cycle: 1977," *University of Toronto Quarterly*, 48 (1978), 1-9; David Parry, "The York Mystery Cycle at Toronto, 1977," *Medieval English Theatre*, 1 (1979), 19-31.

[30]Reviews by Stanley J. Kahrl and John R. Elliott, Jr., in *Research Opportunities in Renaissance Drama*, 15-16 (1972-73), 117-30.

[31]Joseph Papp, *William Shakespeare's "Naked" Hamlet: A Production Handbook* (New York: Macmillan, 1969).

[32]Review by Gail McMurray Gibson of the Toronto production in *Research Opportunities in Renaissance Drama*, 20 (1977), 116. The matter-of-fact tone of this play and the "grace under pressure" of Christ appealed to Ernest Hemingway, according to Robert D. Arner, "Hemingway's 'Miracle' Play: 'Today is Friday' and the York Play of the Crucifixion," *Markham Review*, 4 (1973), 8-11.

[33]Tony Harrison, *The Passion* (London: Rex Collings, 1977); Peter Happé, "Mystery Plays and the Modern Audience," *Medieval English Theatre*, 2 (1980), 98-100; review, citing critical reactions, by John R. Elliott, Jr., in *Research Opportunities in Renaissance Drama*, 21 (1978), 96-99; a selection of further critical reviews (including that by Benedict Nightingale in *Harpers* and *Queen*) in *Research Opportunities in Renaissance Drama*, 22 (1979), 137-41; Heather O'Donoghue, *Times Literary Supplement*, 1 February 1985, p. 121.

Notes

[34]A. M. Nagler, *The Medieval Religious Stage: Shapes and Phantoms* (New Haven: Yale Univ. Press, 1976), a work concerned with none of the points I pursue.

Chapter I
The Wakefield Master and the York Realist

[1][For a different view of the stanza than presented here, see the argument set forth by Martin Stevens, "Did the Wakefield Master Write a Nine-Line Stanza?" *Comparative Drama*, 15 (1981), 99-119.]

[2]Cf. A. C. Cawley and Martin Stevens, Introduction, in *The Towneley Cycle: A Facsimile of MS HM 1*, Leeds Texts and Monographs: Medieval Drama Facsimiles, 2 (Leeds: Univ. of Leeds School of English, 1976), pp. ix-x, xvii.

[3]M. G. Frampton, "The Date of the Flourishing of the Wakefield Master," *PMLA*, 50 (1935), 631-60.

[4]Charles M. Gayley, *Representative English Comedies*, p. xxviii; Charles M. Gayley, *Plays of Our Forefathers* (New York: Duffield, 1907), p. 175.

[5]*The York Plays*, ed. Richard Beadle (London: Edward Arnold, 1982), pp. 10-11, 442-52.

[6]Gayley, *Representative English Comedies*, p. xxv; J. W. Robinson, "The Art of the York Realist," *Modern Philology*, 60 (1963), 241-51; Clifford Davidson, *From Creation to Doom: The York Cycle of Mystery Plays* (New York: AMS Press, 1984), pp. 117-34; Rosemary Woolf, *The English Mystery Plays* (Berkeley and Los Angeles: Univ. of California Press, 1972), p. 245; Jeffrey Helterman, *Symbolic Action in the Plays of the Wakefield Master* (Athens: Univ. of Georgia Press, 1981), pp. 8-10.

[7]*La Seinte Resureccion*, ed. T. Atkinson Jenkins *et al.*, Anglo-Norman Text Soc., 4 (Oxford: Blackwell, 1943), p. 1 (l. 3).

[8]*York*, ed. Alexandra F. Johnston and Margaret Rogerson, Records of Early English Drama (Toronto: Univ. of Toronto Press, 1979), I, 11; hereafter references to this edition are given as REED *York*. The phrase is not uncommon in this context.

[9]Siegfried Wenzel, "An Early Reference to a Corpus Christi Play," *Modern Philology*, 74 (1977), 390-91.

Notes

[10]*Dives and Pauper*, ed. Priscilla Heath Barnum, EETS, o.s. 275, 280 (London, 1976, 1980), I, Pt. 1, 293.

[11]REED *York*, I, 37.

[12]Quoted by A. C. Cawley, ed., *The Wakefield Pageants in the Towneley Cycle* (Manchester: Manchester Univ. Press, 1958), p. 125.

[13]Diana K. J. Wyatt, "Performance and Ceremonial in Beverley before 1642," unpublished D.Phil. (York, 1983), p. 7: the Corpus Christi play was supported in 1411 by craft guilds "that the honour of God and the credit of the town might be exalted more devoutly and worthily."

[14]REED *York*, I, 43.

[15]*The Riverside Chaucer*, 3rd ed., gen. ed. Larry D. Benson (Boston: Houghton Mifflin, 1987), III.555-68 and p. 855.

[16]*A Tretise of Miraclis Pleyinge*, in *A Middle English Treatise on the Playing of Miracles*, ed. Clifford Davidson (Washington: Univ. Press of America, 1981), p. 51.

[17]*A History of Yorkshire: York*, ed. P. M. Tillott, Victoria County Histories (London: Oxford Univ. Press, 1961), p. 86 (hereafter references to this series will be cited as VCH); *Coventry*, ed. R. W. Ingram, Records of Early English Drama (Toronto: Univ. of Toronto Press, 1981), p. xix (hereafter cited as REED *Coventry*). See also Charles Phythian-Adams, *Desolation of a City: Coventry and the Urban Crisis of the Late Middle Ages* (Cambridge: Cambridge Univ. Press, 1979), *passim*.

[18]Davidson, *From Creation to Doom*, pp. 6-11; E. F. Jacob, *The Fifteenth Century, 1399-1485* (Oxford: Clarendon Press, 1961), pp. vii, 684-87.

[19]John Leland, *The Itinerary*, ed. Lucy Toulmin Smith (1907; rpt. Carbondale: Southern Illinois Univ. Press, 1964), I, 42; Herbert Heaton, *The Yorkshire Woollen and Worsted Industries* (Oxford: Clarendon Press, 1920), pp. 68-79.

[20]A. C. Cawley, ed., *Wakefield Pageants*, p. 125. [For a discussion of the Burgess Court records and the forgeries of John Walker, see Barbara Palmer, "'Towneley Plays' or 'Wakefield Cycle' Revisited," *Comparative Drama*, 21 (1987-88), 318-48.]

[21]Large cycles of plays appear, from the records so far published, not to have been the norm; "Corpus Christi" plays were usually short works: John Wasson, "Records of Early English Drama: Where They Are and What They Tell Us," in

Proceedings of the First Colloquium, ed. JoAnna Dutka (Toronto: Records of Early English Drama, 1979), pp. 138-39. "Clerk's plays" are established as a genre by Ian Lancashire, *Dramatic Texts and Records of Britain to 1550* (Toronto: Univ. of Toronto Press, 1984), pp. xiv-xviii. It is perhaps unnecessarily scrupulous to point out that the only good evidence that the Wakefield Master's plays were in fact ever presented is their eminent playability (a central theme of this book); the same is true of *Everyman*.

[22]Arnold Williams, *The Characterization of Pilate in the Towneley Plays* (East Lansing: Michigan State College Press, 1950).

[23]*Ordo Repraesentationis Adae*, l. 292.1, as quoted for convenience from *Medieval Drama*, ed. David Bevington (Boston: Houghton Mifflin, 1975), p. 94; Karl Young, *The Drama of the Medieval Church* (Oxford: Clarendon Press, 1933), II, 539.

[24]For music in the English drama, see especially JoAnna Dutka, *Music in the English Mystery Plays*, Early Drama, Art, and Music, Reference Ser., 2 (Kalamazoo: Medieval Institute Publications, 1980).

[25]*Tretise*, pp. 38-39; *Canterbury Tales* III.559.

[26]*Tretise*, p. 50.

[27]REED *York*, I, 37.

[28]Alexandra F. Johnston and Margaret Dorrell, "The Doomsday Pageant of the York Mercers, 1433," *Leeds Studies in English*, n.s. 5 (1971), 29-34, and "The York Mercers and Their Pageant of Doomsday, 1433-1526," *Leeds Studies in English*, n.s. 6 (1972), 10-35; REED *York*, I, 55-56, 241-42.

[29]Parry, "The York Mystery Cycle at Toronto, 1977," pp. 26-27.

[30]*The Pride of Life* (ll. 470.1-502); *The Castle of Perseverance* (ll. 490.1-525); for these plays, see *Non-Cycle Plays and Fragments*, ed. Norman Davis, EETS, 262 (London, 1969).

[31]The direction at the beginning of the N-town Second Passion play seems to call for such a procession, as do the texts of a number of the longer liturgical plays (Young, *Drama of the Medieval Church*, II, 404).

[32]There is no sign in the York or Towneley plays of the hangings which apparently sometimes concealed from view the occupants of Scaffolds until they

took part in the action as, for example, in the N-town Second Passion play (l. 356*sd*). There are very few such references in the English plays; the reference in the *Pride of Life* (ll. 303-06*sd*) appears to be a bed curtain.

[33]*Meditations on the Life of Christ*, trans. Isa Ragusa (Princeton: Princeton Univ. Press, 1961), p. 38. In many paintings and woodcuts of the annunciation to the shepherds—the Hours of the Blessed Virgin Mary (Paris, c.1520, STC 15929), sig. f1[v], for example—the silhouette of the town of Bethlehem is shown, distant but reachable, in the background. Sometimes the stable is in the foreground, the shepherds in the middle distance, and the town in the far distance.

[34]Allardyce Nicoll, *The Development of the Theatre*, 5th ed. (New York: Harcourt, Brace, and World, 1966), p. 250.

[35]"The Cambridge Prologue" (before 1300), the "Rickinghall (Bury St. Edmunds) Fragment" (early fourteenth century), and the *Pride of Life* (mid-fourteenth century) fully attest to this tradition; see *Non-Cycle Plays and Fragments*, ed. Davis. The speaker treats his audience as if they were his subjects. Antoinette Greene, "An Index to the Non-Biblical Names in the English Mystery Plays," in *Studies in Language and Literature in Celebration of the Seventieth Birthday of James Morgan Hart* (New York: Henry Holt, 1910), pp. 313-50, provides a list of references to "Mahound."

[36]*Meditations on the Life of Christ*, pp. 49, 51; concerning Love's translation, see Elizabeth Salter, *Nicholas Love's "Myrrour of the Blessed Lyf of Jesu Christ,"* Analecta Cartusiana, 10 (Salzburg: Institut für Englische Sprache und Literatur, 1974), pp. 16-18.

[37]Sister Mary Immaculate Bodenstedt, *The Vita Christi of Ludolphus the Carthusian* (Washington: Catholic Univ. of America Press, 1944), explains the origin, significance, and influences of this work. Elizabeth Salter, "Ludolphus of Saxony and His English Translators," *Medium Aevum*, 33 (1964), 26-35, shows that an early sixteenth-century English adaption was in the possession of the Towneley family (Lords of the Manor of Wakefield) by 1603, that is, at about the time the same family acquired the collection of biblical plays now known as the Towneley manuscript. At least one fifteenth-century copy (Worcester Cathedral Library MS. F. 140) is recorded in N. R. Ker, *Medieval Libraries of Great Britain*, 2nd ed. (London: Royal Historical Society, 1964), p. 212.

[38]F. P. Pickering, *Literature and Art in the Middle Ages* (Coral Gables, Florida: Univ. of Miami Press, 1970), pp. 253-85; fully developed in James H. Marrow, *Passion Iconography in Northern European Art of the Late Middle Ages*

Notes

and Early Renaissance: A Study of the Transformation of Sacred Metaphor into Descriptive Narrative (Kortrijk: Van Ghemmert, 1979), *passim*.

[39]G. L. Remnant, *A Catalogue of Misericords in Great Britain* (Oxford: Clarendon Press, 1969), p. 176; Thomas R. Tanfield, *Beverley Minster Misericord Seats* (Beverley, n.d.), Nos. 25-26.

[40]Remnant, *Catalogue*, p. 175. Geese are as common as owls in this kind of work, the former presumably representing folly and the latter wisdom. In the present case it is hard to know who is the sillier, the man or the goose.

[41]Ibid., p. 176 and Pl. 42d; and p. 177 (the interpretation is mine).

[42]Barbara Palmer, *The Early Art of the West Riding of Yorkshire*, Early Drama, Art, and Music, Reference Ser., 6 (Kalamazoo: Medieval Institute Publications, 1990), p. 34; hereafter EDAM *West Riding*.

[43]Remnant, *Catalogue*, p. 174 (the interpretation is mine).

[44]C. J. P. Cave, *Roof Bosses in Medieval Churches* (Cambridge: Cambridge Univ. Press, 1948), p. 201; Remnant, *Catalogue*, p. 177.

[45]The glass is fourteenth-century. For another example, c.1515, a crozier fixed in a tun inscribed BA ("=Bamtun"), once in Easby Abbey, North Riding, see Remnant, *Catalogue*, p. 182.

[46]David Starkey, "The Age of the Household," in *The Later Middle Ages*, ed. Stephen Medcalf (New York: Holmes and Meier, 1981), p. 265.

[47]EDAM *West Riding*, p. 39.

[48]For roof bosses in Selby Abbey and York Minster, see Cave, *Roof Bosses*, pp. 209, 222; and for painted glass at Thornhill and other West Riding examples, see EDAM *West Riding*, pp. 98-100.

[49]*Dives and Pauper*, ed. Barnum, I, Pt. 1, 92.

[50]*The Register of the Guild of Corpus Christi in the City of York*, [ed. R. H. Skaife,] Surtees Soc., 57 (Durham: Andrews, 1872), pp. 1-9 (Latin); Paula Ložar, "The 'Prologue' to the Ordinances of the York Corpus Christi Guild," *Allegorica*, 1 (1976), 94-113.

Notes

[51]W. H. Quillian, "'Composition of Place': Joyce's Notes on the English Drama," *James Joyce Quarterly*, 13 (1975), 21.

[52]*The City of God* XI.30. There are explanations of numerical composition in Ernst Robert Curtius, *European Literature and the Latin Middle Ages*, trans. Willard R. Trask, Bollingen Ser., 36 (New York: Pantheon Books, 1953), pp. 501-09, and Christopher Butler, "Numerological Thought," in *Silent Poetry: Essays in Numerological Analysis*, ed. Alistair Fowler (New York: Barnes and Noble, 1970), pp. 1-31.

[53]Gordon Kipling, "The London Pageants for Margaret of Anjou: A Medieval Script Restored," *Medieval English Theatre*, 4 (1982), 5-27, esp. 20. In this text, but not in the manuscript of the play (where capitalization is not to be expected), the word is capitalized: "Armonie."

[54]Towneley play of the Magi (ll. 1-36); *Pride of Life* (ll. 165-67, 177-80, 195-200).

[55]Cf. Stevens, "Did the Wakefield Master Write a Nine-Line Stanza?" *passim.*

[56]Michael J. Preston and Jean D. Pfleiderer, *A KWIC Concordance to the Plays of the Wakefield Master* (New York: Garland, 1982), is based on Cawley's edition, which includes the play of the Killing of Abel, includes different inflectional forms and spellings of the same word, and excludes the Wakefield Master's contributions to other plays; my "perhaps 3,000 or more" is an educated guess based on this concordance. It is only my impression that the York Realist's vocabulary is not quite as extensive. Chaucer's vocabulary, based on a count of Tatlock's concordance and again counting all the inflectional forms as one, is given as 8,072 words by Joseph Mersand, *Chaucer's Romance Vocabulary* (New York: Comet Press, 1939), pp. 42-43. *The Concordance to the Complete Works of Geoffrey Chaucer* of John S. P. Tatlock and Arthur G. Kennedy (1927; rpt. Gloucester, Mass.: Peter Smith, 1963) is based on the Globe edition of Chaucer's works (ed. A. W. Pollard *et al.*, 1898), which contains in excess of 43,000 lines.

[57]George C. Taylor, "The Relation of the English Corpus Christi Play to the Middle English Religious Lyric," *Modern Philology*, 5 (1907), 18; Erich Auerbach, *Mimesis: The Representation of Reality in Western Literature*, trans. Willard R. Trask (Princeton: Princeton Univ. Press, 1953), p. 72: "a new elevated style, which does not scorn everyday life and which is ready to absorb the sensorily realistic, even the . . . physically base."

[58]These figures, which may be too low, are extracted from Bartlett Jere Whiting, *Proverbs in the Earlier English Drama*, Harvard Studies in Comparative Literature, 14

Notes

(1938; rpt. New York: Octagon Books, 1969). See also Whiting's *Proverbs, Sentences, and Proverbial Phrases* (Cambridge: Harvard Univ. Press, 1968), which I have frequently cited in this study (abbreviated in my text as Whiting).

[59]G. C. Britton, "Language and Character in Some Late Medieval Plays," *Essays and Studies*, n.s. 33 (1980), 1-15.

[60]"Browyd lyke a brystyll" (*MED* broued ppl and bristel n; Whiting B553); "wett hyr whystyll" (*OED* whistle 2; Whiting W225).

[61]J. A. W. Bennett, *Poetry of the Passion* (Oxford: Clarendon Press, 1982), pp. 62-84.

[62]Towneley plays of Noah (ll. 222, 362) and the Talents (ll. 185, 195). See also Noah (l. 394), the Buffeting (l. 202), the Second Shepherds' play (l. 468), and the play of the Conspiracy (l. 622), the first three by the Master. Chaucer's Parson indicates that "harlot" is colloquial.

[63]Thorlac Turville-Petre, *The Alliterative Revival* (Cambridge: D. S. Brewer, 1977), pp. 122-23.

[64]Peter Meredith, "John Clerke's Hand in the York Register," *Leeds Studies in English*, n.s. 12 (1981), 245-71. Clerke apparently sat at the first station, following the script on behalf of the corporation from c.1542 to c.1567.

[65]Chiefly, the Norwich play of the Creation (in *Non-Cycle Plays and Fragments*, ed. Davis, pp. 8-18); the Chester plays of the Purification and the Shepherds' play (*Chester*, ed. Lawrence Clopper, Records of Early English Drama [Toronto: Univ. of Toronto Press, 1979]; hereafter referred to as REED *Chester*); the York plays of the Last Supper and the Last Judgment (in REED *York*); the Coventry play of the Purification (in REED *Coventry*). Except for York, these are sixteenth-century accounts. There are also instructive accounts of money spent on properties for plays no longer extant, particularly at Coventry.

[66]*Meditations on the Life of Christ*, pp. 15-16; Meg Twycross and Sarah Carpenter, "Masks in Medieval English Theatre: The Mystery Plays," *Medieval English Theatre*, 3 (1981), 7-44, 69-113.

[67]Nicola Coldstream, "Art and Architecture in the Late Middle Ages," in *The Later Middle Ages*, ed. Medcalf, pp. 193-94.

[68]The effectiveness of a crucifix is exceeded only "whanne a quyk man is sett in a play to be hangid nakid on a cros and to be in semyng woundid and scourgid"

Notes

(Reginald Pecock, *The Repressor of Over Much Blaming of the Clergy*, ed. Churchill Babington, Rolls Series [1860], p. 221).

[69]Woolf, *English Mystery Plays*, pp. 98-101. An audio-visual tape (NTSC 5 25) of Meg Twycross' production of the Chester Play of the Purification is available from MSU Productions, University of Lancaster.

[70]REED *York*, I, 25, 109.

[71]William Tydeman, *The Theatre in the Middle Ages* (Cambridge: Cambridge Univ. Press, 1978), pp. 199-200; Meg Twycross, "'Transvestism' in the Mystery Plays," *Medieval English Theatre*, 5 (1983), 123-80, reviews the evidence from the English records, 1428-1584, which include payments to males for playing the part of Eve, the Virgin Mary, the Mother of the Innocents, and Pilate's Wife, among others. The published northern records provide no information. The parts of Eve and Noah's Wife were played by men at Mons in 1501. The "Bessy" of the folk plays, a man dressed in woman's clothes, is medieval: E. K. Chambers, *The Mediaeval Stage* (London: Oxford Univ. Press, 1903), I, 190-92; Richard Axton, *European Drama of the Early Middle Ages* (London: Hutchinson, 1974), p. 40.

[72]Lancashire, *Dramatic Texts and Records*, p. xx and No. 1567.

[73]REED *York*, I, 75.

[74]Cawley, ed., *Wakefield Pageants*, p. 111, n. to l. 565; p. 122, n. to ll. 354-55. Christ's height is echoed in the play of the Dice by Spill-Pain (l. 130, literally, and l. 235, ironically, using a standard term of abuse, 'mytyng,' or insignificant or small person; the Wakefield Master provided the beginning for this play.

[75]Copies of Terence's plays were owned by the College of Jesus at Rotherham in 1484 and earlier by the Augustianian Priory at York; see Lancashire, *Dramatic Texts and Records*, Nos. 1343, 1558.

[76]Lancashire, *Dramatic Texts and Records*, No. 583; also Nos. 1376 (Selby), 680 (Fountains Abbey).

[77]Chambers, *Mediaeval Stage*, II, 259-62; John Walker, *Wakefield: Its History and People*, 2nd ed. (Wakefield: West Yorkshire Printing Co., 1939), pp. 90-91. Robert Weimann, *Shakespeare and the Popular Tradition in the Theater* (Baltimore: Johns Hopkins Univ. Press, 1978), pp. 51-55, stresses the plebeian origin of many of these entertainers.

Notes

[78]REED *York*, I, 70-72. The texts of two such skits are extant: *Interludium de Clerico et Puella* (a fragmentary northern text, one of whose characters is also called Malkyn), printed in *Early Middle English Verse and Prose*, 2nd ed., ed. J. A. W. Bennett and G. V. Smithers (Oxford: Clarendon Press, 1968), pp. 196-200, together with its analogue, which is perhaps a polylogue, *Dame Sirith*, pp. 77-95; and an untitled Cornish fragment, c.1400, printed in *Revue Celtique*, 4 (1880), 258-63.

[79]Lancashire, *Dramatic Texts and Records*, No. 1487.

[80]The B text has "saute" (leap) for "sautrien." Details of the minstrel repertoire may be gathered from surveys of European scope by Chambers, *Mediaeval Stage*, I, 1-86; II, 230-39; Allardyce Nicoll, *Masks, Mimes, and Miracles* (London: George C. Harrap, 1931), pp. 135-75; J. D. A. Ogilvy, "*Mimi, Scurrae, Histriones*: Entertainers of the Early Middle Ages," *Speculum*, 38 (1963), 603-19; and, for the United Kingdom specifically, from G. R. Owst, *Literature and Pulpit in Medieval England*, 2nd ed. (Oxford: Basil Blackwell, 1961), *passim*, and Anna Jean Mill, *Mediaeval Plays in Scotland* (1924; rpt. New York: Benjamin Blom, 1969), pp. 36-45, 293-306. In addition, for puppets: Richard Beadle, "Dramatic Records of Meltingham College, Suffolk, 1403-1527," *Theatre Notebook*, 33 (1979), 129; for a drunken monologue: *Secular Lyrics of the XIVth and XVth Centuries*, 2nd ed., ed. Rossell Hope Robbins (Oxford: Clarendon Press, 1955), No. 117; for other details: Sydney Anglo, "The Court Festivals of Henry VII: A Study Based on the Account Book of John Heron, Treasurer of the Chamber," *Bulletin of the John Rylands Library*, 43 (1960), 12-45. Axton, *European Drama of the Middle Ages*, pp. 17-32, suggests that mimicry was central to the minstrel's art. The Vice in the sixteenth-century interludes is given to transparent lying. Louis B. Wright, "Vanity-Show Clownery on the Pre-Restoration Stage," *Anglia*, 52 (1928), 51-68, and "Juggling Tricks and Conjury on the English Stage before 1642," *Modern Philology*, 24 (1927), 269-84, lists some similar activities in later plays.

[81]Lobe (a real surname, but also a "lazy lout," a "lubber") was one of Henry VIII's jesters; Clodd was a real surname but also a "coherent mass or lump," esp. of earth (*OED*); Swaggar is not a recorded Christian name or surname but a "drunken staggerer" (Mill, *Mediaeval Plays in Scotland*, pp. 39, 322); Reginald and Pearl, the former possibly merely Reginald the Story-Teller and the latter Pearl-in-the-Eye (or a blind minstrel) (Chambers, *Mediaeval Stage*, II, 238); "Scot the fole" (Anglo, "Court Festivals," p. 29 [1495]); "Robyn the Rybaudoure" and "Iakke the Iogelour" are fictitious (*Piers Plowman: The B Version*, ed. George Kane and E. Talbot Donaldson [London: Athlone Press, 1975], VI.72, 75). For "Mak," see my chap. 4.

Notes

[82]St. Catherine's Chapel: [W. C. B. Smith], *St. Mary's Church Beverley* (1979), p. [8]; Whiting F394.

[83]Remnant, *Catalogue*, p. 176. These were carved in 1520.

[84]*Jacob's Well*, ed. Arthur Brandeis, EETS, o.s. 115 (London, 1900), p. 295.

[85]*Tretise*, p. 39.

[86]REED *York*, I, 67 ("one player from Wakefield").

[87]Unless the York Realist's play of Christ before Annas and Caiaphas, in which Annas replies to Jesus, "Say ladde, list the make verse?" (l. 310), provides an example.

[88]REED *York*, I, 30.

[89]VCH *York*, p. 84.

[90]Meg Twycross, "'Places to Hear the Play': Pageant Stations at York, 1398-1572," *REED Newsletter*, [3, No. 2] (1978), 18.

[91]Robert Wright, "Community Theatre in Late Medieval East Anglia," *Theatre Notebook*, 28 (1974), 32-33.

[92]*Dame Sirith*, l. 77; *Pride of Life*, ll. 285, 301-02; *Castle of Perseverance*, ll. 201, 2421.

[93]On the location of Horbury, see Cawley, ed., *Wakefield Pageants*, p. 110.

[94]C. Steinberg, "Kempe Towne in the Towneley Herod Play," *Neuphilologisiche Mitteilungen*, 71 (1970), 253-60.

[95]On Watling Street, see Leland, *Itinerary*, V, 146-47.

[96]Baines' *Account of the Woollen Manufacture of England*, ed. K. G. Ponting (New York: A. M. Kelly, 1970), pp. 16-17; Walker, *Wakefield*, pp. 384-88.

[97]Margaret Jennings, *Tutivillus: The Literary Career of the Recording Demon*, in *Studies in Philology*, 74, No. 5 (1977), 38-39.

[98]*Tretise*, p. 39; see also p. 43.

Notes

[99]J. W. Robinson, "The Late Medieval Cult of Jesus and the Mystery Plays," *PMLA*, 80 (1965), 508-14; the examples given here could be increased by some from Yorkshire. In a York Hours of the Blessed Virgin Mary printed in Rouen in 1517 (STC 16104) and illustrated with woodcuts: "vnto all them that deuoutly say thys lamentable contemplation of our blessyd lady stondynge onder the crosse wepyng and hauyng compassyon wyth her swete sone iesus vii. yeres of pardon and xl. lentys" (fol. xliv); see also REED *York*, II, 855, 859.

[100]Lancashire, *Dramatic Texts and Records*, No. 800.

[101]*Meditations on the Life of Christ*, pp. 2-3.

[102]Ibid., pp. 38-40, 320.

[103]Ibid., p. 50.

Chapter II
The York Play of the Nativity

[1]*Meditations on the Life of Christ*, p. 5.

[2]Beadle, ed., *York Plays*, pp. 426-27.

[3]*Pseudo-Matthew* 8-10; see *Evangelia Apocrypha*, ed. Constantinus de Tischendorf, 2nd ed. (Leipzig: Herman Mendelssohn, 1876), pp. 71-72.

[4]*Meditations on the Life of Christ*, p. 32.

[5]This Joseph can also be seen in painted glass, about 1335, in York Minster (EDAM *York*, p. 46) and, about 1500, at Leicester (David T.-D. Clarke, *Painted Glass from Leicester* [Leicester: Leicester Museums, 1962], p. 7); in the illumination of the Nativity in the Bolton Hours, fol. 36 (see n. 12, below); in woodcuts in York Hours printed in France in the early sixteenth century (STC 16104, fols. xv-xvi, STC 16104.5, fols. x^v, xvi); and in fifteenth-century wall paintings. C. P. Deasy, *St. Joseph in the English Mystery Plays* (Washington, D.C.: Catholic Univ. of America, 1937), provides a fuller account of Joseph in the plays, especially as an old man with characteristics associated with the aged (pp. 84-101). My references to York art in this chapter are the result of personal observation which would not have been possible without the guidance of EDAM *York*, pp. 46-56.

[6]*Meditations on the Life of Christ*, p. 31.

Notes

⁷Barry Harrison and Barbara Hutton, *Vernacular Houses in North Yorkshire and Cleveland* (Edinburgh: John Donald, 1984), pp. 4-7, quoting fifteenth-century accounts from the manor of Bedale; painted glass in the chapter house at York Minster, fourteenth-century (EDAM *York*, p. 47), and at Leicester, about 1500 (Clarke, *Painted Glass*, p. 7).

⁸*Meditations on the Life of Christ*, p. 36.

⁹Christopher Woodforde, *The Norwich School of Glass-Painting in the Fifteenth Century* (London: Oxford Univ. Press, 1950), pp. 25-26; A. M. Hind, *An Introduction to the History of Woodcut* (New York: Dover, 1963), II, 717 (a London woodcut, c.1485); G. McN. Rushforth, *Mediaeval Christian Imagery* (Oxford: Clarendon Press, 1936), fig. 165.

¹⁰Henrik Cornell, *The Iconography of the Nativity of Christ*, Uppsala Universitets Årsskrift (Uppsala, 1924), pp. 1-44.

¹¹*The Revelations of Saint Birgitta*, ed. William P. Cumming, EETS, o.s. 178 (London, 1929), pp. xiii-xxxix; *The Orcherd of Syon*, ed. Phyllis Hodgson and G. M. Liegey, EETS, 258 (London, 1966), p. vii; EDAM *York*, p. 143.

¹²York Minster Library, MS Add. 2. Two articles in *Friends of York Minster Annual Report*, 16 (1944), 14-18, and 17 (1945), 27-28, provide an account of the date and provenance of this work.

¹³EDAM *York*, p. 51.

¹⁴In an illumination in the Bolton Hours (fol. 185ᵛ) and in a glass painting, 1470, in Holy Trinity, Goodramgate, York, both of the Virgin and Child, she has long golden hair; and in printed York Hours (STC 16104, fol. xxxiii, etc., and STC 16104.5, fol. xᵛ) she has long hair as she does in two York woodcarvings (J. B. Morrell, *Woodwork in York* [London: Batsford, 1949], figs. 36, 96. Wigs are among the properties recorded from 1560 to 1574 as owned by the Smiths at Chester who performed the play of the Purification (*Chester*, ed. Lawrence M. Clopper, Records of Early English Drama [Toronto: Univ. of Toronto Press, 1979], pp. 66, 78, 105— hereafter REED *Chester*); at Coventry in 1576 the Cappers, who performed a play of the Passion, paid for repairing the Maries' wigs (REED *Coventry*, p. 277). Wigs for angels are recorded in York and for Adam and Eve at Norwich.

¹⁵The description of the play in the York list originally written in 1415 has been written by a later hand over an erasure and now includes *obstetrix* (Beadle, *York Plays*, p. 424, citing Peter Meredith; REED *York*, I, 18).

Notes

[16]Young, *Drama of the Medieval Church*, II, 3-196; REED *York*, I, 1.

[17]*Miracle de Nostre Dame par personnages* [Conge MS.], ed. Gaston Paris and Ulysse Robert, SATF (Paris, 1876), I, 203-48.

[18]Cornell, *The Iconography*, p. 12.

[19]W. L. Hildburgh, "English Alabaster Carvings as Records of the Medieval Religious Drama," *Archaeologia*, 93 (1949), 51-101 and Pl. XIc; woodcuts in York Hours (STC 16104, fol. x^v, and STC 16104.5, fol. x^v); John Baker, *English Stained Glass of the Medieval Period* (London: Thames and Hudson, 1978), fig. 74 (Great Malvern Priory Church, about 1500).

[20]See also Bernard of Clairvaux, *Sermo III In Vigilia Nativitatis*, in *S. Bernardi Opera, IV: Sermones*, ed. J. Leclercq and H. Rochais (Rome: Editiones Cistercienses, 1966), I, 218; *Meditations on the Life of Christ*, p. 40.

[21]Other examples: Francis Cheetham, *English Medieval Alabasters* (Oxford: Phaidon-Christie's, 1984), Pls. 107-10, 112-15, fifteenth-century alabaster retables.

[22]Cornell, *The Iconography*, p. 12.

[23]Bernard, *Sermo III In Vigilia Nativitatis*, in *Sermones*, IV, 216-17.

[24]*The Early English Carols*, 2nd ed., ed. Richard Leighton Greene (Oxford: Clarendon Press, 1977), No. 47.

[25]Ibid., No. 37; woodcuts in printed York Hours (STC 16104, fols. xvi, xxxiii, etc.); painted glass in York Minster, about 1420, and in All Saints, North Street, about 1340 (EDAM *York*, pp. 54-56).

[26]Cornell, *The Iconography*, p. 26.

[27]Ibid., p. 10.

[28]Rosemary Woolf, *The English Religious Lyric in the Middle Ages* (Oxford: Clarendon Press, 1968), pp. 148-49.

[29]Greene, *Carols*, No. 11.

[30]*Meditations on the Life of Christ*, p. 42.

Notes

[31]Greene, *Carols*, No. 86; *Religious Lyrics of the XVth Century*, ed. Carleton Brown (Oxford: Clarendon Press, 1939), No. 79; *Breviarium ad usum insignis Ecclesie Eboracensis*, Surtees Soc., 71 (Durham, 1880), I, 520.

[32]Bernard, *Sermo V In Nativitate*, in *Sermones*, I, 267; *Meditations on the Life of Christ*, p. 38.

[33]*Meditations on the Life of Christ*, p. 40.

[34]*Religious Lyrics of the XIVth Century*, 2nd ed., ed. Carleton Brown (Oxford: Clarendon Press, 1924), No. 87.

[35]Greene, *Carols*, No. 50.

[36]Ibid., No. 44.

[37]Ludolphus, *Vita Christi* I.ix.10; see Ludolphus de Saxonia, *Vita Jesu Christi*, ed. L.-M. Rigollat (Paris: Palme, 1870), I, 83.

[38]Greene, *Carols*, No. 64.

[39]*Glossa Ordinaria*, in *Patrologia Latina*, CXIII, 249.

[40]Bernard, *Sermo I In Nativitate*, in *Sermones*, I, 246.

[41]STC 16104, fol. x^v.

[42]*Meditations on the Life of Christ*, p. 39.

[43]Greene, *Carols*, No. 36b ("Wylyam northe of yorke").

[44]She carries a floral scepter in painted glass in York Minster, early fourteenth-century (EDAM *York*, p. 49), and flowers decorate the recurring woodcuts in a York Hours (STC 16104, fol. xxxiii, etc.)

[45]Greene, *Carols*, No. 67.

[46]Lancashire, *Dramatic Texts and Records*, No. 377.

[47]Bernard, *Sermo IV In Nativitate*, in *Sermones*, I, 265.

[48]Ludolphus, *Vita Christi* I.ix.10; ed. Rigollat, I, 83.

[49]*The Life of Saint Anne*, ed. Roscoe E. Parker, EETS, o.s. 174 (London, 1928), p. 27 (ll. 1032-44); and the N-town play of the Nativity, ll. 253-96, for which see *Ludus Coventriae*, ed. K. S. Block, EETS, e.s. 120 (London, 1922). For the Chester plays, see *The Chester Mystery Cycle*, ed. R. M. Lumiansky and David Mills, EETS, s.s. 3 (London, 1974).

[50]R. H. Wilson, "The Stanzaic Life of Christ and the Chester Plays," *Studies in Philology*, 28 (1931), 425-31.

[51]See *Two Coventry Corpus Christi Plays*, 2nd ed., ed. Hardin Craig, EETS, e.s. 87 (London, 1957).

[52]Lancashire, *Dramatic Texts and Records*, Nos. 376, 1543.

Chapter III
The York Shepherds' Play and the First Shepherds' Play

[1]Beadle, ed., *York Plays*, pp. 427-28, and more fully in his "An Unnoticed Lacuna in the York Chandlers' Pageant," in *So meny people longages and tonges*, ed. Michael Benskin and M. L. Samuels (Edinburgh, 1981), pp. 229-35.

[2]*Meditations on the Life of Christ*, p. 36; Bernard, *Sermo III In Vigilia Nativitatis*, in *Sermones*, I, 213.

[3]Lancashire, *Dramatic Texts and Records*, No. 376; M. D. Anderson, *The Medieval Carver* (Cambridge: Cambridge Univ. Press, 1935), p. 151 (the lamb with vines is carved on a vaulting boss in the fourteenth- or fifteenth-century porch of St. Martin, Bremhill, Wilts.; Remnant, *Catalogue*, pp. 174, 182.

[4]REED *York*, I, 188ff (records of rent for storing the pageant, 1501-28).

[5]In the liturgical *Officium Pastorum* statuettes were sometimes employed (Young, *Drama of the Medieval Church*, II, 26), but the style of the vernacular plays requires live actors except in the case of (here) the ox, ass, and baby, for practical reasons, and except in the case of attempts to present angels of a very small size (such as are sometimes to be seen busy in the sky in art), as in the elaborate York pageant of the Last Judgment, whose decorations included some mechanically moving angels.

[6]Fig. 15 shows the gown, hood, boots, hose, tar-boxes, and crooks (as well as the dog) in a mid-fourteenth-century misericord in Gloucester Cathedral of the

shepherds on their way to Bethlehem (see also Remnant, *Catalogue*, p. 50). A woodcut in *The Kalendar of Shepardes* (London: Julian Notary, 1501), sig. I6ᵛ, also shows a bagpipe-playing shepherd with a gown, belt, hat, and staff and two dogs, while on the ground nearby there is a tar-box; a dog is frequently the companion of shepherds and is mentioned in the Chester Shepherds' play. The shepherds wear full-length gowns in versions of the Adoration in Norfolk, in painted glass at St. Peter Mancroft, Norwich, and St. Peter and St. Paul, East Harling; reproduced in Woodforde, *Norwich School*, frontispiece and Pl. XI. For the Shrewsbury Fragments, see *Non-Cycle Plays and Fragments*, ed. Davis, pp. 1-7.

[7]Richard Rastall, "Music in the Cycle," in R. M. Lumiansky and David Mills, *The Chester Mystery Cycle: Essays and Documents* (Chapel Hill: Univ. of North Carolina Press, 1983), p. 118.

[8]Burrell Collection 29/2; STC 15929, fol. 41ᵛ. The middle shepherd on the Gloucester Cathedral misericord is shielding his eyes from the light of the star while he gazes at it. The shepherds' reaction is also depicted in an illumination in a fifteenth-century English devotional miscellany containing a psalter and Book of Hours, Bodleian MS. Douce 18, fol. 10ᵛ.

[9]*The Holkham Bible Picture Book*, ed. W. O. Hassall (London: Dropmore Press, 1954), fol. 13, pp. 89-91; *The Anglo-Norman Text of Holkham Bible Picture Book*, ed. F. P. Pickering, Anglo-Norman Text Soc., 23 (Oxford, 1971), p. 22.

[10]*Meditations on the Life of Christ*, p. 38.

[11]REED *York*, I, 18.

[12]The following usefully explore the unity and meaning of this play, although none is interested in its staging or goes very far to explore its biblical sources or its meaning for a fifteenth-century audience: A. C. Cawley, "The Wakefield First Shepherds' Play," *Proceedings of the Leeds Philosophical and Literary Society*, 7 (1955), 113-22; Margery M. Morgan, "'High Fraud': Paradox and Double-Plot in the English Shepherds' Plays," *Speculum*, 39 (1964), 678-89 (a seminal essay); John Gardner, *The Construction of the Wakefield Cycle* (Carbondale: Southern Illinois Univ. Press, 1974), pp. 77-84; Alicia K. Nitecki, "The Sacred Elements of the Secular Feast in *Prima Pastorum*," *Mediaevalia*, 3 (1977), 229-37; Walter E. Meyers, *A Figure Given: Typology in the Wakefield Plays* (Pittsburgh: Duquesne Univ. Press, 1978), pp. 62-67; Helterman, *Symbolic Action*, pp. 73-94; Suzanne Speyser, "Dramatic Illusion and Sacred Reality in the Towneley *Prima Pastorum*," *Studies in Philology*, 78 (1981), 1-19; Lois Roney, "The Wakefield *First* and *Second Shepherds Plays* as Complements in Psychology and Parody," *Speculum*, 58 (1983), 696-723.

Notes

[13]Cawley numbers 502 lines, not counting the two lines from Virgil following line 387, which give stanza 44 eleven lines.

[14]The number of stanzas is not in doubt, but counting by lines is difficult because stanza 15 has only seven lines (and so is assumed by Cawley to be defective, although the sense is intact) and stanza 44 has eleven lines if the two lines from Virgil are counted. The playwright may therefore have thought of his play as containing 502, 504, or 506 lines (always provided that he thought of the frons as a quatrain and not an octave). Only 504 is (like 56) divisible by 7, and it is therefore perhaps likely that the extra two lines in stanza 44 are meant to compensate for a deliberate shortage of two in stanza 15. The final seventh of 504 lines begins at line 433, Slowpace's crucial "Then furth lett vs ron; I wyll not abyde." Cawley's line 431 (if intended to be l. 431) might mark the end of the 430 years the Israelites stayed in Egypt (*Exod.* 12.40) and thus suggest that before they set out for Bethlehem the shepherds are in darkness.

[15]Jacobus de Voragine, *Legenda aurea*, trans. William Caxton (London: Wynkyn de Worde, 1512), fol. ii.

[16]*Speculum Sacerdotale*, ed. Edward H. Weatherly, EETS, o.s. 200 (London, 1936), p. 6.

[17]John Peter, *Complaint and Satire in Early English Literature* (Oxford: Clarendon Press, 1956), p. 47; *Religious Lyrics of the XVth Century*, ed. Brown, Nos. 149-170.

[18]Greene, *Carols*, No. 415.

[19]V. J. Scattergood, *Politics and Poetry in the Fifteenth Century* (London: Blandford Press, 1971), p. 336.

[20]J. P. Oakden, *Alliterative Poetry in Middle English* (Manchester: Manchester Univ. Press, 1935), II, 268, 316. Oakden's lists (II, 236-378) are the bases for my subsequent comments about the presence or absence in alliterative poetry of alliterating phrases in the plays.

[21]"On the Times," a late fourteenth-century work in *Political Poems and Songs*, ed. Thomas Wright, Rolls Ser., 14 (London: Longman, Green, Longman, and Roberts, 1859) I, 274, contains the phrase "Galauntes, purs penyles."

[22]A. Abram, *Social Life in England in the Fifteenth Century* (London: George Routledge and Sons, 1909), pp. 22-30; M. L. Ryder, *Sheep and Man* (London: Duckworth, 1983), pp. 457-58.

Notes

[23]See Psalm 11.6: *propter miseriam inopum, et gemitum pauperum.*

[24]*Historical Poems of the XIVth and XVth Centuries,* ed. Rossell Hope Robbins (New York: Columbia Univ. Press, 1959), p. 120.

[25]Peter Meredith, "The York Millers' Pageant and the Towneley *Processus Talentorum,*" *Medieval English Theatre,* 4 (1982), 104-14.

[26]Owst, *Literature and Pulpit,* p. 372; Walker, *Wakefield,* p. 115.

[27]Scattergood, *Politics and Poetry,* p. 341. This man's head is "lyke a clowde" (l. 65), however, and so his hair appears to resemble Absolon's in the Miller's Tale (I.3314-15).

[28]Owst, *Literature and Pulpit,* pp. 309-11.

[29]As in "The Tournament of Tottenham" (ll. 75-76), in *Middle English Metrical Romances,* ed. Walter H. French and Charles B. Hale (1930; rpt. New York: Russell and Russell, 1964), pp. 989-98.

[30]Gordon Hall Gerould, "Moll of the *Prima Pastorum,*" *Modern Language Notes,* 19 (1904), 225-30.

[31][Andrew Boorde,] *Merie Tales of the Mad Men of Gotam,* ed. Stanley J. Kahrl, Renaissance English Text Soc. (Evanston: Northwestern Univ. Press, 1965), p. 2. This work, published about 1565 (the unique copy was not discovered until the 1960's), contains the earliest known version of the tale. Horace A. Eaton, "A Source for the Towneley 'Prima Pastorum'," *Modern Language Notes,* 14 (1899), 265-67, first pointed to this tale (in a version published in 1630) as the source of this episode in the play. The men of Gotham were proverbially fools at least by the thirteenth century (Owst, *Literature and Pulpit,* p. 166).

[32]Some attempts, of which the most recent is by H. Cooper, "A Note on the Wakefield 'Prima Pastorum'," *Notes and Queries,* 218 (1973), 326, and which all involve a serious emendation in a good text, have been made to show that Jack Garcio and Slowpace are the same person. He is, however, needed to point to the moral of the tale, and to remove the horse, and also for his youth (as I try to show in chap. 4); the Chester play is on this point perfectly analogous.

[33]Ludolphus, *Vita Christi* I.ix.5, 10; ed. Rigollat, I, 80, 83.

[34]W. G. Hoskins, "Provincial Life," *Shakespeare Survey,* 17 (1964), 18.

Notes

[35]Meg Twycross and Sarah Carpenter, "Materials and Methods of Mask-Making," *Medieval English Theatre*, 4 (1982), 30. There are four ways to act this episode: (a) with real food—the foods mentioned; (b) with property food modelled after the foods mentioned; (c) with bread or very ordinary food which the shepherds joke about as if it were a sumptuous feast, and (d) with no food—property or otherwise—but by miming. I think *a* is impossible; *d* is almost out of the question, there being no evidence for such miming in medieval English biblical plays; *c* has its attractions, linking, as it does, the episode to the traditional wish-fulfilling Land of Cokayne, and the episode can be successfully performed in this way, as at Toronto in 1985; but the evidence from Chester suggests *b*.

[36]Reginald Scot in 1584 in his *Discoverie of Witchcraft*, introd. Hugh Ross Williamson (Carbondale: Southern Illinois Univ. Press, 1964), pp. 258-311, describes some some juggling (i.e., conjuring) tricks, and says that there "be divers juggling boxes with false bottoms wherein manie false feates are wrought" (p. 283). Chaucer's Canon, who also knew such tricks, used his sleeve and a hollow stick (the Canon's Yeoman's Tale VIII.1160-66, 1265-82, 1314-21). Wright, "Juggling Tricks and Conjury on the English Stage before 1642," pp. 269-84, lists tricks performed in plays from the fifteenth century onwards.

[37]A. C. Cawley, "The 'Grotesque Feast' in the *Prima Pastorum*," *Speculum*, 30 (1955), 213-17; Lauren Lepow, "'What God has cleansed': The Shepherds' Feast in the *Prima Pastorum*," *Modern Philology*, 80 (1983), 280-83.

[38]*Meditations on the Life of Christ*, p. 39.

[39]Ludolphus, *Vita Christi* I.ix, esp. sec. 11; ed. Rigollat, I, 83.

[40]Aelred of Rievaulx, *First Sermon for Christmas*, 9, in *Treatises and the Pastoral Prayer*, Cistercian Fathers Ser., 2 (Spencer, Mass.: Cistercian Publications, 1971), p. 7n.

[41]T. J. Jambeck, "The 'Ayll of Hely' Allusion in the *Prima Pastorum*," *English Language Notes*, 17 (1979), 1-7.

[42]Dutka, *Music in the English Mystery Plays*, pp. 80-81.

[43]Ibid., p. 10.

[44]Theodore R. DeWelles, "The Social and Political Context of the Towneley Cycle," unpublished Ph.D. diss. (Univ. of Toronto, 1980), sees satire on foolish

dreams of social equality here and elsewhere in this play (pp. 240-45). Gib's summary is not unreasonable, although the eclogue does not support "Good luf and charyté/ Blendyd amanges vs." It especially supports peace and miraculous plenty; see the text in Joseph B. Mayor *et al.*, *Virgil's Messianic Eclogue* (London: J. Murray, 1907).

[45]Helterman, *Symbolic Action*, pp. 91-92.

[46]Roney, "The Wakefield *First* and *Second Shepherds Plays*," p. 721.

[47]*The Lay Folks Mass Book*, ed. Thomas Frederick Simmons, EETS, o.s., 71 (London, 1879), p. 38, indicates that a "litille belle" is rung at the Elevation; Ludolphus, *Vita Christi* I.ix.24 (ed. Rigollat, I, 92-93); Whiting N191; Robert Trow-Smith, *A History of British Livestock Husbandry to 1700* (London: Routledge and Kegan Paul, 1957), p. 158; Woodforde, *Norwich School*, Pl. XI.

[48]Lauren Lepow, "Middle English Elevation Prayers and the Corpus Christi Cycles," *English Language Notes*, 17 (1979), 85-88.

[49]First pointed out by Taylor, "The Relation of the English Corpus Christi Play to the Middle English Religious Lyric," p. 18, who, however, omitted the heading to the poem, "A preyer at the leuacioun" (*The Minor Poems of the Vernon MS.*, ed. Carl Horstmann, EETS, o.s. 98 [London, 1892], p. 24).

[50]*Meditations on the Life of Christ*, p. 38.

[51]Mary is recorded as wearing gloves at Coventry, 1539-56 (REED *Coventry*, pp. 152-74). She is not otherwise recorded as doing so, but payments for gloves for other and also unspecified players are recorded at York in the fifteenth century and at Chester, Newcastle, and Norwich in the sixteenth century. The only example of gloves in West Riding art appears in the Betrothal of Mary and Joseph at Elland; see EDAM *West Riding*, p. 71.

[52]Owst, *Literature and Pulpit*, pp. 483-84.

[53]Bernard, *Sermo III In Vigilia Nativitatis*, in *Sermones* I, 211.

[54]Greene, *Carols*, No. 74.

[55]*Meditations on the Life of Christ*, p. 38.

[56]Ludolphus, *Vita Christi* I.ix.25; ed. Rigollat, I, 93.

Notes

[57]Bernard, *Sermo II In Vigilia Nativitatis*, in *Sermones*, I, 206.

[58]See *Minor Poems of the Vernon Manuscript*, ed. Horstmann, I, 148-49.

[59]Ludolphus, *Vita Christi* I.ix.13; ed. Rigollat, I, 86.

[60]Ludophus, *Vita Christi* I.ix.24; ed. Rigollat, I, 93.

[61]Ludolphus, *Vita Christi* I.ix.17; ed. Rigollat, I, 89.

[62]Ludolphus, *Vita Christi* I.ix.13; ed. Rigollat, I, 86.

Chapter IV
The Second Shepherds' Play

[1]Woolf, *English Mystery Plays*, pp. 189, 388.

[2]William Empson, *Some Versions of Pastoral* (London: Chatto and Windus, 1935), p. 26. Real enjoyment of this play in modern times perhaps begins with Professor Moorman and his students. Serious criticism of it begins with Millicent Carey (*The Wakefield Group in the Towneley Cycle* [Baltimore: Johns Hopkins Univ., 1930]) and Empson and can be followed from them to 1971 in the chronological listing in the *New Cambridge Bibliography of English Literature*, ed. George Watson (Cambridge: Cambridge Univ. Press, 1974), I, 734-36.

[3]Roney, "The Wakefield *First* and *Second Shepherds Plays*," pp. 697-98 and *passim*.

[4]*Legenda aurea*, fol. i.

[5]Butler, "Numerological Thought," p. 3 and *passim*.

[6]Isidore of Seville, *Liber Num.* XV.76, in *Sancti Isidori, Hispalensis Episcopi Opera Omnia*, ed. Faustino Arevalo, Corpus Christianorum, 83 (Turnhout: Brepols, 1977), p. 193.

[7]*Legenda aurea*, fols. viii^v-ix.

[8]The sixths begin with stanzas 1, 15, 29, 43, 57, 71, or lines 1, 127, 253, 377, 503, 629. The structural significance of the division by 3 is explored by M. F. Vaughan, "The Three Advents in the *Secunda Pastorum*," *Speculum*, 55 (1980),

484-504, and in "Mak and the Proportions of *The Second Shepherds' Play*," *Papers on Language and Literature*, 18 (1982), 355-67.

[9]Daw interrupts the sequence at lines 449, 452, and 636, and (following Cawley's sensible correction of the manuscript) at 370. Coll, at the end of his tether, interrupts (again following Cawley's correction) at line 621.

[10]Owst, *Literature and Pulpit*, p. 320.

[11]See Abram, *Social Life in England*, p. 87, who cites *Rotuli Parliamentorum* (London, 1767), IV, 344; legislation of 1429 commands that lords should not "receive, cheryssh, hold in houshold, ne mayntene, Pillours, Robbours, Oppressours of the poeple, Mansleers, Felons, Outelawes, Ravyshours of Wymen ayens the lawe," etc.

[12]DeWelles, "Social and Political Context," pp. 27, 33, 56, 67, 72, and chap. 5, *passim*; VCH *Yorkshire*, III, 474-76; *The Cambridge Economic History* (Cambridge: Cambridge Univ. Press, 1941), I, 524-26; William George Hoskins, *The Age of Plunder: King Henry's England, 1500-1547* (New York: Longman, 1976), p. 68. Coll's lines 11, 13, and 20 seem vague unless he is referring to enclosing.

[13]Bernard, *Sermo II In Vigilia Nativitatis*, in *Sermones*, I, 206.

[14]*Legenda aurea*, fol. ii.

[15]Bernard, *Sermo II In Vigilia Nativitatis*, in *Sermones*, I, 206.

[16]The stage direction in the Digby play of the Conversion of St. Paul, "Her Saule ys in comtemplacyon" (l. 261*sd*), has been mistaken as a recognition of the soliloquy (by J. W. Robinson, "Medieval English Acting," *Theatre Notebook*, 13 [1959], 86); it merely explains Paul's speech in accordance with *Acts* 9.11, "For behold he prayeth." For the Digby play, see *The Late Medieval Religious Plays of Bodleian MSS Digby 133 and e museo 160*, ed. Donald C. Baker, John L. Murphy, and Louis B. Hall, Jr., EETS, 283 (London, 1982).

[17]Greene, *Carols*, Nos. 403, 411; *Secular Lyrics of the XIVth and XVth Centuries*, ed. Robbins, Nos. 40-44.

[18]Bernard, *Sermo II In Vigilia Nativitatis*, in *Sermones*, I, 205.

[19]Walker indicates that in the West Riding a laborer's wages were apparently much less than £10 per year in 1495 (*Wakefield*, p. 103).

Notes

[20]*Lay Folks Mass Book*, p. 48 (C text, ll. 285-87).

[21]F. P. Manion, "A Reinterpretation of the Second Shepherds' Play," *American Benedictine Review*, 30 (1979), 44-68, writes enthusiastically of Daw and well of the play as expressing the doctrine of the mystical body of Christ.

[22]Trow-Smith, *A History of British Livestock Husbandry*, p. 159.

[23]St. Augustine, *Confessions*, trans. Vernon J. Bourke (Washington, D.C.: Catholic Univ. of America Press, 1953), p. 284.

[24]Cherrell Guilfoyle, "'The Riddle Song' and the Shepherds' Gifts in *Secunda Pastorum*," *Yearbook of English Studies*, 8 (1978), 208-19. A version of this song, entitled "My Young Sister," is printed in *Secular Lyrics*, ed. Robbins, No. 45.

[25]The drops of blood in triplets, a very common feature of devotional images of Christ, possibly inspired the "cherries." See also Lawrence J. Ross, "Symbol and Structure in the *Secunda Pastorum*," in *Medieval English Drama*, ed. Jerome Taylor and Alan H. Nelson (Chicago: Univ. of Chicago Press, 1972), pp. 192-96.

[26]Walker, *Wakefield*, p. 115.

[27]On East Harling glass, see Woodforde, *Norwich School*, pp. 46-47.

[28]Isidore, *Liber Num.* XV.75.

[29]VCH *Yorkshire*, III, 403-09.

[30]C. Willett and Phillis Cunnington, *Handbook of English Mediaeval Costume* (London: Faber and Faber, 1952), pp. 102-03. J. H. Smith, "Another Allusion to Costume in the Work of the 'Wakefield Master'," *PMLA*, 52 (1937), 901-02, distinguishes Mak's sleeve as the particularly capacious "bagpipe" sleeve, about 1400 to 1440, but the evidence is only that such sleeves appear to have been characteristic of the households of the great.

[31]Ann Wierum, "'Actors' and 'Play Acting' in the Morality Tradition," *Renaissance Drama*, n.s. 3 (1970), 189-214.

[32]*Legenda aurea*, fol. iii.

[33]*Cursor Mundi*, ed. Robert Morris, EETS, o.s. 62 (London, 1874-93), III, 1265 (ll. 22,111-12).

Notes

[34]The only other houses in the English plays which require doors occur in the N-town plays of Joseph's Return (ll. 1-9), the Woman Taken in Adultery (l. 121), and the Assumption of the Virgin (ll. 161*sd*, 169*sd*); other conversations on both sides of a gate or door take place in the York play of Pentecost (l. 175) and in the plays of the Harrowing of Hell.

[35]The alternative—make-believe walls—is not un-medieval, but does not help express the meaning of the play.

[36]Harrison and Hutton, *Vernacular Houses*, pp. 10-11. The evidence is scanty.

[37]*Piers Plowman*, B-text, XVIII.339, 357.

[38]*Glossa Ordinaria*, in *Patrologia Latina*, CXIII, 1181.

[39]Ephraim Lipson, *The History of the Woollen and Worsted Industries* (London: A. and C. Black, 1921), p. 64.

[40]Walker, *Wakefield*, p. 131.

[41]*Canterbury Tales* VII.1891-1923.

[42]Remnant, *Catalogue*, p. xxxviii; EDAM *York*, p. 182 (painted glass in York Minster, c.1320); Greene, *Carols*, No. 403.

[43]David Lindsay, *Ane Satire of the Thrie Estaitis*, ll. 25-100, 897-982, 1199-1243, 1423-65, in *Four Morality Plays*, ed. Peter Happé (Harmondsworth: Penguin, 1979).

[44]*Canterbury Tales* I.472; *Sir Gawain and the Green Knight*, l. 967, for which see the edition by J. R. R. Tolkien and E. V. Gordon, 2nd ed. (Oxford: Clarendon Press, 1967); "balȝ" is an emendation (for "bay") generally accepted.

[45]*Piers Plowman*, B-text, XVII.334.

[46]*Mankind*, ll. 198-200; quoted from *The Macro Plays*, ed. Mark Eccles, EETS, 262 (London, 1969).

[47]In the top right quarry of the central window of the third row; EDAM *West Riding*, p. 244.

[48]Ian Roberts, "Another Parallel to the Mak Story?" *Notes and Queries*, 213 (1968), 204-05 (the thief's name was Scott).

[49]Caedmon Records TC 1032 (1962).

[50]REED *York*, I, 17. Eve's spinning is also alluded to in the Chester (l. 503) and N-town (l. 408) plays of the Expulsion. The play is missing from the Towneley manuscript.

[51]Gail McMurray Gibson, "'Porta haec clausa erit': Comedy, Conception, and Ezekiel's Closed Door in the *Ludus Coventriae* Play of 'Joseph's Return'," *Journal of Medieval and Renaissance Studies*, 8 (1978), 137-56, cogently explains the locked door of the N-town play of Joseph's Return in terms of Ezechiel's metaphor (44.1-2) and also suggests that Jill's locked door is a "perverse human version" of the same metaphor (pp. 152-53).

[52]Ludolphus, *Vita Christi* I.ix.14; ed. Rigollat, I, 86.

[53]Bernard, *Sermo V In Nativitate*, in *Sermones*, I, 267.

[54]Ludolphus, *Vita Christi* I.ix.12; ed. Rigollat, I, 85.

[55]Whoever put the Towneley collection together may have felt obliged to try to find a play of the Nativity for it, but failed. It is also possible that the Shepherds' plays were felt to be sufficient substitutes for the Nativity proper. It is further possible that the Nativity, the birth of Christ, is shown silently in the Second Shepherds' play, just before the angel sings. "[N]ow is he borne," "thys nyght is he borne," and "now at this morne" (ll. 638, 640, 641), phrases more emphatic than in the First Shepherds' play (l. 302), suggest this possibility, especially since the *Meditations on the Life of Christ* reports that an angel flew "immediately" when Christ was born to announce the birth to the shepherds.

[56]Bernard, *Sermo II In Vigilia Nativitatis*, in *Sermones*, I, 211.

[57]Trow-Smith, *History of British Livestock Husbandry*, p. 159.

[58]Lauren Lepow, "Drama of Communion: The Life of Christ in the Towneley Cycle," *Philological Quarterly*, 62 (1983), 403-13.

[59]It is not certain, however, that he knew plays 10-11, 14-15, or 17-18 (the play of the Annunciation to the play of John the Baptist), since he wrote no stanzas for them.

Notes

[60]Morton W. Bloomfield, *The Seven Deadly Sins* (East Lansing: Michigan State College Press, 1952), pp. 165, 197, 199, 205, 212, 226.

[61]Bernard, *Sermo II In Vigilia Nativitatis*, in *Sermones*, I, 205.

[62]*Glossa Ordinaria*, in *Patrologia Latina*, CXIII, 306.

[63]The play is explored on these terms by Linda E. Marshall, "'Sacral Parody' in the *Secunda Pastorum*," *Speculum*, 47 (1972), 720-36, and more generally by T. P. Campbell, "Eschatology and the Nativity in English Mystery Plays," *American Benedictine Review*, 27 (1976), 297-320.

[64]T. J. Jambeck, "The Canvas-Tossing Allusion in the *Secunda Pastorum*," *Modern Philology*, 76 (1978), 49-54.

[65]The boss, in the sacristy, is probably of the fourteenth century; it shows a soul being carried in a cloth by two angels (Cave, *Roof Bosses*, p. 182). See also EDAM *York*, p. 112.

[66]Bernard, *Sermo III In Nativitate*, in *Sermones*, I, 260.

[67]Good pastors would keep their sheep better (*Jer.* 10.21). David L. Jeffrey, "Pastoral Care in the Wakefield Shepherd Plays," *American Benedictine Review*, 22 (1971), 208-21, interpreting the two plays in this way, postulates that the playwright had a particular interest in the clergy in his audience.

[68]John Speirs, "The Towneley 'Shepherds Plays'," in *The Age of Chaucer*, ed. Boris Ford, Guide to English Literature, 1 (Harmondsworth: Penguin, 1954), p. 174.

[69]Bernard, *Sermo II In Vigilia Nativitatis*, in *Sermones*, I, 208.

Chapter V
The York Play of the Slaughter of the Innocents and the Play of Herod the Great

[1]Beadle, ed., *York Plays*, pp. 437-38.

[2]REED *York*, I, 19, 107, 136-37; Beadle, ed., *York Plays*, p. 438.

[3]REED *York*, I, 68; II, 746.

Notes

[4]Young, *Drama of the Medieval Church*, II, 102-09. The text of the thir-teenth-century York liturgical presentation of the three kings is lost (REED *York*, I, 1). The four other English plays are in the Chester, Coventry, Digby, and N-town collections.

[5]Rushforth, *Mediaeval Christian Imagery*, pp. 287-88. [For a West Riding example of the Massacre of the Innocents (at Ingleton), see EDAM *West Riding*, pp. 85, 89-90.]

[6]Wyatt, "Performance and Ceremonial," p. 1: "Childer of ysraell," following the Flight to Egypt; Lancashire, *Dramatic Texts and Records*, records what might be plays on the subject at Cambridge in 1353 and at Edinburgh in 1494 (Nos. 435, 1661).

[7]Young, *Drama of the Medieval Church*, II, 109-24; Gertrud Schiller, *Iconography of Christian Art*, trans. Janet Seligman (Greenwich, Conn.: New York Graphic Soc., 1971), I, 115.

[8]Charles M. Gayley, *Plays of Our Forefathers*, sees the York Herod as the "model" for the Towneley Herod (p. 175), and Marie C. Lyle, *The Original Identity of the York and Towneley Cycles*, Studies in Language and Literature, 6 (Minneapolis: Univ. of Minnesota, 1919), lists the many parallels between the two plays.

[9]Schiller, *Iconography*, I, 115.

[10]Ibid., I, 116; EDAM *York*, pp. 58-60.

[11]EDAM *York*, pp. 58-59. He may also be seen, crowned and with a sword on his canopied throne taking part in the slaughter, in a glass painting in St. Peter Mancroft, Norwich; see Woodforde, *Norwich School*, Pl. III. Sometimes he has a devil crown; see Miriam Skey, "Herod's Demon-Crown," *Journal of the Warburg and Courtauld Institutes*, 40 (1977), 274-76, and EDAM *York*, p. 60, for an ex-ample at St. Michael Spurriergate in York.

[12]Owst, *Literature and Pulpit*, p. 310.

[13]Beadle, ed., *York Plays*, p. 423.

[14]Owst, *Literature and Pulpit*, p. 321.

[15]Ludolphus, *Vita Christi* I.xi.7; ed. Rigollat, I, 104.

Notes

[16]A line is missing from the York play; as originally written it consisted of 282 lines.

[17]M. H. Marshall, "The Dramatic Tradition Established by the Liturgical Plays," *PMLA*, 56 (1941), 969-70.

[18]REED *York*, I, 25.

[19]Woolf, *English Mystery Plays*, p. 204; Helterman, *Symbolic Action*, pp. 115-38.

[20]Stewart Perowne, *The Life and Times of Herod the Great* (New York: Abingdon Press, 1959), p. 176.

[21]Schiller, *Iconography*, I, 116. For Rachel in the Fleury play, see Young, *Drama of the Medieval Church*, II, 110-17.

[22]"The Cambridge Prologue," in *Non-Cycle Plays and Fragments*, ed. Davis, p. 115.

[23]The more austere Chester collection generally avoids such play-openings, but nevertheless (if the text compounds with the records) the two tyrannical boasts appear to have been intended to provide a lively start to the second and third days of the performance; the play of the Innocents begins with Herod's boast and the play of Resurrection with Pilate's.

[24]J. W. Robinson, "The Late Medieval Cult of Jesus and the Mystery Plays," p. 513n.

[25]Cawley, ed., *Wakefield Pageants*, p. 114, glossing the play of Herod the Great, ll. 4-5.

[26]*Original Letters Illustrative of English History*, ed. Henry Ellis, 2nd ser. (London: Harding and Lepard, 1827), I, 268-69; and *Foedera*, ed. Thomas Rymer (1704-32), X, 67, 508, etc.

[27]*Religious Lyrics of the XVth Century*, ed. Brown, p. 322.

[28]*Legenda aurea*, fol. xi; Ludolphus, *Vita Christi* I.xi.7; ed. Rigollat, I, 104.

[29]A few of these are mentioned by Charles Elliott, "Language and Theme in the Towneley *Magnus Herodes*," *Mediaeval Studies*, 30 (1968), 351-53.

Notes

[30]As always, I do not list all these collocations, of which there are many in this and subsequent speeches. For example, for ll. 51-54, compare *OED* tongue II 4 and Whiting T379.

[31]Meyers, *A Figure Given*, pp. 71-73.

[32]*Dives and Pauper*, I, Pt. 1, 109; *Lay Folks Mass Book*, p. 163.

[33]Gardner envisions him as possibly "a piping, squawking midget" (*Construction of the Wakefield Cycle*, p. 99).

[34]Willett and Cunnington, *Handbook of English Mediaeval Costume*, pp. 134-43.

[35]*Legenda aurea*, fol. xi.

[36]Ludolphus, *Vita Christi* I.xi.8; ed. Rigollat, I, 105.

[37]*Cursor Mundi*, ll. 11538-54.

[38]Young, *Drama of the Medieval Church*, II, 55, 66, 95, 105, 111.

[39]Cawley proposes alternatively that Herod be accompanied by his knights as he enters the Place; if this is the case, Herod's failure to have received their report earlier is not easily explicable. It can be argued that Herod would not have ventured forth without a bodyguard; on the other hand, such recklessness is well within his character.

[40]*Canterbury Tales* VIII.471-72.

[41]Roscoe E. Parker, "The Reputation of Herod in Early English Literature," *Speculum*, 8 (1933), 64.

[42]J. W. Robinson, "'As Small As Flesh To Pot'," *Folklore*, 80 (1969), 197-98. The expression, if the "pot" is omitted, is of wider currency than Whiting, Palmer Morris Tilley (*A Dictionary of Proverbs in England in the Sixteenth and Seventeenth Centuries* [Ann Arbor: Univ. of Michigan Press, 1950]), or R. W. Dent (*Proverbial Language in English Dramas Exclusive of Shakespeare, 1495-1616: An Index* [Berkeley: Univ. of California Press, 1984]) reveal. In the Chester play of the Magi, Herod says, "I shall hewe that harlott with my bright brond so keene/ into peeces smale" (ll. 336-37), and in John Redford's *Wit and Science* (Malone Society Reprints, 1951), Tediousness says, "In twenty gobbets I showld have squatted them" (l. 216).

Notes

[43]Ian Lancashire, "The Corpus Christi Play of Tamworth," *Notes and Queries*, 224 (1979), 509.

[44]*Legenda aurea*, fol. xi.

[45]Ibid., fol. xii.

[46]Ludolphus, *Vita Christi* I.xi.8; ed. Rigollat, I, 105.

[47]"Here" (1. 120) and "wonys" (1. 169) mean Jerusalem and the surrounding area, although Cawley glosses the latter as "dwelling," unnecessarily, I think.

[48]Ludolphus, *Vita Christi* I.xi.7; ed. Rigollat, I, 104.

[49]E.g., *English Lyrics of the XIIIth Century*, ed. Carleton Brown (Oxford: Clarendon Press, 1932), No. 26: "Tho heroudes herde the kinges speken,/ of alle his blisse he was skere;/ ful ney is herte wolde to-breken/ and than he madam glade chere" (ll. 33-36).

[50]*Jewish Antiquities*, ed. and trans. Ralph Marcus and Allen Wikgren, Loeb Classical Library (Cambridge: Harvard Univ. Press, 1963), VIII, 449 (XVII.vi.5). Josephus also describes the disease in similar terms in his *History of the Jewish War*. Perowne, *Life and Times of Herod the Great*, pp. 185-86, provides a different translation and comment on these symptoms. Peter Comestor's version is given in Woolf, *English Mystery Plays*, p. 393.

[51]*Jewish Antiquities* XVI.viii.5.

[52]M. D. Anderson, *Drama and Imagery in English Medieval Churches* (Cambridge: Cambridge Univ. Press, 1963), Pl. 11b.

[53]*Canterbury Tales* I.3384.

[54]*Paston Letters and Papers of the Fifteenth Century*, ed. Norman Davis (Oxford: Clarendon Press, 1976), II, 426. "More agreable to hys pageaunt" must mean "more in keeping with his part in the play."

[55]See Ludolphus, *Vita Christi* I.xiii.10; ed. Rigollat, I, 137. The point is preserved by the Anglo-Scots paraphrase: "for Symeoun ye ald,/ The Gentel licht, till Iserall ye king,/ Had him before into ye tempill tauld" (ll. 170-72). [Full bibliographic information is not available for the Anglo-Scots translation of Ludolphus.—Ed.]

Notes

[56]Young, *Drama of the Medieval Church*, II, 71, 75, 84.

[57]Ludolphus, *Vita Christi* I.xi.8, I.xiii.10; ed. Rigollat, I, 105, 137.

[58]VCH *Yorkshire*, III (1913), 475 (a flagrant case at Temple Newsam).

[59]Anglo-Scots Ludolphus, p. 173.

[60]*The English and Scottish Popular Ballads*, ed. F. J. Child (1882-98; rpt. New York: Dover, 1965), I, 242 (stanza 11: "turmentowres").

[61]Lancashire, *Dramatic Texts and Fragments*, Nos. 217, 267, 365, 387, 501, 554, 768, 1208-09, 1630, 1712, 1736; REED *Coventry*, pp. 25, 73.

[62]Owst, *Literature and Pulpit*, pp. 320-38 *passim*.

[63]EDAM *York*, p. 59.

[64]Hooked noses sometimes appear on alabasters and misericords. Snub noses, sometimes amounting to a pathological condition, are seen in a glass painting, about 1370, of workmen (?) nailing Christ to the cross now in All Saints, Pavement, York (fig. 22), and another in St. Peter Mancroft, Norwich (Anderson, *Drama and Imagery*, Pl. 15a); on a fourteenth-century embroidered English chasuble (Victoria and Albert Museum, *Gospel Stories in English Embroidery* [1963], Pl. 24); and on the face of the fourteenth-century "Beverley Imp" carved in the chancel of St. Mary's, Beverley ([W. C. B. Smith], *St. Mary's Church Beverley*, illus. on p. [7]). The second worker in the glass painting in All Saints has a singularly vacuous and dog-like appearance.

[65]Craik, *Tudor Interlude*, pp. 51-53.

[66]Owst, *Literature and Pulpit*, p. 337.

[67]R. W. Ackerman, "Armor and Weapons in the Middle English Romances," *Research Studies in the State College of Washington*, 7 (1939), 104-11; J. G. Scott, *European Arms and Armour at Kelvingrove* (Glasgow, 1980), p. 4.

[68]Gervase Mathew, *The Court of Richard II* (London: John Murray, 1968) describes the ideal code of chivalry (pp. 118-28).

[69]Ludolphus, *Vita Christi* I.xiii.13; ed. Rigollat, I, 138-39.

[70]Woodforde, *Norwich School*, Pl. 3. Herod, himself the butcher, is here about to slice a child in half with a curved sword. Blood is not particularly in evidence in these paintings but much mentioned in the play. "Dummies," rag dolls, must have been used for the infants; they are tossed around in the paintings and perhaps in the York and Towneley plays. They might have had pierceable bags of blood in them (as in a St. Thomas Becket show at Canterbury in the early sixteenth century). In the Towneley play the bodies are said to be "strayd" (l. 481, "strewn") in the street, as in the painting by Hans Memling on a panel from his *Seven Joys and Seven Sorrows of Mary* (1480). Fake daggers (whose handles swallow their blades) are described and illustrated by Reginald Scot, *Discoverie of Witchcraft* (p. 294), but are not called for in the Towneley play.

[71]The episode is at least in part farcical in the Chester, Coventry, and Digby plays, where the women are armed with distaves (like Jill) and a pot-ladle. The misericord is described in Remnant, *Catalogue*, p. 84.

[72]Michael Paull, "The Figure of Mahomet in the Towneley Cycle," *Comparative Drama*, 6 (1972), 195.

[73]DeWelles, "Social and Political Context," chap. 5.

[74]Ludolphus, *Vita Christi* I.xiii.10; ed. Rigollat, I, 137.

[75]The Devil can speak snippets of French in the Middle English poem *The Harrowing of Hell*, ed. William Henry Hulme, EETS, e.s. 100 (London, 1907), for example, where he tries to keep Adam in Hell, "par ma fay" (l. 85). And Sir John Fortescue wrote (c.1471-76) that Herod was a French tyrant, not an English limited monarch (*The Governance of England*, cited in Robert E. Jungman, "An Analogue in Fortescue to the Wakefield *Magnus Herodes*," *American Notes and Queries*, 14 [1975], 2-3). "I can no more franch" (there is, of course, no capital F in the manuscript) might also mean, "I do not know how to devour any more [people just now]" (*OED* Franch v).

[76]Woolf, *English Religious Lyric*, pp. 172-79; and Richard W. Pfaff, *New Liturgical Feasts in Later Medieval England* (Oxford: Clarendon Press, 1970), pp. 62-83. The long Yorkshire poem sometimes attributed to Rolle in which almost every stanza begins with "Sweet Jesu" or "Jesu" is an expansion of the hymn *Dulcis Jesu Memoria*; whoever recites it often shall find grace, it says.

[77]"Now Crystys holy name be vs emang," cries Mak hypocritically but nevertheless forming the line (l. 378) which exactly concludes the first half of the Second Shepherds' play.

[78]Daniel C. Boughner, "Retribution in English Medieval Drama," *Notes and Queries*, 198 (1953), 506-08.

[79]Ludolphus, *Vita Christi* I.xiii.12; ed. Rigollat, I, 138.

[80]Weimann, *Shakespeare and the Popular Tradition*, pp. 64-72, insists that the "biblical" is overshadowed by the "contemporary" and, since he is also concerned with the related (as he sees it) matter of tracing the line between the "non-representational" and the "mimetic," sees "clowning self-consciousness" in the play, especially since the dramatic experience is that of the man who bows down before power but does not recognize its claim to privilege.

[81]John Mirk, *Festial*, ed. T. Erbe, EETS, e.s. 96 (London, 1905), p. 35.

[82]*Canterbury Tales* X.400.

Chapter VI
The York Play of Christ before Annas and Caiaphas and the Wakefield Master's Play of the Buffeting

[1]John Bale wrote a play *De pontificum consilio*, perhaps in about 1538-40 (Lancashire, *Dramatic Texts and Records*, No. 282), presumably on the subject and if so probably depicting Caiaphas and Annas as Roman Catholics.

[2]See [EDAM *West Riding*;] EDAM *York*, p. 73. Only two alabaster carvings of the Appearance of Christ before Caiaphas are recorded as opposed, for example, to over fifty of the Scourging (Cheetham, *English Medieval Alabasters*, p. 56).

[3]The two plays fall into Lyle's third group showing "a similarity in structural outlines and verbal reminiscenses in isolated passages"—Lyle, *Original Identity of the York and Towneley Cycles*, pp. 87, 90-91.

[4]Listed as a proverb in Whiting, *Proverbs in the Earlier English Drama*, p. 10, but not in Whiting, *Proverbs, Sentences, and Proverbial Phrases*, where, however, B135 is "To beat one as a Beast" and B473 is "He who is Bound must bow."

[5]Lawrence L. Besserman, *The Legend of Job in the Middle Ages* (Cambridge: Harvard Univ. Press, 1979), p. 56.

[6]*Patrologia Latina*, LXXVI, 525.

Notes

[7]Isidore, *Allegoria quaedam scripturae sacrae* 53, in *Sancti Isidori . . . Opera omnia*, ed. Arevalo, Corpus Christianorum, 83, p. 108.

[8]Isidore, *In Libros Veteris Proemia* 48, in *Opera omnia*, ed. Arevalo, Corpus Christianorum, 83, p. 167.

[9]J. Fewterer, *The Myrrour or Glasse of Christes Passion* (London, 1534) [STC 14553].

[10]Elizabeth Salter, "Ludolphus of Saxony and his English Translators," pp. 27-28.

[11]The fifty stanzas are divisible only by 2, 5, and 10, and these divisors seem not to mark any key moments in the play, except that the second fifth of the play begins (probably incidentally) with the line "Men call hym a kyng and Godys son of heuen" (l. 91).

[12]*The Northern Passion*, ed. Francis Foster, EETS, o.s. 145 (London, 1912).

[13]Grace Frank, "Popular Iconography of the Passion," *PMLA*, 46 (1931), 333-40. Another tradition, not confined to elaborate works produced for wealthy patrons, introduced oriental costumes and properties. In British Library MS. Royal 6 E.vi (a fourteenth-century English Encyclopedia), for example, Caiaphas has a turban and scimitar (fol. 12); in a woodcut in a York Missal (Paris, 1533; STC 16224) the high priests wear Jewish hats (fol. iv); and in the N-town First Passion play Annas is costumed "*after a busshop of the hoold lawe*" with "*a mytere on his hed after the hoold lawe*," and his messenger is a Saracen (before l. 1).

[14]Rushforth, *Mediaeval Christian Imagery*, p. 27.

[15]*Canterbury Tales* I.200.

[16]Gregory, *On Job* II.76.

[17]*Meditations on the Life of Christ*, p. 325.

[18]Ludolphus, *Vita Christi* II.lix.28; ed. Rigollat, IV, 491-92.

[19]EDAM *York*, p. 73.

[20]Ludolphus, *Vita Christi* II.lix.28; ed. Rigollat, IV, 491-92.

[21]*Meditations on the Life of Christ*, p. 325.

[22]Ibid., p. 326.

[23]Ibid., p. 325.

[24]Fewterer, *Myrrour*, fol. 76ᵛ.

[25]Ludolphus, *Vita Christi* II.lix.28; ed. Rigollat, IV, 492.

[26]Fewterer, *Myrrour*, fol. 76ᵛ.

[27]Ludolphus, *Vita Christi* II.lxi.12; ed. Rigollat, 522.

[28]See also Ludolphus, *Vita Christi* II.lx.16; ed. Rigollat, IV, 507.

[29]Fewterer, *Myrrour*, fol. 77.

[30]See Ludolphus, *Vita Christi* II.lix.28; ed. Rigollat, IV, 492.

[31]*Meditations on the Life of Christ*, p. 319.

[32]Ludolphus, *Vita Christi* I.lx.6; ed. Rigollat, IV, 499.

[33]"Motu corporus insaniam mentis demonstrat"—Ludolphus, *Vita Christi* II.lx.6; ed. Rigollat, IV, 499.

[34]*Anglo-Scots Ludolphus*, pp. 442-43.

[35]Owst, *Literature and Pulpit*, p. 510.

[36]Ludolphus, *Vita Christi* II.lx.4; ed. Rigollat, IV, 498.

[37]*OED* game 1c; on ambiguity in the meaning of the term 'game,' see John Coldewey, "Plays and 'Play' in Early English Drama," *Research Opportunities in Renaissance Drama*, 28 (1985), 181-88.

[38]Fewterer, *Myrrour*, fol. 66.

[39]Rudolph Willard, "Chaucer's 'Text that seith that hunters ben not hooly men'," *Texas Studies in English* (1947), pp. 209-51.

240

Notes

[40]See also *Piers Plowman*, B-text, XIX.306-18.

[41]See *The Mirror of the Blessed Life of Jesu Christ*, trans. Nicholas Love (London: Burns, Oates, and Washburne, 1926), pp. 142-44.

[42]*Meditations on the Life of Christ*, p. 319.

[43]Bernard, *Sermo III In Nativitate*, in *Sermones*, I, 261.

[44]*Meditations on the Life of Christ*, pp. 327-38.

[45]Christ before Annas and Caiaphas, ll. 176-212; Christ before Pilate, ll. 229-64, Christ before Herod, ll. 58-91.

[46]REED *York*, I, 6, 8-9, 26.

Index

Index

Index

Index

1. Dijon Nativity, by the Master of Flemalle. Courtesy of Musée des Beaux-Arts de Dijon.

2.

4.

2. Shoeing the goose, misericord, Beverley Minster. Courtesy of B. T. Batsford Ltd.

3. Fox preaching to geese, roof boss, Church of St. Mary, Beverley. Courtesy of the Royal Commission on the Historical Monuments of England.

4. Man with head in sack, misericord, Beverley Minster. Courtesy of B. T. Batsford Ltd.

5. Tuning bells, glass painting, York Minster nave, north aisle. Courtesy of the
Royal Commission on the Historical Monuments of England.

6. Agnus Dei, held by John the Baptist. York Minster, south choir aisle, tracery. Courtesy of the Royal Commission on the Historical Monuments of England.

7. God with a gold face, Te Deum window, York Minster. Reproduced by kind permission of the Dean and Chapter of York.

8. God wearing a gold mask; production by Lords of Misrule. Photograph: David O'Connor.

9. Dancing fools, misericord, Beverley Minster. Courtesy of the Royal Commission on the Historical Monuments of England.

10. Contortionist, pulling faces, misericord, Beverley Minster. Courtesy of the Royal Commission on the Historical Monuments of England.

11. Magi, Mary and Child, and Joseph. Alabaster. The Burrell Collection, Glasgow Museums and Art Galleries.

12. Nativity with Shepherds, painted glass, St. Peter Mancroft, Norwich, east window. Courtesy of the Royal Commission on the Historical Monuments of England.

13. Nativity, Bolton Hours. York Minster Library, MS. Add. 2, fol. 36. Reproduced by kind permission of the Dean and Chapter of York.

14. Shepherd with dog, supporter on misericord, Beverley Minster. Courtesy of B. T. Batsford Ltd.

15. Shepherds following star of Nativity, misericord, Gloucester Cathedral. Courtesy of the Royal Commission on the Historical Monuments of England.

16. Distributing food to the hungry, painted glass, All Saints, North Street, York. Courtesy of the Royal Commission on the Historical Monuments of England.

17. Angel, with feathered tights, painted glass. The Burrell Collection, Glasgow Museums and Art Galleries.

18. Fox carrying away goose, misericord, Ripon Minster. Courtesy of B. T. Batsford Ltd.

19. Agnus Dei, painted glass, Church of St. Michael, Thornhill, West Riding. Courtesy of the University of York.

21. Herod, carving on font, Church of All Saints, Aston, West Yorkshire. Courtesy of Barbara Palmer.

20. Tomb of Robert, Lord Hungerford, 1459, Salisbury Cathedral. Courtesy of the Royal Commission on the Historical Monuments of England.

22. Torturers nailing Christ to the cross, All Saints, Pavement, York. Courtesy of the Royal Commission on the Historical Monuments of England.

24.

23. Bed of well-to-do person; deathbed scene of Richard Beauchamp, MS. Cotton Julius E.iv, fol. 26^v. Courtesy of the British Library.

24. Trinity, showing wounded Christ, painted glass, York Minster; formerly in Church of St. John, Micklegate. Reproduced by kind permission of the Dean and Chapter of York.